WAHIDA CLARK PRESENTS

NUDE
Awakening
A NOVEL

VICTOR L. MARTIN

Wahida Clark Presents Publishing, LLC
60 Evergreen Place
Suite 904
East Orange, New Jersey 07018
973-678-9982
www.wclarkpublishing.com

ISBN 13-digit 978-0975964620
ISBN 10-digit 0-9759646-2-3

Library of Congress Catalog Number 2011905654
1.   Urban, Porn, South Beach, Miami, Florida, African-American, Street Lit – Fiction

Cover design and layout by Oddball Design
Book interior design by Nuance Art.*.
nuanceart@acreativenuance.com
Contributing Editors: Linda Wilson, Maxine Thompson and Rosalind Hamilton

Printed in United States
Green & Company Printing, LLC
www.greenandcompany.biz

Acknowledgments

Here I still stand coming with title #8. I am still pushing to become a better author with each new book and topping *The Game of Deception* was not easy.

Much thanks goes to my publisher/friend, Wahida Clark. You and your staff at WCP are the best. This is my second book under WCP and I'm hoping there will be a third. Get the contract ready. Hadiyah, thank you for all you do behind that desk.

To my editor Maxine Thompson, thank you for your review on how I could make my story better. I listened and I respect your views and criticism.

Also to my first review editor that told Wahida my first draft was not fit for publication, you were 100% right. Thank you for bringing out my best.

To my fans behind bars, A. Cee, Sinz, Pretty Soon, Yang, Jr., Da Dirt Road Bully, Sha, B.B. from the "K", Face, Ant, Dirt Bagg, Wesley Thomas, Dean Newnan, Ron J, Natt Turner (Red Gorrilla), Curtis Tyson, A-Drop, T-Dot, Dutch, D.B., Keith Fraizer, Mack, Shell, Weezy, Black, Red Prince, Choppa, Bird, Pimp C, Twan, Viper, Stick, and you know I can't forget ya, Robert Williams aka Blac-O.

Yeah, I know I left someone out, but don't take it personal. I'll catch you in book #9.

Oh yeah, to a few new supporters, Felicia Williams, Hadiya McDuffie, China Ball, Temeeka McKenvie, Kierra Scott, Charlene Lopez, Chelsea, Savvy Sistahs Bookclub, Jennifer Willis and again, thank you.

To my fam, cuzos Kenneth Latraz McMillan, Shonda Dobbins, LaWanda Neal, Lisa McMillan, Jeff Fields, I love and miss you all. Sorry I forgot y'all in my past books . . . Oh, and my Aunt Doris.

Kimberly McCallister, thank you for just being yourself. Now spread the word on my books like you promised. LaShawn Terry, a true friend. You will love this book. Francesca Walker of my hometown Selma, NC. Happy Birthday ... December 23rd (the release date for this book is on your B-Day!) Levires Richardson, Temica C. Sutton, Leo Sullivan, Tamika Razz, Toya and author Sabrina R. Daniels. Your book of poems "Forever Love, Eternally Yours" left me without words. You are special. Day by day. Quovadis N. Shaw, you've been my friend and motivator since book one. Thank you. Renita M. Walker, keep your head up.

Mom, I love you deeply. My big sis, you're the best! Bruh-in-law Duke, 2018 and it's on, fam! My niece and nephew, you know who you are. Your uncle loves you.

Okay, time to bring this to an end. You got this book for my story, not to read my shoutouts.

To you, the reader, thank you for buying my book and for all it's worth, you are appreciated!

Author Victor L. Martin 11/16/11
Keep your eyes dry & Your heart easy
You can reach the author directly @
Mr. Victor L. Martin #0549353
P.O. Box 506
Maury, NC 28554

Prologue

Summer of 1996 - Miami, Florida

Not guilty! Not guilty! Not guilty!

Eighteen-year-old Trevon Harrison could still hear those unjust words ringing in his anger-clouded mind. Six days ago, he had sat in the courtroom and watched the man accused of raping his thirteen-year-old sister await his verdict. Trevon sat with his mother as the ruthless attorney cross-examined his sister Angie to the point of tears. Because of his mother's presence, Trevon held his peace. The entire trial was bullshit. He doubted not a word of what happened when Angie stormed into his bedroom with tears in her eyes.

Trevon hated how the defense attorney weakened Angie's testimony. Since Angie's teacher had given her a failing grade, the attorney claimed her testimony was false. A simple act of revenge. There was no physical evidence to back up Angie. Trevon's testimony, a retelling of his sister's version of events was helpless.

It was so fresh in his young mind when the judge gave the verdict. The sick, child-molesting teacher had sunk back in his chair with a smile of relief on his pale face. Angie and his mother slipped out of the courtroom in tears. Trevon remained seated as a taste of detest filled him fully. There was no *justice* here. None. The only *justice* that made any sense was the type Trevon was willing to give. As the days turned over, he watched Angie turn into a quiet soul. His mother felt it was best to move them away.

Four days after the trial, Trevon heard the teacher on a local radio station speaking on the horror and pain of being falsely accused. Trevon listened to every lying word as his mother and sister packed up for the move to North Carolina. The radio host had asked the teacher how he felt toward Angie.

"I forgive her. She's just a troubled child. But in the end. One day she'll have to answer to a higher calling for telling that lie on me."

Trevon called Angie into his room with fresh tears filling his eyes. He did not question if she had told him the truth. To do so would have crushed whatever glimmer of life she still kept inside. He told her he knew the man had raped her and that she was not the young, scheming, lying, revengeful girl the attorney labeled her.

"The judge said he ain't guilty." Angie sobbed on his shoulder.

Trevon, at eighteen, had too much to shoulder. He would never be at peace without *justice*. No justice . . . no peace.

"Promise me you'll finish school when you get to North Carolina." Angie nodded, too deep in her sorrow to understand that Trevon was not planning on making the trip.

"I love you, lil sis."

Trevon stood hidden in the bushes under the sweltering sun. In his hand he held a slightly rusted snub–nosed .38 that was prone to misfire. Mr. Falston, Angie's English Lit teacher was standing in his manicured front yard peacefully watering the lawn. His back was toward Trevon. A green Acura Legend was parked in the driveway with a small poodle sitting under the front bumper cooling off. The front door of the house Mr. Falston shared with his wife was open. Music from a radio flowed out of the house. Trevon thought about the sick things Mr. Falston had done to his sister. No *justice* . . . no peace. Closing his eyes, Trevon mumbled a short prayer. He wanted the best for his mom and sister. Though he felt he was doing the right thing, he had yet to learn the danger of acting on anger. Opening his eyes, he saw Mr. Falston moving down a row of yellow and blue flowers with the water hose. The day was perfect. One of peace and quiet.

The poodle raised its head when Trevon emerged from the bushes. Its tail began to wag. Mr. Falston paused to wipe a coat of sweat off his forehead. He was almost done with his yard work. He was doing his best to put the trial behind him. At forty-four years old, he had to be more careful with his pickings of young girls. Angie was not the first underaged girl he had molested at school, nor would she be his last. He would learn from his mistakes with Angie. In his thinking, he felt he had not taken his time with her. When his poodle yelped, he turned around.

"What's the fuss, Missy?" Mr. Falston dropped the water hose when he spotted Trevon standing two feet away with Missy jumping and yelping around his legs wanting to play.

"You-you shouldn't be here." Mr. Falston took a step backward, quickly looking around for help. "I'm going to call the police if you don't leave . . ." His words ran into a gate when Trevon raised the .38.

Trevon held his aim true and dead center of Mr. Falston's chest. The poodle circled his feet. "Why did you do those things to Angie?"

Mr. Falston took another step backward, crushing the flowers. "You're . . . you're—her brother. Look. Just put the gun down. I know you're upset, so—"

"You don't know how I fucking feel!" Trevon's voice was loud and sharp. The poodle froze, tilted its head, then scampered off back toward the car.

"Son . . . please listen—"

"Ain't your damn son! The only father I knew . . ." Trevon blinked and raised his free hand to steady the pistol. "You said my sister would have to answer to a higher calling, right!"

"I—please put the gun down."

Trevon's head snapped to the left. A police siren. Across the street he saw a curtain falling back in place. Trevon kept the .38 pointed at Mr. Falston. His hands began to shake. A quick vision of the smile Mr. Falston wore at the verdict hearing flashed in Trevon's mind. The police siren grew louder.

"Put the gun away," Mr. Falston pleaded. "Just calm down, okay?"

"I came here for a reason!" Trevon took a deep breath.

"Please . . . Don't shoot me!" Mr. Falston threw up his hands then rushed Trevon. Trevon stood his ground. No *justice* . . . no peace. He closed his eyes, pulling back hard on the trigger. Not once, but twice.

Three and a half months later, Trevon found himself back inside the courtroom. Behind him in the packed limited seats sat two women who were his solid source to continue living. Angie and his mother sat in silence as the judge read the verdict.

"Trevon Harrison," Judge Holmes said as he removed his glasses. "It pains me that you felt justice could be carried out by your hands. This system was built to be fair. If your actions were allowed to go unpunished . . . this country would be in utter chaos."

Trevon held his head down, punishing himself by straining his wrist against the handcuffs. Focusing on the pain was better than facing the reality.

When the judge saw that his words were not reaching Trevon, he cleared his throat and asked, "Is there anything you'd like to say before you are sentenced."

The female bailiff helped Trevon to his feet. He glared briefly at the judge with contempt. Silence. When he turned to face his mother and Angie, he did so with his head held up high. He was unable to wipe the tears off his face.

In the third row, Angie and his mother stood.

"I—I'm sorry, Momma." He sniffed. "But I can't have . . . no peace knowing that . . . man . . . what he did to Angie . . . I know Angie told the truth. We both know it."

The bailiff felt pity for Trevon and wiped the falling tears from her eyes. Glancing around the courtroom, she saw a few others reaching up to dry their eyes.

"You said enough, son," his mother said as Angie leaned on her shoulder, sobbing.

"I love you, Momma. You too, lil sis. And remember my promise."

At that moment, Angie broke from her mother's embrace and made a beeline toward Trevon shouting, "DON'T TAKE MY BROTHER AWAY FROM MEEE!"

The understanding bailiff allowed Angie to crush her brother in her arms. The judge grumbled, "I demand order in this court!" The bailiff ignored the judge and motioned Trevon's mother to come and help calm Angie down.

Once order was restored, the judge moved on with the sentencing. "In this judgment, the defendant, Trevon Harrison, having pled guilty to first degree murder, the court orders that he be imprisoned in the Florida Department of Corrections for—"

"Nooooo!" Angie screamed. "That man raped me! Why won't y'all believe meee!"

"ORDER IN THIS COURT!" Judge Holmes roared and rose to his feet.

Trevon managed to rise to his feet. He did so on his own.

"Bailiff!" Judge Holmes pointed at Angie. "Remove her from my courtroom!"

"I believe you, lil sis!" Trevon shouted. "Always did — and always will!"

Before the day was over, Trevon was sentenced. He begged his family to leave, knowing the system was unfair and would come down hard on him. Trevon kept his head up as Judge Holmes sentenced him to twenty–one years with the possibility of parole.

CHAPTER
ONE
August 26, 2011
Friday 10:23 a.m. - Miami, Florida

Thirty-three-year-old Trevon Harrison sat in the back of the non-air conditioned cab. Even with the windows down, it felt like 1,000 degrees and did little to stop the sweat beading up on his baldhead. An irritating drop of sweat and cheap deodorant trickled down his armpit. Even in his discomfort he had a reason to be happy. "We almost dere," the Haitian cab driver said with a hand-rolled cigarette between his cracked lips. "'Nother hot day, huh?"

Trevon nodded. If there was one virtue Trevon had, it was patience.

"Hey!" The cab driver peered at Trevon in the rearview mirror. "Didn't I pick you up—few days ago? Yeah. Took you to the dog track for job," he said.

"A job I didn't get." Trevon leaned up a bit to see the cab driver's ID tag. Through the scratched plexiglass, he saw the cab driver's name. Manuel.

"Why not? What is hard to do dere?"

Trevon shrugged his massive shoulders. "Don't know. Once they heard 'I'm fresh out of prison' I was shown the door."

"Life no fair sometimes," Manuel said, snuffing the cigarette in the ashtray.

7

"That it ain't," Trevon replied, looking out the window.You look for new job again?"

"Yeah. This will be my sixth interview since I've been out."

"How long you do?"

Trevon glanced down at his hands. "Fifteen years. Just got out nine days ago."

"You wise to look for job. These streets—" Manuel gestured. "Not the same no more. Young kids wild. Gangs, drugs, nothin' fair no more."

"I feel you on that."

"What type of job you look for?"

"Any job that will keep me gainfully employed. I'll shovel cow shit to avoid going back to prison."

"You on parole?"

"Yeah."

"I wish you luck with your effort today. If it not turn out good—" Manuel slid a slot open on the plexiglass and handed Trevon a business card. "I might can get you down at station washing cabs. I put in a good word for you. You seem like nice guy."

"Thanks." Trevon slid the card in his pocket. "Oh, my name is Trevon Harrison."

"Nice to meet ya." Manuel slowed the cab then switched lanes to pass a delivery van.

Trevon's sweat was a mixture of nervousness and anxiety. Adding the relentless Miami heat to the pressure of trying to find a job was slowly taking a toll on Trevon. He was trying hard to do right. Each time he was turned down for a job, it only pushed him to try harder. Angie and his mother were still up in North Carolina, so his support system in Miami was not in his corner. Trevon had left the streets at a young age when he needed support the most. Today, he was a grown man. Most important to him, he was a free grown man. His reason to be happy.

"Ah, here we are my friend," Manuel said, slowing the cab in front of a glass front modern building on Biscayne Boulevard. "Timing good?"

"Perfect," Trevon said then stepped out of the cab. He reached in his pocket for cab fare.

Leaning across the seat, Manuel shook his head, smiling. "This one on me. Keep your money."

Trevon thanked Manuel then waved at him as he drove off. Trevon stood on the sidewalk as people walked by him. It took only a few seconds to see that he was the only one without a cell phone. Looking up, he had to shield his eyes from the sun. Seven pencil straight palm trees stood in front of the building Trevon was about to enter. Turning around, he waited for an opening in the crowd, then moved closer to the glass mirrored door. He paused a moment to study his reflection. His clothes were casual. Black dress shoes, black cotton pants, and a crisp, white, button-down shirt. His prison built muscular frame was hard to hide. Straightening the collar, he inhaled the sea-scented air, then pulled his pants up an inch. *Please, let me get this job,* he thought.

Reaching the doors, he paused to look at the chrome plated nameplate. Amatory Erotic Films.

Stepping inside the air-conditioned building, he walked up to the security desk. Two stocky white men, both armed, eyed him like a suspect. The smaller of the two guards greeted Trevon with a stern, unsmiling approach.

"Welcome to Amatory Erotic Films. How may I help you?"

"I um, have an eleven o'clock interview with Ms. Babin," Trevon said.

The second guard checked the computer after Trevon told them his name.

"Trevon Harrison, I see it," the second guard replied.

Trevon was asked to show his ID. Once it was fully scrutinized, it was given back along with a visitor's pass that was clipped to his shirt.

"Just head for the elevator and push the button for the third floor, Mr. Harrison." The short guard pointed to the left.

Trevon nodded, then made his way across the soft black carpeted floor. There was no indication that connected the office to an adult film company.

After pressing the button for the elevator, he took a moment to gather his thoughts. *A porn star!* he thought. Under no circumstances was he going back to hustling. Trevon reflected briefly on his past as the elevator began to move. When he gave up his freedom back in '96, he had a side hustle of selling weed and slanging a few small pieces of crack. All done for the strength of his family. His street-earned money placed food on the table and kept the water and power on when his mother was facing hard times making ends meet. Looking at his feet, he hoped he could meet the standards if the chance was given to do a new type of slanging—dick slanging!

The ride up to the third floor was taken alone. When the doors slid open, they revealed a new setting. Everything was white and chrome. Taking a step out, he froze. To his left was a receptionist desk. Behind it sat a cute, young looking black female.

"Welcome to Amatory Erotic Films, Mr. Harrison," the receptionist said with a toothy smile. "Someone will be with you momentarily. You can have a seat to your right." She nodded.

Trevon headed for the cozy waiting lounge. A white horseshoe-shaped leather sofa was the centerpiece. At both ends of the sofa were a few hard core adult magazines on the end tables. The 52-inch flat screen plasma TV was flushed into the wall, currently showing the news. Trevon sat down as the receptionist went back to work. His expectations had not been met. He had assumed the building would be filled with half-naked women prancing around and doing all types of freaky shit. Trevon had come across Amatory Erotic Films by reading an ad in an adult magazine that someone had snuck inside the prison. He only had two years left on his bid when he saw the ad. The fact that Amatory was based in Miami, Florida and not in California had drawn his attention. He leaned over to pick up a magazine when a soft voice called him by his full name. Her accent was definitely Hispanic.

"Trevon Harrison," the woman rolled the letter 'r' as she pronounced his name.

Trevon stood, staring with his mouth agape. The woman was stunningly beautiful. Never during his fifteen-year bid did he think he would be in the presence of a woman of her caliber. He dropped the magazine back on the table as the woman paused to talk to an older female in a cream pantsuit that had gotten off the elevator with her. He cleared his throat as she neared him. Raven black, lustrous curls tumbled past her olive-toned bare shoulders. The clingy colored camisole exposed the cleavage of her succulent breasts with its plunging neckline. Her denim jeans were tight against her juicy appealing thighs, ass and hips. Even in her platform wedge-heeled shoes, she still had to look up to meet his eyes with his 6'4" stance.

"Hi," she said, extending her jeweled wrist and manicured hand. "I'm Jurnee Cruz, Janelle Babin's personal assistant." She shook his large hand, eyeing him openly. She blushed at the size of his arms. They were swollen! His size reminded her of her ex-boyfriend who was a linebacker in the NFL.

Trevon fought hard to keep his eyes from falling into her sea of cleavage. Her top did nothing to hide the size and roundness of her breasts. She had worn the too small camisole without a bra to see how he would react.

"Let's head up to my office," she said, releasing his hand. "Are you nervous?"

"A little bit," he replied, being honest.

They walked beside each other toward the elevator.

"That's to be expected," she said, looking at the size of his arms again. "We'll go up to my office and wait until Ms. Babin is ready to see you."

Trevon nodded.

Reaching the elevator, they waited for two black men in business suits to exit. They both greeted Jurnee with a curt nod.

"Up we go," she said, cheerfully ushering Trevon into the elevator. Neither said a word on the short ride up to the sixth floor. When the doors slid open, she stepped out first. Trevon followed and easily allowed his eyes to fall on her round plump ass.

"Care for anything to drink or eat?" she asked over her shoulder.

"I'm good," he said, following her down the hall.

Walking past an office, a skinny white dude stuck his head out and asked Jurnee if she would reply to his e-mail.

"I'll get to it later," she said without looking back or stopping. Nearing the end of the hallway, she stopped at the second to last door on the left. Trevon stood aside as she unlocked the door. Stepping inside, he felt a bit awkward being alone with her once she closed the door. Her office was roomy, with cool warm hues of green painted walls, modern-styled furniture, plush carpet and pictures and awards displayed in a built in wall case. In all four corners sat large tropical potted plants. The huge picture window behind her desk was covered with drapes. He sat down on the green leather bonded couch as she slid behind her desk and into the soft-looking chair.

"So," Jurnee asked, leaning back. "How has your morning been thus far?" She wanted him to be relaxed before meeting the boss.

"Okay," Trevon replied, keeping his eyes on her exotic-looking face. "Just hoping I'll get a chance to um—"

"Have sex with beautiful women on film and get paid for it?" Jurnee stated bluntly.

"Since you put it like that, yeah." Trevon broke into a sheepish grin.

"No need to beat around the bush with me." Jurnee adjusted the camisole over her breasts. "You don't look like you're thirty-three, but I guess the myth is true about prison keeping you looking young."

He shrugged. "It's true in my case, but it ain't true for everyone."

"I'll agree," she said. "But to be honest, I had my doubts about you because of your age."

"Why?"

"Well, in this business, looks are a major asset to success. I'm aware that sex will sell in just about any form. Different people have their lust or fetish for which type of sex they wish to view. I know some men that will only buy hard core DVDs with women featured at two-hundred pounds or better. Women of all shapes and colors can get by. But with men, it can be very selective. Also, in most films that we produce, the male is the supporting actor. Males are our biggest consumers, so it's only right that we cater to them."

"How do you know so much about porn?" he asked.

Jurnee smiled, crossing her shapely legs behind the desk. "I take it that you weren't allowed adult magazines inside prison?"

"I had my fair share. Actually, I had one that had a promo ad for Amatory in it."

13

She casually brushed a strand of hair out of her face, then reached down to open a drawer on the desk. "My porn name was Honey Drop. And I'm heartbroken that you never heard about me," she teased.

Trevon leaned up to pick up the magazine. Settling back in the couch, his eyes widened. The cover featured Jurnee wearing nothing but a pair of black platform heels and a black leather choker. She was looking back over her shoulder with a finger stuck promiscuously in her mouth. Her naked ass glimmered with oil, looking good enough to eat.

"Y-you-you used to do porn?" he stuttered.

Jurnee nodded up and down. "For nine years." She stood up. "Read the article. I have to use the restroom right quick."

He watched her leave then quickly moved his attention on the magazine. Turning to page twenty-seven, he read up on Jurnee, aka Honey Drop, and what she had accomplished in her nine years of porn. A big surprising fact came when he read that she was forty-one years old. His attention was yanked from the written article after he viewed several hard core pictures from her films. Two small pictures had her with two men. She took one doggy style while filling her mouth with the second. His dick got hard as he viewed each picture of her getting fucked in a number of positions. Adjusting his throbbing erection, he then closed the magazine to calm himself. He had not been with a woman in fifteen years! Trevon was single at the time of his sentencing, so there was no female waiting for him with legs wide open when he was released from prison. He was leaning back with his eyes closed when Jurnee returned.

"Was it that boring?" she asked, easing back behind her desk.

"No." He sat up.

"I was just thinking about something."

"I bet you were." She noticed the magazine on his lap. No doubt, hiding his erection that she was hoping to see. So far his outer appearance had gotten him through the door. Her concern was if Trevon had the *tools* to be a male adult actor. What good was a handsome face and a pussy moistening body with a little dick? Unemployed when it came to Amatory's standards. Jurnee held this thought process in the office as well as in her personal life.

"Why did you show me this?" he asked after she sat down.

"Reason one, I have no shame of my past. Porn to me is liberating. I enjoy having sex, and with me, I'm able to do it without my emotions playing a big part. Reason two, of course, the money and fame was good, but I didn't let them control me."

"So what do you do now?"

"You forgot already." She laughed. "I'm Ms. Babin's assistant—remember?"

"Oh, yeah." He looked down at the magazine and held it up. "So you're really done with porn?"

"One hundred percent, if you're asking if I get in front of the camera."

"How does your man feel about you being a former adult film actress?"

Jurnee laughed, she knew this question was coming. "I didn't mention anything about being in a relationship in that interview you just read, and as the saying goes . . ." She held up her left hand showing no ring. "I've had my share of relationships. I prefer being single."

"Do you have any regrets about doing porn?"

"Nope," she said, glancing at her watch. "I'll share this with you. Many men have high hopes of being a porn star. It's not an easy job. If you think it's all about getting your dick hard and ramming it in and out of a willing female, then you'll be in for a big surprise. You'll have to act. You'll have to sell yourself to the camera. Think you can stop in mid-stroke of the director's cue? Think you'll be able to get hard in a room with ten or more faces focused on you? I'm not trying to discourage you. I'm just telling you the true facts of this business."

"I guess I have much to learn."

"Just be willing to learn and listen and you'll go far in this business. You can trust me on that." Jurnee winked.

"Okay, since you know everything that goes on in this business, what can you tell me to keep in my mind as a golden rule?"

"A golden rule you ask?" She thought for a minute.

"One that you hold the closest."

"This is all assuming you'll be signed to Amatory, right?"

"Call it positive thinking," he said, grinning.

"Well." She smiled. "If you're signed, I'll tell you my golden rule. But right now, I need to get you up to see the boss lady."

"What do I call her? Janelle or Ms. Babin?"

"Ms. Babin. And with her, it would be a good idea too."

"Can I keep this?" He stood up with the magazine.

"Sure." Jurnee winked as he tucked it under his arm. "You can leave that here and come back and get it after your interview, okay?"

Walking down the hall toward the elevator, he enjoyed the backshot. Her ass was soft looking, making him want to squeeze it. The temptation was strong, but Trevon was able to beat it. Reaching the elevator, she boldly reached up to fix his collar. He had no choice but to gaze at her breasts. She showed no protest as he looked.

"There." She smiled. "Perfect."

"Thanks," he muttered, wishing he could spend more time with her.

"Okay. This is where we part. When you get up to Janelle's floor, just step over to the receptionist desk and she'll take care of you. And be yourself, okay?"

"I will," he said as the elevator doors parted.

She took a step back and waved playfully as the doors slid shut. Pulling out her Smartphone, she made a quick call to the receptionist on Janelle's floor.

"Ruby. Hi, this is Jurnee. If you see Kandi up there tell her to come to my office. It's urgent."

CHAPTER
TWO

"Ms. Babin. Your eleven o'clock interview is here."

"Thank you," Janelle said, turning her radio off. "Go ahead and send him in."

"He's sexy!" the receptionist, Ruby said through the wireless intercom.

"Don't let me check his pockets and find your phone number," Janelle joked.

"Oh, I wish, but my husband would kill me."

"I hear you. But if you'll excuse me, I have to go back to work." Janelle pressed the OFF button then tapped a secret key on the keyboard to disengage the lock on the door. It silently popped open on its own. She rose to her feet, tugging at the hem of her white tailored Michael Kors tuxedo jacket. A picturesque smile formed on her dark brown face when Trevon eased inside her office. So far, she was feeling his first impression.

"Come in and have a seat." She motioned toward a purple leather chair placed in front of her desk. Her light hazel eyes did a quick scan of him from head to toe. Personally, she preferred her men to have hair, but with Trevon, the baldhead suited him.

Trevon sat down. Immediately, he was put off his square by her beauty. Straight, jet-black shoulder length hair, and her flawless dark brown skin without a heavy mask of makeup. The linen pantsuit formed noticeable taut lines over every curve of her body. Diamond stick earrings laced her ears. Janelle Babin was drop dead beautiful.

"Welcome to Amatory Erotic Films," she greeted him as she walked around the desk with her hand held out. Her presence had Trevon at a loss for words. "I'm so glad you could make it." She shook his hand. "How are you doing?"

"Fine." He sat down, eyeing her tight frame as she strolled back around her desk. Her office was twice the size of Jurnee's. Ornate leather sofas lined both sides of the office. The walls were olive green with numerous framed pictures on the wall. To his left were twenty framed cover arts for films Amatory had produced. Six of them showed Jurnee as the star actress.

"So, we finally meet," she said enthusiastically. "When you first wrote me two years ago, I had strong doubts that I would ever meet you. I'm glad you stayed in touch with us."

He cleared his throat. "I, too, want to thank you for giving me this interview, Ms. Babin. I'm still surprised that my letter was even answered in the first place."

"Oh, we had our doubts, Mr. Harrison. You won't believe the amount of mail we get from guys locked up. Some want to venture into the business and the rest merely seek to be a pen pal with some of my actresses they have seen in a magazine. Like I just said, you were not the only one to write about doing porn, and I'll go ahead and tell you what sets you apart. Those pictures you sent with your shirt off caused a few of my actresses to act crazy. I had one girl saying how she would like to lick every part of your body until her taste buds got numb.

"You have two of the three assets that I look for in men that I hire. First, you are extremely handsome. Two, your body! Those years of pumping iron has really paid off

for you. And last, we will have to find out at another time."
She smiled, looking down toward his crotch.

"I have your blood test and I'm happy to see there are
no signs of any STDs. Now, tell me this. Have you had sex
since you've been out?"

"No such luck," he said, forcing himself to relax at the
level of her blunt talk.

"What about masturbation?" she asked with a straight
face.

Trevon shifted in the chair.

"Nothing to be ashamed of, Mr. Harrison. Hell, I had
to break myself off twice last night just to go to bed."

Trevon pictured the vivid erotic sight of her playing in
her pussy. Rubbing his baldhead, he admitted that he had
jacked off two days ago.

Janelle smiled. "Women view men such as yourself as
a rare stone. You're like a virgin. Fifteen years is a long
time to go without sex. Just that fact alone would be a
strong marketing tool. My vision is to capture your very
first sexual act on film!"

Trevon leaned forward as his heart rate sped up.
"You're giving me the position?"

She wagged her finger. "Rule number one. Patience is
a must. If we can reach an agreement, I can set the filming
to begin within two weeks. There will be legal items that
need to be taken care of and they can't be passed over.
Remember, above all else, this is a business, okay? Here at
Amatory, all of our filmed scenes are done practicing safe
sex." She allowed her words to sink in before she
continued. "I do have a few questions I would like to ask
you." She turned toward the keyboard then adjusted the flat
widescreen monitor.

"First question. Have you ever had any sexual relations
with a member of the same sex?"

"Nope, and I'm not going to start." He frowned.

"Just routine questions, Mr. Harrison. No need to take it personal," she said easily.

"My bad."

"It's all good. But let's move on. Okay, have you ever had sex filmed? Any homemade sex tapes?"

"Nah."

She nodded while typing. "Have you ever had anal sex with a female?"

"Nope."

"Really?" She paused.

"I'm telling the truth." He shrugged.

"Okay, what about a threesome?"

"I can only wish."

"How about you and another guy with one female?"

"Um . . . I ran a train on a few girls. But I never did it with another man in the same bed, if that's what you're getting at."

"That's what I was getting at," she said, grinning. "How do you feel about double penetration?"

"Well um, like I said, I never did it, but I've seen a few pictures and read about the experience."

"And?"

"I won't knock it, so I'm game to try it . . . and anal sex."

"Good answer," she said, sitting back and crossing her arms. "How do you feel about eating pussy?"

"I can hold my own."

"I hope so. If not, you'll learn."

"I'm open to learning all that I can," he said, feeling pre-cum seeping from his dick. Talking about sex with her fine ass was messing with his head.

"Did you know a woman can climax from anal sex if it's done right?" She was speaking from experience, not hearsay.

"Really?"

She nodded yes. "Sexually, I see that you are behind when it comes to the knowledge of sex. No need to feel bad. I'm sure you won't mind being taught."

He was about to respond, but her iPhone rang.

"Hold that thought for one moment." She answered the call and surprised him by switching flawlessly to Spanish. He had no other option but to admire her sexy looks. The suckable glossy lips. Perfect straight white teeth and in Trevon's view, she sorta favored the singer Keri Hilson. He was caught looking at the outline of her titties when she ended the call.

"Sorry about that, but I have to go meet my lawyer." She took another scan of him, getting a closer look at his clothes. None of the items were up to her standards.

"Is everything okay?" he asked.

"Yes. But I'll need to finish this interview at another time."

Trevon could not mask the disappointment on his face.

"How did you get here?" she asked.

"A cab. I don't have a car yet."

She bit her bottom lip, pondering. Making up her mind a few seconds later, she pressed the TALK button to speak to her receptionist.

"Could you please send Kandi up to my office now?"

"I'm on it," Ruby said in return.

"Thank you." Janelle then turned her attention back to Trevon. "I'm terribly sorry about this." She sounded sincere.

"Will you be setting another interview for me?" He hoped she would.

"Sure. In fact, I'll make sure to tell Jurnee to reschedule my itinerary to fit you in at the soonest. Are you free for the rest of the day?" she asked.

"Me? Yeah."

"Well, if you're up to it, I have a surprise for you."

"I'm listening."

"I'm throwing a party at my place tonight and I'd like you to attend."

Trevon looked down at his cheap clothes. "I'll need to change because—"

"I'll take care of that—" She paused. "If you'll allow me. It's part of my surprise. Just accept it as a welcome home gift."

"And the interview?"

"Patience," she reminded him.

"I'm working on it." He smiled. Building up the courage, he asked her how she earned her position.

"Hard work, foremost," she said, turning her computer off. "I used to be a fashion model a few years ago. My ex-boyfriend released one of our personal sex tapes and it ruined my career. Instead of denying the tape, I decided to capitalize off it once I saw how the tape was selling. This company was formed off that tape and two more that I starred in and produced myself."

Trevon envied the lucky men who had fucked her in front of the camera.

"In case you're wondering—" She smiled. "I do all of my work from behind this desk and behind the camera."

"Ms. Babin," the receptionist broke in over the intercom. "Kandi is on her way up."

"Thank you," Janelle replied. "Before I forget. Can you alert the guards that I'll be leaving soon and to make sure that nobody is blocking my car in?"

"I'll call them now," Ruby replied.

"Thank you."

Janelle walked to the door to unlock it since her computer was shut down. "I want you to meet someone." She unlocked the door, then headed back behind her desk.

Trevon turned in the seat just as the door was pushed open. He rose to his feet when he laid his eyes on Kandi.

"Trevon, I'd like to introduce you to Kandi."

Trevon was again at a loss for words. Kandi entered the office in a pair of blue ice pick heels and skin-tight black spandex Capri pants. The loose blue Jersey shirt draped over her large breasts and exposed her flat belly and pierced navel. He was unable to pull his eyes away from the size of her hips and ass. Dark golden ringlets reached the middle of her back. Her pouty lips were coated with a nude-pink colored gloss that looked wet. Along with her lust-enticing frame, she had a major element that ensnared him. She was a redbone sistah. Her thighs, ass and hips stretched the spandex to its limit. Her eyes were hidden behind a pair of tinted designer shades. Trevon rubbed his face to get himself together, no doubt, deeply embarrassed.

Janelle paid close attention to their chemistry. "I need a favor, Kandi," she said. "Could you please take Trevon to see Larese? He'll be expecting the visit."

"Now?" Kandi asked.

"Yes."

"Yeah, I can do it," Kandi said, brushing a piece of lint off her wide baby-making hips.

"Good and be sure to give me a call when you're done," Janelle added and escorted them out of her office.

Out in the hall, Trevon followed the two women toward the waiting elevator. They rode down to the main floor. The women were engaged in their own conversation, leaving Trevon to his thoughts. He second-guessed himself, thinking this environment was out of his league. He was led out through the back door where a black security guard met them. The guard nodded at Janelle and Kandi as they strolled by. Trevon followed in the wake of Janelle and Kandi's sweet-smelling fragrances. They were still chatting to each other when they stepped out of the building.

Trevon took a few steps then stopped. Squinting from the sun, he laid his eyes on the row of expensive cars and

SUVs lined up. For the first time in his life he trained his gaze on an Oregon yellow Lamborghini Aventador. Trevon had seen the new beast in magazines and knew the price tag for the flagship Lambo sat in the range of $380,000. He looked at Janelle in awe when she came to a stop in front of the vehicle. By remote, the driver's side scissor door slowly raised.

"You're in good hands with Kandi," Janelle said before pulling out the key for her ride. Keying the alarm, she waved Kandi and Trevon goodbye, then slid into her car.

Trevon watched her rolling off on chrome with the system bumping "Pieces of Me" by Ledisi. Shit seemed surreal to be around business-minded women pushing three hundred thousand dollar cars. He was so caught up in Janelle that he had forgotten all about Kandi. She regained his attention by calling out his name. Turning, he found her stepping into a diamond black Escalade riding on chrome 28's. The sun glinted on the chrome mesh grill and rims.

"Ready to go?" She watched him closely as he moved to the passenger side.

Inside the Escalade, Trevon settled in the tan leather seat as Kandi slid off her shades, revealing natural green eyes.

"I like black," she said out of the blue. "It's my favorite color . . . and my favorite flavor if you know what I mean."

Trevon looked at her as she drove toward the gated exit.

"You really did fifteen years in prison?" she asked openly.

"Day for day," he said, hoping she would not press him to speak about his time in prison. He was having a hard time dealing with his nightmares that kept him up at night. He assumed it was normal since he was fresh out of the joint. Having to discuss it during his awake time was punishment.

Kandi sensed the uneasiness in his reply, so she changed the subject. "I know Janelle is real picky of the men she hires. I see you got the looks and the body." She paused and smiled at him as she slowed down for a red light. "How big is your dick?"

Trevon looked away, grinning and shaking his head at her blunt candor. "Big enough," he said. He quickly glanced away out of habit. It was hard on him and he tried to be normal, to act like it was all good. Even now, he was rubbing his wrist. It seemed like he was in the wrong to not be in cuffs and chains. Prison had forced him to be cautious around new faces, but he was finding it hard to place any judgment on Kandi. His weakness would always be a female. Rubbing his face, he tried to relax. He wanted to fit in. He needed to do this to survive in the free world.

Pulling from the light as it turned green, Kandi reached over to rub his knee. "Why are you so tense?" She smiled. "I hope you're not nervous being around me?"

"Nah, just trying to take things all in."

"Don't try too hard, okay? If you do get signed, you'll be with a good company because Janelle knows what she is doing."

"How long have you been with Amatory?"

"Four years. I did my first amateur film when I was twenty. I'm twenty-four now and I do enjoy what I do for a living. Maybe one day we can hook up." She squeezed his knee, then placed both hands on the steering wheel. By voice command, she filled the SUV with music. They found their first common link when the hit by Rick Ross "Aston Martin Music" flowed through the system. Kandi loved hip-hop. She was feisty and hated when things did not go her way. In order for her to make it in this industry, she had to grow some balls of her own. She was a freak on and off the screen, but moved as a true DIVA. She loved looking fly, feeling fly and like her ex-rapper boyfriend once told her, "Stay on your swag." That was the only advice she took from him. Kandi was over him and did not fuck with him in any form.

CHAPTER
THREE

"You think Janelle will sign me?" Trevon later asked as the wind blew through Kandi's hair. They were cruising down the palm tree-lined boulevard within the thick traffic.

"Hard to tell with her. I say your chances are good, but it's not up to me."

He nodded that he understood.

"You don't like to talk much, huh?" she figured. "That's okay, because I like to talk and you'll make a good listener. I do have one question though."

Trevon pulled his eyes from the road ahead. "Let me guess. You want to know what I was in prison for?"

"Um, no," she lied. "But since you mentioned it. Yeah. Why were you in prison?"

Trevon glanced up through the tinted sunroof. "I killed a man that raped my sister when she was thirteen," he said flatly with a deadpan look on his face. He assumed she would judge him, thus pushing her to the point of fear.

"I hope you made that sick bastard suffer," she stated.

Trevon lowered his eyes and looked away. He, too, had suffered. He held no doubt of what happened to Angie when she came home from school with tears falling down her face. The man accused of the crime was a well-known white teacher at Angie's school. Trevon never missed a court date of the three-week long trial. Not guilty. Trevon could not accept how fate had freed a guilty man. Acting on pure anger, he gunned the man down in broad daylight as he stood watering his lawn only six days after the unjust verdict. Even now he was being pulled in two directions. Knowing what Angie had gone through had him morally doubting his move to jump into the life of porn. He knew his sister would not understand his choice.

"Where are we going?" he asked, pushing the painful thoughts from his mind.

"It's a surprise, remember?"

"Okay, I'll wait."

"You don't have a choice because I'm good at keeping a secret," she said, turning the music down. "You gotta girlfriend?"

"Not right now I don't."

"Good." She smiled.

"Why do you say that?"

"Because it will be less drama when we get our freak on. I told you my favorite color is black."

Again she reached over to rub his knee. "Do I make you feel uncomfortable, Trevon?"

"If you did, you'd know by now."

She took that as the go-ahead to inch her hand up his thigh. "I think you and I will get along like sand at a beach," she said without a doubt in her mind.

Trevon took a deep breath as Kandi rubbed his bold dick print under his pants.

"Here's your surprise!" Kandi entered the Gucci store swiveling her hips. "Janelle wants you to ditch those clothes and get upgraded!"

The Gucci store was brightly lit and smelled of leather and perfume. The walls were brown and white with the Gucci logo embedded in the paint. Kandi's loud entrance turned a few heads as her heels clacked on the mirror black marble floor.

Trevon had a new open chemistry with Kandi after the brief pleasure she gave him with her hand. He was trying to just relax and go with the flow. Stepping past the front desk, he looked around and easily noticed that he was the only black male in the store. His massive arms drew stares that Kandi noticed, but told him to ignore.

"My money ain't where it's supposed to be for me to be up in here," he said to Kandi.

"Boy, miss me with that." She laughed, reaching into a black python Fendi bag strapped over her shoulder. After digging around, she pulled out a Visa Black Card. "This one is on Janelle! She wants you to look your best, and I do agree because what you have on is so Walmartish, boo."

Trevon smiled at her honest view of his clothes. "Are you going to the party too?"

"Wouldn't miss it!" Kandi pulled him toward the back.

"I don't think I'm ready for a party."

"Are you serious! A party is just what you need."

They slid by a married couple and were a few feet from the men's cologne counter when a soft, feminine voice called out for Kandi.

"And you must be the man of the hour! Trevon?"

Trevon turned toward the voice, instantly picking up on the accent and over-stressed words of a man trying to sound feminine. He knew immediately that it was a man.

"Larese, I'd like you to meet Trevon. Larese is the pint-sized manager here."

"I'm not in the mood, Kandi! Don't make me get bitchy up in here!" Larese snapped.

Trevon took a step back as the three-foot ten-inch midget walked bowlegged from around a shirt rack of solid colored silk shirts.

"Larese is gay," Kandi said as she squatted to his eye level to tease him.

"Out of my face. Poof! Be gone." Larese tried to push her aside. "Who is my VIP?"

Kandi stood up and quickly introduced the two. Trevon had no phobia being around homosexuals. In prison, he had to learn to deal with living with them. True, many straight men had fallen and were turned out—straight men thinking that getting favors from another male did not make them gay. Gay was gay. It did not matter if you were on the receiving end or giving end.

"Janelle wants you to—"

"Girl, I spoke to the Boss Diva and I know what to do to this fine piece of eye candy." Larese snapped. "Follow me."

Trevon was taken to the back and treated with VIP status. Larese had to stand up on a table to measure Trevon. Kandi rolled her eyes at Larese fanning himself while measuring Trevon's arms and swollen chest. Kandi sat down crossing her legs when Trevon took his shirt and tank top off. It was tossed in the trash and replaced with Gucci linen. Everything that touched his skin was Gucci. Button down shirts, pullovers, linen pants, jeans, gator shoes, ties, suits, hats, socks, boxers, belts and shades. He lost count of the number of times he went in and out of the dressing room. In the end, he kept on an all white loose linen set, laced down to a pair of square-toed white gators.

"Fabulous!" Larese clapped his tiny hands as Trevon pimped out of the dressing room. His 6'4", 245-pound frame had Kandi lost with sexual ideas. Kandi stood with her tongue twisted. His new gear changed his look dramatically for the better. She still had the vision of his naked body from the waist up planted in her mind. That V-shape of his back had made her nipples hard. Ducking off to head outside, she pulled out her cell phone.

Trevon ended up with a tab totaling $7,530 charged to Janelle's credit card. No one had ever given him such a large gift. Reverting back to his prison state of mind, he knew there was no such thing as a 'free gift.' If something was given, then you damn well better have something to give in return. It took him a moment to notice that Kandi was missing. With help from the store personnel, he headed outside with his large bags. The sun instantly began to pounce on his baldhead. At least now, he had on a new pair of tinted shades.

"Where are you parked, sir?" one of the sales reps asked, breaking Trevon's gaze.

"Oh, my bad. Follow me." Trevon led the way. He was a few feet from Kandi's SUV when he saw her walking away from him gesturing wildly with one arm while beefing with someone on the phone. Pedestrians on the sidewalk parted out of her way. Most of the men were looking and pointing at her ass. Trevon placed his bags on the curb, then asked one of the Gucci employees to watch them. Trevon jogged toward Kandi as she kept ranting over the phone.

"What the fuck do you keep calling me for?" she shouted as Trevon finally reached her.

"Kandi," he said. "Yo, what's up? You okay?"

Kandi spun around, causing Trevon to bump into her. She gasped then ended the call. They stood without saying anything. Kandi fingered loose hair from her face.

"You look good," she said, circling him. She was not open to sharing her drama.

Trevon turned, trying to figure her out. Who was he to care or worry about who she was talking to on the phone? If she had a man, so what. Trevon shrugged, then followed Kandi back toward the ride.

"You got some place to be?" she asked as she pulled away from the curb.

"Not really. What time does the party 'spose to start?"

"Eight or nine," she said with both hands on the wheel.

Trevon looked at his new Gucci watch. It was twenty minutes to 3 p.m. and the heat outside was still roasting.

"Wanna get something to eat?" she asked, taking a glance at his lips.

"Yeah. I was in a rush this morning so I didn't get to eat much. I think we passed a Burger King down the block on our way here."

"Burger King!" she blurted. "I wouldn't dare." She laughed.

"Food is food," he said, smiling as she whipped the Escalade through the traffic.

"True. But I think we can have more privacy at this cozy beach front restaurant on south Miami Beach."

"Do I have a choice?"

"Nope."

"I figured that."

Along the short trip, he lowered the tinted windows and just mellowed out with the wind in his face. Trevon had no idea what tomorrow would bring. All he wanted to do was make money and stay free.

"I can't believe you haven't had sex in fifteen years! I wouldn't know what to do," she said, breaking the silence. "Oh, I know I would have lots to do. I like women too. I would be just fine."

They both shared a laugh while Trevon made a mental note of his new discovery about Kandi. He saw no wrong with her going both ways.

CHAPTER
FOUR

At the trendy restaurant, Kandi caught Trevon off guard by hooking her arm inside his. The owner of the Chophouse personally came from the back office to greet Kandi. The woman was in her late fifties and met Kandi with a big warm hug. Making her own assumption, she glanced at Trevon, blushed, then told Kandi she had a keeper.

"Who was that lady?" Trevon asked when they were seated in a quiet secluded booth.

"She's one of my biggest fans."

"Yeah, right." He laughed at the thought of the older woman watching porn.

"You have a lot to learn, Trevon."

"Are you going to teach me?"

Kandi looked up over the glass of iced tea she was drinking. Finally, she noticed signs of him opening up to her. She wanted to figure him out. Was he hood, a G, a hustler? Hell, she just wanted to know something! She lowered the glass from her wet lips.

"I can teach you a lot of things about sex."

"I'm down with that," he said. "So when is my first lesson?"

"Oooohhhh, look who is coming out of their shell," she teased.

34

"Well," she whispered, licking her lips. "Lesson one, I can show you how I can do it with no hands. Then after that, I can show you why they call me Kandi."

"Tell me now."

"Sure you want to know?"

"Positive."

Kandi leaned back in the booth, never taking her eyes away from Trevon. Parting her thick legs, she raised one finger to her pouty lips and slid it inside her mouth. Next, she used her other hand to pull up the elastic band of her spandex Capri pants. Keeping eye contact, she slid her wet finger down into her pants and under her thong. Her eyelids fluttered when her fingers brushed over her sensitive clitoris. Holding her breath, she inserted her middle finger inside her moist pussy.

"Mmmmm," she moaned, fingering herself at the table.

Trevon thought she was bullshitting. Looking under the table, he saw her hand down in the front of her Capri pants. "Damn!" he said, enjoying her freaky show.

Kandi released a deep breath, pulling her fingers from her pussy. With glassy eyes, she looked at him, then slid her wet slippery fingers into her mouth and sucked them clean.

"They call me Kandi because my pussy stays sweet."

Trevon sat back in the booth as Kandi smiled at him. "That was—wild!" He panned the room.

"Relax. No one can see us. And if they did . . . who gives a fuck?"

Trevon had no idea what to expect from Kandi. When the food arrived, it did nothing to push sex from her mind.

"How often did you jack off when you were in prison?" she asked while cutting a piece of steak.

"A lot," he said and quickly realized how easy and comfortable it was to talk to her.

"What did you think about?"

"Women."

"I know that, silly." She laughed. "But seriously, did you think of any wild fantasies?"

Trevon slowly chewed a piece of steak before answering. "Well, to be straight up, I usually think about having um . . . backdoor sex with a woman."

"Anal sex," she said a tone too loud for him.

"Damn! Stand up in the chair and yell it out."

Kandi sat back, looking at him funny.

"What?" Trevon asked, looking confused.

"You've never fucked a girl in the ass?"

"No, Kandi, I haven't."

Grinning, she winked. "I'll keep that in mind. And FYI, I love taking it in my ass."

"You got a man or anything?"

"No. I'm not currently fucking anyone off the set if that's on your mind."

"A lot is on my mind," he said, wondering what it would be like to finally have sex after fifteen years.

"Why do you want to do porn?"

"I need the job, Kandi. All bullshit aside, I have to find a job or my parole officer will send me back to prison. I've been to five job interviews since I've been out and this is my last chance."

Kandi felt sorry for him. "Does Janelle know about your parole issue?"

"Yeah. I told her about it the day I got out over the phone. I doubted I would get this chance, so I went ahead and looked for some jobs. My parole officer ain't the best person to get along with."

"How much time do you have to get a job?"

"A month. After that, I know she'll start acting stupid and press to send me back to prison."

"How long would you have to stay?"

"Six years."

"Umm, if you get signed, can you tell your parole officer what you're really doing?"

"Why wouldn't I? She told me to find a job and stressed that any job would do as long as it is legal. Hell, I'll be getting a check, so it will be a legal job."

Kandi reached across the table to grasp his hand. "Janelle will sign you and then you can tell that P.O. to kiss your ass." She tried to assure him of the best.

"I hope so."

"Cheer up, boo. You're free and dining with a world class *diva*, so enjoy the moment."

Trevon was indeed free. He had to stop thinking about failure before chance.

Kandi suddenly excused herself to the restroom. Trevon's eyes traveled straight to the fat print between her juicy legs. It looked like a miniature boxing glove. This was the fourth time in five hours that his dick grew hard. If this did not stop, he might not make it to his first film.

Back inside the Escalade, Kandi turned the system down. "I spoke to Janelle while I was in the bathroom and she wants us at the party around eight."

Trevon looked down at his watch. "It's four-twenty now. Can you run me by my spot so I can drop my clothes off?"

"Janelle told me that you're living in a boarding home in Liberty City?"

"Yeah," he said, slightly embarrassed of the fact.

Kandi nodded. "Well. Janelle and I spoke on it. I know that Janelle seems all business, but she knows about the streets too. And she knows the risk you'll face over in Liberty City. Janelle will protect her investment by any means necessary."

"The boarding home is all I can afford right now."

Kandi smiled. "I understand that and so does Janelle, which is why we have an idea."

"What is it?"

Kandi drove with one hand as the air conditioner blew over her smooth skin.

"How would you like to stay with me and be my roommate?"

Trevon sat and waited for her to say she was only kidding. She had to be.

"Roommate? With you? You don't know me like that nor do I—"

"Whatever." She laughed. "You can dead that talk. You'll have your own room and I also have a pool. Can you swim?" she asked, trying to be persuasive.

"No, I can't swim, but me moving in with you is different." Trevon was not about to make a quick decision. He weighed the pros and cons of moving in with her. It would be a challenge because he had never shared a place with a female other than his mom and sister.

"You'll have much more room and a ton of privacy," she offered. "At least come to visit. Just chill with me until it's time for the party."

Trevon knew she would be persistent, so he shrugged and said, he would chill with her.

"You don't have a cell phone, do ya?" she asked as a slow moving car changed lanes in front of her.

"Not yet."

"I gotcha."

Kandi stopped at a cellular phone store and told Trevon to pick out one. He reminded her of his time in prison and she was shocked to learn that he had never owned a cell phone. She ended up picking out a pre-paid touch screen phone for him. It was tiny in his large hands and he was amazed with the different applications it could do. Out in the parking lot, she showed him how to take a picture using his new phone. Kandi stood beside her gleaming SUV in a mean stance as Trevon took the picture. Before they drove off, she showed him how to use her picture as the screen saver.

CHAPTER
FIVE

"Welcome to my crib," Kandi said, opening the door to her spacious three bedroom home. She lived in a gated community with 24-hour security in Coconut Grove, Florida.

"This is nice." Trevon followed her inside as her heels clacked on the glossy hardwood floor.

"I can't front," she said over her shoulder. "Janelle owns this place. Some companies have cars. Amatory has houses!"

"What do you mean?"

Kandi strutted down into the sunken living room, tossing her Fendi bag on the floor by the sofa. She flopped down and reached for the TV remote.

"This is a bonus for bringing a certain amount of bread to the company from the films I made."

Trevon sat down next to her on a purple crescent moon-shaped leather sofa. "How long have you been living here?"

"Just five months," she said, removing the heels from her sore feet.

Trevon looked at the 70-inch 3D TV in front of her. The largest he had ever seen. Kandi surfed through the channels until she reached a music video channel.

"Same old videos." She turned the TV off, then pulled her feet up off the floor. She turned to face Trevon. "Let's talk."

Trevon sat back with his arms crossed. "So, Janelle really wants me to move in with you?"

Kandi nodded yes.

"Is it safe to assume she'll be signing me to a contract?"

"Yeah, or she's just courting you to fuck her silly." She laughed. "Just kidding. But for real, I think you'll get your chance, so don't blow it."

Trevon unfolded his arms. He needed to relax!

"If you do stay, I only have one house rule and that's no smoking up in here."

"I don't smoke."

"Good," she said, looking at him. He was just . . . so big, but not in a steroid taking type of look. She reached over to rub his arm. "Anybody ever told you that you favor Tyrese Gibson?"

"You're the first," he lied, having heard it while he was in prison.

"Didn't I see some tats on your chest?"

"I have a few."

She sat up. "Take your shirt off and show me!"

Trevon complied. As he stood up, she took the opportunity to look between his legs. She could just make out an imprint of his dick. She wanted it to get hard again. She wanted it out and in her hands.

"I um . . . keep noticing how much you favor—"

"Nicki Minaj, right?" She rolled her eyes skyward. "I've heard it too many times, so please don't go there."

Trevon left the subject alone as he removed his shirt. Kandi slowly traced her fingers down his chest. Without her heels on, she stood on even ground at 5'7" and weighed 150 pounds. Using her fingertips, she outlined the hard muscled lines of his chest, touching the letters on his left chest that read 'For the Strength of You' and the date, October 25.

"Tell me about this." She spoke in a low tone, seemingly in a trance. Her hands stayed on his dark smooth skin.

"It's for my sister and that is her birth date." He knew the game they were playing by their contact. Her touch sent signals throughout his body that he wanted to answer. Looking down into her top, he noticed she did not have on a bra. There was no doubt of his attraction to her.

"Where is she now?

"Up in North Carolina."

Kandi nodded, then moved her fingers to the tattoo on his stomach. It was a highly detailed lion's head. "You a Leo?"

He nodded yes, struggling to keep his hormones in check. He could only picture the temptation he would have to deal with if he moved in with her.

Kandi had the same dilemma going through her mind. Acting on what she was feeling inside, she slid her hands up and down his rippled stomach. She heard him take a deep breath.

"You want to touch me?" she whispered. When he remained silent, she looked up into his face.

Trevon could not believe he had frozen up. Kandi sensed it. She lowered one hand to his, then guided it to her ass.

"Can I see what you're working with?" She slid her hands back up his chest.

Trevon felt heat coming from her palms. Looking into her eyes, he moved his other hand on her ass. Even with his large hands, he had a lot of ass to explore. He lowered his hands to the bottom roundness of her luscious ass.

"Why are you so tense?" she purred as he squeezed both of her cheeks.

He swallowed. "It's been a long time, Kandi," he said, pulling her up against his body. "Plus, I never been with a chick as fine as you."

"Dang, you never?" She smiled.

"Honest."

"I can't believe that." She pushed her breasts against him, deeply enjoying him rubbing all over her soft ass. "So, if I do this"—She rose up on her toes, sliding a hand up and around his bald head, and bringing his lips to meet hers. Playing the aggressor, she pushed her wet tongue against his and lowered her free hand between them, down to his crotch. A moan eased from his lips when she squeezed his dick. She kissed him with a hint of passion, playfully blocking his tongue from sliding inside her mouth.

Trevon breathed heavily as his body reacted to her touch. Kissing her seemed like a need to him. At this moment, he thought about what she did for a living. He thought about the risk of an STD. When Kandi allowed his tongue past hers, it seemed to awaken a dormant part of him. He squeezed and molded her ass while kissing her deep and slow.

Kandi unfastened his belt and wasted no time reaching inside his boxers to stroke his hard flesh. Breaking their kiss, she tugged his pants and boxers down a bit. She gasped at the ebony dick weighing heavy in her hand, having correctly judged that he was packing a nice nine-incher. Slowly, she stroked it with one hand.

"You so big, Daddy," she said, rubbing under his long hard dick.

Trevon licked his dry lips as Kandi licked all over his chest. She now had both hands on his thick dick. Her pussy moistened.

"Yessss," he moaned into the top of her fresh smelling hair. Filled with a new drive, he slid his hands up and under her top. Cupping her bare titties filled him with desire.

Kandi started a slow hand job, forcing a clear drop of pre-cum to seep from his dick. Suddenly, she imagined his dick between her lips. She wanted to suck it.

"Baby, I wanna—" she began, but was halted by the doorbell.

CHAPTER
SIX

Kandi hurried to the front door, leaving Trevon in the living room. She had a slim list of visitors who would show up unannounced. *I know this motherfucker ain't at my front door*! She stomped barefoot across the floor with an irritated expression on her face. Unlocking the door, she yanked it open without looking through the peephole.

"What are you doing here!" She fumed at the sight of her ex-boyfriend, Swagga and stepped out onto the front porch shutting the door behind her.

"Here to see you," he said through his mouthful of gold and platinum teeth.

"Damn this bullshit! I don't even want you calling me, so why would you think I would want to see your ass?" She crossed her arms with her face balled up. The humid air warmed her chilled skin within seconds.

"I know you ain't still trippin' ova me fuckin' Cindy? Fuck that bitch!"

"You played me!" Kandi shouted. "By doing just that— fucking that bitch!"

Swagga looked over his shoulder at his idling midnight blue wide-body kitted Bentley GT. His personal bodyguard, Yaffa leaned against the ride with his black heavily tattooed arms crossed. In plain view, a chrome .45 was holstered on his waist.

"Why you taking it so serious, yo?" Swagga asked while openly looking at her pussy print. "You fuck and suck dick for a living and you actually thought our relationship was on some exclusive type shit?"

"Why did you try to hide it from me and lie about it, huh?"

Swagga shrugged his skinny shoulders. Lifting weights was not his thing. Smoking weed and popping pills was his only routine that came second to his successful rap career. The only two rappers above him were Lil Wayne and Rick Ross.

"Shit is in the past," he said, towering over her with his 6'2" lanky frame.

"Yeah it is, and I left your ass along with it!"

Swagga laughed. "You buggin' for real." His slightest movements caused his long pencil thin dreads to sway.

Kandi hated him. *I should have never fell for that wack ass game!* Kandi took a step backward when he reached for her hand.

"Oh, you don't want me touchin' you now?"

"I don't even wanna talk to you! You had your chance, but you hurt me."

Swagga was iced out on both wrists and always wore his custom made platinum chain and chunky medallion. He was only twenty-four years old with three platinum albums to his name.

Grinning, he pulled out a knot of money. "How about I take you shoppin' and make up for my wrong?"

"I don't want your money," she said, crossing her arms.

Back inside Kandi's house, Trevon had his clothes back on. He was far from slow as he put two and two together. He would bet anything that the visitor was a dude. Why else would she not invite them in? He paced the floor.

His curiosity wanted to pull him to the window to see who she was talking to. *I'm trying to get a job, not a damn girl!* he thought.

Swagga's ego was hurt as he shoved the money back into his fitted Evisu jeans. "So you gonna handle me like this?"

"Swagga," Kandi said annoyingly. "It ain't all about you, and I'm sorry you got me mixed up with one of your um . . . groupie bitches. What we had is over. Yeah, I suck dick and get fucked for a living, and obviously, it ain't a big deal to you since you are so pressed with getting back with me."

Swagga laughed. "Damn, you feelin' yourself, huh?"

"No." She smiled. "I already have someone inside that's feeling on me."

His smile slowly faded. Looking down, be noticed she was barefoot. His jealousy could not be hidden even if he tried.

"Who?" he asked, looking past her shoulder at the front door.

"You don't know 'im," she said, enjoying the fact that she could get up under his skin.

Swagga had four kids by three different women and was still fucking two out of the three. His link to Kandi was built on emotions. Hands down, she had that bomb pussy. Even though he was clowned by his crew for being seen out in public with her, he just could not stay away. The short ten-month affair he shared with her left him with a yearning for freaky sex unmatched by any other female. In his words: *Couldn't no bitch do it better than Kandi!*

"I'd very much like it if you didn't come here anymore." She reached back for the doorknob.

Swagga wiped his dreads out of his face. "You actin' like a real bitch, yo!"

"Actin' is what I do for a living, remember? And for your info, I did it a lot when you were *trying* to fuck me! Now if you'll excuse this bitch. I gotta nice juicy, fresh, black dick inside waiting on me."

Swagga balled up his fist. "Jump off, bitch!" he shouted.

Kandi blew him a kiss and turned to go back inside.

Swagga remained silent inside his Bentley GT as Yaffa drove with one hand.

"Why you even playin' your face over that bitch is beyond me, my nigga," Yaffa said as his deep baritone voice filled the interior.

"Fuck dat bitch! She ain't shit!" Swagga snapped.

"Told you that before we came over here." Yaffa turned on the two-lane road, then sped off with the tinted windows up. His big frame filled the driver's seat in an imposing look. With his thick Rick Ross like beard and freshly designed cornrows, he could be judged by his looks. He was thirty-four with no kids. He was licensed to carry the chrome .45 and held no weight in using it when it came to protecting Swagga. At 6'3", he pushed the scales at 310 pounds.

"That bitch done crossed the wrong nigga!"

"Let that shit fly, bruh," Yaffa said, scanning the three mirrors. He had to stay on point 24/7. "Call Trina or somebody. You actin' like you pressed for some pussy, my nigga. What about them two West Indies strippers you had up in the room last night. Call 'em back over tonight."

Swagga grinned. "I bet you would want to call 'em since you fucked ol' girl."

Yaffa grabbed his dick. "Doing my job. I was just doin' a cavity search to make sure she wasn't stealin' none of your rings and shit."

Swagga laughed. "Nigga, please! You was diggin' her back out 'cause your black ass was horny. Yeah, I might call them hoes back over to the crib tonight after the party."

"I know you ain't bouncin' to Janelle's party. You know Kandi and her girl Jurnee will be there."

"Fuck them hoes! Janelle invited me, so I'm going."

Yaffa could not debate with Swagga. His job was keeping Swagga alive, not telling him how to run his life.

Reaching I-95 North, they headed back to Fort Lauderdale where Swagga lived on an Oceanfront Estate.

Kandi went to the kitchen to fix a drink before facing Trevon. She figured she would need to offer him an explanation about Swagga. Allowing her nerves to settle, she stood in the open refrigerator drinking from a bottle of fruit punch. The TV was back on. She could hear it from where she stood. *A shower is what I need*! She tossed the empty bottle in the trash, then made her way back into the living room.

Trevon was messing with his new cell phone when Kandi snuck up behind him easing her hands down his chest.

"Whatcha doing?" she asked, resting her chin on top of his baldhead.

"Trying to figure this phone out," he said, telling himself not to stress the issue of her visitor.

"I got a better idea." She pulled the phone from his hands and turned it off. "Come take a shower with me."

Trevon followed her down the hall and into her bedroom. Kandi showed no shame nor timidness when she pulled her top up and over her head. She faced him topless as he stood in the doorway staring at her huge golden titties that sat up high with thumb-sized dark brown nipples.

"Yes, they're real," she said, rubbing her 36D twins.

"I um . . . need to get a change of clothes out of your ride," he said, ogling the ripe fullness of her breasts. *I want to fuck her so bad!*

"Hurry up," she said, tugging the tight spandex bottoms off her plump ass. "I'm going to jump in the shower."

Trevon turned and hurried out of the room. He knew he was going to fuck her. The urge was there and ignoring it was not an option. He wondered why she was on his dick so hard, not that he had any beef with it. All he knew was this: If she wanted the dick, he would serve it to her red ass.

Kandi was soaping up her titties when Trevon slid the glass shower door open. She smiled at the sight of his light chocolate naked frame. Immediately, her eyes fell between his stout legs.

"Come on in, Daddy," she said, loving every inch of his flesh. *This nigga got it goin' the fuck on!* she thought, biting her bottom lip. Looking down at his feet, she frowned. "Hold up. Why you got those things on?" she pointed at the Gucci sandals on his feet.

"I'm taking a shower so I'm wearing shower shoes," he said as if it was normal.

"Shower shoes? What the hell are you talking about?"

Trevon explained. "I always wore shower shoes in prison. Niggas be jacking off in the shower, pissing on the floor and all types of shit. Ain't no telling what type of foot fungus be on them nasty ass floors, so I—"

"Trevon." She touched his shoulder. "You are not in prison no more, okay? And my shower ain't got no fungus in it. My shit stay clean. You can take those thangs off 'cause you ain't getting up in here with me wearing them."

Trevon looked down at his feet. She was right. *Damn, I'm bugging.* He slid his feet out of the shower shoes, then stepped into the shower with Kandi. Playfully, she turned her back toward him. "See anything you like?" she said, handing the soapy rag over her shoulder.

Trevon looked at her wide ass and small waist. Before he even had the time to admire her body, his dick grew hard and solid.

"I feel you do," she said when she felt the tip of his dick poling against her ass. She inched backward causing his dick to slip up and settle into the soft crevice of her ass. "That feels real good." She licked her lips, then reached down to rub her pussy as the shower sprayed onto her titties and belly. His dick was hot and throbbing against her ass.

Trevon grabbed his dick with one hand and teased her by sliding it up and down the length of her wet crack. Getting bold, he pushed the tip between her soft ass cheeks.

"I like that," she said, opening her meaty pussy lips. "Mmmm."

Trevon dropped the soapy rag, then reached around her to fondle her breasts. "Your ass so phat!" he said against the back of her neck.

Kandi knew she was in the wrong. Janelle told her about the plan to save Trevon's first piece of pussy for the film. *This nigga got me so open! I wanna fuck him so damn bad*! He kept teasing her by sliding his dick up and down her ass.

Trevon lowered his mouth behind her ear and started kissing her there. She melted back into his body as his hand continued to tweak her nipples. His dick was now between her legs. She closed them, trapping his dick under her pussy and between her soft inner thighs. She reached back and circled an arm around his baldhead. She gasped and looked down to see his dick sliding between her thighs.

Trevon moaned against her neck when her hand gripped a few inches of his dick. He could feel her wet pussy on the top of his piece.

"Wait Daddy." She panted. "We shouldn't . . . be doing this."

"I want you!" He squeezed her left breast.

"I want you too," she whined.

Trevon released her and turned her around. "What's up? You playing games with me now?"

"No." She shook her head, looking down between his legs. "I know what Janelle told you about saving yourself for the film."

He closed his eyes. *This is some straight up bullshit!* he shouted in his head.

Kandi wanted to help him out. She knew he wanted some pussy and her attraction to him was strong. *Fuck this shit!* she vented.

Trevon had to keep his cool. Just as he opened his eyes, he felt her hands rubbing and stroking his dick.

"Do you want to cum?" Kandi licked his chest before he spoke. "Janelle said she wanted to save your first piece of *pussy* for the film. But as for this—"

Trevon felt his breathing change as she leisurely lowered to a squat. Picking up the rag, she proceeded to wash him. She did it slowly, rubbing the fruit scented rag over his balls. His long dick sat on her shoulder. He ran his fingers through her hair as she began washing his shaft. Soaping up her hands, she took him to the edge by rubbing it up and down. Trevon gasped and moaned. Washing the soap off, she remained in her position. She looked up into his face with his dick in her grasp.

"Yes! Please suck my dick! Look at those lips. I hope I don't cum too fast. Fuck it, I just want to cum! Trevon laid his eyes on hers as she brushed her closed lips over his tip. His slick pre-cum clung to the corner of her sweet, silken lips. She did it twice more, each time forcing more pre-cum to exit. Her eyes lowered to what she held. She licked her

lips, tasting him. With the water pelting her back, she gripped his shaft causing his dick to swell.

"Welcome back to the free world," she purred.

Trevon instantly rose up on his toes as Kandi licked the tip. She did it unhurried with all of her tongue. His hand flew to the towel rack for support as her wet mouth slid over his throbbing tip. He had truly forgotten how good it felt to have his dick touched and sucked. Kandi kept to her promise. She laid her hands on her knees, bobbing her lips over his dick with no hands.

"Ooohhh . . . please . . . d-d-don't stop." He tripped over his words as she sucked him.

She was focused. Sucking and humming. Of his nine-inches, she ate up seven. When his moans changed to a chorus, she moved her hands into the circle. Cupping and rubbing his balls while pumping his shaft had his knees shakey. She was in her zone now. Sucking and pumping and rubbing his balls all at once.

"Mmmmmmmm," she purred, making her tongue firm under his erection as it slid in and out of her mouth. She loved how the friction of his tight skin made her lips tingle. Above her, he was groaning and saying twisted words that she did not understand. In and out. In and out. Lick, kiss, in and out. In and out. Slow. Fast.

Trevon felt his neck roll. He could not hold back any longer. Kandi sensed what was about to happen. She lightly raked her nails over his balls.

"Ohhhh . . . Kandi . . . I'm gonna cum!" he panted. "Ooohhh shhhit!"

Kandi sped up, lips tightening around his dick. Slurping and sucking, she tried to pull his climax up through his feet. Trevon felt as if he could pull the shower rack from the wall as his climax spilled into her mouth. Her mouth remained, giving him that eye-rolling pleasure as his cum spurted to the back of her throat. She swallowed it all, then slowed down to inch her lips all the way down to his thick base, stretching her jaws. She stayed there, deep throating him with her nose buried in his pubic hairs. This was how she got down for hers.

Trevon woke up from his needed rest at 6:30 p.m. Kandi had sucked his dick once more after the shower episode. She swallowed his release as he leaned back on her bed palming her head.

"Time to get ready for the party," she said, nudging his muscular shoulder.

"Get up!" She pulled the sheets off his naked body. *Shit! I put this nigga out with some head! He'll go in a coma afta I break 'im off with some pussy.* She was proud of her skills. It took a little effort to get Trevon out of the bed and dressed. She was standing in front of the bathroom mirror putting on some eye shadow when Trevon asked what her measurements were from the bedroom.

"Thirty-six D, twenty-eight, forty-eight."

"Damn!" he said amazed. "Your ass is bigger than Buffie the Body! Plus you look better so I guess I'm one lucky nigga! Okay, how tall are you?"

"Five-seven."

"You smell good," he said, walking into the bathroom sporting a black Gucci wife beater. She turned from the mirror.

"Damn, you look delicious," she said, rubbing his shoulder.

A sequinned black, tight provocative mini dress emphasized her small waist and award-winning ass. She had her hair pinned up and a diamond necklace circled her neck.

Trevon eased his arms around her waist. A smile formed on her mouth at the touch of his hands firmly squeezing her ass.

"In due time," she purred, reading his thoughts of wanting to be inside her.

For a reason that neither understood, they shared a slow, wet kiss in the bathroom. She could not remember the last time a man had kissed her like this. Before they lost control, they pulled apart, looking deeply into each other's eyes.

Almost an hour later, the two were ready. Outside she told him to drive. He surprised her by walking to the passenger side to open the door for her. The courteous act was the first ever for her. She had only seen it in old movies, but never in real life. The only thing Swagga had opened was her legs.

Resting a hand on his thigh, she quickly sat up. "Wait! Um, do you think you um . . . still know how to drive?"

Trevon looked at her sideways as he started up the Escalade. "I got this."

"Well, excuse me, Big Daddy." She laughed, easing back into the soft leather.

He smiled. *Damn it felt good to be free!*

CHAPTER
SEVEN
8:10 p.m.
Sunset Island, Miami Beach

Janelle's waterfront two-story Mediterranean mansion was a mesmerizing architectural seven bedroom, 4.9 million dollar mansion. Trevon slowed the Escalade at the front of the gated driveway. Two guards walked up to the gate as a third suddenly appeared at the driver side window. Trevon lowered the window.

"Name?" the guard asked.

"Kandi and Trevon Harrison," Kandi said from the passenger side.

The guard leaned in for a closer look. "Hi, Ms. Kandi!" he said, grinning. He was a big fan of her hard core fuck flicks. They were directed through the gate and down the palm tree-lined driveway.

Look at this fucking crib! "This is Janelle's place?" Trevon asked as he pulled up behind a sunset yellow Jaguar XKR-S.

"Yep. Bought and paid for." Kandi checked her hair and makeup in the visor mirror.

The mansion was brightly lit by bluish lawn lights. Trevon had never seen a house this big up close. Glancing at Kandi, it all seemed normal to her. It made him feel out of place. Stepping out of the SUV, they headed for the front mahogany double doors. Kandi again hooked her arm in his. Along the way, they walked by a young white couple stepping out the back of a black and silver Bentley Mulsanne.

"They're swingers," Kandi told Trevon when they were up near the front doors.

"Swingers?" He had no idea what she was talking about.

"They fuck other people. I guess it's a thrill to them. A lot of married people do it."

Trevon shook his head. "That would be too hard for me to do."

She shrugged, leaning closer into him as they went up the granite steps. Nearing the door, they heard the first sounds of music.

Kandi smiled as Trevon opened the door for her. Her thank you was drowned out by the loud thumping music. Three people called Kandi's name the second her stilettos touched the glassy blue marble stone flooring. Two were men that she had done a film with and the third was a female that she had also worked with. To Kandi, she was able to treat her time in front of the camera as a job. No emotions were carried over. She put both men in check and told them she would get back up with them later. Tonight she was all about Trevon.

The female was given the same treatment.

The large living room was too big to be labeled as such. *You can put a damn full basketball court up in this shit!* Trevon judged correctly as he looked around. He wanted to have this type of living. He eyed the scantily dressed women that walked by or were dancing. All of them looked their best and had no shame with showing off their body. Kandi shouted in his ear that half of the women were porn stars as she guided him around the dancing group. Trevon noticed the first sexual spark when he bumped into two females tonguing and feeling each other up. Moving past the gourmet kitchen displayed a scene of three topless women popping bottles of champagne. A group of men stood around them with glasses waiting to be filled.

All this pussy around me! Trevon thought. *And still I ain't seen nobody with an ass like Kandi's!*

She was still latched on his arm and he did not mind.

I need to find Janelle and see what's up about her signing me. "Where Janelle at?" he asked as they stepped down into a lavish appointed sitting room.

"Around here somewhere," Kandi replied, squeezing his arm. "Hey, take a seat over in the corner and I'll go get us something to drink from the bar."

He nodded, then headed for the cozy looking black velvet armless chair in the corner. The atmosphere around him was an overload. He slid around two sexy looking females drinking Henny and speaking a language he could not understand. Ornate paintings hung on the wall that drew a few guests to gather and speak on them. They did nothing for Trevon. He really felt lost and out of place by not knowing any of the faces around him. This life was not his life, but he would damn well try to adapt to it. All he needed to do was get a job and enjoy his freedom. *And fuck plenty of fine willing dimes!*

Out by the pool, Swagga and his crew passed around two blunts of Kush with a heavy haze floating. Swagga stepped from the group when he saw Yaffa approaching. Two Latina girls noticed Swagga, then asked if they could take a picture with him. He did so, knowing he had to show love to fans of his music.

"You find out who that nigga is?" Swagga asked Yaffa as they stood at the far end of Janelle's Olympic-sized infinity edge pool.

"Some dude named Trevon Harrison," Yaffa said, after having asked one of the guards to check the guest list.

"Trevon Harrison? Who the fuck is he? He play football or sumthin'?" Swagga had seen Kandi when she arrived with her new friend.

Yaffa shrugged, wishing Swagga would get over Kandi. Sure, she was fine as fuck and had a banging ass body, but she was an adult-film star.

Swagga looked toward the back of the mansion. *Bitch think she can just bump me to the curb! I'm that nigga! Damn, I miss that fiyah ass pussy.* "I'ma go holla at this nigga right quick." Swagga puffed up his flat bird chest.

"Dawg." Yaffa grabbed Swagga's skinny arm. "Let that shit go."

Swagga snatched his arm away, grilling Yaffa. "Fuck that! I'ma find out who dis nigga is!"

Trevon spotted Swagga and his seven-man entourage the instant they pushed through the tinted glass and polished stainless steel trimmed double doors. Trevon sat up out of habit. He kept his eyes on them because they all had their eyes on him. He rose to his feet and glanced at the young skinny dude in the front, then focused on the biggest dude walking slightly behind him. Trevon sized the big dude up.

Swagga paced boldly up to Trevon then stopped. *Damn, this nigga big as fuck!*

Swagga began to doubt if Yaffa could handle Trevon if a fight broke out.

"What's up?" Trevon said in a challenging tone. He had to shout over the loud music.

"That's what I'm tryin' to find out." Swagga gestured wildly with his arms.

Trevon smiled. "Y'all must got me mixed up with somebody else because—"

"You fuckin' Kandi?" Swagga blurted. "You Trevon Harrison, right?"

How this clown ass nigga know me? I bet he's one of Kandi's niggas. This is drama that I don't need. Trevon knew that a simple assault charge would send his black ass back to prison. He had to control his anger. If a fight broke out, he knew it would not be a one on one. He kept his eyes on the group. The tension was growing. Trevon began to feel the edginess that sped up his temper when shit was about to pop off. Out the gate, he would try to break the first niggas jaw that broke bad. His ego and pride would not allow him to back down.

"Swagga!" Kandi shouted, shouldering through his crew. She placed the two glasses on a table, then confronted Swagga. "What the fuck you all up in Trevon's grill for!"

"His bitch ass can't talk, so I guess a bitch gotta talk for 'im!" Swagga shouted.

"Nigga, you is so playin' yourself!" she shouted.

"Hold up," Trevon said, gently moving Kandi aside.

"No, Trevon!" She tried to stay in front of him, but he was too strong.

Swagga took a step back.

"Repeat what you just said." Trevon's focus was on Swagga. His upper lip began to twitch. At his sides, his beefy hands curled into fists as he moved his weight to the front of his feet. He was ready to fuck some shit up.

Yaffa pulled Swagga back, then took up his position in front of Trevon. "We all gonna chill right now," Yaffa stated with his eyes challenging Trevon. The commotion had gained everyone's attention, including three guards who quickly intervened.

Kandi glared at Swagga as he strolled away heading for the front door. *Dumb ass nigga! I hate his black ass!* She lowered her head, rubbing her temple as the crowd of nosey onlookers went back to minding their business.

Trevon sat down with a flat expression on his face. Kandi sat down beside him.

"Let's go outside so we can talk," she said over a song by Waka Flocka Flame.

"I'm good," he said, looking away from her.

Kandi placed her hand on his wrist. "Please. Just let me explain what's going on. Come on." She pulled him to his feet.

Kandi took him outside by the pool. They found a secluded area by the diving board. A light breeze pushed at Kandi's hair. On this night the starless sky left the moon solo. Kandi looked across the green landscaped lawn toward the dark water reflecting broken images of the moon.

"Look," he began. "All I want to do is get on my feet and make money. I'm not trying to go back to prison for no bullshit! I don't know who that nigga was and I don't give a fuck, so—"

"Just let me explain—okay?" She turned toward him, hoping he would listen.

Trevon could not be mad at her. *Why would a girl so fine be doing porn? I know she can have any nigga she wants. Shit is crazy!*

"I'm listening." He crossed his arms.

"He's my ex-boyfriend."

"How recent?"

"I broke up with him two months ago."

"And he still trippin'?" *Hell, I don't blame the nigga!*

"He's just stupid."

"Who were those clowns with him? He important or something?"

"The big guy with the beard is his bodyguard, Yaffa. The others are just a bunch of lame ass followers."

"Bodyguard? What is he? A professional shit talker?"

Kandi laughed. "He's a rapper. I can't believe you never heard of him. He came out six years ago. He's the one that made that song 'Trapped Up.'"

"I heard that song, but I ain't feeling it though."

Kandi shrugged. "I really don't fuck with him no more."

"You really don't have to explain anything to me. Hell, we just met today."

"And I already sucked your juicy dick twice." She smiled.

Trevon could not hold back his grin. "Yeah, you did," he said, looking at her hips filling out her outfit.

"So," she said as she slid her nails up his arm. "Have you made up your mind about being my new roommate?"

Trevon thought back to the bullshit with Swagga. "Did your—ex come by your crib today?"

"Yes. But it won't happen again. I forgot to remove his name from the visitors list. If he's not on it, they won't let him through the gate," she said, speaking of the armed guards at the front gate.

"Before I make that move, shouldn't I wait to see if Janelle will sign me or not?"

"Why wouldn't she? She bought you some clothes and it was her idea for you to stay with me." She took her hand away from his arm.

Trevon knew she was making sense. "What's your real name?" he asked, catching her off guard.

"Why?" She crossed her arms, tilting her beautiful face.

"Kandi is your porn name, right?"

62

She nodded.

He looked around. "I don't see no cameras, so why should I call you Kandi?"

"Does it matter?" She looked away only for him to gently turn her face back toward his.

"What's your real name?" *Damn, she's so damn fine!*

"My real name is LaToria," she said reluctantly.

"LaToria what?"

"Damn!" She smiled. "You the police?"

"Yeah." He stepped closer. "And I'ma punish you if you don't tell me."

"Punish me? How, Big Daddy?" She unfolded her arms.

"I'ma beat that pussy up first chance I get."

"Mmmm! Well, in that case, I'll never tell you my last name because I do want to be punished."

Trevon rubbed his face. *This girl is a damn trip!* "What's your full name?"

"LaToria Nicole Frost. Now quit bugging me."

He smiled. "LaToria. That's what I'm calling you from here on out."

"Whatever!" She rolled her eyes and then looked at her pink gator band watch.

"You okay?" he asked, placing his hands on her shoulders.

She nodded yes. "Let's go back inside and try to find Janelle." She walked off because her emotions were starting to trip. *Girl, you just met this nigga, so chill!* she scolded herself.

CHAPTER
EIGHT

Back inside, the party was still jumping. Trevon and Kandi entered the living room and found the floor packed. It looked like a club instead of a living room.

"Wanna dance?" she shouted over the loud music.

"I'm not much of a dancer!" he shouted back.

"Huh?" She pretended not to understand as she pulled him deep into the sea of bodies.

"I tried to warn you!" he shouted as she turned to shake her ass against him.

"Just hold on then!"

Trevon was having too much fun to stress over his lack of dancing skills. Following Kandi's advice, he held on to her winding hips, loving how her ass felt bumping against him. The deejay had the hundred plus crowd dancing and singing along to "Oh My" by DJ Drama featuring Fabolous, Wiz Khalifa and Roscoe Dash. Reality hit Trevon in a flood. He was finally free. They both danced through three songs before they squeezed out of the dancing mob.

The two were heading for the wet bar when Jurnee spotted them. Kandi greeted Jurnee with a big hug then whispered a few words into her ear. Jurnee smiled, keeping her eyes low.

Trevon looked at the two women, twenty cent. Two dimes. Hands down it was hard for him to pick between the two. Jurnee and her Cuban accent and sexy looks were tough to pass on. And then her age could be thrown in as well. Tonight she was killing it with a black shoulderless Nicole Miller collection silk twill dress. The deep scoop neckline showed off her juicy breasts. The tight dress looked glued to her body. Trevon admired her fully. He could not help it.

"Well, hello, Mr. Harrison." Jurnee stepped up to him, fingering a loose strand of hair over her shoulder. "You look . . ."

"Delicious." Kandi playfully elbowed Jurnee on her arm.

Jurnee pursed her red glossy lips. "That fits." Jurnee blushed then looked at her dress. She wanted everything to be in order in front of Trevon.

"Jurnee." Trevon nodded. "You look nice tonight."

Kandi rolled her eyes. "This nigga is an all around gentleman. He even opened doors for me."

"Then you should feel honored," Jurnee told her without taking her eyes off Trevon.

"Where is Janelle?" Kandi asked, looking around.

"Up in her office. She would like to speak to you, Mr. Harrison, or would you rather wait till business hours on Monday?"

"No, I'll see her now," Trevon said eagerly.

"I figured you would," Jurnee stated. "If you'll follow me, I'll take you up to her office."

"Y'all go on without me." Kandi winked at Trevon. "Good luck," she added, then stepped off and intentionally swished her big ass for him to lust over.

Jurnee and Trevon headed up the stairs and away from the party. Two more guards stood at the top of the stairs and their presence pushed Trevon to ask why they were needed.

"Janelle had a bad experience with a stalker last year. The guy somehow made it onto the estate, but one of the dogs got ahold of him. We also had a few issues with common thieves, so the security is needed. Tonight you're seeing more than the usual because of this party."

"Does Ms. Babin live alone?"

"No. She has three women staying here. They are signed with Amatory."

"Sorta like the Playboy Mansion." Trevon grinned as he followed Jurnee down the hall.

"Something like that. But don't compare her company to any other. Janelle is very serious about her business and she's not to be underestimated because she's a female."

"That thought never entered my mind." Trevon stole a glance at Jurnee's sexy legs.

"Well, here we are." Jurnee came to a stop at a closed door. She looked Trevon over, smiled, then knocked on the glossy oak door.

Twenty-eight-year-old CEO of Amatory Erotic Films, Janelle Babin looked up from her Apple iPad tablet. She smiled as Jurnee walked in followed by Trevon.

"Stay, Dino," she said, giving a command to her loyal pit bull who sat by her feet.

"I found Mr. Harrison," Jurnee said, pulling at the hem of her tight dress before sitting.

"Glad you could make it, Mr. Harrison." Janelle had to admit to herself that he was looking good.

"I don't think LaToria gave me a choice," he said, sitting next to Jurnee in a separate leather chair.

Janelle and Jurnee exchanged a quick glance. Jurnee shrugged.

"I see you're already on a first name basis with Kandi." Janelle was surprised at this because Kandi rarely spoke about her private life. She wanted to be branded as the best in the adult-film industry, which is why she used her screen name exclusively.

"I think I would be with the two of you wanting me to move in with her."

"Have you made up your mind yet?" Janelle asked him.

Trevon made sure he sat up straight. "Do I have a job?"

Janelle folded her hands. "As I said at my office, you have two of the three assets that I look for. Before I sign you, we need to find out what's up with the last item."

Jurnee coughed then stood up. She knew what was about to go down.

"You can stay," Janelle said with a small grin. "In fact, would you like to see if Mr. Harrison has what it takes to be a porn star?"

Jurnee looked at Trevon and saw the lost look on his handsome face. "I'd love to," she said.

"Could you stand up and drop your pants, Mr. Harrison?" Janelle whispered.

Trevon looked at the two lovely women. Both returned his incredulous stare. "You serious, right?"

"This is business, Mr. Harrison," Janelle said without smillng. "I want to see how big your dick is and Jurnee is going to help you get it up."

Trevon ran a hand down his face. *She's dead ass serious. It does make sense. I'ma be slangin' dick, so I might as well show them what I'm working with. Please don't freeze up on me, boy. It's showtime!* Trevon boldly stood and unfastened his monogrammed Gucci belt. Coming up behind him, Jurnee slid her hands up his hard shoulders, brushing her soft lips against his back.

Janelle watched the two without saying a single word. She studied how Jurnee's hands traveled all over his body.

Trevon had the belt undone and was tugging his pants down when Jurnee suddenly shoved her hand down his pants. He groaned, closing his eyes as she pressed her breasts hard into his back. She wrapped her fingers around his dick then slowly jacked her grip up and down its length.

"Pull it out." Janelle said and crossed her legs. Her pussy throbbed in response to the sight before her.

Jurnee yanked his pants and boxers down, exposing his semi-hard dick. She began to stroke faster while licking and nibbling on his ear.

Janelle moved around the desk for a better view of his dick. Big and black with protruding fat veins. Jurnee stroked it as it continued to grow, elated to see that it was circumcised. Uncircumcised dicks were ugly to her.

"Rub his balls," Janelle said, standing beside the two. She waited until Jurnee massaged his balls before she wrapped her hand around his shaft.

Trevon moaned again as he felt two warm hands moving all over his dick.

Damn . . . feels so good! I want to bust! I want to fuck something! Trevon opened his eyes and looked at Janelle slowly pumping his dick. He wondered how far the two were willing to go. Suddenly, Janelle released him. Jurnee did the same, walking around to get a clear view of Trevon. He felt a bit awkward as the two women observed his swollen dick.

"You can put him up," Janelle said with a big smile on her face.

Trevon was afraid to touch himself. He knew he would make a fool of himself if he lost control and bust all over the desk. Taking a deep breath, he reached down to fix his clothes. Gradually, his dick began to shrink. While he was fastening his belt, Janelle gave Jurnee a silent signal to leave.

"I need to use the bathroom," Jurnee lied, excusing herself from the office.

Trevon sat down once they were alone.

"That's very impressive." She nodded toward his crotch from behind her desk. "I believe we could use your talents at my company." She lowered a hand to rub her pit bull. "I'm willing to give you a chance, Mr. Harrison, so if you're ready, I have a contract you can read and sign if it's what you're expecting."

Hell, yeah I'm ready! Trevon wanted to jump up and shout, "Let's do it."

Janelle reached into the drawer, then pulled out a fifteen page contract.

"Take your time and read it. If you wish to have someone go over it for you, you can do so."

"I trust you," he said, knowing he was taking a big risk, but other employment options were not in his favor. If he signed the contract, he would have a job. Not having a job was the root of his issues.

"Read the contract, Mr. Harrison. In this business, trust is rare. Remember that, okay?" She gave him a warm smile, then turned her attention back to the tablet as Trevon started to read the contract.

It was hard for him to focus on the contract because he could not get over one fact. *Just mere minutes ago, she had her hand all over my dick!* He became focused when he came across the money aspect in the contract.

Swagga had ditched his entourage at Club Bed, then headed to the condo on Fisher Island. Yaffa was lounging in the colorful art deco den on a plush peach leather sofa watching TV.

Outside on the thirtieth floor balcony Swagga and Cindy aka Déjà Pink were smoking Kush and sipping on

Patron. The view was amazing. Across the bay was the brightly lit spectacular skyline of downtown Miami and Biscayne Bay. Déjà Pink was a white urban model who had the game on smash. Swagga had featured her thick, sexy ass in three of his rap videos. She had blonde dreads with brown highlights hanging to the middle of her back. Her ocean blue eyes were glass-like from the Kush. Swagga was so open on her body that his safe combination at the crib matched her measurements: 32-25-42. She stood at 5'5" with natural C-cup breasts that Swagga flicked his tongue across as she pulled hard on the Kush while straddling his lap. Swagga had been fucking her for six months. His fetish was her pierced tongue and creamy white skin. The cool breeze coming off the bay blew against her wet pointy nipples. Cindy squealed.

"Stand up and take these off," Swagga said, tugging at the skintight silver boy shorts. Her dark brown nipples brushed against his lips.

"Let me suck you first." She tossed the tiny joint over the balcony rail, then slid her pierced tongue inside his mouth while running her fingers through his dreads. Swagga roamed his hands up and down her sexy back as they kissed at a slow pace. Pulling her hands from his dreads, she stood but kept her lips against his. Reaching back, she slid her bottoms off, exposing her naked heart-shaped ass to the world. Goosebumps formed over her butt as another bay cool breeze blew over her ass. Swagga kicked his Jordan's off and lifted his skinny ass off the chair to push his boxers and jeans down.

At the young age of twenty-two, Cindy had the oral skills of a woman twice her age. Dipping to her knees, she grabbed his dick with both hands, blowing on the tip. She did it a few more times while stroking his shaft.

Swagga watched her. "Don't tease a nigga," he said, touching her shoulder.

She ignored him. Licking the tip, she lowered one hand to his balls then eased her pink lips down his dick. She did it slowly while humming.

"Ohhhh . . . suck it right," he moaned as her mouth slid up and down. "Mmmm . . . yeah, rub my balls. Yessss . . . suck it for me just like I taught you."

Up and down she slurped at his meat while bouncing his balls on her fingertips. Soft wet pops mixed in with the sound of his escaped moans.

"Don't stop," he gasped as he watched her deep throating him. "Damn!"

Déjà Pink had no intentions to stop. She was always out to please him in any form. Anal sex, licking his ass, swallowing his cum, she did it all. She sped up when he began to breathe faster. She had sucked him off enough times to know when he was about to bust. Swirling the steel ball on her tongue around his tip made his eyes cross. Modeling had earned her fame, but not fortune. The condo, the Range Rover, and the monthly vacations were all due to Swagga. She would admit in secret that she only fucked with Swagga because of his money. The dick really was not all that, but she had him fooled. She jerked him off inside her mouth as he began to cum.

Now I can ask him to buy me a new Louis Vuitton bag. She schemed as his milky cum slid down her throat. Cindy turned, bending over the rail. She did not have to wait long before feeling his tongue flicking over her pussy. Deja Pink bit her bottom lip as Swagga began to suck on her pink wet pussy. Life could not get any better.

Back at Janelle's mansion, Trevon was on the last page of the contract. It stated that he would be given six months to film six DVDs to the company's requirements. Trevon held the contract in his hands not fully knowing what his future would hold. He hoped he would not freeze up in front of the camera.

All I gotta do is fuck. Eat some pussy and slang dick. That's it. He was trying to convince himself that it would all work out. Looking up from the contract, he cleared his throat.

Janelle looked up from the tablet after pausing the adult-film she was watching.

"I would like to sign the contract," Trevon said.

Janelle rubbed her ear. "Will you be able to stay sex free until we film?" she asked.

"I've waited fifteen years. What's a few more weeks?"

She studied him closely from where she sat. She would give him his chance. A chance that she knew he needed. "I hope you'll take my advice and move in with Kandi."

He took a few seconds to run the idea through his mind. He did not want to start out by *not* taking her advice. "Yeah, I'll move in with her."

"Good! Now, how about we take care of business." She slid a pen across the desk, then smiled as Trevon signed his name on the dotted line.

CHAPTER
NINE

Trevon found Kandi at the wet bar surrounded by a group of men. He was about to turn around until she saw him. His ego grew when she rudely jumped from the stool to rush toward him.

Damn, she's so fucking fine! And all that ass! I hope I can—

"How did it go? What did Janelle say? Did you sign?" Kandi asked.

"Calm down," he said, breathing in her sweet perfume. "Yes, I got the—"

"Yes!" She jumped into his arms. "I told you not to worry."

Trevon eased his arms around her waist. *Hell, she's happier than I am.* Since she was so happy, he went ahead and hinted toward some more equally good news.

"I'm ready to go home," he said, fighting the urge to squeeze her ass in front of everyone.

She assumed he was speaking of the boarding home. Her wide smile faded.

"I want to see my new room."

Kandi gasped. "You're moving in with me?"

He nodded yes.

"Good. Let's blow this bitch." She laughed.

They made their exit from the party with Trevon behind the wheel. He was driving with some sense because he had yet to obtain his driver's license.

"This is where you'll be sleeping." Kandi stood in the spacious bedroom as Trevon walked up to the window. "Looking for somebody?" She walked toward the bed and sat down.

"No." He turned around. "Just taking all this in. One minute I'm an ex-con living in a boarding home and the next I'm staying with a beautiful woman—"

"*And*, you've signed a contract to make some adult films."

"That's right."

Kandi looked at her watch. It was now two minutes to midnight.

"You expecting any company tonight?" he kidded.

To his surprise she answered, "In fact, I am."

Trevon looked at her, thinking she was bullshitting. He had asked if she had a man and she said no. Did she tell him a damn lie? He knew of Swagga being her ex, so now he assumed she did have a nigga. A midnight visit was a straight up booty call. Trevon was confused. The way she was all over him earlier had him thinking she was feeling him on an emotional level. *Shorty ain't shit but a straight up freak! I can't trip though. At least she broke me off twice with that bomb head game.* His simple male ego challenged him to accept that she was about to get her freak on with a nigga other than himself. *If that's how she gonna be, fuck it! Ain't 'bout to sweat it.*

"Well, I guess you better get ready before he gets here," he said, picking up his shoes to put them in the walk-in closet.

Kandi was about to say something, but she held back. "I'll catch you in the morning," she said, eyeing him. *I need to leave his sexy ass before I be all over that dick!*

"A'ight," he said without looking at her. He wanted her to know that he did not care about her late night booty call. When she left him alone, he sat at the foot of the bed looking aimlessly around the bedroom. He tried to think of anything that did not involve Kandi. Rubbing his baldhead, he thought about his mom and his sister Angie. He would call them tomorrow to see how they were holding up.

Knowing he would also need to visit his P.O., he figured it was time to bring his day to an end. He dropped to the floor and did ten sets of pushups in reps of thirty for a total of 300. Trevon took a quick shower then found comfort on the soft bed. He was thinking about who he would fuck in his first film, when a pair of headlights moved across the wall, shortly followed by the sound of a door closing. Trevon could not ignore his curiosity. He jumped from the bed and rushed to the window, wanting to see the lucky dude that would be with Kandi tonight. The lighting outside hid the figure stepping away from a red Black Series Benz SL65 two-door coupe. Trevon figured it had to be a baller with money. Easing back on the bed, he rolled over on his stomach, folding the pillow over his head. Closing his eyes, he again tried to push any and all thoughts of Kandi and her late night guest from his mind.

Fifteen years in prison had forced Trevon to be a light sleeper. Rolling to his side, he rubbed his face. The sounds that pulled him from his sleep registered in his mind. Through the closed door he heard Kandi moaning over a slow song. Trevon rolled to his back, pulling the pillow over his face and ears. It did not help.

"This some bullshit!" he murmured into the pillow. Sitting up, he looked at the digital clock on the dresser. 2:33 a.m. It was hard to ignore the kitten like purrs that eased into his ears. His dick got hard. "Fuck!" He kicked the covers off and got out of bed and paced the floor. The moans were constant. Trevon slid on the Gucci slippers, then headed for the door in his boxers. He needed a drink. Something strong. Opening the door, he stepped out into the dark hallway. Kem's "I Can't Stop Loving You" flowed from the half-open bedroom door. Trevon eased down the hall as Kandi kept moaning at the top of her lungs. He allowed his mind to picture what was going on, wishing he was inside her, beating the pussy up.

"Damn!" He grabbed his hard rock dick.

Kandi tried to keep one eye focused on the door while her lover lapped at her wet, juicy pussy.

"Yesss!" she shouted. "Eat my pussy. Uuhhhhmmmm . . . my clit!"

The music was turned up loud. The lights were on as well for a certain reason. Kandi grabbed her titties, squeezing them. Between her juicy thighs was Jurnee.

The two had been sexing each other for nearly a year. Jurnee slowly licked her pussy using all of her tongue. It got so good to Kandi, that she missed the sight of Trevon strolling past the door.

Trevon looked back twice to take in the sight of Kandi and Jurnee. He had assumed wrong about a dude coming to see Kandi. In the kitchen he sat at the table with a glass of orange juice. He had changed his mind on the alcohol. He was lost in his thoughts when Jurnee tiptoed into the kitchen.

"Did we wake you up?" Her voice was gentle and warm.

His head snapped up. Jurnee leaned against the wall with her arms crossed under her breasts. A mesh silk gown wrapped around her sexy frame. Just as he started to answer, Kandi strutted down the hall butt ass naked. She stopped behind Jurnee and ran her hand under her gown, palming her bare ass. Jurnee winked at Trevon, and turned to kiss Kandi on the mouth. Trevon slid his chair away from the table. Kandi opened Jurnee's gown and Trevon licked his lips at the sight of Jurnee's shaved pussy. Kandi had a small strip of hair between her thighs. The two women kissed briefly, before facing Trevon.

"We know about the contract," Kandi said, striding up to him and pulling his dick out of his boxers. "You can't get no pussy until you make your first film," she purred, looking at his hard dick.

Trevon looked at Kandi as Jurnee came up beside her. The two women exchanged a quick glance. Jurnee went down to her knees in front of Trevon and rubbed her hands up and down his legs.

"Lindo," Jurnee murmured in Spanish. "Nice," she translated the word.

"It tastes as good as it looks." Kandi stood beside Trevon rubbing his shoulders and chest.

Jurnee took his hardened flesh in her hands. "May I?" she asked, gazing up at him. "Oh, my golden rule. Just go for what you know, papi."

Trevon ran his fingers through her hair as Kandi stuck her wet tongue in his ear. The spark was lit. Inches from the kitchen table, he sat moaning and twitching with his dick in Jurnee's mouth. She took her time to savor every inch of him. Her soft lips massaged his full length in ways that made his knees weak. She flicked and twisted her tongue all over his manhood, while juggling his balls in her palm. Three minutes ticked off with no change in her steady pace.

"I wanna see you do it, Big Daddy," Kandi purred against his ear. "Let me see you cum in her hot mouth."

Jurnee had a smooth medium pace set. The top of her head moved back and forth, titties wobbling nonstop.

"Oooohhh . . . Jurnee," Trevon moaned, looking at the top of her head. Suddenly she stopped and stood to wipe the corners of her wet lips. Grinning, she looked at Kandi. The two gave each other a high five, leaving Trevon speechless.

"We tag teamin' up in here!" Kandi squatted in front of Trevon and took over where Jurnee had stopped.

Trevon, through all the lust and excitement, could sense the difference with Kandi. She seemed to be more impassioned with sucking him. Her soft whimpers were driving him over the edge. Beside him, Jurnee placed one foot up on the chair, vigorously fingering herself toward a climax. Her eyes zeroed in on his dick pumping in and out of Kandi's mouth. All three chanted their ecstasy as if in chorus.

Kandi was in fact, deep into sucking Trevon's dick. Right now she could not explain why she was so open with him. She had not known him for twenty-four hours and for the what—third or fourth time his dick was in her mouth punching her throat. Lost in her zone she urged him to thrust deeper by palming his ass. Breaking the connection, Jurnee gently pulled her away. Again, Trevon was left unattended.

"Let's take this to the bedroom." Jurnee looked down at his dick and could tell he was close to his climax. Even the look on his face gave truth to her thoughts. "Learn to control yourself, Trevon. On film you'll face times like this when you'll have to stop."

"She's right, Smooch," Kandi added while kneading Jurnee's ass.

"Smooch?" Jurnee frowned.

Kandi giggled. "I just made that up. Look at his lips. When I first saw him I just had the urge to kiss him. So . . . Smooch. Get it?"

"Girl, the only smooching you've been doing is sucking that—" Jurnee nodded at his still hard penis. "Succulent piece he's working with. And I don't blame you at all."

"What's going on here?" Trevon asked with a lost look on his face.

"Business." Jurnee crossed her arms. "Mixed with a bit of pleasure. We see you love some good head, but I wanna see how good you can give it."

"Me first," Kandi said.

Trevon followed Jurnee and Kandi into the bedroom. Once they were all undressed, Jurnee made him lie still and watch as she and Kandi ate each other out. Jurnee was serious when she spoke to him and showed him how a woman wanted to be touched. Paying attention to this course was one he planned to ace.

CHAPTER
TEN
August 27, 2011
Saturday, 9:38 a.m. - Coconut Grove, Florida

Trevon's morning began with Kandi pulling the sheets off him. He was dead tired after their freak oral session. They made sure he had not broken the guideline in the contract. Trevon was given a lesson in the art of orally pleasing a woman. At one point, Jurnee sat on his face as Kandi bobbed up and down on his dick. Jurnee again said it was business. She wanted to make sure he knew how to eat pussy. Business or pleasure, Trevon enjoyed every moment.

"Jurnee said you forgot this," Kandi said, posed at the foot of his bed.

Trevon sat up, rubbing his eyes as Kandi tossed a magazine on the bed. It was the magazine with Jurnee on the cover.

"Damn, why are you up so early?" He yawned.

"I'm going to get my hair and nails done with Jurnee." Kandi sat on the edge of his bed. "Have fun last night?" she asked with a guilty grin.

"What do you think?" he lay back down, closing his eyes.

"We wore your ass out, huh?" She stood up. "You can use my ride if you want to 'cause Jurnee is coming to pick me up."

He forced himself to sit up. "Gotta see my P.O. and plus I need to get my damn driver's license."

"You need some money?"

"Um . . ." He was hesitant to take any money from her.

"It only requires a yes or no reply, Smooch." Kandi grinned.

"Don't call me that," Trevon said, lying back down hoping to catch some more rest.

"Why not? I should be able to call you that. It means I like you."

"Did you have one for your ex, Swagga?"

Kandi frowned. "Damn. You sure do know how to steal my shine. But for the record, no. I didn't have a pet name for his no-good ass."

"My bad."

"I know, Smooch." She smiled then pulled him back up. "You have some sexy ass lips."

Trevon rolled unwillingly out of bed.

"That morning wood looks tempting." She nodded at the bulge under his boxers and crossed her legs, eyeing him as he headed for the bathroom. "I had a wild dream about us fucking last night."

"Something tells me not to doubt that," Trevon replied, reaching for the toothpaste.

"Yeah. It got me looking forward to doing it with you."

Trevon looked at her. "Business or personal?"

Kandi was caught off guard by his direct question. "I guess time will tell."

"I've heard that a lot."

Kandi tugged the fitted cream-colored sundress down over her wide hips. "I have to get ready to go. I'll leave you some money and the keys to my truck on the kitchen table. And I added your name to my visitor's list so you'll have no problem at the front gate."

Trevon could only nod okay since he was brushing his teeth. Seven minutes later he was alone. Once he got dressed he found the keys and $1,200 on the kitchen table and a note from Kandi:

Be safe, Smooch. I'll call you later on. Oh yeah . . .
I'm missing you much already!
Sweet Kandi

Trevon sat down at the table smiling. She was indeed sweet. Last night he held nothing back in licking and sucking on her flesh. Everything so far was drawing him in toward Kandi. He just needed to draw the line between his building emotions. Business or personal.

Trevon made it to the downtown probation and parole building in Miami after stopping at a fast food restaurant for breakfast. Without Kandi at his side he was nervous to drive without a license. Down in Miami the Escalade was flashy, but by no means was it exotic. It was nothing special to pull up at a red light and spot a Ferrari or a Porsche.

Stepping out of the Escalade he took a moment to take in the scene. Horns blew nonstop in the heavy flow of traffic. Again, he noticed everyone walking with a cell phone glued to their ear. All types of nationalities were merged together within his view. On one corner stood a shouting Arab behind a hot dog stand. A few yards to his left sat a heavy dreaded black man singing a song in a lost language Trevon could not understand. What stood out most to him were the police posted around every one or two hundred yards. Seeing them pushed the visit with his P.O. back into his mind. Above him, the towering building blocked out the sun, but as usual, it was still hot as hell.

Trevon made his way inside, hoping the visit with his P.O. would be a productive one. At the front counter, a thin, short-haired black female sat typing on a keyboard. The wooden name block on the counter read Nikki Conner.

"Um, I'm Trevon Harrison and I'm here to see Ms. Paige," he said placing his hands on the waist leveled counter. He stood ramrod straight.

"How about *good morning* or something?" Nikki said, looking up from the computer screen and rolling her neck.

Trevon sighed. "Good morning." He glanced at the name block again. "Ms. Conner. I'm here to see—"

"I heard you the first time. Gimme your I.D. and sign in." She nodded at the sign-in sheet to his left. "How long you been outta prison?" she asked impatiently.

"Since the seventeenth," he replied, signing his name. He could feel her ogling him.

"Of what?"

"This month."

"Umph! Ain't been out two weeks and you wearing Gucci! What type of drugs you selling?"

Trevon ignored her bullshit assumption. He was told to sit and wait.

The waiting room was packed. Trevon could feel the hopelessness emitting from the other parolees who also sat in the waiting room. Across the room, two females complained about the lack of jobs while a thugged-out teenager paced the floor. A few of them eyed his clothes. Trevon could feel the envy. Twenty minutes went by before his name was called. After passing through a metal detector, he was directed to the elevator. His parole officer was located on the fifth floor.

Thirty-nine year old Kendra Paige was in an ill mood today. In truth, it was the norm for her. She associated it with her daily dealings with ex-cons. Law enforcement was in her blood. She started out in the military and served three and a half years until she was medically discharged for lower back pain. After a year of depression, she got back on her feet and found a job as a correctional officer. She found the job rewarding and sometimes stressful, but she refused to give up. In six years, she moved up to the rank of Sergeant. After becoming pregnant with her firstborn, she left the prison to take a job as a parole and probation officer. She was a single mother of a three-year-old little girl who was the center of her life. As for the baby's father, she despised him, but respected the support she received financially. Kendra pushed up her designer glasses as she typed on the wireless keyboard. Her frame was naturally thick, but not in the lines of an exotic dancer's body. Her only flaw was her ever sour attitude. She looked up at the door when Trevon knocked. The door was open.

"Name?" the dark, brown-skinned sister asked, looking down at her appointment sheet.

"Trevon Harrison."

Kendra found his name. "You can sit down, Mr. Harrison." She frowned and briefly scratched her short, curly hair.

Trevon eased his large frame into the hard metal chair, hoping the R&B singer Jill Scott look alike would lighten up with the attitude.

Kendra pulled up his file while trying to ignore the scent of his cologne. She had a good memory and could recall when she first met Trevon two days after his release from prison. She had driven to the boarding home to introduce herself and to lay down the rules she expected him to follow. No drug use, no drug selling, no possession of a firearm. He could not leave the state and he had to find a job. She knew he had no family in Florida and he only had $130 to his name. Once his file was on the monitor, she looked at him.

"How's life treating you, Mr. Harrison?" she asked in a flat emotionless tone.

"Okay," he began. "Just trying to catch up with everything. All this new technology and stuff is crazy, but I'm learning." He wanted to get on good terms with her.

"Found a job yet?" she pressed.

He suddenly remembered a clause in his contract that prevented him from telling anyone about his deal with Amatory. Janelle wanted Trevon to stay focused. She said it was okay to share the news with Kandi.

"Um . . . not yet, but I'm working on something."

"Mm hmm." She sat back, crossing her arms over her large breasts. "So you don't have a job. Well, how about you explain those clothes."

"It's all a gift."

"A gift?" she asked skeptically. "From who?"

"From a friend."

"Hmm . . . and does this *friend* know that you need a job? And does this *friend* have a criminal record?"

"No, she doesn't."

"Oh, I see. Your girlfriend. Well, that was nice of her, but you still need to find a job. I don't care what you find, just as long as it's legal. You know what will happen if you don't find a job, right?"

"How could I forget?" he said with a slight ill attitude.

Kendra smacked her lips. "Don't get fly with me, Mr. Harrison. You might look like somebody in all that Gucci shit, but you're still property of the state. As long as you're on paper, you have to deal with me! Now these can be two years of peace or you can make it hard on yourself and end up back in prison. It don't make a difference to me. Matter of fact—" She sat up and grabbed the telephone, then pushed the buttons for an extension. *This fool got me mixed the fuck up if he think I'ma be tripping over his ass! I'll show his black ass that I'm not the one to fuck with! Send his big ass right back to prison where he can lift weights for—* She glanced at the monitor—*Six years!*

"Sherwood, this is Kendra. I need to send someone down for a drug urinalysis test. Can you squeeze him in?"

Trevon began to hate Kendra and bit down hard on the inside of his jaw. *Stupid ass bitch!*

Kendra slammed the cordless phone down then told Trevon to go down to the main floor to see the drug urinalysis officer. She stared at him hard as he sprung up to his feet.

"Fail the test and I'll personally take you back to prison!" she said as he barged out of her small windowless office. Instantly, her mood changed by picking up the digital picture frame off her desk. She sat back and smiled while flashing through the twenty pictures of her daughter.

Trevon walked back into her office thirty minutes later having passed the drug testing. Kendra visibly gave him a side smirk.

"Your next contact with me will be the twenty-sixth of next month and you better be able to show me proof of a job. In between time you can expect random visits to the boarding home by me or another parole officer and be subject to a search and drug testing and—"

Trevon cleared his throat. "I'm not at the boarding home no more."

"Excuse me? What do you mean you're not living there no more. Since when? And why haven't you informed this office?" She pointed down at the desk.

"I'm moving out today and I'm telling you now."

"And where are you moving to? You are aware that you must let us check the place out first. You're not allowed to be in a high crime rate area."

"So why is it okay for me to be in Liberty City?"

"It was the only place that had space, so we made an exception."

"Well, I've found a better and safer place to stay."

"Where?"

"Coconut Grove."

Kendra asked, more like demanded the address. She warned him that if the address was fictitious, that she would lock him up. Seeing he also had a new cell phone, she *told* him to give her the number. She was very suspicious of all the new material items he had. *This nigga selling drugs. I know he is. Either that or he robbed somebody.* She would enjoy catching his ass in the wrong. She typed his new contact information on the computer, then told him that she would be in touch.

Trevon had no idea how he would manage to deal with her hateful ass for two years. *She can't have no man at home. Too fucking hateful!* he thought as he stood up to leave. His mood was low as he headed back outside. *Nigga, you free!* he told himself, then jumped in the shiny black Escalade and rode off with the system bumping. Trevon would not let one stuck up miserable P.O. steal his shine. *Fuck her!*

Cindy aka Déjà Pink, woke up late in the afternoon with her naked body curled against Swagga. She had knowledge of the other bitches he fucked, but none of them mattered to her. Currently, he was the only man sliding dick up in her and she was content because the money was endless. She knew what Swagga was worth. Last year alone, he had earned $2.3 million in record sales. For that reason, Cindy had an exclusive sexual relationship with him and was happy with herself when her affair with Swagga caused tension with Kandi. Cindy was pulled into Swagga's life by his money. Hanging out with his entourage and people in the rap industry, she tightened up her slang and became a bigger fan of hip-hop. Katy Perry was long gone from her playlist. She could now recite the lyrics to her theme song, "Five Star Chick," word for word.

Slipping from the bed, she walked barefoot and stark ass naked out of the bedroom. Hearing the TV on in the den, she smiled.

"Morning," she said and waved at Yaffa as her perky breasts swayed and juggled.

"Afternoon," he corrected her, lusting hard at the size of her creamy ass.

Cindy trotted by slowly, letting Yaffa get an eyeful of her body. She had lost count on the number of times Yaffa had seen her naked. Just last week, she had screwed Swagga in the studio booth doggy style while Yaffa and the production crew watched. That shit was a huge turn on for her. While Swagga was doing her, she was having a graphic fantasy that everyone in the studio would take turns. One line she knew Swagga would not cross would be allowing her to fuck someone else.

In the kitchen, she pulled out a wine cooler and sauntered back to her bedroom. She knew Yaffa was looking at her and it made her nipples hard. She loved to tease and flirt.

Flopping on the bed, she nudged Swagga to wake him. When that did not work, she reached under the sheets and grabbed his dick with her cold hands. He woke up shoving her hand away. "What the fuck!"

"Wake up, baby." She smiled. "I have to go to the gym."

"Why you wakin' me up?" He rubbed his face, then reached out to rub between her tanned legs. She was slick. It was the norm for him to wake up with sex on his mind. She pushed his hand away.

"Didn't you want me to call my friend Chyna about what we talked about last night?"

"Oh yeah!" He sat up. "What time is it?"

Cindy picked up his yellow diamond encrusted watch from the mass of jewelry on the nightstand by the bed. "One-twenty."

"Damn, I was knocked out, yo!" He rubbed his stiff neck.

"Good pussy tends to do that to a man." She smiled.

Without asking, he took the wine cooler from her then drank half of it. "Shit too damn sweet!" He frowned, giving it back.

She finished the rest then slid back in the bed. "Now tell me again what you want me to tell Chyna," she said, lying next to him.

"Just tell . . ."

"*Her.*"

"Yeah. Um, say I got somebody for them to meet and the rest will just fall in place."

"I'll see if she'll do it. She be on some bullshit, but she's my girl."

Swagga again reached down to play in her pussy. "Damn, you stay wet!"

"Only 'cause of you." She played on his ego, opening her legs. She rubbed his face as he pushed two fingers inside her. Pulling his face toward hers, she circled her tongue around his lips then into his mouth.

The sex was rushed and Cindy was rarely pushed to a climax. She faked it as he pounded her from the back while spanking and rubbing her ass. He had enough dick to please her, but his skills of throwing the dick were lacking.

In the shower, she asked him who Trevon was and why he wanted Chyna to hook up with him.

"Don't worry 'bout all that," he said, scrubbing his dick. "Just make the call and see if they will do it. Better yet, if they say yeah . . . give 'em my number."

Cindy said fine and inwardly thought it was silly of him to refuse to refer to Chyna as 'she' or 'her.' She knew Swagga was up to some bullshit and had a feeling that this Trevon guy would be the recipient of it.

Swagga was immersed in his thoughts as Yaffa drove the Bentley GT back to Fort Lauderdale. He was unable to get over Kandi. He was used to having things his way. Money took care of everything. Cindy was in line. He knew for a fact she was not fucking around on him. He had tried to run the same game on Kandi, but she was not having it. It was simple; he wanted what he could not have. Swagga hated to lose. When he thought of Trevon having the pleasure of being with Kandi, it got under his skin. *Maybe she's just tryin' to make a nigga jealous?* He continued to flip his jealous thoughts around. Swagga wondered if Kandi had told anyone about that night he proposed to her and gave her a chunky diamond ring. She had said yes through real tears. Deep down through all the bullshit, he knew she was the only woman that genuinely loved him through all his drama and not for his money. When he told a few of his friends, he was clowned.

"Nigga! You musta been on the Kush fo' real!"

"Man, how you gonna marry a bitch dat eat dick for a livin'?"

Swagga was dissed hard by his crew and a few other known rappers. To save his street reputation, he made a move to erase his sucka for love status by hooking up with Deja Pink. He purposefully allowed the sex tape to leak. Kandi was crushed when she found out about it. Swagga could not be viewed as a sucka for love, so he fronted as if he did not give a fuck. Behind closed doors, he was heartbroken to have loved and lost. His mind was made up. Somehow, he would get this Trevon bama out of the picture and find a way to get Kandi back. Once that was done, he would cut all the side bitches off, including the two baby momma's he was fucking and just focus on loving Kandi. *Fuck what people gon' say!*

CHAPTER
ELEVEN
Sunset Island, Miami Beach

Janelle lay out by the pool with her pit bull reading a paperback novel when Jurnee sashayed toward her. She lowered the book by Ne Ne Capri, *The Pussy Trap*, then rubbed the hackles down on the dog's thick neck.

"How did it go?" Janelle asked as Jurnee slid a chair beside her.

"Wild," Jurnee replied, sitting her brown gator purse on her lap. "Trevon will need to tighten up on his oral skills, but I think he'll work out."

"Was it tempting?" Janelle sat up from the chaise lounge to adjust her yellow triangle bikini top.

"Girl, you better be glad I'm a professional, because it was a challenge not to jump on that dick!" Jurnee stated, telling the truth.

"How did Kandi do?" Janelle asked, grinning at Jurnee's comment.

"She sucked his soul out. Their chemistry was . . . Wow! They both wanted to do it so bad that they became frustrated. When you do let him fuck Kandi, I will envy her because Trevon is going to go wild!"

Janelle smiled. "I want their attraction and lust to pour into the camera. I will let Kandi be with him in his debut film. Where is Kandi anyway? I thought she went with you to get fancy."

"I dropped her off. She's home."

Janelle looked down at her pedicured toes. "There is something unique about Trevon that I can't put my finger on right now."

"Why do you say that?"

"I think he—I don't know, but he just seems different. I just get these vibes from him."

Jurnee looked down at the sharp crease lines on her Carolina blue slacks.

"Got an idea on how the theme will be for the film?" Jurnee asked.

Janelle sat back, crossing her ankles as the sun heated her oily skin. "A coming home from prison theme will work. That's the idea I want to run with for the first film."

"Any anal?"

"Not yet. We'll just stick with oral sex and full penetration. For his first anal film, I might pair him with Black Pearl."

"Good idea because she needs to bring up her DVD sales."

Janelle turned her wrist up to check the time. 3:40 p.m. "I want to start on his first film within two weeks. Get the production team together and make sure there will be no delays."

"What about the filming location?" Jurnee wanted to know.

Janelle bit her bottom lip. "Um, we'll rent an apartment and just try to keep it as authentic as possible."

"I have a suggestion. Remember that married couple in Opa Locka? They have a three-bedroom home they are willing to rent. Times are hard and this isn't a new thing. People are desperate for money."

"You're right," Janelle agreed. "See if they are still open to it. If so, make sure we will have full time security during the length of the filming."

"I'll get on it first thing Monday morning." Jurnee reached inside her purse.

"Also, get with Temica in accounting and make sure she has the advance check for Trevon ready for my signature. I know we have thirty days to pay him part of his advance, but he really needs the money. Make sure it's ready and on my desk by the end of business hours on Monday." Janelle smiled when she saw Jurnee typing the notes into her Blackberry. When it came to being on point and professional, Jurnee was one she could depend on.

"Anything else?" Jurnee asked, looking up.

"Yes. Let Trevon know that I want his dick to be completely shaven before we film. Now, tell me all the juicy details about last night."

"Gurl, let me tell you!" Jurnee rubbed her neck. "Trevon has the nicest black ass! I even kissed it. You know I tried to lick his ass, but he tensed up on me."

Janelle laughed. "The man has been in prison since he was eighteen. Your nasty butt trying to break him in too soon."

Jurnee had not thought about that fact. "Damn! Really, it's like he's still eighteen when it comes to sex. Think he'll be down to letting someone suck his dick with a finger up his ass?"

"I seriously doubt it. I will give him the same respect as I do with the women. If he doesn't feel comfortable, the camera stops."

"I agree," Jurnee said seriously. "But back to last night. OMG—that dick! Gurl, I know I sucked on it for ten minutes nonstop. Mmm, I can still feel and taste him in my mouth." Jurnee closed her eyes, reminiscing.

"Calm down, bitch." Janelle laughed.

"And yes, I swallowed . . . All of it. Kandi did her thang, too. She had his eyes rolling and he ate both of us out. Overall, his body is so fucking hot! No lie, Janelle. I've seen many naked men and plenty of big dicks, but Trevon has it all! The looks, the body. Mmm, his chest, shoulders and arms, his legs and that sweet dick. My pussy was dripping! When we put him to sleep, I made Kandi dick me down with a strap on. I just needed something in me!"

"What's up with you and—"

"He got too emotional," Jurnee blurted. She did not want to speak on her *former* male friend. "Started trying to keep tabs on me, so his ass had to go."

"But he was cute."

Jurnee rolled her eyes. "You want his number?"

"I said he was cute. Did not say I want to fuck him. You know I don't do the white milk."

"People change." Jurnee shrugged.

"They do. But not my preference for dick," Janelle explained. "The only thing the white man can do for me is business."

"Speaking of men. What's up with you and Victor?"

Janelle looked at her nails. "He called me last night."

"And?"

"We talked about some things."

"What things?"

Janelle looked off toward the pool. "He um . . ."

"Spill it."

"He—he asked me to marry him."

Jurnee gasped. "For real! Are you for real, gurl?"

Janelle nodded. "I let him hit it raw when he came to visit me last week."

"Damn that! What did you say? Yes or no?"

"Girl, I said yes!"

"Ooohhh, you lucky bitch you."

"Ain't I!"The two friends gave each other a high-five. Jurnee was happy for Janelle to have found true love. Deep down, Jurnee wished she could find someone, but she allowed her past as a porn star to create doubt that a man could love and most importantly, respect her. She had no problem finding a man to cater to her sexual needs, but when it came to emotions, she would run. The day she learned to focus on today and not the past, would be the day she could balance her life.

"I'm not a star, somebody lied, I got a pistol in the car, a .45..."

Rick Ross blared from the Escalade as Trevon cruised slowly through his old neighborhood in Liberty City. He had moments ago checked out of the boarding home and left his old clothes behind for donation. The hood still looked the same to him. The only pointless change was the size of the rims the D-Boys were stunting on. Bums were still on the corners, trash bins were overloaded with dirty diapers, and numerous brass shell casings littered the ground. Mangy, rail thin dogs roamed in packs while ducking the rocks thrown at them by bored kids. Young mothers walking with kids with no fathers. It all looked the same. Trevon shook his head when he stopped at the corner he once sold drugs on. A young looking boy with long dreads and gold teeth glared at Trevon while sitting on the hood of a Lemon Heads themed 2011 roofless Dodge Charger. It was his block now. Trevon ignored the look, sad that the teen was caught up in the cycle.

Trevon did not wish to return to this life. He wanted out. Leaving the hood, he swore he would not take his freedom for granted. He looked back in the rearview mirror as he left Liberty City and the boarding home behind.

"Shit gotta change," he said, looking ahead.

He was still riding around twenty minutes later when Kandi sent him a text. At a stoplight, he tried to open the text to read it, but was unable to do it. Giving up, he hit the button to call her.

"Hey, what's up? I got your text," he said when she answered.

"Why didn't you text me back so we could instant message each other?"

"That shit is wack. I'd rather talk to you."

"Whateva." She laughed. "You just don't know how to work that phone yet."

Trevon smiled. "Okay, you're right."

"You're hopeless, Smooch. Anyway, I'm home now and I was wondering if you would like to go to a movie? I figured we could catch one together, if you want to."

Trevon slowed to turn off the avenue. "What time are you trying to go?"

"Are you done with whatever you had to do?"

"Yeah. Saw my P.O. and I checked out of the boarding home."

"Well, we can catch the six o'clock show if you want to?"

Trevon saw no reason not to take her up on the offer. "Yo, is this a date?"

"Boy, just get here and stop talking silly. You're going to be staying with me, so we might as well spend some time together."

"I like your hair." Trevon commented on Kandi's new look.

"Thanks, Smooch." Kandi touched her small spiral, springy curls and new color. Jet-black. She relaxed in the passenger seat of the Escalade as Trevon drove.

"Why did you cut your hair?" he asked, turning the music down.

She turned in the seat. "You trying to be funny or something?"

"Funny? What's funny about me asking you about that?"

"I had weave in my head, boy. Couldn't you tell?"

"Nope."

She punched his arm then told him to shut up. The two were opening up to each other with no reservation. At the Omni Mall, they walked together holding hands. Kandi drew all types of looks as her ass poked out the custom made black denim jeans. Because of Trevon, the men kept their comments silent.

In the dark theater, they took their seats two minutes before the movie began. As the movie played, he pulled his attention from the screen and thought about his personal life. He wanted to have kids one day. It would be a one handed juggle to have a girlfriend and do porn at the same time. *Damn. I need this job, but at the same time, I'd like to settle down with one woman and just chill. I'll do these six films, stack my money and then try to find a new hustle.*

"This movie is stupid!" Kandi muttered. "I knew we should've gone to see that other movie."

"Shhhh."

"Don't shhhh me!"

Trevon smiled in the dark, then leaned over to kiss her cheek. Knowing what he was about to do, she turned her face. Their lips met. Instantly, their lips parted and their tongues darted out. Kandi raised her hand to his face and twirled her tongue over and around his. Turning slightly in the seat, he lowered a hand on her thigh and rubbed it. No one was behind them so they acted freely on their lust.

"Pull it out," she spoke against his lips. When he did not act fast enough, she moved her hand to his crotch.

Trevon moaned from her touch while sucking on her tongue. She jerked his belt loose, shoving a hand down his pants. He was already solid when she wrapped her grip around him. He winced when she pulled it out roughly.

"Sorry," she mumbled against his full lips.

Trevon felt his legs turn mushy as her hand slid up and down his dick.

Kandi showed her boldness even more by pulling up her shirt to expose her left titty for him to lick.

"Mmmm. Suck my titty, Daddy." She kept pumping his dick as his mouth blew, sucked and licked her swollen nipple. She looked around. No one was paying them any attention.

Trevon rubbed and molded her breast. When Kandi had enough of the tease, she pushed his mouth away then leaned over the armrest to lick the pre-cum off the tip of his throbbing masterpiece. Trevon gripped one armrest then laid his other hand on her shoulder. Before he took his next breath, Kandi stole it by lowering her glossy lips down his pole. Up and down, her head bobbed. Slow and softly.

"LaToria," he groaned, lifting his ass off the seat.

She gripped and squeezed the bottom half while licking the rest as if it were coated with honey. Her luscious lips sent chills up his stiff spine. He had never done anything sexual in a public place. He looked down at the back of her head bobbing in the dim flickering light. Any second now, he knew he would reach his climax. Kandi sensed it also, slurping and sucking him with a smooth up and down pace. He was closing his eyes when he caught the glimmer of light over his shoulder. Looking back, he saw a female theater employee strolling down the aisle with a small flashlight.

". . . Comin'. . ." he gasped, squeezing her shoulder.

Kandi reached down to rub his balls while moaning. "No . . . coming. Stop! . . . ahhhh. Somebody coming." She kept sucking. "Stop!" he moaned. "Some —somebody coming!"

Finally understanding, she sat up quickly but kept a tight grip at the base of his wet throbbing penis. She wiped her mouth, grinning.

Trevon sat motionless with his hands gripping the armrest. The woman with the flashlight walked by with the light held toward the ground. When she reached the front, Kandi quickly lowered her lips back on his dick.

"You tr-trippin'," he stuttered as she sucked him rapidly up and down before sitting back up. The thrill of being seen or caught pushed Kandi to commit her wild freaky acts. A small smirk spread on her face as the woman turned to head back out. She was seven rows from Trevon and Kandi when a lone man motioned her to stop her. The few minutes of the two talking, broke the spell between Trevon and Kandi.

"Why didn't you stop when I said someone was coming?" he asked, fixing his clothes.

"I thought you said *you* were cumming." She giggled.

"Yeah, right. You just crazy as hell. We could've gotten an indecent exposure charge or something."

She rolled her eyes. "Smooch, relax."

Trevon realized that sex was like a drug to LaToria. *Might as well call her Kandi because her freaky nature is turned on twenty-four fucking seven! Not that I mind. What I really want is a shot of that pussy! Gotta wait. Gotta wait. Gotta wait.*

Kandi complained tirelessly about how dull the movie was. Trevon had reached his patience with her and suggested they leave. It seemed normal that their hands met as they walked around the mall. Being spontaneous, he stopped at a flower kiosk and bought her six white roses.

"Who are those for?" Kandi asked him.

"They're for you."

Kandi did not know how to react. She never had such a gift given to her. Seeing the flat look on her face, he led her to a bench to sit down.

"Why you trippin'?" he asked as a white overweight lady ambled by holding a baby.

"What are you talking about?" she asked.

"You know what I'm talking about." He nodded at the flowers. "You don't like flowers?"

She shrugged, looking away. "These are . . . mushy things. You didn't have to buy them."

Trevon knew it was going to be hard to break her walls down. "Kandi, I mean, LaToria. Just because you do porn doesn't mean you shouldn't be treated nice. I got the flowers as a way to say thank you."

"What are you thanking me for?" she asked, looking into his eyes.

"Be serious."

"I am being serious. I don't know! Shit! Is it 'cause I got some bomb head? I just don't know, okay? All this shit you're doing. You got me off balance."

"And what is this *shit* I'm doing?"

"Actin' like . . . you really feeling me. This is a business, Trevon, and that's all it is. Dealing with emotions in this business is like selling dope and trying to smoke it at the same time. It don't mix. I don't deal in emotion, not anymore. Besides, you just met me yesterday. Once you do your first film, you'll change and I promise that. All this mushy shit will be the last thing on your mind."

Trevon sensed the hurt in her voice that she tried to conceal. He wanted to get to know her. Even though she did porn, he felt he could overlook her job. At least he would try. *Maybe I do need to slow down. I have not been with a woman in so long. Now I'm free and her fine ass got me so wide open. Damn, she just so damn cool. Why can't I be the man in her life? She gave that skinny ass nigga, Swagga, some play. Wait, I can't forget that he has money and I don't.*

"So it's just business, huh?" he said after running his thoughts through his mind.

"That's all it is, Trevon," she lied. *Girl, this nigga is uugghhh! Now I know what Nicki Minaj meant by that nigga seeing right through her. Youuu seeee right through me. How do you do that shit! Now I'ma be stuck with this damn song in my head all fucking damn day. I can't be real with you, Trevon. Lord knows I'm feeling you too, baby. And I ain't even got a shot of the dick!*

CHAPTER
TWELVE
September 8, 2011
Thursday 11:10 a.m. - Miami, Florida

Twelve days later, Trevon found himself filled with a strong urge to fast forward to tomorrow. He was still sex free, no pussy, and still living with Kandi. Strictly business. Tomorrow would be the first day of filming. Kandi suggested a week ago that she stop her regular oral favors so he would be ready to bust on film. He agreed. They both placed their emotions aside and fronted like it was *only business*.

Trevon was slowly adjusting to his freedom and the speed of things. When he was not going over the movie script, he was chilling with Kandi. She showed him how to wash his own clothes and how to cook basic meals. Their friendship grew, but each refused to act upon anything that dealt with emotions. Trevon had bought a year old car with some of his advance money and had obtained his driver's license. If he was not at home, he was out cruising the streets in his pearlescent white 2010 Jaguar XJL. He kept it clean and with Kandi's help, the MP3 player was loaded with old school classics ranging from Biggie Smalls to the Lost Boyz.

He was cruising down 54th Street with the system thumping, leaning hard in the black leather seat. *I'ma be a star! A porn star!* He nodded to the music. He had yet to tell his mom and sister of his new career. He only assured them that the money he wired was earned legally.

With Kandi ignoring his wants to become closer, he began to flirt more openly with women he met randomly in the street. He had close to ten different phone numbers and pictures of new women stored in his cell phone. At times, his communication skills came to a halt when he dealt with older women. He had yet to go out with any of the women. One reason was his unfairness to compare them to Kandi. Being exposed to this new life had him wanting more. Coming up on 12th Avenue, a shapely female caught his eye. Her back was toward him as she pumped gas into a tinted forest green brand new Jeep Grand Cherokee. Her heels showcased her leggy stance in the tight-fitting blue jeans.

I got to see who she is. Damn, look at those hips! He switched lanes to slow down and turned into the gas station. Feeling himself, he quickly changed up the music then thought about what he would say to this new honey. Even if she turned out to be ugly, he would still give her a call just for the view of her ass and legs. He hit the button to lower all four of the tinted windows.

Kendra Paige kept her eyes on the digital counter. *Gas is too damn high!* The price was $50.72 and counting. Suddenly, a soft mellow thump from a car system made her turn her head. She hated all that bumpity bump shit, but at least it was one of her favorite songs.

When the pump clicked indicating the tank was full, she again glanced over her shoulder. Kendra wanted to be sure it was Trevon Harrison before she walked over. *Yep!*

That's Trevon. She eyed him hard as he pulled up to a pump. Now she *knew* he was up to something illegal!

Trevon almost drove into a light pole when he locked eyes with his parole officer. "What the fuck!" He eased the British sedan to a stop with the system still playing The Dream, "Falsetto."

Damn. Here come the parole officer from hell. This is what I get fo' chasin' a piece of good looking ass! Trevon stepped out of his ride and tried to front like he was surprised to see her.

"Ms. Paige! What's—"

She held up a hand, shutting him down. "Show me your driver's license, Mr. Harrison. I seriously hope you're not driving without one."

Trevon was not in the mood to be dealing with her salty ass. He reached into his loose black Gucci jeans and pulled out his wallet. "I got it last week," he said and held the license out between his two fingers.

"I know how to read!" She swiped it from his hand. *Please let it be fake so I can lock his ass up!* Seeing it was authentic, she handed it back. She looked at his ride and the big chrome rims wrapped in thin glossy rubber band tires.

"Can I get some gas?" he asked since she stood in his path.

"This your car?" She had to squint from the gleam sparkling off the polished chrome rims.

"Yeah," he answered, hoping she would stop tripping.

"Oh really, Mr. Harrison?" She crossed her arms. "Please enlighten me how *you* can afford a ride like that? Wait! You're about to tell me you found a job. And even if you did, I doubt you would get a check so soon. Not one to afford that." She nodded at the sleek four-door Jag.

"I—" he began, but stopped himself. *Fuck her! Ain't doing shit wrong. If she wanna act stupid, then fuck it.*

"I what?" She pulled her cell phone seemingly from out of thin air. In truth, it was so small that Trevon had not noticed her holding the tiny flip phone. "I'll tell you what I can do and what I'm about to do since you can't explain this car. How about I get on this phone and call the police, huh? What will they find if that car is searched?"

"Leather seats!"

"Oh, you still wanna be funny with me?"

"Listen. You want to call the police, do it! Ain't got no place to be."

Kendra flipped the phone open. *This nigga think I'm bluffing! I'll show his ass 'cause I ain't the—"*

"Mommy!" a tiny voice whined from the back of her SUV.

Kendra scolded herself, having forgotten about Carmelita, her three year old. *Shit! I'm really out here tripping! What if this fool was on some dumb shit? I got my baby in the ride and I got her around this ex-con. What if . . . he has a gun? Okay, calm down and fall back. I'll just file a suspicious activity report on his ass. At the rate he's going, he'll get popped for whatever he's doing. Let me take my baby to the park.* "Coming baby," she said, closing the phone. "You need to get your shit together, Mr. Harrison."

"What?" Trevon pulled out his cell phone. "Your phone dead? Need to use mine?"

"Don't push me!" she warned.

Trevon glared back, holding his ground. *She cute. Just stupid.* When she turned to stomp away, he had to admit that she had a nice country thick frame. Without effort, he compared her to Kandi. Kandi was still that top-notch-dimed-out-fly-ass-all-around-the world-DIVA.

106

Bayview Condo, Fisher Island

"Girl, where ya been?" Cindy said while out on the balcony sunbathing. She lay on her back wearing nothing. The sun was basking her tone to a deep golden hue that would drive Swagga silly. In her ear, hidden under her dreads was a tiny wireless earpiece.

"I've been out of town," Chyna responded with a true Asian accent.

"For two whole weeks?"

"Two and a half. So what's up? I got your message on my Facebook."

"I need a small favor," Cindy said, reaching for the peach scented tanning lotion.

"A favor? Uh-oh." Chyna giggled.

"It's nothing crazy. Just need you to be an escort for somebody." Cindy squeezed a small dime drop of tanning lotion on each breast.

"You know my fee?"

"Yes, I know your fee, Chyna. I doubt you would let me forget." Closing her eyes, she began to rub the lotion into her skin. She intentionally squeezed her nipples between her thumb and index fingers on both perky tits.

"Who's the guy?"

"Um ..." She released her slippery tits as a shadow appeared over her. "You'll have to speak to someone else about all the details and stuff." Cindy raised her feet up, then opened her legs. Her pussy lips were small and delicate looking.

"Will this somebody have my money up front?"

"Yes, Chyna." Cindy slid her hands toward her recently waxed pussy and opened her outer lips. "How did your operation go last month?"

"Huh?"

"Your operation. The sex change. How did it turn out?"

"Oh! Fine. Everything is good?"

"So, you have a pussy now?" Cindy dipped her middle finger inside her pussy, then slid it back out.

"The juiciest in Florida!"

"I doubt it, bitch."

"Suck it, ho!"

The two friends laughed. Cindy gave Chyna the phone number to reach Swagga.

"Swagga? The rapper!" Chyna said excitedly.

"Calm down, ho. He's my meal ticket, so erase dem dollar signs out 'cha eyes."

"Bye bitch. He just betta have my bread."

"Whateva."

Cindy ended the call, then gazed up at the sexy concierge from the kitchen.

He was jacking his pink, hard dick while standing over her. She began to finger herself while rubbing and squeezing her slippery titties. Her eyes moved from his face to his dick.

"Pump that cock! Pump it. Look at my pussy. You wanna ram that dick all up in me? Yesssss . . . pump it fast. Faster!"

The concierge's fist was a milky blur as he masturbated over Cindy's perfect body. She kept rubbing her breasts and fingering her dripping pussy at his feet. He moaned. He grunted. Easing up on his toes, he pumped his climax free.

Cindy lost her breath as a long stream of warm milky cum landed from her tits to her pussy. His last release landed on her chin.

"You made a mess," she said, pointing at the mass of cum sliding down her waxed pussy. "Lick it off. All of it."

Nude Awakening

Under the warmth of the soothing sun, she finger combed the concierge's beach blond hair. He took his time slurping at her damp pussy, thankful she was allowing him this freaky pleasure. Cindy held him in place until she popped one against his lips. She was still down for Swagga. The concierge could only fantasize about running his dick up in her.

CHAPTER
THIRTEEN

At the same time up in Fort Lauderdale, Swagga was home up in his state-of-the art studio. He looked at his music producer through the soundproof glass while bobbing his head to the bass filled beat. He pressed the Dr. Dre headphones against his ears. He had to come with some fire to dethrone Lil Wayne and Rick Ross. His music producer D-Hot gave him a nod from the soundboard.

"My shit hot like the hood in Opa Locka, where bricks get chopped cookin' coke wit straight Vodka, Make you lose blood like you drainin' your bladder, That's for any cock sucka dats aimin' at Swagga, Fish scale, Nigga I'm raw, now clap your hands and gimme an encore . . ."

D-Hot stood up. "That's a good take, Swagga!"

Swagga pulled the headphones off and turned to glance over his shoulder. Lounging behind him on a white sofa was a new groupie he had met last week. He had already fucked her twice and was ready to make it a third by day's end. She had a bag of Kush on the table and was ready to smoke.

Just as he sat down beside her, his mobile phone vibrated on his waist. Viewing the number, it was one he had never seen.

"Yeah?" he answered as Yaffa walked into the booth with a bottle of Moet and two glasses.

"Hello. May I um . . . speak to Swagga?"

"Dis he. Who dis?" He changed his tone hearing a female voice.

"Chyna. Cindy told me to call you."

Swagga stood and walked to the far corner of the booth. "Did Cindy tell you what was up?"

"A little bit. Said something about me being an escort for somebody."

"Yeah. My man . . . He um—would like to get up with you, but it has to be on the down low."

"That's normal in my line of business."

"Yo, how do I know you really look like a bitch? My nigga wants you to look like a female all the way around. You ain't manly lookin', are you?"

Chyna laughed softly. "How about you meet me face to face? Then you can judge for yourself."

Swagga looked over at Yaffa and the groupie. "That might be a good idea. How much you charge?"

"Eight hundred for a date. Oral sex is an extra two hundred and the pussy is a flat fee of fifteen hundred."

That was nothing to Swagga. "You a transvestite, right?"

"No, sugah." Chyna laughed. "I'm a transsexual, also called a transgender."

"What's the damn difference?"

"A lot, honey. A transvestite is a man that likes to dress and act like a woman. As for me, I had a full sex change. I got it all. Pussy, ass, breasts and the best head on this coast."

"Yeah, well you can brag 'bout all that shit to my nigga."

"Still want to see what you're paying for?"

"Yeah. Also, I'm dealing in cash."

"Fine with me."

"Aiight. Where can we meet?"

"Um, there is an Asian bar in downtown Miami near Bayside. I can meet you there tonight at eight."

"How will I know what you look like?"

"You won't miss me, baby. I'll be the only Asian chick with blonde hair, green eyes and a nice firm booty."

Swagga was pissed off! *Where the fuck dis bitch at? Got me up in dis funky ass spot wit' all these Jackie Chan lookin' motherfuckers!* Swagga looked at his iced out watch. It was ten minutes past eight. He had tried to call Chyna five minutes ago, but his call was forwarded to voice mail. Snatching up his phone he called her again.

"Chyna! Where the fuck you at, yo! I'ma give you . . . ten mo minutes then I'm leavin' this—Just call me or hurry the fuck up and get here!" Swagga ended the call, then motioned for one of the tiny Asian hostesses to come to his table.

Yaffa declined a drink as Swagga made his order. Yaffa was staying focused on his surroundings to spot any threats toward Swagga. "What this chick look like?"

"Um . . . blonde hair, green eyes and a nice ass." Swagga had not told Yaffa that Chyna was a transgender.

Yaffa had eyed every female in the bar. The only blonde haired female in the bar was a small-breasted white girl over by the pool table.

The bar was loud. Too loud for Yaffa. The language being spoken was lost to both Yaffa and Swagga. Neither knew one word of Chinese or Japanese.

Swagga settled back in the booth with a cold beer checking out the women.

Shit! Ain't never had no Asian pussy! Damn, that bartender do look sexy as fuck. Wonder if she ever had any Mandingo dick?

"Yaffa." Swagga stood. "I'ma go spit game to the bartender. She keep looking over here at a nigga." Swagga made his way to the bar. Heads turned as he walked by. His dreads, bulky jewelry and skin color was a rarity inside the bar. Swagga had all the confidence in the world as he took a seat at the crowded bar. He eased his lanky frame between two Asian men and smiled at the short, cute faced bartender. Her jet-black hair was tied up in a bun. She had a nice set of thin lips that went natural with her Asian features. Overall, she was a small petite female in Swagga's view. All he wanted to do was fuck or get some head. Once he gained the bartender's attention, he forgot all about Chyna and laid his game down. He told her he was a rapper, but she thought he was telling a lie.

"You lie." she said and laughed, while cleaning the bar top.

"Look ma," he said, looking at her small breasts. "I got a big ass mansion up in Fort Lauderdale. Ain't gotta front 'bout nothin'," he boasted. "I got racks on racks."

"You rich?" the bartender asked while fixing a drink for another customer at the bar.

Swagga nodded. "I'll make it rain up in this bitch. What time you get off?"

"Two hours. Why is that important to you?" she asked with a smirk.

"You coming home wit' me tonight?"

Ten minutes later, he finally got the call back from Chyna. Swagga listened while watching the bartender work. Chyna explained that a family issue had come up and they could meet tomorrow.

"Yeah. Just call me." Swagga had his mind on the bartender. *Chyna on some bullshit.*

Swagga ended up talking the Asian bartender into coming to his mansion. His mind was still focused on setting up Trevon with Chyna, but for now, he wanted to see how he would fair with his latest quest.

CHAPTER
FOURTEEN
September 9, 2011
Friday, 7:00 p.m. - Opa Locka, Florida

Finally! Finally! Finally! Trevon kept repeating in his mind. He was alone in the bathroom looking in the mirror. "Time to show and prove," he said, glancing down at his hairless crotch. *I hope I don't freeze up in front of everybody.*

The sex scene would take place in a small bedroom already packed with lights and cameras. The home was being rented out by a married black couple in their late fifties. Neither was a big fan of porn, but the money was needed. Trevon took a deep breath, then sat down on the closed toilet. He picked up the film script off the sink.

He had his dialogue down pat, having practiced alone and with Kandi. He saw another side of Kandi during their practice sessions. Kandi took things seriously when it dealt with her time in front of the lights and camera.

Trevon moved beyond the dialogue to read up on the action. He was to enter the bedroom and find Kandi stepping out of the shower. Janelle wanted to keep it real. Any man coming home after fifteen years would not be down for much talking.

"Trevon. We're ready for you," Jurnee said, knocking on the door and waiting for it to open.

Trevon wore an all white outfit. He had to look as if he had just come home from prison. He took a deep breath and opened the door to the start of his future.

Trevon stood at the closed bedroom door waiting for his cue to enter.

"Scene one. Take one. Action!" the director shouted, followed by the snap of the digital clapper board being closed. Trevon opened the door and messed up by looking directly at the camera.

"Cut! Cut! Stop the damn film!" the black male director screamed. "Don't look at the camera! We are not here. Walk in and look toward the bathroom. Let's do it again people."

Trevon closed his eyes as he turned around. *Damn! I'm fucking up already!*

"Trevon," Kandi said, stepping out of the bathroom with nothing but a large green towel wrapped around her succulent soft frame.

Trevon turned to face her.

"Trevon," she said, looking into his eyes. She knew he was nervous as hell. "Relax, okay? Just walk through that door and come to me. Ignore the camera. Just focus on me. Come and fuck me like I know you want to. I know you can do it."

Trevon looked at his feet then up into her eyes. "Okay, I'll do it."

Exiting the room, he glanced at Janelle and Jurnee sitting in the corner.

"Okay, let's do it again," the director ordered.

Trevon again waited in the hallway. The film's title was *Home Cumming* and they had four days at the max to film it. He took a deep breath with his eyes toward the ceiling. *I can do this. I'm going to fuck Kandi. Give her all this dick! I'm 'bout to fuck a woman that men can only imagine fucking! I'm that nigga! I will do this! I will do this!*

"Scene One. Take Two. And . . . Action!"

Trevon stepped into the bedroom then closed the door. Right on cue, Kandi eased out of the bathroom with a towel wrapped around her wet body.

"Baby!" she squealed, running into his arms letting the towel slip from her body. She jumped on him, locking her arms around his neck and her legs around his waist.

"Surprised to see me?" he said as his hands cupped her big red wet ass.

"Hell yeah! I thought you was getting out next week!"

"I got some good behavior credit, so they let me out a week early."

Kandi rubbed his face then slid her tongue over his lips. "Welcome home, baby."

"I won't be home until I'm balls deep up in this," he said, squeezing her ass.

Kandi slid from his grip. On cue, Trevon removed his shirt and white wife beater as Kandi undid his belt.

"I wanna suck your dick!" She yanked his pants down as he kicked his boots off. "I wanna feel you in my mouth."

The camera zoomed in to focus on Kandi's face and Trevon's rapidly growing dick.

Standing only in a pair of socks, he reached down to rub Kandi's face. She stroked him slowly, using both hands.

"Yeah, that feels so good, baby," he moaned hoarsely as his dick swelled from her touch. She squatted in front of him with a bright warm klieg light behind her. To her left was the bed and one of the cameras. Only those who were needed for the film production were in the crowded bedroom. The director, Janelle, Jurnee and the film assistant, two cameramen, one lighting technician, and one sound operator. None of them distracted Kandi from Trevon.

"So . . . big," she murmured, grazing his dick across her lips. She did it a few more times, slowly sliding it across her puckered lips.

Trevon's neck turned to jelly when Kandi stuck her tongue out. She circled it around and around his tip while caressing the shaft with a two-hand grip. Kandi used her thumb to press it up and under the length of his dick. When she neared the tip, her reward was a clear globule of pre-cum. She licked it off, using only the tip of her tongue.

"Mmmm," she purred. "You taste so good!"

Trevon was breathing hard. "Please!" he moaned. "Put your lips on it, baby."

"Ready baby?" She lifted his dick to her lips and slid the tip in. She paused with her lips wrapped around it. Catching him off guard, she flicked her tongue over his slit before engulfing him to the back of her throat.

Janelle crossed her legs as she watched Kandi slowly devoured Trevon's dick as the cameraman lowered in over her shoulder for a super close-up.

Kandi swallowed Trevon's dick. The script called for an oral scene of three minutes. Trevon had to control himself.

Kandi made sure she sucked him at a slow pace. His dick was shiny and reflected the lighting. It would look good on film. *This dick is soooo good! I know mad bitches are gonna envy me!* Kandi took his dick from her mouth then kissed and licked her way to his balls. The second cameraman was already waiting. A shot between Trevon's parted legs showed an extreme close-up of her tongue licking under and over his balls. Trevon looked down as Kandi slid her thumb over his throbbing tip. She sucked on his balls and licked her way back up.

"Annnnnd cut!" The director clapped his hands. "Good job, Trevon!"

Kandi walked to the bed. One of the cameramen tossed Trevon a robe.

"Okay," the director said. "We'll fade in on a shot of Kandi playing in her pussy. We'll zoom out and then Trevon, do your thang. Okay people, let's set it up!"

Kandi was already on the bed with two fingers slipping in and out of her wet pussy. She had her eyes closed, sliding her tongue around her lips. She was on her back with her knees bent.

Trevon stood against the wall as the cameraman moved in for the shoot.

"Scene two. Take one. Action!"

Kandi worked her fingers over her clit and pussy. She whined and moaned softly as she opened her outer pussy lips.

The director pointed at Trevon as the cameraman slowly zoomed out.

Trevon walked into the scene and stood over Kandi. His dick was still an impressive sight, even though it was semi-hard. Sitting on the bed he lowered his lips to her pointy nipples. His tongue circled her nipples four times.

"Lemme taste that pussy," he said, licking up her neck. Kandi slid over rubbing her tits. Trevon rolled to his back as Kandi positioned herself over his face.

"Ahhh . . . Yesss . . . lick my pussy," she moaned the instant his tongue slid inside her. She sat on his face with her hands braced on the bed. Tossing her head around made her dizzy. From the TV in the corner, she could see what the cameraman was shooting. The close up of her wide ass filled the screen. Trevon was smacking at her dripping pussy, and rubbing all over her ass.

"Feels sooo good!" she squealed. "Oooohhhh right . . . there! Suck me out!" She pulled at the sheets.

Trevon slurped at the tangy juices flowing from her pussy. His skill had greatly improved and Kandi was reaping the pleasure. Her butt was so big that it covered all of his face. She squirmed over his mouth as his gentle licking made her toes curl. Slowly, she began to rock back and forth. His tongue stiffened inside her. Moaning tenderly, she acted outside of the script and lowered her mouth down the length of his dick. The director glanced at Janelle. She nodded and motioned for the cameras to keep rolling. Janelle wanted to see how far they would go. Trevon lapped his tongue firmly against her pussy as her slow head job made his balls tighten. What was happening now was real.

Jurnee shifted in the chair as Kandi kept slurping up and down on his ebony dick. Sitting up on his face, she arched her back while moaning and purring. She reached back and opened her big ass cheeks apart.

The cameraman zoomed in on her asshole only seconds before Trevon began to tongue it out.

Janelle reached for her bottled water. She never took her eyes away from Trevon and Kandi. The way Trevon was licking her ass out was mind twisting. *Dang! He definitely has his lickin' license!*

Kandi felt her stomach twisting in knots at the feeling of Trevon's tongue in her ass. She rolled off his face, trying to catch her breath.

"Cut! Great scene you two!" The director stood up from his chair with his dick hard.

Kandi sat up and looked around the room. "Someone give me a wet rag. It's hot up in here!" She glanced down at her sweaty breasts.

Janelle walked up to the bed with the script in her hand. Trevon assumed they were about to be chewed out for veering off the script.

"Which one of you added in that anal licking?" Janelle asked as she slowly flipped through the script.

"I did." Kandi raised her hand.

"Did you know about it, Trevon?" Janelle asked.

"Um . . . no," he said uneasily.

Janelle smiled, looking up from the script. "Good of you not to freeze up. That shows promise for you."

"Thanks," he modestly replied.

Janelle handed the script to the director. "Throw it away." She then turned her attention back to Trevon and Kandi. "I'll let you two freestyle it. Don't make me regret this."

"Scene three! Take one . . . action!"

Kandi sat on the bathroom sink with Trevon between her legs. She spiraled her tongue around his while pumping his dick with her hands. They did this for a few minutes then pulled apart to open a rubber. Sliding off the sink she sucked his dick at a fast pace as he tore open the pack. Once she rolled the rubber down with her lips, she stood up and trembled when he bent her over the sink. He came up behind her, caressing her hips and big red ass. She arched her back, begging him for the dick. Janelle held her breath as Trevon slid his dick around Kandi's pussy. Kandi had a dip in her back, tits hanging beneath her.

Trevon took a deep breath and guided the first few inches of his dick inside her. Once her pussy gripped it, he let go of his shaft and placed his hands on her waist. He took another deep breath, then pushed forward. Kandi gasped as Trevon inched his entire dick into her wet hole.

"Yessss," she moaned. "Push it deeper . . . Uhhhh . . . deeper! Ahhh."

Trevon forgot how to breathe as he buried himself balls deep. She was tight and slippery. Neither moved.

Trevon moved his hands to her ass then back up to her waist. She looked back at him wincing and licking her lips.

"Hit dis pussy!" she gasped as he placed a grip on her shoulders.

His first full thrust took her breath away. It was followed by another and another. In and out, in and out.

"Fuck . . . me!" she moaned with his dick thrusting between her legs.

Her breasts swayed with each contact of his waist against her jiggling ass. Pussy farts mixed with their moans filled the bathroom. Kandi's ass rippled like jello as he long dicked her. He sped up. Pounding her with a long tip to shaft thrust as she whimpered and twisted at the waist. He laid it down for seven full minutes until he stopped to change positions.

Throwing a towel on the floor, she pushed him to his back. Kandi got on top of him, placing her bare feet by his waist.

Jurnee wanted to cheer Kandi on when she lowered her pussy down Trevon's dick. *Ride that motherfucker, girl!* Jurnee nodded at the sight of Kandi's dick riding skills. The soft smacks of her ass filled the room.

"Ohhhh . . . dick so good!" Kandi bounced hard and fast, taking him deep up inside her. She pinched her nipples as he smacked her hips.

Trevon moaned beneath her. She whirled her pussy in circles. Her desire for him was so strong. She was so lost with him, that her mind could not grasp when and how they ended up on the bed. She wanted him to cum.

Trevon was behind her, fucking her doggy style. Her huge bouncing ass wobbled all over the place.

"Pussy. So. Damn. Juicy!" he moaned each time his balls slapped against her. He showed her no mercy.

Kandi bit the pillow with her ass raised high in the air while braced on her knees. She gripped the wooden headboard as it thumped against the wall. Sweat rolled down his face as he pumped himself into her. She spilled his name from her lips like a drink into the pillow.

"You-you're killin' me!" She pulled at the sheets. "Give it to me!" she said in one breath. "Cummin' . . . I'm cummin'! All. Over. That. Dick!"

Trevon kept pumping her pussy. When she came, he forced himself to pull out so the cameraman could zoom in. Soon the world would see the milky cream oozing out of her swollen pussy.

To everyone's shock, Trevon suddenly stood up on the bed. He moved over Kandi. She was still on her face and knees.

"Oh. My gawd!" Jurnee gasped. From the rearview, she watched Trevon push his dick into Kandi's asshole. Kandi spread her cheeks apart. She cried into the pillow as he dropped his dick into her ass by bending his knees. The position was odd looking, but deeply pleasing to both Trevon and Kandi. He slid his dick slowly into her tight ass. Gripping the top of the headboard, he moaned out her name. Catching his breath, he moved his legs, slowly fucking her in the butt. Once he got the movement down pat, he had her crying into the pillow. His dick reached deep into her ass.

"Don't . . . stop! I . . . love this!" she wailed. "Mmmmm. Fuck it good!"

Trevon was in a zone. Her tight, wet ass was too good to be calm. Closing his eyes, he rocked in and out with short hard thrusts. *Yes! This ass so good! I wanna do this forever!* He praised her in his mind.

Kandi reached up to play in her pussy as Trevon turned her world out. Each time he poured his nine inches into her, she squealed. His huge dick stretched her wide open.

Jurnee felt caught up. She was horny as hell. She could not remove her eyes from the sight. Trevon's dick slid in and out of Kandi's ass like a piston. She felt her own pussy beginning to throb and get moist.

Kandi's ass was tight around his plunging dick. Everyone was on edge. Trevon reached down and fumbled at pulling the condom off as he eased out of her ass. His sudden exit left her ass gaping open. Still on his feet, he managed to remove the rubber only seconds before his explosive burst. His fist-clenching climax shot into her asshole. He shivered as he jacked himself off against her tooted up ass. His cum slid into her ass, down her back, over her ass and some over her pussy.

"And cut!" the director yelled.

CHAPTER
FIFTEEN
September 10, 2011
Saturday, 9:18 a.m. - Fort Lauderdale, Florida

Swagga moaned in his sleep. Opening his tired eyes, he found the Asian bartender kneeling over him rubbing his dick. He quickly thought back to last night.

Bitch wanted to make a nigga beg last night. All I could get was a handjob and now she all on me. Yeah, suck it hoe. Damn, I done forgot her fuckin' name.

Swagga slid his hands under his head as his Asian treat pumped his long organ with two small hands.

"Suck it slow for me," he moaned. "Yeahhhh. Lick it, too."

Yaffa was down on the first floor eating breakfast in the kitchen. He hated when Swagga would bring strange women to the crib. Yaffa trusted no one! A female could pull a trigger just as quickly as a man. At least the bartender was sexy; Yaffa had to give her credit. He stayed up late and watched Swagga fail at getting some pussy. He assumed the chick had bounced last night until he saw her car still in the driveway. After he ate his breakfast, he took the elevator up to the second floor.

Swagga's oversized master bedroom was at the end of the hall. Yaffa was the only person other than Swagga who knew the security codes to the mansion. Reaching the closed bedroom door, he walked right inside without knocking. He never knocked and Swagga knew not to lock the doors for his own safety. Yaffa was two steps in the bedroom when he came to a halt. The topless bartender lay aside Swagga sucking the hell out of his dick. Swagga moaned like a bitch with his eyes closed pulling at the sheets. Yaffa shook his head then eased back out. Before he closed the door, he thought of something. *Just in case this bitch try to yell rape or some grimy shit, I'll just film a few seconds to prove the bitch was willing.* Pulling out his cell phone, he pulled up the video recorder app, then aimed the camera toward Swagga and his guest. He recorded for thirty seconds, then left them alone.

Swagga had not seen Yaffa either time. He was still thrusting his dick upward into the bartender's mouth. The head was the best he ever had!

"Oooohhh, fuck! You suckin' it soooo good, ma-!" he groaned. Up and down he gazed at the pink thin lips racing along his dick. "Swallow it, yo! Eat it all up! I'm cummin'!"

Swagga's ass and hips lurched up off the bed as he started to cum. Soft fingers went to his balls to tumble them. Swagga ran his fingers through the soft fine black hair that brushed against his throbbing dick.

"Good morning," the bartender said in a soft intimate tone.

Swagga slid his hand down to rub the small grapefruit sized breasts with oversized brown nipples.

"You enjoy?"

"Hell, yeah!" Swagga replied, hoping she was ready to fuck.

The bartender pushed her hair back then sat up.

"What you grinnin' about?" he asked, sliding his thumb over her nipple.

"Nothing."

"Yo, don't feel bad. But ummm, I forgot your name." He sat up grinning.

"My—name isn't what I told you last night."

"Say what?"

"My name is Chyna. I'm Cindy's friend."

Swagga's mouth fell open. Before he could stop himself, he blanked all the way out.

Yaffa was entering his bedroom when he heard shouting. At first, he thought it was Swagga blasting music. Stepping back into the hall, he stood and listened. Again, he heard Swagga yelling and cursing. A glass shattered, followed by a high-pitched scream.

"Oh shit!" Yaffa took off running, pulling out his .45 in case it was needed. He bolted up the stairs wishing he were a few pounds lighter. Reaching the top floor, he heard Swagga shouting at the top of his lungs. Coming up on Swagga's bedroom, he found the two. Swagga stood over the bartender, punching and kicking. Yaffa slid his gun back in his waistline then rushed Swagga.

"Get the fuck offa me!" Swagga yelled as Yaffa pulled him back in a tight bear hug. "Let me go! I'ma kill that muthafucka!"

"Calm down, nigga!" Yaffa shouted. He handled Swagga back into his bedroom as Chyna fled past them.

Swagga tried to break free, but it was hopeless. "Let me go!"

"Nigga, chill! What the fuck you beatin' on that bitch fo'?"

"Man! That muthafucka a . . ." Swagga caught himself.

"What she do? You caught her stealin'? What the ho do?" Yaffa released him.

Swagga spun around and grilled Yaffa. *I can take his gun and go murder that trick ass ho right now! Damn! That bitch tricked me! Man, this shit get out and my name is trash. Think nigga, think! Hell, even Yaffa think it's a bitch. Shit! He, she—a man. Damn!*

"What the fuck is goin' on, dawg?" Yaffa pressed.

Swagga flopped down on the bed, hanging his head. *I can't tell NOBODY about this! Not even Yaffa. I trust 'im wit' my life, but not this.* Swagga raked his fingers through his dreads then snapped his head up to whip his dreads back. "I'm good, yo."

"The fuck you ain't." Yaffa pointed toward the hall. "Look what you did to her. You know damn well she gonna press charges on you."

"Naw . . . she ain't," Swagga forced himself to say.

"And why the fuck she ain't?"

"'Cause she just ain't, gotdamnit!" Swagga shouted. "This shit is personal, yo. My life ain't in no jeopardy, so fall back!"

Swagga looked back over his shoulder. Chyna limped back into the bedroom holding her ribs. She sat down slowly onto the bed, still topless with a pair of yellow boy shorts on.

"You okay, shorty?" Yaffa asked.

"I said she—"

"Chill, nigga!" Yaffa turned to face Swagga. "I'm talkin' to *her*, not you!"

Swagga took a step back. *Your dumb ass is a fool too! But that faggot . . .*

"You okay, shorty?" Yaffa asked again.

"I'm fine." Chyna nodded. "We just had a small misunderstanding. I won't call the police or anything."

"See! Told you so!" Swagga jumped in.

Yaffa rubbed his face and looked at Swagga. "Don't expect me to pull you outta this bullshit!"

"Chill, nigga. All it was, was just a small misunderstandin' like she said. Shit good up here." Swagga turned toward Chyna when Yaffa walked out slamming the door.

"I didn't mean to trick you," Chyna whispered. "I really mean it."

"Just shut the fuck up! Sit there and just shut up!" Swagga paced the floor with his hands balled in a fist. *Okay. I got money. Money can solve anything. The bitch must want something since she ain't callin' the police.*

"Why you ain't callin' the police?" He stood above her with his arms crossed.

"Because I know you have a lot to lose."

"Yeah, I do! And you got a lot to lose—like your fuckin' life!"

"I'm sorry, okay? I didn't plan for this to happen."

"Bitch please! Yo, hold the fuck up! How the fuck did you call me when I was at the bar with you? Explain that since you ain't fuckin' plan for this shit to happen!"

"It was a friend of mine that sounds like me."

"She know you're here?"

"No."

"Cindy got anything to do wit' this bullshit?"

"No. And please don't tell her I did this."

"Fuck!" Swagga kicked the air.

Chyna looked up at Swagga. "Just help me out and what happened here will not leave this room."

"You tryin' to blackmail me! Fuck around and *you* might not be leavin' this bedroom!" Swagga shouted then lowered his voice.

"How much do you want to keep shit quiet?"

Chyna looked at her feet. "I want you to pay for the rest of my operation."

"Huh? What operation? Cindy said . . . hell, you said you had a—"

"I still have—a penis."

Swagga closed his eyes. "Ain't. No. Fuckin' way!"

Chyna was still physically a man. The voice was feminine, the Adams apple was shaved down, the breasts were soft. Hips and waist were curvy and female-like, but Chyna was still cuffing a dick and a pair of balls.

Swagga was glad he did not have a gun. *This—nigga! Muthafucka fooled me! Shit, I might as well push his ass on Trevon. Only he'll be exposed for fuckin' with this—faggot ass Kung Fu fucker! Okay, this here will be my secret.*

Swagga looked at this issue as a small bump in the road. He still wanted to be with Kandi. *Ain't a damn thang changed! Trevon, I got a surprise comin' for your He-Man lookin' ass!*

Swagga calmed down then told Chyna the deal. Chyna had no choice but to listen. All he had to do was to trick Trevon as he had done with Swagga.

Swagga said he wanted it on film.

"Freak him. You pull it off, I'll pay you double on top of the bread for . . ." He paused. "Your operation. And yo, don't tell nobody about what happened between us! Nobody!"

Chyna promised him. Promised him that he would do what he wanted.

Opa Locka, Florida

Trevon was back on the set and in front of the camera by 7 p.m.

Today, the director wanted to film him fucking Kandi in various positions. The mental connection between Trevon and Kandi was shown without words. At one point, he slowly fucked her with her ass halfway off the bed as he held her ankles up high, and pounded his dick in and out of her gushy pussy. The director yelled cut, but Kandi whined, "Don't stop!" Trevon kept pumping, long dicking her with sweat coating his muscular frame. Kandi later told everyone that she was so sorry for the slight delay. Everyone understood, including Janelle and Jurnee.

It took them five different takes to film the shower scene. Trevon fell into his role and became at ease with fucking in front of other people. His trick was easy. He kept his attention on Kandi.

A surprise occurred during a break in the filming. Trevon noticed the wife that owned the house had been chatting with Janelle for a while. He was lounging on the sofa in a robe, drinking an energy drink, when Janelle came to sit with him. Trevon listened as Janelle laid a small proposition on him. She told him that the wife was willing to cut the rent fee by ten percent if she could be with him.

"Be with me how?" He glanced over at the attractive older lady.

"She—wants to have sex with you."

"Ain't she married?"

"Her husband is okay with it. So, will you do it?"

"You serious?"

She nodded yes.

Trevon finished his drink then told Janelle he would do it.

The filming did not end until 11:38 p.m. Kandi had worn Trevon out and she had to admit that her pussy was sore. After everyone left with the production crew, Janelle introduced Trevon to Mrs. Linda Rorie, who acted star struck when Trevon spoke to her. All she could do was shy away and cover her face. She looked good to be fifty-six years old.

Janelle pulled Trevon to the corner before leaving the bedroom. "Take it easy on the woman, okay? Don't kill her with that thang. I'll be in the den."

Trevon's ego soared through the roof. Yes, he was willing to fuck Mrs. Rorie, so he wasted no time in getting down to business. They were alone in her bedroom with no rolling film. He undressed her slowly, intending to go slow and be tender, but she had other plans.

When she pulled her wet panties off, her shyness came off as well. He sensed she was a bit self-conscious of her sagging breasts, but he went ahead and sucked on them. She had a nice round ass, but had no hips. No longer shy, her hand slid inside his robe to rub between his legs.

"No need for the tender soft stuff," she said, looking at the biggest dick she had seen in years. "I would like for you to fuck me."

Trevon was speechless when she eased down on her knees. To his surprise, she had his toes curling in the shag carpet. She was unable to swallow him whole, but Trevon gave up no complaints as she slowly flicked her tongue around his swollen tip. This was cougar loving at its best.

Janelle looked at her watch. It was 12:14 a.m. and Trevon was still in the bedroom fucking Mrs. Rorie. She could hear the constant, genuine moans and the headboard thumping into the wall. *Damn! I told him to fuck her, not make love!* She smirked. Getting up from the sofa, she tiptoed back to the bedroom and peeked in. Trevon was throwing dick to her doggy style, going balls deep.

Trevon did not ease into his bed until 2:20 a.m. He was so tired that he slid under the sheets, wet from his shower. Kandi was in her bed knocked out to the world. *What a day! That old lady. Damn, that pussy was good!*

Trevon rolled to his back and fell asleep. This was day number two of his new life as a male adult-film actor. He recalled what Jurnee had told him when they first met. It was not all about fucking. That damn director wanted everything to be perfect. Trevon went to sleep with the director's voice ringing in his head.

"Cut! Kandi, you're sucking his dick too slow!"

"Cut! Trevon, long stroke her!"

"Cut! Grab her titties! Both of them!"

"Cut! Kandi, make your ass bounce more!"

"Cut! Cut! Cut! Cut! Cut!"

At the same time, Swagga was out riding around smoking Kush in his charcoal gray Chrysler 300. The 300 allowed him to keep a low profile. He had snuck out without waking Yaffa. Swagga had the world pushing down on his shoulders. The bullshit with Chyna was too much to deal with. He tried to build up a deep hatred toward Chyna, but he failed. Any thoughts of Chyna made his dick hard.

"Dis bullshit!" He punched the steering wheel, angry at himself. Inhaling the Kush, he drove with the light traffic in silence.

All because of Trevon fucking my bitch! And Chyna. Muthafuckin' he-she. Titty, ass, dick swingin', chop-chop rice. Damn, dis Kush got me trippin' fo' fuckin' real! Swagga laughed at himself. "Damn, I'm high as hell."

Feeling the need to assure himself, to assure his manhood, he headed for Cindy's condo.

"I ain't fuckin' gay!" he said. "Bitch just tricked a nigga, that's all!"

Swagga made it to Fisher Island without being pulled over by the police. Parking his car, he strolled to the elevator and rode it up to the thirtieth floor. He had a key so he did not have to knock.

Cindy woke up scared when she heard the front door close. Filled with fear, she reached under the mattress and wrapped her hand around her .380. She now regretted having slept in the nude and eased from the bed with her heart pounding. Just as she reached down to lock the door, Swagga called her name. Her body relaxed. She tossed the gun on the bed, then walked out of her bedroom rubbing her eyes and yawning. Cindy stepped into the den.

"Swagga?" She turned the lights on and found him passed out on the floor. She shook her head at the sad sight. Forcing him to wake up, she showed some down-ass-chick traits by putting his ass in bed. He was fucked up. She smelled the weed all over his clothes. Searching his pockets, she found half an ounce of Kush and a bunch of money. She took half of the money, stashed it, and slid back under the sheets. Her job was done. Before she fell back to sleep, she noticed that Yaffa was not tagging along. *Odd*, she thought.

CHAPTER
SIXTEEN
September 24, 2011
Saturday, 10:48 p.m. - South Beach, Miami, Florida

Two weeks blew by for Trevon. His new lifestyle was slowly becoming second nature. His debut sex film had been completed last week. Tonight gave him time to unwind and fully enjoy his freedom. Things were still the same with Kandi. They were now having sex even when no cameras were rolling. Safe sex was practiced and both were still ignoring their emotions toward each other. To keep it leveled, Kandi made sure she never woke up in his arms. It was mainly up to Kandi and how she was feeling, and some nights Trevon felt as if he was just being used as some in-house dick.

Trevon was feeling himself and his ego was high. He slowed his Jaguar on Collins Avenue, turning into the parking lot for Club B.E.D.

Through Amatory and Janelle's clout, all signed actors and actresses had VIP status at the club. This was Trevon's first night out alone in the city. He hoped he would fit in. Kandi elected to stay home, so Trevon was rolling solo.

Stepping inside the club he forced himself not to get wide-eyed. He knew it was called Club B.E.D., but to have real beds up in the joint was stunting. He played it cool and composed as he was directed toward VIP. The club was packed with all assorted flavors of women from exotic to erotic looking. Courtesy of Kandi, he was laced down in a green pullover long sleeve Coogi top and a pair of denim Coogie jeans that were cuffed over his tan clear bottom Timberlands. Around his neck hung a gift from Janelle. Trevon proudly wore the long rose gold chain with a small rose gold encrusted medallion that read *A.E.F.* With his own money he copped a platinum ring and matching bracelet. His brown tinted stunna shades were framed in chrome. He knew his shit was tight when a fine, leggy black chick sauntered by with her man. She eyed Trevon openly and nodded. Shit was fabulous up inside Club B.E.D.

Trevon put the trip up to VIP on hold when he spotted a sexy female dancing her ass off on the dance floor. She stared dead at him while dancing seductively to the loud music. Under the constant changing lights, she slid her hands up and down her sides then made the *come here* motion with her jeweled index finger. Her slender body was molded in a black and yellow mini dress.

Trevon showed no lack of courage as he eased behind her, dropping his hands to her soft hips. She favored Gabrielle Union, but her skin was darker. Trevon got free with her. Moving in sync with her sexy body, he began to lose his tense feelings. Closing his eyes, he nuzzled her neck, inhaling her sweet perfume. The scent was a subtle hint of flowers. They stayed hooked up through three songs. Feeling it was time to break the locks, he leaned in toward her diamond jeweled ear.

"What's your name?" he asked, filled with confidence.

She smiled, twisting and shaking her hips to the beat. "Patrice," she told him.

"I'm Trevon. How about we head up to VIP for a drink?"

She kept dancing under the constantly changing lights. "Can't honey."

"Why not?" he asked as she rocked her hips.

Moving with the beat, she held up her left hand. "I'm married. Sorry." She shrugged.

Trevon respected her honesty and scolded himself for not noticing the ring. Knowing she showed no promise beyond a dance, he managed to politely leave her after two more songs. It was too early in the night to lose hope. Heading up to VIP, he wondered how Kandi would react if he brought a female to the crib. *Wouldn't dare!* was his short thought process on that issue. Even though he was not dating Kandi, he knew there were certain lines he could not cross.

Up in the VIP area, he was taken to a new level of living it big. The tranquil atmosphere went beyond mere words that Trevon could use to explain it. Gorgeous women were all around him. It would be a challenge to pick one. Making it to his booth, he walked by two light-skinned women sitting on a peach colored canopy bed drinking champagne. The music in VIP was not as loud compared to downstairs. Everything and everyone seemed mellow and laid back.

Damn! Everybody up here is balling! Trevon started to feel out of place. He knew no one. He seriously doubted he'd bump into anyone from Liberty City. Club B.E.D. was for the elite status in Miami. Reaching his booth, he ordered one drink. Knowing he had to drive home was reason enough to limit his drinking. From where he sat, he was able to view the entire VIP area. Easing in the soft, cream plush seat, he wanted to get a feel of the spot before he tried to push up on a female. He settled back, nodding to music.

A few minutes later, a group of four good looking, classy black women stepped up in VIP. He eyed them one by one as they headed for a king-sized bed across the room. He checked out the shortest and last female in the group.

"Of all people and of all places," Trevon said, shaking his head as he laid his eyes on his parole officer, Kendra Paige. Instead of feeling anger toward her, he admired how beautiful and sexy she was looking. When she glanced toward him, he quickly lowered his face in the shadows. He stole a glimpse of her a few seconds later. She was now lounging on the bed with her friends. Trevon watched her. Her personality was nothing like he had viewed her. Tonight, she was a happy beautiful black woman. Men appeared out the cut and swarmed around their bed. Trevon sipped his drink as he watched her turn three men down. He assumed it because each time she shook her head signaling no, the man would walk off. Kendra had that aspect of rare natural beauty in Trevon's view. The glasses she wore added to her look in a small, sophisticated fashion. He started to trip on himself when he had the urge to go and talk to her.

Knowing her hateful ass, she might try to arrest me or some dumb shit. She is looking fly as hell though. Shit, she look so different with that smile on her face. In a different world, that's wifey material.

Trevon grinned at the idea of being with Kendra. He then thought about reality and having to deal with her for two years. It seemed as if she wanted him to fuck up. *Why couldn't I get hooked up with a helpful parole officer instead of her hateful ass?*

Finishing his drink, he glanced at his watch. It was now midnight. Looking back up, he saw Kendra getting up from the bed. Trevon again admired her looks. Suddenly, he had a new sense of purpose. He wanted to make peace with her. He took a deep breath then went after her.

Nude Awakening

Kendra stood in the bathroom washing her hands. Glancing up in the mirror, she was pleased at the sight. With her heels, she stood 5'10". She knew she could stand to lose a few pounds, but it was nothing to stress over. *Shit, girl you still got it! Almost pushing the big four-zero and still attracting men half my age.* She dried her hands and took one more look at herself. The Versace backless dress placed an emphasis on her legs, waist and hips. Kendra was not conceited, but she knew she was looking fly as hell tonight. *Maybe I should find a man. Hell, I do miss some good loving. Let me stop fronting. I need some good ol' dick. But not just any dick. A good, nice black big one!* She laughed at her silly thoughts as she turned from the mirror. She figured she could stop being so damn picky and at least flirt. Stepping out of the bathroom with her beautiful face held high, she spotted Trevon.

Her face and posture changed in a heartbeat. Her smile flipped to a frown.

Instantly Trevon regretted his move as he stepped toward Kendra. *Fuck it. Ain't no turning back now.* Trevon willed himself on and ambled up to her with a forced smile on his face.

"What are you doing here!" she asked with an authoritarian tone.

Trevon rubbed his chin. "Free country, ain't it? Besides, my probation doesn't bar me from coming to a club."

"I know what you can and can't do," she said, switching back to her ill attitude. "I want to know how *you* are up in *this* club, and VIP at that. You just got out of prison last month and you look like—"

"Look like what? That I'm doing something with my life," he butted in. "Let me guess. If I was still at the boarding home in some bummy ass clothes, you wouldn't be sweating me. But since I'm exceeding your expectations, you gotta assume I'm doing something wrong. Of all people, I would expect a black woman to help me get adjusted to freedom. But you—all you talk about is sending me back to prison."

"I'm doing my job!"

"And what do they pay you these days for being a ..."

I know he ain't about to call me a bitch! If he do, I'ma show my ass up in here.

Trevon closed his eyes, releasing a deep sigh. "Kendra, I—"

"It's Ms. Paige, Mr. Harrison!" She made his name taste like dirt in her mouth.

"Look, I don't wanna beef with you, okay? Matter of fact, can I buy you a drink?" Trevon asked sincerely.

Kendra gasped. "Are you high? You must be out of your mind! Who do you have me mixed up with? You? Buy me a drink? Not gonna happen." She crossed her arms.

Trevon was crushed. *Well, at least I tried.* His ego deflated, slowly falling back to earth.

Kendra rolled her eyes then walked around him without saying a word. Her actions said one thing but her mind said another. *Damn, he is looking so good!*

Seeing Kendra had spoiled his night, Trevon was in a sour frame of mind as he exited Club B.E.D. Slipping inside his XJL, he felt the need to let some music ease his mind. With no regard for the city sound ordinance, he pushed the four loud subwoofers to the max. Young Jeezy's, "Put On" shook the pavement as Trevon cruised out of the parking lot.

Kendra was leaving the club when her best friend, Dani pointed at Trevon's XJL.

"That shit is fly!" Dani said, nodding her head to the music. "That's that new Jag!"

Kendra ignored Trevon. She was glad he had not seen her. "Why you acting all silly over a damn car?" Kendra scolded.

"Girl, chill. You just need some dick in ya life. And who was that baldhead dude you was talking to? Yeah, we all saw your ass."

"Nobody," Kendra said and pulled out the keys to her ride.

"Nobody my ass! Girl, that brutha was fine. I know you got his number, right?"

Kendra waved her best friend off. She was ready to go home and go to bed. Alone. *Why can't I find a good man? One without a damn criminal record!*

CHAPTER
SEVENTEEN

Kandi took a quick look at the time when she heard Trevon coming through the front door. 1:38 a.m. *He's home early!* She lay in bed with the sheets down, intentionally exposing her big naked ass. The door was wide open and the light brightened up the hallway. Closing her eyes, she pretended to be asleep, hoping Trevon would bite at the hook she threw out. She was in the mood tonight. Sleep was hard to find because her thoughts had been on Trevon. She remained still. His boots made a soft thump on the floor as he came down the hall. Her feet were facing the door. Taking a peek, she saw his shadow blocking the light from the hallway.

Trevon stood in the doorway, looking at Kendra's ample bare ass. It was normal for her to sleep naked with the door open. His attraction for her was so strong. He had fucked her in positions unknown to mankind, and his lust for her had yet to waver.

Kandi smiled into the pillow when she felt him sit on the bed.

"LaToria," he said, softly tapping on her shoulder.

She ignored him at first. *I love it when he calls me that!*

"Wake up, baby." He leaned down to lightly kiss her naked shoulder. Kandi could've won an Oscar for her performance. She rolled over, yawning.

"Damn, how you gonna wake up smiling?" he said, leaning over her.

"Because I woke up to you." She grinned.

Trevon looked at her sexy face then down at her breasts.

"Enjoy the club?" she asked, rubbing his arm.

"Not really. You see I'm home early."

"Meet anyone?"

"Um, yeah."

She stopped rubbing his arm. "Oh, you did?"

He nodded yes. "She's . . . in the living room. I hope you don't mind me bringing her here."

Kandi looked at him like he was stupid. "Um, you might need to take that *bitch* to a motel! You are not about to be fuckin' no ho up in my crib!"

"Ain't this Janelle's crib?"

Kandi pushed him. "Nigga, you got the game all—"

"Girl, chill!" He laughed, standing up. "I'm just fucking with you."

She sat up in the bed. "Stop playing!" She smiled, pulling him back on top of her. They rolled over a few times until she ended up on top.

"So you just fucking with me, huh?" She traced his lips with her thumb. "I love your lips, Smooch."

"You know I wouldn't play myself like that," he said, rubbing her hips.

"Hmm," she said and lowered her lips to his.

They kissed softly in the dimly lit bedroom. Easing a hand between them, she undid his belt.

"Sleep in my bed tonight," she purred, kissing behind his ear.

"I doubt we'll be doing any sleeping," he added while stroking the sides of her tits.

"Fine with me, Smooch. As long as it's hard, I'mma be up on it."

"How do you want it?" he asked, touching her breasts.

"I want all three. I want to have sex. I want to fuck. And, I need you to make love to me."

Everything seemed to stop. She lowered her head, wishing she could take back those last nine words.

"I'm just playing." She tried to pull her emotions back in.

Trevon gently turned her over. "Don't lie to me, LaToria."

She could not pull her eyes away from his face. "I . . . don't feel like talking.

"What do you want from me?" he asked.

"I want the same thing you want from me, Trevon." She slid her hands up to his face and pulled him close until their foreheads touched.

"Please, make love to me, Trevon. Tonight I want to be with you."

Trevon firmly stood behind the adage of actions speaking louder than words. He wanted it to happen. They both knew the difference between sex, fucking and making love. The latter dealt solidly with emotions.

Their lips met five times with slow pecks. When their tongues met, it seemed to release those pent up emotions. She did not think of herself as Kandi the porn star. She was LaToria Nicole Frost now. Her hands slid down his body, seeking the removal of his jeans and boxers. He toed his boots off then pushed his jeans down his legs. Everything seemed new about LaToria. Her mouth had a new taste that had him greedy. Her breasts seemed softer pressed against his chest. His hands explored her fresh nakedness. His touch was tender.

"So beautiful," he groaned between her cleavage.

LaToria gasped, arching her back and rubbing his baldhead. His tongue circled her nipple until he covered it with his mouth. Trembling, she purred out his name as he stroked the sides of her breasts. She slid her hands down and palmed his ass.

"Let me," he moaned, licking behind her ear, "turn some music on."

She nodded yes, reluctantly releasing him from her hands. She sat up as he walked over to the digital sound system in the corner. "Hurry," she said, feeling how wet she was between her thighs.

Trevon had excellent taste in music. At least that was his opinion. He wanted the mood to be perfect.

"Please hurry," she whined, rubbing a finger over her clit.

"Good things come to those who wait," he teased, programming the playlist on the MP3 player.

LaToria yanked him in the bed when he finally finished. She rolled him to his back as the first song came on. "Cupid" by 112 melted into their ears.

"Relax, baby," she said, licking his chest. "I'm gonna suck on your dick through this song."

She did just that. Going with the slow tempo, she sucked up and down his solid length. Her tongue twirled and twisted over his tip in ways that were new to him. Up and down, her rhythm had him squirming. He enjoyed it most when she pumped downward with her grip as her lips went upward. She never removed him from the grip of her lips. He had to fight back his climax only one minute into the song. Up and down, she took him deep into her mouth. When the song ended, she licked at his pre-cum slicked tip until he begged her to stop. Grinning, she swallowed him again as the second song came on. She reached for his balls as R. Kelly, "Seems Like You're Ready" kept the mood flowing. Squeezing his shaft, her lips glided over his vein-mapped dick. She was loose with it now and liked how it opened her jaws.

"LaToria! Suck your man's dick! Mmmm . . . make me cum!" Trevon urged her on as she continued sucking his dick.

"Not yet." She crawled up his body with her nipples grazing his flesh. She dipped her tongue back inside his mouth. His dick was hard and flat against his stomach. She teased herself by grinding her clitoris against it. Without a rubber, she could feel the heat pumping off his dick. Slowly, she rocked her pussy back and forth over the length of his dick.

"You so wet!" he groaned, gripping her ass as her pussy juices flowed down his balls.

"I know," she whined, licking his ear. She kept grinding on top of him.

"Whose pussy is it?" he asked, caressing her ass.

"Trevon's," she panted as she rocked back and forth at a faster pace.

Trevon gripped her waist and guided her movements. Her slippery pussy felt so good skating over him. She pulled at the sheets. He smacked her ass.

"Rubber!" he said, humping up against her pussy.

"No . . . wait! This . . . feels so good!" She kept grinding and hunching hard against his dick.

Wanting to put more friction on her clit, she slid up a few inches. She misjudged her movement, but realized it was too late. When she shifted her hips backward, the head of his dick slipped inside her up to the shaft. He was balls deep inside her without a rubber.

"Ooooohhhhh, Trevon!" She clenched her walls around his bare dick.

"LaToria, it's—"

"I know! I know! I know! It's in, baby." She twirled her tongue in his ear.

"Don't move!" he panted hard. "Pussy . . . so hot!"

LaToria could feel his heart beating through his dick.

She sat up slowly, dragging her nails down his chest. "I'll—go get the rubber," she said with her body quivering. "Just . . . ahhh. Let me sit on it for a second."

Trevon eased his hands to her waist. Biting her bottom lip, she eased up off his dick. Trevon was lost at the erotic sight of her pussy lips being pulled out, wrapping around his dick. LaToria swore she could feel each bump of his veins. It felt like his dick was up to her throat. She kept rising, but the dick seemed to keep growing. She stuttered his name when she was halfway off, but purposely came to a halt to flex her inner walls. Trevon lost his sense.

Without thought, he shoved her back down while simultaneously rocketing his hips up off the bed. LaToria felt her titties bounce as Trevon filled her. The tone was set. Gripping the sheets above his head, she took control and rode him. Their moans were loud.

"LaToria! Baby, don't stop!" he begged, rubbing all over her ass.

"Smooch!" she screamed, rocking hard on his dick. The feeling was too sensual for her to stop. Moaning and pulling at the sheets she continued to give herself away to Trevon. His hands latched on to her waist as her hips and ass jiggled. His dick plunged in and out of her. Panting heavily through her mouth, she rose up on her arms, bouncing her ass up and down.

"Yesss! Ride dis dick!"

"Smooch!"

"Ohhhh . . . my pussy now!"

LaToria bit her bottom lip. She could feel him reaching far up inside her. Her ass clapping against his flesh was new music to her ears. They knew the line had been crossed. She showed her mind was set as she rode him through one song. Tirelessly, she bounced up and down on him as her juices flowed. In the middle of Marsha Ambrosius' "Far Away" she reached her climax.

"Yess! Urrrrgggghh!" she growled, digging her nails in his chest. "Cummin' all over you, Smooch! All over your dick! Keep . . ." She rolled off and on her stomach. ". . . Fucking me please. Put it back in me."

Trevon lifted her waist until she was on her knees. Sensing his hesitation, she looked back at him.

"Put it in, Smooch."

Trevon pushed himself inside her. Speechless. Trevon's strokes were slow and steady. He wanted the moment to last. How far was he willing to go? What would he do when he reached his climax? Pull out? Or stay in the softest place on earth?

CHAPTER
EIGHTEEN
September 25, 2011
Sunday, 10:40 a.m. - Coconut Grove, Florida

LaToria woke up with Trevon spooning her. She smiled. His slow in and out breathing warmed her ear. His arms were wrapped possessively around her waist and best of all, she could feel his manhood pressed against her butt. Her mind pulled her back to last night. After he came inside her the first time, it proved only to be the beginning. He pleased her thoroughly and made love to her so good that she cried. She lost all control of her once confined emotions as he stroked her missionary style. She experienced something deep inside her when she looked into his face as he came inside her for the second time. Each stroke had her voice cracking. Emotionally, she felt open and exposed to him. Now, she would have to deal with the morning after issues. For now, she was at peace in his arms.

Trevon lay wide awake. Each time he inhaled, it seemed a part of LaToria swirled inside him. She was so warm and soft. Last night had awakened him. This moment was what he sought emotionally. To go to bed and wake up with a beautiful woman in his arms. *This is no lust!* he told himself. He knew his bond with her was to some degree built on sex. But that was then. What concerned him was now. Closing his eyes, he thought about how things started off. That rare raw feeling of being inside her was . . .

LaToria smiled. All at once, she sensed the change in Trevon. His breathing sped up, along with his heartbeat. She felt his dick growing and pushing itself between her soft thighs.

"You up, baby?" She squeezed her thighs. "Are you dreaming?"

"I'm up." He kissed her shoulder, moving a hand up to her breast.

"I can feel that." She twisted at the waist then reached down to rub his erection.

Looking at his handsome face, she touched her lips against his. She knew what was about to happen when he lifted one of her legs. Before she could get adjusted, she felt him pushing deep inside her.

"Yessss! Do it, baby." She found his tempo and tossed it back to him. They both took notice of the gushy sounds they made under the sheets.

"LaToria!" he groaned, long dicking her while she lay on her side. Their increased rocking caused the sheet to fall off her hiked up leg. He sped up at the sight of his dick sliding in and out. A guttural moan eased through his lips when he felt her fingers moving over his balls. Trevon had never had such a meaningful sexual experience that could match what he was feeling now.

Gripping her leg, he slid closer, pumping hard. She winced, now rubbing her throbbing clitoris as his dick plunged in and out, in and out. A spasm rocked her body. They shared each other openly.

"Tre-Tre-Trevon! I'm cummin', baby!" she shouted several minutes later.

"Pussy!" He slammed his balls deep. "So." He kept pumping. "Good!"

LaToria felt her pussy explode around his dick. She came in waves. Her eyes rolled, her body shook, and she stopped breathing as he pounded himself to his own climax, only seconds behind hers.

After the morning sex, Trevon and LaToria sat relaxing in the tub. She sat between his legs while he gently rubbed her breasts with a soapy rag. Her eyes were closed.

"Feel like talking?" he asked.

"About what?"

"You. Honestly, you've never opened up to me about your past. Why you started in porn. Your family . . ."

"Umm, you never asked."

"Well, I'm asking now." He twisted the rag, wringing it out then dropped it on the edge of the tub.

"Kinda late to wanna know all that."

Trevon slid his hands up and down her shoulders. "I wanna know you beyond the bedroom, LaToria. Why you gotta be so . . . defensive?"

"I'm not being defensive."

"Then talk to me, okay? Tell me about yourself."

LaToria opened her eyes. "I don't have a family. Happy now?"

"Everybody has a fam—"

"I was an orphan, Trevon. I don't know a damn thang about my mother or father so everybody don't have a family, okay!" She crossed her arms with her face balled up.

"I'm sorry to hear that."

LaToria shrugged. "I had six different so-called foster parents as I grew up. Some things happened to me that shouldn't happen to young girls and . . . I just didn't understand it. I was touched by this lady when I was sixteen. She and her husband would encourage me to bring my boyfriend over. They made me feel like it was okay to have sex in front of them."

"Did the husband ever touch you?"

"No. Just his wife. But he was still sick to sit and watch me do it with guys. They made sure to keep me happy. I had all the fly clothes, all the freedom, but I was being used."

"Did you tell anyone what was going on?"

"No," she murmured. "Anyway, I started to get too wild. Skipping school, fucking all the guys in the neighborhood. Letting niggas run trains on me . . . I just didn't care. Then my foster parents got upset because I wasn't feeding their voyeurism fetish. They started hooking me up with all these guys. Most were college students. I was nineteen then. It took me three months to catch on to what my foster parents were doing to me."

"They were still watching you have sex?"

"Yeah. But one day I came out of my bedroom and I overheard Mrs. Driskill, that's her name. Anyway, she was on the phone telling someone about me. She was telling whomever what I looked like and the things I would do sexually. All types of shit. I listened to her negoitiate a price for someone to have sex with me."

"They were pimping you!"

LaToria nodded. "For fifty bucks. I was mad as hell! I got mad about the wrong thing though. Instead of being upset about being used as a prostitute, I got pissed because I wasn't getting my cut of the money. I never said anything. I kept up with the routine for three more weeks before I ran away with only two hundred and twenty dollars to my name."

Trevon was unsure of what to say. He felt sorry for her and the pain she went through. Anger was also boiling inside him.

"I was staying up in Atlanta," she continued. "I had a friend from school that was a stripper and she got me a spot at a club. Oh yeah, I dropped out of school in the tenth grade. Well, my looks had the money rolling in at the club, knowing that men would pay for sex changed my view of being promiscuous. I danced in the club for two years and I had my share of boyfriends and girlfriends. One day, a local big time drug dealer tried to holler at me, but I wasn't falling for his game. Come to find out, he had a cousin that was an urban model manager."

"Was he legit?"

"Hell yeah! I went to his studio with one of my girlfriends and he signed me on the spot. A week later, he had me booked to be in a music video. I ended up doing three within two months. Next, he took me up to New York and I had a six-page spread and interview for the *Straight Stuntin'* magazine. I answered one question about if I was open to doing porn or not. I said yes. My big break came a month later when Janelle reached me through my manager."

"What happened to your manager?"

"Janelle bought out my contract with him. A week later, I moved down here . . . and now I'm Kandi. A month after I turned twenty-one, I did my first adult film. I left all that pain behind me."

"And you're seriously happy with your life and doing porn?"

"Don't feel sorry for me, Trevon."

"How can I not? I—I care about you."

She smacked her lips. "You don't even know me like that."

"What? You doubting how I feel about you?"

"Just leave me alone." She frowned, folding her arms.

"No. I wanna talk about what we did last night and this morning."

"Well, I don't!" She pushed herself up. "I'm tired of talking. I done told you shit that I never told any other man."

"LaToria, wait!" He stood up in the tub. "Are you on birth control?"

LaToria stepped out of the tub hiding her face and her fresh tears. Yanking the door open, she ran into the bedroom sobbing.

"LaToria!" Trevon snatched the towel off the sink, wrapping it around his wet waist. Before he took a step to chase after her, his cell phone began to ring. He was going to ignore it until he saw it was his sister, Angie calling. Looking into the bedroom, he saw LaToria shoving her wet legs into a pair of jeans. He wanted to talk to her. Seeing that she was upset, he assumed it was best to give her space and a moment to calm down. Sitting on the edge of the tub he answered his cell phone.

In the bedroom, LaToria threw on the first items of clothes that reached her hands. Out the corners of her blurry eyes she saw Trevon sitting in the bathroom on his cell phone. She was hurting inside. She had run from him, but her heart was crying out for him to follow. Seeing his attention was on the phone, she broke into a chest-heaving sob. *He doesn't care about me!* rang inside her confused mind as she stormed out of the bedroom and out of the house. She was running away . . . again.

Kendra was having breakfast at IHOP with her daughter, Carmelita, who had gotten full and was playing with her food as Kendra talked on her cell phone.

"Girl, are you coming or not?" her BFF Dani bugged her.

"I said I'll be there. But there better not be no foolishness going down."

"I promise. Okay, I did go overboard with those male strippers. But we did have a ball!"

"No." Kendra grinned. "*You* had a ball. Four of them from what I've heard."

"Honey, it's true! When all y'all left, I got me a taste of them two bruthas. And girl, they put it down on me. I did both of 'em. But not at the same time though."

"I'm   trying   to   eat   breakfast."

"My bad. But look, eight o'clock. Sex toy party at my place."

"I'm coming."

"You'll do just that if you buy some of these sex toys."

"Girl, bye!" Kendra laughed at her crazy friend and ended the call.

"Who is that, Mommy?" Carmelita asked with syrup all over the table.

"Nobody important. Now stop playing in the syrup before it gets on your clothes."

"Okay. I'll stop now."

"Thank you, baby."

Kendra would keep her word and attend the sex party. Instead of women getting together to buy plastic bowls and cups, this party would feature sex toys. If anything, she would trip off the other women. The last sex party she attended, a lady in her early seventies had bought a ten-inch dildo and promised to use it. Kendra swore she would hear it on the breaking news. *Old lady found dead in her bed with ten-inches up her ass!* Kendra felt guilty as she laughed at her thoughts.

Within ten minutes of its start, Kendra lost full interest of the party.

The petite, dark-skinned talkative hostess stood in front of the eighteen women holding a black flesh-colored eight-inch dildo.

"This is our best seller," the hostess claimed. "It cums." She grinned. "No pun intended, with a money back guarantee."

Dani softly elbowed Kendra. "YOU should buy that one." Dani snickered.

"*You* should shut up," Kendra promptly replied. "I can't believe I let you talk me into coming to this mess." Kendra glanced around the living room at the other women. They all seemed to be so engrossed with the hostess' every word. The women, ranging in ages from 21 to 58 were all attractive in Kendra's view. A few wore wedding rings and that made Kendra wonder if their married sex life had lost its fizz?

"Do you have anything bigger?" This came from a light-skinned woman that looked to be five months pregnant. The hostess nodded yes and reached behind her display.

Kendra inhaled sharply, covering her mouth.

"This big boy," the hostess said, grinning. "We call it, The Intimidator!" She held the imposing eleven-inch dildo with two hands.

A few women gasped or moaned.

"I'll call it . . . ain't no damn way!" Kendra said, shaking her head.

One woman in her early 40s spoke what was on her mind. "Anybody find a piece like that swinging from a breathing man, let me know, honey! Mmmm."

Two other women agreed with her. A discussion started. It centered on how big of a dick anyone had seen. Mostly everyone in the room admitted to seeing a few in porno films. A lady with a short haircut that framed her oval face claimed that her ex-boyfriend had a ten-inch dick.

Nude Awakening

It took only one female to say she was *stretching* the truth. The short-haired woman backed up her claim by pulling out her cell phone. She had some pictures to prove it. One picture showed it in its fullness with her hands on it.

"Why aren't you two together?" a middle-aged woman asked.

The short-haired woman looked at her sideways. "He was killing me! He's the prime example of having too much of a good thing."

When the topic of men died down, the hostess took over. Her next items to sell were different types of sex lotions that came in assorted scents and flavors.

Kendra was prudish when it came to sex. She thought, *I'm just not a freak like Dani. Yeah, I have sucked a few dicks in my lifetime. Hmm . . . David, Kevin, and that manipulative ass Marcus! I shoulda bit that skinny shit off! Been too long; I can't lie. Damn, the last time I had some dick was . . . nine damn months ago! Maybe I need to try out some on-line dick. I know one thing! When I do get some, I'ma fuck his ass to death and suck him 'til my jaws are sore and then—*

"Kendra." Dani nudged her.

"What girl!"

"Ho, you just zoned out on me. Looking all slack faced. Thinking 'bout some dick, ain't cha?" She laughed.

Kendra blushed. "Girl, leave me alone."

"I knew it! I can hook you up with my—"

"No."

"Girl, just—"

"No. Shut it down."

Kendra hated how Dani could see right through her. About an hour later, Dani stood up in front of the group as the hostess took up all the new orders she made.

"Okay, y'all. I won't be up here too long, okay? Well, I do have a surprise ending for this party, but it has to stay between us, okay?" Dani winked at the group.

Everyone nodded except Kendra. She lowered her face into her hands. *I knew she would do something crazy. I should leave right now. Ain't no telling what she's about to do.*

"A few of y'all know about my cousin that works at Amatory. For those in the dark, Amatory is an adult film company based right here in Miami."

"She's a porn star?" someone asked.

"No," Dani replied, rolling her eyes. "She's one of their receptionists. Anyway, I have an unedited copy of the next DVD they'll release later this year! All of us are going to watch it. My cousin told me it's a film of a fine handsome brutha that just got out of prison. And she said it's his actual first time doing it! Hold your questions. I know some of you have some babysitter on the clock, so let's watch this film. Tammy, hit the lights!"

Kendra slid next to Dani on the sofa when the lights went off. "Girl! Ain't about to waste my time watching no porno film."

"Kendra, relax please."

Kendra settled back into the sofa crossing her arms. *This is really a waste of my time! I can be home reading my Kindle!*

Everyone turned their attention to the flat screen TV. Since the film was unedited, they would be viewing the raw footage. The scene started with a view inside a bedroom. To the left of the screen someone was wrapping a towel around her body.

Her butt is so big! Look at her small waist. Wish I had a body like that. I wonder if her butt is real. I know them perky titties ain't. Kendra was about to make an excuse to leave when on the screen, Trevon Harrison walked into the bedroom and looked directly into the camera.

CHAPTER
NINETEEN
Fort Lauderdale, Florida

Later that night around ten o'clock, a white BMW drop top slowed to a stop in front of Swagga's mansion. Swagga hurried down to the first floor to meet his guest. Yaffa was knocked out in a deep sleep and Swagga wanted him to stay that way.

Chyna was not surprised when Swagga himself opened the front door. This was their first time meeting since Swagga's discovery of Chyna's mixed gender. He fought hard to overlook how sexy Chyna appeared. The high heels, tight miniskirt and tube top with no bra had Swagga lusting if but for a second. Truth be told, Chyna was a dime in the face with a firm fit body.

"You late!" Swagga's voice boomed.

"I was pulled over for speeding," she informed him and followed Swagga into his mansion.

Swagga took Chyna to the entertainment room at the far end of the mansion. It was the furthest room from Yaffa's bedroom.

Chyna sashayed into the entertainment room that was nearly the size of his two-bedroom house. The walls were covered with black and red felt with matching leather furniture placed around the room. There were 40-inch plasma TVs on the walls plus a minibar to the left. Two chrome and black pool tables sat in the middle of the room with chrome plated pool sticks.

Swagga flopped down on the sofa, picking up a wireless remote. He turned the lights off at the bar then sat back folding his arms. Chyna sat on another sofa across from him.

"What did you find out about, Trevon?" Swagga asked, trying to stop his eyes from lowering to the jutting nipple prints on Chyna's tube top.

"A lot. He just got out of prison back on—August the seventeenth."

"How much time he do?"

"Fifteen years."

"Damn! That will make it more believable to expose him as a nigga on the down low when we—you—do your thang with 'im."

"Just because he did a lot of time doesn't mean he's into men."

"I don't give a fuck if he ain't! We gonna make it so that he *is*! Now tell me what else you found out."

Chyna crossed his legs. "Trevon goes to get his car hand washed at a spot in Liberty City. My cousin said he has seen Trevon there every Friday since he got that Jaguar."

"And what's your plan?"

"I'm thinking that I can bump into him at the carwash. Start up a conversation and just go from there. My only issue is him being attracted to me or not."

"He will. Trust me," Swagga admitted, then regretted his comment.

Chyna smiled. "Do you find me attractive?"

"Bitch, don't play me!"

Chyna kept smiling. *Yeah nigga, you said it right because I am a Bitch!*

"Anyway," Chyna said, blowing off Swagga's weak reply. "If I can get up with Trevon at the carwash, I'll see if he's down to come to my crib."

"And then what?"

"I'll try to seduce him. I also have this . ." Chyna reached into his tote bag and pulled out a small clear liquid in a tiny glass bottle.

"What the fuck is that?" He sat up, peering at the bottle.

"Date rape juice."

Swagga jumped to his feet. "You used that shit on me!"

Chyna looked up at Swagga. "Didn't need to."

"Fuck you!"

"Anytime you want it, you can get it."

Swagga sat back down. "Fuckin' faggot!"

"Call me what you like. But you still can't erase what I did to you. I know for a fact that I sucked your dick better than Cindy!"

Swagga was feeling that Chyna was going to be hard to control. Chyna had too much sass.

"Fuck all this shit, okay!" Swagga fired back. "I slipped up, so fuck it! You said once I pay you, that all this bullshit will be dead."

"Your—*our* secret is safe, if that's what you're worried about. I'll do what you need to be done to Trevon and then I'm gone. Maybe I can come back to visit you once I get my full sex change. How about it? Wanna be the first to fuck me? It will be like breaking in a virgin pussy."

Swagga stared at Chyna with his emotions brewing. *I see right now I'ma end up killing dis faggot ass muthafucka!*" When will you try to hook up with Trevon?"

Chyna knew he was pissing Swagga off. "This Friday. I'll need your help though."

"How?"

"I'll need a fly ass whip. I want all eyes on me. I will handle the rest."

Swagga shrugged. "I'll have something for ya by Thursday. And film that shit wit' Trevon."

"Make sure the ride is white. Cum white is my favorite," Chyna added.

Swagga was happy when Chyna finally left. He stayed in the entertainment room and found his peace in a bag of weed. Dealing with Chyna was a big regret.

Chyna stepped into his car when Yaffa appeared out of nowhere.

"What are you doing here?" he firmly demanded.

Chyna spun and stumbled back against the BMW. "Damn! You scared me."

"I know that. Now answer my question."

Chyna waited a few seconds. "Yaffa, do you get a kick out of sneaking up on a beautiful woman at night?"

"Listen, I'm Swagga's bodyguard and I need to know when he has a guest over here."

Chyna shrugged. "He didn't mention my visit?"

"If he did I wouldn't be wastin' my time out here talkin' to you."

"I guess you need to take that up with Swagga. But as for you wasting your time talking to me, why does it have to be like that?" Chyna flirted.

Yaffa glanced back toward the mansion. The lights were off in Swagga's bedroom.

"Are you worried about Swagga seeing you talking to me?"

"Ain't worried 'bout a muthafuckin' thang. What I don't get is why some women will put up with a man beatin' on 'em. Swagga beat the shit outta you and you still bouncin' on his heels."

Chyna maintained a straight face at the knowledge of Yaffa not knowing about his gender problems. *Umph! Swagga didn't even tell the man that's trusted with his life about me!* Chyna took a step closer to Yaffa. "I'm not bouncing on his heels and I don't put up with men hitting me."

"Okay. Back to question number one. What are you doin' over here so late?"

"Nothing important."

"Yeah right."

"Look, can I thank you for pulling Swagga off of me?"

Yaffa folded his arms. "I was lookin' out for Swagga, not you. I can't get paid if he's sittin' up in jail for beatin' your ass."

"I still want to thank you."

"Whateva, yo."

"I'm not seeing Swagga if you think it's like that," Chyna replied softly.

"Shit, I can't tell. Not the way I saw you suckin' his dick."

Chyna blushed. "You saw us? How?"

"That ain't none of your business. Just doin' my job."

"Okay, I still appreciate what you did and I'd really like to thank you. A good deed should not go unrewarded." Chyna took a risk by lightly touching Yaffa's elbow. "If you want me to reward you, I think we could both find some pleasure behind it." Chyna's fingernails skated up Yaffa's arm.

When Yaffa reached down to adjust his dick, Chyna knew it was a wrap.

Yaffa knew Chyna's type. A jump off. He fell for Chyna's advance and was now following Chyna's BMW in his silver Lexus LX570. They ended up at a city park in

Northwest Miami. The park was dark and deserted. The only light was that of the pale moon. Chyna told Yaffa to relax as they walked past the gate and into the park. Yaffa had his .45 out and he had no thoughts of putting it up.

"I think we'll be okay here," Chyna said, standing under a mango tree waiting for Yaffa to step around the swing set.

"So what's up?"

Chyna reached down toward Yaffa's dick. "I hope you'll be up." Chyna squeezed him.

"You on some outdoor freaky shit, huh?" Yaffa smiled, a rare emotion.

Chyna nodded yes. "It's that time of the month for me. But you can fuck my mouth as much as you like."

Yaffa began to relax as Chyna's little hands unfastened his belt. The weather was still warm so Yaffa was not bothered when Chyna pulled his dick out and went to work on him. The deception was a risky rush for Chyna, but it was done. Chyna just hoped that these actions that were done in the dark would stay in the dark.

CHAPTER
TWENTY
Sunday, 11:30 p.m.
Coconut Grove, Florida

Trevon stormed into LaToria's bedroom slamming the door behind him.

"What's your problem?" she shouted, looking up from the latest issue of *Straight Stuntin*.

"You're my problem! Why do you keep finding ways to avoid talking about what's going on between us?" Trevon stood next to her bed with his big arms folded.

"Why are you yelling?" She threw the magazine down.

"'Cause it seems to be the only way you'll listen to me! You've been gone since . . . eleven o'clock this morning!"

"I'm grown, dammit!"

"Then fuckin' act like it, LaToria! Last night you got all emotional and shit, talkin' 'bout make love to you. And now you acting like ain't shit happened!"

"Big deal! I got caught up, okay! We fucked without a rubber. What now? We supposed to be in love, huh?"

"You buggin'!" He threw his arms in the air.

She rolled out of bed and got up in his face. "You the one that's buggin', nigga!"

"How!" He crossed his arms again.

"How? How, motherfucker. You the one that pulled me back down, remember? I told you to wait so I could get a rubber!"

"Oh, so you saying I *took* the pussy?"

"Fuck you Trevon!"

"Why are you actin' like this? All I want to do is talk to you."

"We ain't got shit to talk about, okay? We made a mistake last night."

"A mistake! You call last night a damn mistake! What about this morning? Oh, I guess that's what you call business, huh?"

"All of it was a gotdamn mistake! I don't love you! I don't give a fuck about you, Trevon! Why do you have to try to make this something that it ain't?"

Trevon grabbed her arm as she tried to walk away. "You're not running from me this time."

LaToria snatched her arm away. "Nigga, you betta slow the fuck down! You ain't the only nigga with a big dick! Ain't my fault you got wide open on me! And for your info, I been out fuckin' somebody else. And ain't no need to look stupid!"

"Well, I guess I better go get my shit checked for STDs since you being a ho off the camera, too."

LaToria slapped him hard. "Fuck you!" she shouted with tears in her eyes. "Get out!" She pointed toward the door. "GET OUTTA MY FACE!"

Trevon had no idea why she was tripping on him. *All I'm doing is trying to treat her with respect.* He gave up. *I'll just give her time to calm down,* he thought as he walked toward his bedroom.

"No!" She ran to the door. "I don't want you under this roof no more. Pack your shit and get the fuck out! I hate you!"

CHAPTER
TWENTY-ONE
September 26, 2011
Monday, 9:30 a.m. - Miami, Florida

Trevon was eating his breakfast from Burger King inside his car. Last night he had stayed in a motel. The drama with LaToria was still on his mind. On top of that, he had a ten o'clock appointment with his parole officer. Above him, the bullying sun was trying to burst through the tinted sunroof. Trevon had the cool air running, wishing he could postpone the meeting with his P.O. *Not gonna happen*, he thought. When he finished his food, he turned the car off then headed into the office building.

"I'm here to see Ms. Kendra Paige," he said when he stepped up to the front counter.

"Umph! You again," Ms. Nikki Conner said, rolling her eyes. "I see you're still rude and—" She looked him over. "Gucci'd down again."

Trevon was not in the mood for her drama. "Good morning, Ms. Conner," he said with his jaws tight. "I'm here to see my P.O."

"Yeah, yeah. Sign in and I'll call up to her office."

Now I gotta go sit and wait in that dirty ass waiting room! I hate having to check in like I'm a damn kid! Trevon waited impatiently as Ms. Conner called Ms. Paige.

"Hi Ms. Paige. This is Nikki on the first floor. You have a Trevon Harrison here to—" She paused to listen to what Ms. Paige had broken in to say. "Oh. Well, I'll send him right up."

Trevon was directed up to Ms. Paige's office, thankful that he did not have to wait. *The sooner it's over, the sooner I can leave!* He stepped off the elevator. *Might as well get pissed off some more because this salty ass chick will do or say something to piss me off!* Trevon paused. He had to get his mind right. The most important thing was *not* to piss her off. Turning the ringer off his cell phone, he knocked softly on the door.

Kendra was twisting the top back on her tube of lip-gloss when Trevon knocked on her door. She nearly tripped in her rush to get around her desk. *Small ass office!* she complained. She composed herself, tidied her fitted dress, and reached up to pat a strand of hair in place. Once she felt she was in order, she pulled the door open.

"Glad you could make it, Mr. Harrison," she greeted him with her hand extended.

Trevon was caught completely off guard. The first major difference he noticed was the warm friendly smile on Kendra's face. He was too stunned to accept her hand. The eye shadow, lip-gloss, the hair, the perfume and the tight dress that seemed to turn her curves into a sculpture. He noticed it all, even down to her peep-toed platform heels.

Kendra lowered her hand. *Damn! He ain't even smiling. I'm making a damn fool of myself.*

"Come on in." She ushered him into her office. Taking a risk, she stole a quick look at his crotch.

Trevon sat down as Kendra closed the door. Her perfume was sweet with a subtle peach scent. When she strolled by, the scent turned Trevon's head in her direction. He had to admit that she was looking good. *Yeah, she was looking good at the club too! And she dissed me.*

"So," she said cheerfully once she was seated behind her desk. "How are you doing this morning? I see you're adjusting well back into the free world."

Trevon glanced over his shoulder then back at her. "Am I in the right office?"

Kendra kept smiling as she removed her glasses. "Trevon, I think we got off on the wrong foot."

Trevon noticed she had called him by his first name. *What's going on? First, LaToria tripping on me. Now my P.O. on some other shit. Must be the sun or something baking folks' brain.*

"I um . . . thought about what you said to me at the club and you were right."

"Right about what?" he asked, surprised that she had thought about him.

Kendra touched her hair. "I should be trying to help you. I—know I've been a challenge to deal with and I'd like to apologize."

"Are you serious? This ain't some kind of mental test, is it?" He looked at the ceiling.

"You got some hidden cameras up in here?" he joked.

"If there were, I'm sure they wouldn't bother you."

"What's that suppose to mean?" His smile fell off his face.

"Um, you were in prison and I know they had you under twenty-four hour surveillance."

"Yeah, I was."

Damn, I let that one slip, Kendra thought, putting her glasses back on. "I want to um . . . change my attitude and see if I can help you with your reintegration."

Trevon relaxed his tense posture. This is what he wanted. A cool, laid back parole officer who was willing to help him. Trevon looked at her. Was she real? Even with her so-called *new* attitude, he had his doubts about her. He wanted to see how serious she was.

170

"So, you want to help me?"

She nodded yes.

"Okay, I need your help finding a place to stay."

Kendra gasped. "I thought you had a place?" she said, sounding concerned.

"I did, but um, the living arrangements ain't working out."

"Care to talk about it? You didn't get in any trouble, did you?"

"Nah. My roommate, she just felt that—"

"She?"

Trevon nodded. "Yeah. *She.* Let's just say that she'd rather be alone."

Umph! She must be a dumb bitch to put his fine (and I can now add, BIG DICK) ass out on the streets. Kendra could not get over the unedited porno film of Trevon. Keeping her connection to Trevon a secret, she easily convinced Dani into letting her borrow the DVD. After watching the film in the privacy of her bedroom, she saw Trevon in a new form. She had fingered herself to two orgasms while viewing the film. In all, she was open highly on how Trevon could put it down in bed. Even now, she kept looking between his legs.

Kendra snatched her mind from the gutter. "How soon do you need a place to stay?"

"As soon as possible. I had to stay at a motel last night."

"I can't promise you anything, but I'll try to help."

"Thank you," he said, wondering why she had yet to ask if he had a job. *She actin' weird as hell.*

"I'm really sorry about the other night," she said, expressing deep regret.

"Nah, I understand. You are my parole officer and I know you have certain lines you can't cross."

"I agree." She smiled. "But that gave me no reason to treat you the way I did."

Trevon believed her. *Maybe I should run with this new attitude she is showing. Yeah, she's been a pain to deal with, but that was the past. I have to deal with this woman for two years! Okay, she wanna be friends. I'll roll with it.*

"So . . ." he said with a grin. "Let's say we cross paths again like we did at the club. Would you let me buy you a drink?"

"Publicly, no." She cheesed. *I can't believe I'm flirting with this guy!*

Trevon read between the lines. *Publicly no?* "So, you're saying if we was like . . . alone somewhere, you would say yes?"

"Are you flirting with me, Trevon?"

"If I was?"

"If you were, I'd tell you that my workplace is not the right spot."

"Okay . . . *if* I was flirting, where would the right spot be?"

Shit! We can do it right now on my desk! Kendra pushed her sexual urge and thoughts aside. She knew she was taking a big risk at losing her job if she was caught getting personal with him. *Shit, didn't I take a big risk once before? Sure did, and ended up being played by Marcus.* Kendra reached for an ink pen and wrote down an address.

"There is a nice restaurant up in West Palm Beach. Maybe you should show up around . . . say eightish? Maybe you'll *bump* into someone you know. And maybe, she'll be the one buying you a drink." She handed him the address with a lustful look in her eyes.

He folded the address, slipping it into his pocket. "Eight o'clock?"

"Eight," she replied. She would not back down, figuring the odds of anyone recognizing her with Trevon would be slim up in West Palm Beach. The risk could be the same at a spot in Miami, but she just wanted to be extra safe.

Moving back to being his parole officer, she promised to do her best at finding him a place to stay. Before he left, he gave her the info to the motel where he was staying. When it was time for him to leave, she walked around her desk to show him out.

"Take care," she said and held out her hand. *Mmm! I don't even have to try to undress him with my eyes. I already KNOW what he looks like without any clothes!*

"You too." He shook her hand. *Yo! I know she ain't blushing! She still ain't ask if I had a job? She got to be up to something. Maybe she's trying to set me up for real.*

"See you at eight?" Kendra held his hand longer than a friendly shake.

"Yeah, eight." Trevon released her hand after a brief moment of feeling awkward. *I might have to think about this shit 'cause something ain't flowing right. Buy me a drink! Yeah right! She up to something. Something that won't be good for me.*

Trevon felt at ease riding in his Jaguar. It gave him a sense of control. For fifteen years, in prison he was controlled. If he wanted to go left or right, today it was his choice. His outer looks made it appear that he was fully adjusted back into society. Deep inside, he knew that was not true. In the small motel room, he had woke up at 5 a.m. That was his body still acting on the prison schedule. He had actually waited for someone to call him to breakfast. When Trevon took a shower and washed his arms, he realized he was wearing shower shoes. He left them on, but felt at a low state because he had not *thought* to put them on, he just did it.

He slowed at the intersection of 22nd Avenue and 62nd Street with the system knocking "I Can't Wait" by Redman. The traffic was heavy. Trevon waited for the light to turn green. He saw a cheerless looking guy sitting at the bus stop, clad in mismatched colored ragged clothes. *That could easily be me.* Trevon knew what he had going for himself was rare. Eighty percent of black men being released from prison were back within a year. He thought back to a Positive Thinking course he had taken in prison. The teacher had told him to refrain from what she termed 'stinking thinking.' *I wonder where her sexy tail at?* He grinned.

When the light turned green, he drove off. Suddenly, he hit the turning signal to turn back around. Thoughts about that course pushed his next action. He drove back down 22nd Avenue then crossed over to pull up behind the bus stop. He blew the horn twice, easing the window down.

"Yo, bruh!" He waved the guy over.

The guy looked around, then pointed at himself.

"Yeah, you. Lemme holla at cha'."

The guy timidly approached Trevon as the sun poured down through a gap in the clouds. Trevon got out of his car. The two men stood within arms reach apart.

"Nice ride you got!" the guy said, nodding at the silent running car.

"Thanks. She's my baby." Trevon slid his fingers down the sculpted gleaming white hood. *Yeah, I could easily be at a bus stop. Watching cars go by and wishing I had one. Well, I got one and since I know this means struggle, I'ma help him out if I can.*

"What is it? A Benz?"

"Nah. This the new Jaguar XJL."

"Oh."

"Hey, if you don't mind. Can I ask where you're headed?"

174

"Huh . . . I'm going to the rec center in Liberty City to get something to eat."

Trevon wiped a bead of sweat off his forehead. "What they having?"

The guy looked at Trevon with a strange expression. "Um, collard greens, hot rolls and fried chicken, I think."

"Times are hard out here, huh?"

"Sure is. I've been struggling ever since I got out the joint."

"You did time?"

"Yeah. Did six years. Been out for almost two years. Hard to get a job."

Trevon's attention was briefly drawn to a MetroRail train clacking by overhead on the tracks. In Miami, the train system was built above ground instead of underground like New York.

"Prison ain't the place for ya, brother," the guy said. "Whatever you're doing, legal I hope. Stay at it."

Trevon could not bring himself to tell the guy of the time he had pulled. *This man has been out for almost two damn years! I've been out less than three months. How is life fair?*

"Hey, my bus coming, rap. I gotta go—"

"Wait!" Trevon looked down the avenue at the approaching city bus. "Um, how about I give you a lift?"

The guy looked at Trevon, then glanced toward the bus. "You ain't crazy, is you?"

Trevon laughed. "No, my brother."

The guy shrugged. "What the hell. I always wanted to ride in a Benz."

"Jaguar."

"Oh right."

Trevon eased inside his ride then waited for his new friend to get adjusted in the seat. Trevon introduced himself as he slid the Jaguar back into traffic. He found out his passenger's name was Marvin and he was forty-eight years old. Trevon was acting off what his teacher had told him on his last day of class. "Do good for others to do good for yourself." Trevon told Marvin that he wanted to help him out. He first took Marvin to the USA Flea Market and bought him a few pairs of shoes and five outfits. After that, he took Marvin to a soul food joint in the Brownsville area. Marvin thanked him for everything.

Nearly three hours later, around 2 p.m., Marvin directed Trevon to a small duplex apartment with a shabby fence around it.

"God bless you, brother," Marvin said with tears in his weary eyes. "Ain't nobody never gave me nothing all my life. Why you do this?"

Trevon gripped the steering wheel. "I could have been in your shoes, Marvin."

"Could of, but cha' ain't," Marvin pointed out.

Trevon indeed felt better about himself as he pulled off. He gave Marvin $500 and told him to be safe. Back on the road, he settled easily into his element behind the wheel. Feeling the need to just be wholly free, he ended up on I-95 North. On cruise control, he commanded the big-bodied sedan while letting one of his favorite songs play on repeat, "Sky's the Limit" by Biggie.

CHAPTER
TWENTY-TWO

At the same time, Yaffa was sitting in Swagga's kitchen secretly talking to Chyna.

"Yo, ma. When I'ma get up wit'cha again?"

Before Chyna could reply, Swagga appeared with a bottle of Courvoisier Rose in his hand. Yaffa told Chyna to hold on, then asked Swagga what was up.

"Yo, I wanna go see one of my dumb ass baby mommas." Swagga appeared drunk.

"What time?"

Swagga shrugged. "Don't matter."

Yaffa looked at Swagga dressed in the same clothes he had on yesterday. "How about you ease back off the liquor and Kush and take a shower to freshen up?"

Swagga turned the bottle up and swallowed hard. "A'ight." He burped. "I'ma . . . go . . . take a shower."

Yaffa eased his cell phone back up to his ear as Swagga shuffled out the kitchen. He was pushing hard for a second hook-up, but Chyna was casually stringing him along.

"Yo, when I'ma see you again?" he asked, squeezing his dick.

"Soon, baby. I'm just tied up with some personal things right now."

Yaffa's ego would not let him sweat Chyna. The behind the back affair was not a big deal to him, but Chyna suggested they float things on the down low.

"Yo, let me call you back later, a'ight." Yaffa stood up.

"I'll be waiting, Sugah Bear." Chyna kissed him through the phone.

Yaffa laughed as he ended the call. Back to business. Heading up to his room, he went inside, opened his weapon safe and pulled out two twin Glocks. Nearly forty minutes later, he met Swagga outside. They stood under the blazing sun in front of the four-car garage.

"I pick . . . door numbah . . . two." Swagga pointed. He was drunk and high. The garage door slid up, revealing the chrome mesh grill of his champagne colored Bentley Brooklands. The on duty chauffeur drove the Bentley out of the garage then promptly got out to open the rear door for Swagga.

"I'm rich, bitch!" Swagga fell into the six-figure sedan.

Yaffa got in the front passenger seat and told the chauffeur where to go.

LaToria was fucked up emotionally. In her bed, she soaked the pillow with her tears as the MP3 system filled her bedroom with "Love" by Musiq Soulchild. The soft ballad was on repeat for the third time.

Love . . . so many people use your name in vain . . . Love, but those who have faith in you, sometimes go astray . . . Love . . .

LaToria had no idea how to deal with her emotions. Her pessimistic mind-set reared its head. *It ain't love; it's only lust! Trevon is just hooked on me 'cause I'm his first piece of ass. That's all it is!* She pounded the bed with her fist. So deep in her sorrow, she had not heard nor noticed she had a visitor.

"Girl!" Jurnee turned the music off.

LaToria rolled to her side looking at Jurnee through her blurred vision.

"What is wrong with you?" Jurnee dropped her purse on the floor then sat down on the bed.

LaToria dropped her face on Jurnee's lap, sobbing like a baby. Jurnee tried to console her by rubbing her shoulder.

"Whatever it is, just let it all out, baby," Jurnee whispered.

LaToria gripped Jurnee's blouse, thankful that she was not alone anymore.

Last night had been hard on her. She had stayed up, hoping Trevon would return or at least call. Her guilt was too thick, which stopped her from calling him. It took a few minutes for her sobs to die down. Jurnee lifted up LaToria's tear streaked face. "It's time to talk."

"What time is it?" LaToria sniffed, wiping her eyes.

"Five twenty-eight."

LaToria sat up. "I need to use the bathroom."

"Where is Trevon?" Jurnee asked as LaToria got off the bed. When she got no answer, she assumed that LaToria's grief was over Trevon.

LaToria stood at the sink, head down and her arms braced on the edge. She did not look up until Jurnee walked in behind her.

"Ain't going no where 'til you tell me what's going on." Jurnee stood beside LaToria with her hands on her hips.

"I—just did something stupid, that's all." Latoria looked at herself in the mirror. Her hair was wild and out of place. *I look a mess!*

As if she were a mind reader, Jurnee picked up a comb then stood behind LaToria to straighten her hair.

"What happened?" Jurnee knew that combing LaToria's hair would calm her.

"I—I did it with Trevon last night."

"Tell me something I don't know," Jurnee replied, smiling.

LaToria waited a few seconds. "We um, didn't use protection."

Jurnee froze and looked at LaToria's reflection in the mirror.

"I know it was stupid, but I wanted to—do it, Jurnee."

"How do you feel about him?" Jurnee resumed combing LaToria's hair.

LaToria shrugged.

"Yes, you do."

"I don't. I don't know what I feel for him. I'ma look real stupid to be . . . in love or some dumb shit."

"You trying to end up like me?"

"Like you? What do you mean?"

"You think I'm happy being alone? You . . ." She paused to turn LaToria by her shoulders. "You can't worry about what people will say. To hell with that. If you like Trevon, tell him. Did you?"

LaToria pouted. "No. I told him—that I hated him then kicked him out."

"When?"

"Last night."

"Call him."

"No."

"Stop being stubborn, LaToria!"

"I'm not calling him. What we did—it was a mistake."

Jurnee crossed her arms. "Bullshit. Did you ever have a *mistake* with Swagga?"

"Hell no!"

"Don't lie to yourself. You know it wasn't a mistake and you know you wanted it to happen."

"You don't know what you're talking about." LaToria tried to walk around Jurnee, but her path was blocked.

"I bet you walked out on him when he was trying to talk to you."

"Why do you care!"

"I care because I got love for you! I care enough that I need you to be happy, even if it's not with me. That's why I care!"

LaToria turned her back on Jurnee. "I want to be left alone."

Jurnee laid her hands on LaToria's waist in a sexual manner. "Don't be like that."

Jurnee lowered her lips to LaToria's neck. She gently kissed on her flesh. LaToria closed her eyes as Jurnee began to explore her body.

"Take your clothes off." Jurnee turned LaToria back around then pushed her tongue into her mouth. Piece by piece, their clothes formed a pile at their feet. They took turns pulling off each other's panties. Both nude, they went back into the bedroom. Slipping on the bed, they kissed again while feeling on each other's wet pussy. Wanting more, Jurnee moved on top of LaToria in a 69. Soft moans and slow licks were given for the next eight to ten minutes. Both knew how to pull a climax from the other.

Jurnee blew on LaToria's phat clit, while fingering her pussy in a rapid circular motion.

LaToria tried to push Trevon from her mind as she ate Jurnee out. She wanted him. Wanted him above her, pushing her knees back to her ears. Wanted him to thrust that dick deep. Wanted him to moan her name. Wanted him to . . . she just wanted him.

CHAPTER
TWENTY-THREE
8:21 p.m.
West Palm Beach, Florida

Kendra refused to look at her watch. The fact was already proven. Trevon was late. *Maybe he's just having trouble finding this restaurant. I've been here since seven-fifty. This is so embarrassing. I asked for a table for two and I'm sitting here alone.*

She looked around the dimly lit serene setting. By candlelight, the other couples sitting at their tables were eating and talking softly. There were sixteen tables, all were filled and only Kendra sat alone. She caught the male waiter heading toward her table. She waved him off when he signaled a refill on her glass.

Okay, he stood me up. I can't get mad. Maybe I should call and see what's up before I jump to any silly conclusions. Kendra looked down at her freshly painted fingernails. She had put in a lot of effort to look good for him. *No. I won't call him. If he was coming, he would have been here by now. Suck it up. I just played myself.* Feeling cheerless, she lifted the glass of champagne to her glossy full lips. Setting it back on the table, she reached for her black leather tiny clutch purse. *Suck it up. I'm a big girl. I can handle this.* She slid back from the table when a black waitress approached her from behind.

"Ms. Kendra Paige?"

Kendra turned her head, surprised to see a friendly waitress behind her with an arm full of white roses. "I'm Kendra."

The waitress smiled as she walked to the side of the table. "These are for you."

"Me?"

"Yes." The waitress nodded. "Courtesy of the gentleman behind you."

Kendra spun around and caught Trevon walking toward her between the tables. She smiled, placing her clutch purse back on the table. The waitress left the flowers on the table as Kendra stood to greet Trevon.

Damn! He is so handsome! I gots to keep my cool around him because he got me acting out of my character.

Trevon had never dealt with an older woman. He had left the streets when he was only eighteen years old.Trevon walked toward her with his next move taken from movies he had seen.

"Um, sorry I'm late," he said, standing in front of her.

"You're here. That's all I care about." She smiled at his grown and sexy appearance. He had on an off-white suit with a matching tie.

"You look beautiful," Trevon said truthfully.

"Thank you." She blushed.

Trevon slid her chair back. She sat down and allowed him to assist her moving up to the table. That was how it was done in the movies.

"Thank you for the flowers." She picked one up to smell it.

"I'm late because I was pulled over by the police."

"For what?"

"DWB."

She frowned. "DWB?"

"Driving while black." He shrugged.

"You didn't get a ticket or anything did you?"

"Nah. Just given a hard time."

"Are you okay?"

Trevon could not look into her eyes. He could not admit the paralyzing fear that had gripped him when those blue lights flashed behind him. At one moment, he had thought about running from them. His heart had sped up. Trevon was plain out scared. Scared of going back to prison.

"Trevon." Kendra reached across the table for his hand. "It's okay." Her voice took on a reassuring tone. She noticed the glimmer of fear that had woven into his face. She felt bad for all of her threats to send him back to prison.

The waiter broke the spell when he approached their table to take their orders. Kendra would enjoy herself and dump her diet, just for tonight. They both ordered a steak with seasoned fries and mashed potatoes with gravy. Quiet intruded upon the two, as Trevon got lost in his internal thoughts. Kendra cleared her throat, breaking the awkward silence. She asked Trevon general first date questions until she saw his tense shoulders relax and he seemed comfortably seated. Their food arrived twenty minutes later.

"So, how are you adjusting to being free after fifteen years?" she finally asked the question that had been on her mind.

Trevon briefly fidgeted in his seat. "I must admit that . . . mentally, it ain't easy," he said, cutting his steak.

"Have you ever sought any counseling?" She was glued to his every word, looking at him between lifting the food to her mouth.

"Nah. Kinda . . . just dealing with it myself. I ain't crazy or nothing."

"I would hope not," she kidded.

"I um . . . At times, it just seems unreal. I feel like—like I don't fit out here."

"It will take time, Trevon. I know about prison life. I used to be a correctional officer."

Trevon was surprised. "Prison ain't no place to be."

They spoke openly once Kendra told him not to view her as his parole officer tonight. Trevon reminded himself to go with the flow of things. As their time together increased, his thoughts of LaToria slid away. Soon he had her laughing and reaching across the table to touch his hand. He had *read* in prison that touching from a female was a positive sign of attraction. For now, he was keeping his hands to himself. The attraction was there on his side as well. He caught himself looking at her line of cleavage whenever she lowered her eyes to the plate. He took notice of how her breasts seemed to take up much of her top.

"I have some good news," she later said after the waiter placed their ordered desserts on the table.

"What? I'm getting off parole early?" he asked, finding it easy to look into her eyes.

"No," she said, crossing her legs. "I found a two bedroom apartment over on 103rd Street."

"When can I check it out?" he asked eagerly.

"Tomorrow, if you want to. I can set you up with an assistance program if you need it."

"I'm good. There are others in a needy position that might need it."

"That's very thoughtful of you, Trevon. I know a lot of people on government assistance that don't need it. You're an honest man."

Trevon could not remember the last time he had really felt important. Being with Kendra was a challenge. It seemed that she understood him, when in truth she did.

"Tell me about your family. Why didn't you ask to have your parole moved up to North Carolina to be near them?"

"For starters, I'm not a kid anymore. I love my mom and sister and I'd do anything for them. I'm down here because I want to make it on my own. Times are hard on them as it is and me living off them won't help."

"I can understand that. But you've been away for so long. Have you seen them since you've been out?"

"Yeah." He smiled. "They came down for three days after I got out. We hung out and stuff. I talk to them just about every day."

"What is your sister doing?"

"She's a weather—um—a TV meteorologist for a news station up in Raleigh, North Carolina."

"Wow. That's wonderful!"

"Yeah. She kept her promise to me and finished school."

Kendra crossed her legs. "You know, I had to read up on your case notes, Trevon. I can't say what you did was right. But as a mother, I think I would have lost it, too, had someone violated my child."

"They didn't believe my sister."

"I read about that trial, too."

"My only regret was the pain I placed on my mom and sis."

"What about the life you took?"

"He shouldn't have touched my sister."

"Do you still feel anger? Looking back, would you have done anything differently?"

Trevon laid his fork down then picked up a napkin to wipe his mouth. "Would you think of me differently if I told you that I wished I had my eyes open when I shot him?"

"No."

"I was scared, Kendra. I couldn't even hold the gun straight without two hands on it. I shot twice . . . with my eyes closed. When I opened them he was on the ground. Just on his side. I dropped the gun and just stood there looking at the body as the police rolled up."

Kendra tried to envision Trevon as a young teen committing murder. "Don't let the past drag you down, Trevon. Like you said, you were a kid then. Now you're a man."

"A man that's somewhat stuck with a young mind."

"So what do you want out of life? What is your true desire?"

"I want to just stay free. I want to have a family. A wife, some kids, I just want to be someone."

"You are someone, Trevon."

"Um, you have a little girl, right?" he asked, pushing into her personal life.

"How do you—"

"When we crossed paths at the gas station, remember?"

"Oh, I forgot. Sorry. But yes, I do have a precious little girl. Her name is Carmelita and she's three."

"I hope to be a father one day."

"Really?"

He nodded yes. "Just have to find that perfect woman, I guess."

"There's no such thing, Trevon."

"Why do you say that?"

Kendra waited to answer as a waiter walked by their table. "Everyone has their own issues to deal with. Example, you have your past."

"And you?"

Kendra took her glasses off and rubbed between her eyes. "I'm not perfect."

"Can I ask why you're not with your kid's father?"

"I was never with him."

Trevon did not understand. He was about to change the topic, but she spoke up.

"I met my baby's father when I was working at the prison."

He understood now. "Let me guess. He got out, hooked up with you then left you?"

Kendra wiped a smudge off her glasses. *Should I tell him the truth? How will he view me?* Kendra wanted to vent to him. She wanted him to know that she was human. One that was able to make a mistake. "I met, Marcus while he was in prison. He was only in for a six-month skid. I fell for his game and we had an affair while I was working at the prison." She laid her glasses on the table. "We had sex a few times. And me being silly, I ended up pregnant. It wasn't something I planned. It just happened. I was vulnerable and I wasn't thinking."

Trevon had not expected her to cross that line. During his fifteen years in prison, he had heard about inmates being sexually involved with female guards. Trevon knew it took more than the average inmate to bag a female guard behind bars. *Okay, if she had taken the risk in prison . . . Now I see why she's risking her job once again.*

"Can I assume that you're single?" he asked, already knowing the answer.

"Yes, I am. My last relationship was with one of my co-workers and that didn't work out."

She did not add in the fact of him being white. She had ended the relationship on the strength of her daughter. She was already without a father figure. Why confuse her with an interracial relationship. "How about you?" she asked, hoping he would say no.

"The same."

Kendra opened her clutch purse and pulled out a slim handheld device. She laid it on his side of the table.

"What's this?" He picked it up, flipping it over and around. There was a black screen about the size of a credit card.

"It's a digital picture album. Just hit that left button on the bottom."

Trevon was amazed at the advancement of technology. Turning it on, he viewed pictures of Kendra's little girl from the day she was born.

"How many pictures does it hold?"

"Two hundred. I have a bigger one at home."

"Your little girl is cute."

"And she's a mess, too." Kendra beamed proudly.

Trevon came up on a picture that showed Kendra, her daughter and a face he knew.

"Um, were you and your daughter at a concert?" Trevon turned the screen toward Kendra.

The smile on her face turned into a frown.

"That's Marcus Brooks aka Swagga. He's Carmelita's father."

CHAPTER TWENTY-FOUR

Bayview Condo, Fisher Island

Swagga was in the den lounging with Cindy resting her head on his lap. The two were smoking weed and tripping hard off an old Bernie Mac DVD. Yaffa was out on the balcony talking on his cell phone with the glass door closed.

Swagga had visited two of his three baby mothers. He had sex with one and got his dick sucked by the second. The ony child he *really* loved was his firstborn. He had wanted to see her tonight. After passing the weed back to Cindy, he picked up his mobile phone.

"Who you calling?" Cindy asked, after exhaling a lung full of smoke.

"Dumb ass Kendra," he said, blocking out his number.

"Oh." She shrugged. She knew all three of his baby mother's only because he had told her about them.

Swagga closed his eyes for a few seconds. The line started to ring. On the seventh ring it was answered.

"Hello?"

"Yo, whut up? Been tryin' to call your ass all day."

"What do you want, Marcus?"

"My name is Swagga! I told you 'bout that shit! Look, I wanna see my seed."

"It's almost ten o'clock and I'm sure Carmelita is sleep."

"Wake 'er up then."

"I'm not home, okay? And even if I was I would not wake her up. You need to call at a more sensible time because—"

"Where the fuck you at?"

"I'm at—minding my damn business! Look, you sound high or drunk, so don't be calling me with this bullshit, Marcus!"

"Fuck that! What time you gonna be home? I'm comin' by."

"You can shut that shit down! Carmelita is at the babysitter and you know damn well that I don't want to see you!"

"Fuck you always trippin' fo'? You wasn't being such a bitch when you was suckin' my dick in the mop closet!"

"Try that shit on somebody else, *Marcus!*"

Swagga hung up the phone in her face. "Stupid bitch!"

"Don't let her stress you out," Cindy said and rolled over to her stomach. All she had on was a tank-top and a pair of white panties.

"Can't nobody stress me out!" he said, reaching down to slide his palm over her exposed butt cheeks.

"That feels good," she said, looking at the TV. "Hey, what's the deal with Chyna doing that favor for ya?"

Swagga instantly went on his guard at any mention of Chyna. He did not trust Chyna at all. "Should go down this Friday."

"How much she charge?"

"Um . . . fifteen hundred." Swagga leaned back rubbing his face.

"You staying with me tonight?"

"Yeah," he murmured. "And I want some pussy."

Trevon leaned on his Jaguar as Kendra strutted back across the parking lot. He had seen her shouting into her phone while standing next to her Jeep Grand Cherokee.

"Sorry about that," she said, massaging her forehead.

"That was your baby's father?"

"Unfortunately it was."

Trevon glanced up at the full moon.

"Beautiful, ain't it?" Kendra said, looking up at the moon.

"Yeah. Funny how I realized that I haven't seen it that much. In prison, I was back inside before it got dark. Feels strange to even be outside this late."

"You're free, Trevon." She reached out to touch the side of his face.

Before he could react, she quickly removed her hand.

"When will I see you again?" he asked. "I really enjoyed this date."

"You have a—"

"I'm not talking about an interview at your office," he said, catching her off guard. Trevon pulled her up against his body.

Kendra planted her hands on his solid chest. His hands felt good on her waist.

"I'm your parole officer, Mr. Harrison." She grinned.

"So what? You wanna lock me up now?"

"How about I just put the cuffs on you and have my way with you?"

Trevon took a chance and made a bold move by slipping his hands down to her ass. Kendra felt her nipples getting hard as well as his dick. Her mind quickly jumped back to that porn DVD she had of him.

I KNOW he can slang it! Mmm, I feel it growing. Calm down. I can't act like a ho.

"I have to go pick up my baby, Trevon."

Trevon gave her ass a soft squeeze. "You still haven't answered my question."

"On a personal level . . . we can do another date this weekend."

"I'll be looking forward to it."

"Um, you know we have to be discreet about this."

"Trust me, I understand."

Kendra cleared her throat. "About your family," she pressed. "You didn't say anything about your father."

"He was never in the picture. At least not my real dad. I know it's a harsh thing to say . . . but I don't have no feelings for him."

Kendra looked into his eyes. "Goodnight Trevon," she whispered and smiled.

Minutes later, he was pulling out behind her in his ride. He had no idea how things would turn out with her. She was nothing like LaToria and Jurnee. Shit, Kendra had not allowed a mere kiss to pop off on their first date. Trevon's only issue was the chance of bumping heads with Swagga.

Why out of all the women in Miami I gotta have the sloppy seconds behind Swagga? Shit crazy! I should be straight now. My damn parole officer is feeling me! Trevon looked at the empty passenger seat. One day, he hoped he could fill it with a special someone.

LaToria rolled over in her bed with changing thoughts of calling Trevon. Jurnee was asleep on the other side of the bed. LaToria looked at the digital clock on the nightstand. It glowed 12:37 a.m.

It's too late to call him. Shit! He has not made an effort to call me! Ain't about to sweat no nigga. Fuck no. LaToria squeezed the pillow. *Maybe I need to give Swagga another chance. At least he did ask me to marry him.* Reaching for her cell phone, she sent Swagga a text message.

Cindy had Swagga stretched out on the floor bouncing hard on his dick. She was doing it reverse cowgirl style, so he could see her ass clapping. Her titties flopped loosely as her nails dug into his legs. Swagga had a pillow under his head and his hands gripped the pointy heels of her shoes.

"Ahhhh Swagga!" Cindy moaned as sweat coated her naked body. This was about the only time she could get the best out of the dick. "Yessss! All. Up. In. My. Pussy!"

They did it with the lights on. She threw her head back, whipping her dreads. Slowing down, she eased up off the dick then backed her pussy up to his face. She rolled her pussy all over his face, smearing it with her juices. Taking him into her mouth had him moaning. *At least he's good at sucking pussy.* She torqued her tongue ring all over his dick. Using her special tricks, she began to suck just the tip while pumping his shaft. His legs stiffened, followed by his toes balling up. Keeping her lips wrapped around him, she swallowed the first of his three-spurting climax. Pressing her pussy against his mouth, she squirmed herself to a huge orgasm. She knew he was in a freaky mood when he slid his tongue over her asshole.

When her legs were able, she stood up.

"Where Yaffa?" Swagga reached for his boxers.

"Out on the balcony," she replied, picking up her panties off the floor.

"Go tell 'im I'm 'bout ready. I gotta use the bathroom."

"You still taking me to the beach tomorrow?"

"Yeah. And your ass betta be ready when I get here."

She waited until he closed the bathroom door before giving him the bird. As the norm, she wanted to tease Yaffa again. She left her tank top draped across the arm of the sofa with the intention to go topless. Turning the TV back on, she spotted Swagga's phone on the floor beside his Timberland boots. Her curiosity got the best of her. With a quick search, she viewed all of his recent calls then pulled up the text message application. Her face turned upside down when she came across the text message from Kandi.

She quickly deleted the text, then put his phone back how she had found it. Of all the other bitches, Kandi was the only one she felt could take Swagga's full attention.

Trevon was back in the tiny motel room. He left the lights off. Turning his phone on, he felt a touch of loss when he saw no messages from LaToria. He wanted to hear her voice. *Gotta play my position. I can't call her. If she wanted to talk she know how to reach me.* He turned the phone off then took his shoes off. The dead quiet reminded him of the prison dorms after lock down. He did not want these thoughts or harsh memories. He now realized how a man could be mentally trapped in his own prison. Any dream about prison was a nightmare for Trevon. They broke him out in cold sweats. Sleepless nights.

CHAPTER
TWENTY-FIVE
September 30, 2011
Friday, 11:30 a.m. - Miami, Florida

Trevon managed to make it to Friday without losing his mind. His help came in the surprising form of late night phone calls from Kendra. He now knew the worth of a woman that could carry on a decent conversation that was not centered on sex. He was still staying in the motel, but Kendra promised him that the apartment would be ready next week. Trevon looked forward to having his own crib, no matter how small it was.

On Wednesday, Janelle had called him to the office. She got right to the point and told him that she knew about the issue between him and LaToria. She wanted to know if he would have a problem working with LaToria in the future. He told her he had no beef with LaToria. A surprise came when Janelle told him about Jurnee and LaToria. The two had taken a spur of the moment vacation up to New York. Before he left her office, she told him to be ready to start his next film sometime late next month.

Today he was taking his XJL to be hand washed. This was a relaxing moment for Trevon. Besides, he loved watching the thick bikini clad women washing his ride. Under the cloudless Carolina-blue sky, he turned into the corner parking lot where the hand wash was located. As always, there was a line. Trevon turned in and pulled up behind a '85 Buick Regal sitting on 28s. There were numerous car systems playing at once. Trevon had the only Jaguar on the spot, but all the attention was on a ghost white Ferrari 458 Italia. Even Trevon found himself bending his neck to check out the Ferrari. He had assumed it was being driven by a dude. He was proven wrong when all eyes fell on this bad ass Asian chick strutting toward the 458. Two D-Boys hopped out of a brown Donk Chevy to holler. The chick ignored them. Trevon shook his head. *She's out of my league.* He settled back in the seat, watching the Ferrari as it pulled off. His attention grew when he saw it slowing alongside his ride. He sat up. His window was lowered in sync with the Ferrari. He slid his shades off to get an unobstructive view of the honey behind the wheel.

"Nice ride," Chyna said.

"I can say the same about yours." Trevon nodded at the sports car.

"Forget these rides. I see we have something in common. We both like white. My name is Chyna. What's yours?"

"Trevon."

"Got a girlfriend?"

"If I did, I wouldn't be having this urge to ask for your number."

Chyna smiled. "How about I give you my address? I do have a man, but I feel like having a little fun." Chyna lowered the sunglasses off his face. "But I have a feeling that there is *nothing* little about you."

Trevon smiled. *Damn! I got it going on! Just be smooth. Don't act too pressed.* "Where are you located?"

"I have a crib in Coral Gables."

Trevon noticed a few haters looking his way as Chyna wrote down the address and phone number.

"What time can I expect your company?" Chyna asked after handing Trevon the address.

"Um, how about later on? Like five o'clock or something like that." He wanted to play it smooth and not look desperate. Truth be told, he wanted to follow the Ferrari now. Fuck the car wash.

"Five o'clock is perfect," Chyna agreed.

South Beach, Miami Florida
Same Time

Cindy was easily looking fancy in a skimpy two-piece orange string bikini. She was out enjoying the perfect beach weather with Swagga and his entourage. She made sure she was looking fly for the ever present paparazzi hounding Swagga today. Cindy sat on a huge white beach towel under a yellow umbrella stuck into the warm sun baked sand. Looking out toward the ocean, she watched Swagga and Yaffa speeding around on their wave runners.

To her knowledge, Kandi had not tried to reach Swagga again. With that on her mind, she looked over to her left and spotted Swagga and Yaffa's cell phones and one of Swagga's platinum watches.

I bet that bitch might've tried to reach Swagga through Yaffa. Cindy looked around thebeach. This section was not open to the public. There were about seven other women, all white, laid out on towels getting a topless suntan. Acting quickly, she picked up Swagga's mobile phone and checked it thoroughly. E-mails, text, IMs, phone calls, nothing. She felt at ease. Putting it back, she picked up Yaffa's cell phone. First, she pulled up the calls received. She was going through a second time, when she noticed Chyna's cell number. At first, Cindy did not think much of it. She assumed Swagga was having Yaffa set things up for that mess with Trevon. Just to be nosey, she went to the video app and glanced at a few titles of the video clips on the phone.

> -*Concert in NYC–5 min. 23 sec.*
> -*Strip Club Suck-Off–7 min. 18 sec.*
> -*Ho's at Bike Week–10 min. 24 sec.*
> -*Chyna and Swagga–30 sec.*

Cindy snatched her shades off. She glanced up to see where Swagga and Yaffa were. She judged that they were half a mile down the beach. She pulled up the video clip having no idea what the clip would show. Cindy waited only a few seconds for the clip to download. Sitting up, she at first thought her eyes were playing tricks on her. Her eyes popped open at the sight of Chyna vigorously sucking Swagga's dick. Cindy closed her eyes. She went ahead and jumped to the conclusion that Swagga was a closet homosexual. *Wait! Chyna is a transgender. She has a pussy, so technically Swagga is with a female. I bet this motherfucker only wanted to get up with Chyna. All this bullshit about Trevon is just a front! Something ain't right.* Cindy came up with an idea. She quickly typed in the command on the slider keyboard to forward the video clip to her cell phone. Once it was confirmed, she deleted the command from Yaffa's phone. Cindy felt she was being played and used. She wondered how far Swagga had gone behind closed doors with his sex life. He was becoming *suspect* to her. Swagga allowed a *known* transgender in his home and in his bed. That last thought triggered an instant surge of rage in Cindy.

Swagga only took me to his crib twice since I've been fucking him. And he let this bitch Chyna up in his shit on the first fucking night!

Cindy had her beautiful face balled up when Swagga's mobile phone made a soft chime to indicate an incoming text message. Acting on jealousy and anger, she read the text message once she saw it was from Chyna.

Everything is good! Met Trevon.

He will Cum ☺ see me @ my crib in Coral Gables @5. I will call u when he arrives. Chyna. 9/30/11, Fri. 11:42 a.m.

Cindy was really confused now. *So the deal with Trevon is real. I still don't like this bitch, Chyna dealing with my man!* Cindy knew she would have to tell Swagga she had read the text message. It might backfire in her face if she deleted it. She had somewhat calmed down when Swagga returned with his crew.

"Whut up?" he said, dropping down behind her on the towel.

"Chyna sent you a text."

"Huh?" Swagga's stomach dropped. "You read it?"

"You know I did. Here." She handed him the mobile phone over her shoulder.

Swagga took his phone. *I gotta put a lock on my shit.* His tense shoulders relaxed when he read the text. *Damn! Chyna bagged that nigga already. Well, nigga gonna have a nude awakening when Chyna drops them panties.*

"Where Yaffa at?" Cindy asked as Swagga slid on a pair of shades.

"'Bout to go back out."

Cindy looked toward the surf. Yaffa had a topless Britney Spears look-a-like on the back of his waverunner. "So, what is Chyna supposed to do with this Trevon guy?"

"Expose him for being gay!" Swagga laughed.

"Chyna is a transsexual so how will he be viewed as a guy?"

"Transexual, she-sexual, what fuckin' difference do it make? Chyna ain't no real bitch! The muthafucka is mixed up in the head!"

"Really? So, any man that fucks with a transsexual or transgender is gay in your view?"

"Damn right he is! Shit, Chyna has the same number of ribs as I do! And that makes him a man in my book."

"Why are you trying to set this guy up? What did he do to you?"

"Damn! Where 50 cent at? This the fuckin' remix for 'Twenty-one Questions?'"

"Oh, so now you ain't gonna tell me!"

"Chill, yo. It ain't that serious. Fuck Trevon. He in the way of something I'm trying to gain, so don't worry about it, okay?"

Cindy stood up. "You're being an ass, Swagga!" She picked up her cell phone.

"I'ma be *in* your ass if you don't sit the fuck down and stop yellin' in my fuckin' ear!"

Cindy stormed off, stopped, kicked sand on Swagga, then ran off.

"Bitch!" Swagga let her go. He was used to her bitchy ways. He smiled, shaking his head. Trevon would be setup in a major way.

Cindy felt challenged by Chyna and the re-emergence of Kandi. She hated the fact that Chyna had gone behind her back to fuck with Swagga. Cindy strolled down the beach trying to figure out what was going on. She needed Swagga in her life. It was strictly for his money. Yeah, she was a bit pissed that Chyna had sucked his dick. She only felt this way because it was done behind her back. While walking on the hot sand, she turned her phone on to pull up the video clip of Swagga and Chyna. *Slant-eyed bitch even sucked the dick better than me! Swagga never cries like a ho when I do it. I need to step up my game fo' real.*

"Motherfuckers must think I'm stupid!" she murmured to herself. She came to a stop and looked back down the beach toward Swagga. She balled up her fist. Swagga had the guts to have another bitch massaging his back. *Okay, he wants to play like that! It's on fo' real!*

CHAPTER
TWENTY-SIX
Coral Gables, Florida

Chyna stepped out of the shower when the front doorbell chimed. He looked at the time. 3:40 p.m. Walking into the bedroom, he hit the intercom button.

"Who is it?"

"It's me, girl. Open the door," Cindy replied.

Chyna punched in a code that opened the front door. "I'm in my bedroom." Chyna only had a few friends and Cindy was at the top of that short list. The two had been friends for three years. Both were the same age. Chyna, then Chad, was a homosexual hair stylist that Cindy had met at a photo shoot.

"What you up to?" Cindy asked as she walked into Chyna's bedroom.

"Taking care of that thing for your man." Chyna stood in the bathroom, putting on eye shadow. "He will be here around five."

Cindy placed her purse on the bed then took her earrings off. "Funny you should mention that Swagga is my man."

Chyna walked out the bathroom wearing a robe. "He *is* your man."

"Hmm. So tell me how *his* dick ended up in *your* mouth since he's *my* man?"

Chyna froze by the bed. "Girl,what are you talking about? I—"

"Bitch, don't lie!" Cindy shoved Chyna. "How you gonna go behind my back like that?"

"What are you—"

"Ho, please! I saw the video clip of you sucking his dick in his bed! Did you let 'im fuck that fake ass store-bought pussy you got?"

"Calm down because I—"

"Fuck you!" Cindy shoved Chyna again. This time Chyna lost his balance and fell to the floor.

Chyna jumped back up and shot dead at Cindy's face with a tight closed fist. It connected on Cindy's left cheek. She stumbled back, grabbing her face. Cindy was shocked that Chyna had hit her.

"Bitch, you need to—"

"Ho! It's on now!" Cindy rushed Chyna, landing a wild swing. The blow dazed Chyna and Cindy kept it hot.

"I told you—-" Cindy shouted, punching Chyna in the stomach, "that he was my meal ticket, bitch!"

Chyna folded, holding up his/her arms to ward off the blows. They both started to swing wildly. Chyna tried to rip Cindy's shirt off. They bounced around the room, knocking the lamp table over.

"Cindy please!" Chyna cried.

"Shut up, bitch!" Cindy now had a fist full of Chyna's soft silky black hair.

SMACK!

Cindy's hand set fire to Chyna's face. Chyna screamed as Cindy yanked her/him around by the hair.

SMACK!

Cindy slapped Chyna again.

Chyna ducked the next slap then shoved and tripped Cindy back against the bed. They both fell on the bed in a heap. The two began to tussle, falling on and rolling off the bed.

"Oohh!" Chyna wheezed as Cindy's weight dropped on his stomach.

In the heat of the moment, Cindy shot her knee between Chyna's legs. Chyna howled in agonizing pain, balling up and cupping his balls.

"Get up, bitch!" Cindy stood over Chyna ready to go for some more. Seeing Chyna curled up in pain, she lowered her fist. "What the fuck are you holding?"

Cindy yanked the robe off.

"Stop! Noooo!" Chyna tried to slap Cindy's hands away.

"You lying ass, still dick-having bastard!" Cindy took a step back. She could see the little print of a penis under Chyna's cotton panties.

"Fuck you!" Chyna cried.

Cindy covered her mouth. *Oh my gawd! Swagga is gay!*

Chyna slowly got up and sat down on the bed.

"I thought you had a full sex change!" Cindy stood over Chyna. "Why the fuck you lie to me?"

"I ran outta money, okay!"

"Why of all people . . . Why did you lie to me, Chyna?"

Chyna shrugged and started to cry. Cindy sat down next to her/him. Hell, she was not sure how to look at Chyna. When Chyna stopped crying he opened up and told Cindy how the meeting went down with Swagga. The story started at the Asian bar.

"He thought I was someone else," Chyna explained.

"Does he know you have a—" Cindy looked between Chyna's legs.

"Dick," Chyna broke in. "Yes, but for all it's worth, it was *after* I sucked his dick."

"Chyna, you are playing a dangerous game. You know I don't really care about Swagga. I just don't like how y'all got down behind my back. That was some bullshit and you know it."

Chyna stood up. "I'm sorry, Cindy. But I really need the money to get this operation done. Swagga is going to pay me after I do this thing with Trevon."

Cindy began to think. Her anger was now focused on Swagga. "What are you going to do with this guy, Trevon?"

Chyna looked up with a small bruise under his left eye. "Film the two of us having sex."

"Chyna, you do realize you have a dick, right?"

"Bitch, I know that! I was gonna put something in his drink and then have my fun with him."

"That's crazy." Cindy frowned. "You trippin' fo' real, girl."

Chyna shrugged. "I have to do it."

"Wait! I might have a better idea. We can get a whole lot more money, that's for damn sure."

"*We?*" Chyna pointed out. "Bitch, you just beat my ass and now you think we're on the same team?"

"Ho, sit down and listen. You on the side where dem dollars at." Cindy seemed to speak hood/ebonics as if it were her true identity. In truth, she had grown up upper class, but started what she termed her 'black phase' when she was sixteen. She loved Black culture. The music, the clothes, the food and yes . . . the men.

Chyna flopped down on the bed. "Hurry up. I'll listen to what you have in mind."

Cindy began to pace the floor with her arms crossed. Money was on her mind. She was tired of *only* fucking Swagga. It would have been okay if he knew how to fuck.

"Lemme use your car right quick!" Cindy asked as the plan formed in her mind.

"Where's your Range Rover?"

"I caught a cab over here," Cindy explained. "Swagga has that GPS shit hooked up to my truck and can always find me. But he doesn't know I know about it."

"Why you need my car?"

"I want to be here when Trevon gets here, but I need to get a few items from the store."

"Like what?"

Cindy smiled. "You'll see."

Trevon knew he was at the right address when he saw the white Ferrari. It was 4:55 p.m. with the sun firmly holding a grip on South Florida.

Trevon stepped out of his Jag under a row of palm trees. Looking to his left, he noticed a mango tree in the well-kept front yard. The neighborhood was quiet. Only the sound of a barking dog was heard in the distance. An airliner flying above drew his attention up to the sky. The sight of the airliner reminded him that he had never flown before.

"Didn't think you would show," Chyna said.

Trevon looked toward the front door and spotted her standing in the doorway. He smiled then made his way up the driveway. He was dressed casual in a fresh pair of all black Nike ACG boots, LRG denim and a solid white long sleeved buttoned-up. Chyna looked like a cover model. The white sequin mini dress licked every curve. Trevon nearly tripped over the front step when Chyna turned around. The dress had a scoop back plunging near the top of Chyna's surgically enhanced bubble ass. The way Chyna walked in heels had Trevon lusting to palm that ass.

"Glad you could make it," Chyna said, stepping into the living room with Trevon in tow.

Trevon stepped into the living room and took a seat on a green sofa with matching pillows. Glancing out of the floor-to-ceiling windows, he saw a screened pool in the back. He felt relaxed as he looked around the spacious living room. He wondered where the TV was when suddenly it slid down from the ceiling.

"Care for something to drink?" Chyna asked with the remote pointed toward the flat screen 3D TV.

"Um, not trying to spoil the mood, but you said you have a man, right? Do I need to worry about him popping up?" Trevon nodded at the front door.

"No, you don't. But to relax you, my man is out of the country on business." Chyna lied as easily as telling the truth.

"Okay, in that case I'll share a drink with you."

Chyna smiled and pressed the play button on the remote. "I'll be back shortly."

Trevon allowed his eyes to follow Chyna's pert little ass. Turning back around, he knew what was on Chyna's mind. On the big screen two naked women were kissing each other in a hot tub. A man stood in the background taking his clothes off.

"I hope you don't mind watching porn," Chyna said from the gourmet kitchen behind him.

"It's okay," he said, watching the porn film. *She gonna flip when I tell her that I do porn. Nah, I won't tell 'er.*

Chyna twisted the top off the bottle of Paul Masson brandy, then filled the two glasses on the black granite counter. Keeping an eye toward the living room, Chyna poured a dose of the magic potion into the glass she would give Trevon.

Trevon stood when Chyna came back into the living room.

"Hope you like Paul Masson."

"Never had it," he admitted as Chyna handed him a glass.

"You'll like it." Chyna sat down then motioned Trevon to do the same.

He took another sip of the smooth tasting brandy. The taste was something new. *Tastes good. But I'll just drink this one glass. I came here to fuck, not to get drunk.*

"That's my favorite position." Chyna nodded at theTV.

Trevon looked at the screen and saw the threesome. The man had one of the small-breasted women on her back with her legs up on his shoulders. The female was filling the guy's mouth with her nipple.

"I like to get it like that. Long dicked." Chyna looked down between Trevon's legs and smiled.

"Why do you like it like that?" he asked as his dick grew hard. He took another sip of his drink.

"I like to feel all of the dick. And I love to feel a man's balls slapping my ass."

"You get right to the point, huh?"

Chyna nodded yes. "We only live once, so why let a good thing pass."

"I can agree to that." Trevon looked at Chyna's sexy legs then back to the porn on the screen. He took a few more sips from his glass.

"Do you like rap music?" Chyna was fishing to see if Trevon would mention Swagga.

Cindy told Chyna to ask because she wanted to know why Swagga was beefing with Trevon, and Chyna felt the same way.

"Yeah, but mostly old school rap. Biggie, Lost Boyz and DMX."

"What about the new rappers?"

Trevon felt it was odd how Chyna had changed the subject from sex to music.

"Um . . ." He paused to finish his brandy. "I like Waka Flocka Flame, Rick Ross, Drake and Gucci Mane."

Chyna noticed Trevon's empty glass. From the dose she mixed in his drink, it would take no more than three minutes for it to work.

"I went to a Drake concert back in July. It was fire! Jeezy was there and Nicki Minaj. Gosh, I love her! And Swagga was there, too. It was the Summer Fest on South Beach. Did you go?"

"Nah." Trevon did not want to tell Chyna that he was an ex-con. *I might tell 'er down the line. But not before I get between those legs.*

"What's your favorite position?" Chyna asked, switching back to sex.

Trevon looked up at the porno still playing. The dude was fucking one of the girls in the ass. It was a close up shot.

"I can show you better than I can tell you."

Chyna cocked his head, placing a hand on Trevon's knee. "I like that answer. Now you got me running a bunch of positions through my head."

Trevon looked at Chyna's delicate hand rubbing his knee. *Play it cool. Let her drive this.*

"Can I try to guess what it is?"

"I still won't tell you," he said, playing the game.

Chyna pouted. "No fair."

Trevon shrugged, then sat up to put his empty glass on a coaster.

"Okay, I'll still make one guess." Chyna's hand slowly circled Trevon's thigh. "You like to do it doggy style. That way you can go deep and see it going in and out."

Trevon rubbed his face. *Damn! That Paul Masson a beast! I'm feeling a buzz already. And it got my dick throbbing like a muthafucka! I hope her little ass can take a dick 'cause she ain't fucking no short-winded nigga!*

"Am I right?" Chyna slid closer against Trevon.

Trevon closed his eyes. He lost control of his mind. Simultaneously, he was aware of Chyna's tongue in his ear and a hand rubbing his dick print. He moaned. Then it seemed as if Chyna's soft voice echoed in his ear. His clouded mind snatched only a few words.

"My bedroom. . . . Take your clothes off . . . see your dick . . . going to enjoy."

Trevon was out of it. He was feeling good. The images from the flick spun in his head as Chyna undid his belt.

Trevon was still under the effect of the drug in his system. With little effort, his mind told him a few things. He was blindfolded on his back with his wrists cuffed to the bed. Had he been in his right mind, the cuffs would have triggered harsh thoughts of his incarceration. He was vaguely aware that he was naked. Chyna. He had a fleeting memory of her in his mind. *Yesss . . . Chyna . . . freakin' me.*

Trevon moaned as the teasing lick of a wet, pierced tongue tickled his balls. A hand lifted his dick up and began to stroke it. Trevon was breathing heavily. His body began to tense and quiver as a soft set of lips eased up and down his hard dick.

A camera sat at the foot of the bed. The LED blinking light meant it was recording. Trevon's moans filled the bedroom as a wet, pierced tongue continued to travel up and down the length of his throbbing dick. He could not think straight. His mind only took in the good feeling that stimulated from between his legs. He was not even cognitive of a rubber being rolled down his dick. Somehow his mind told him that he was in *something*. Something tight, wet and hot. The pierced tongue dipped inside his ear.

The shadow on the wall showed a figure vigorously bouncing up and down on top of Trevon reverse cowgirl style. Up and down, the shadows matched the deep moans that filled the sex-scented bedroom.

CHAPTER
TWENTY-SEVEN
Friday, 5:40 p.m. - Coral Gables, Florida

Chyna walked alongside the bed looking down at Trevon's naked body. The camera was still recording. Walking to the dresser, Chyna took off her bra, then reached for a condom. Chyna looked toward the bathroom when the toilet was flushed.

The chime of the doorbell froze her/him in place.

Swagga stood at Chyna's front door looking wasted. He pressed the doorbell again and then looked at Trevon's Jaguar. Swagga had managed to duck away from Yaffa to come check out Chyna.

"What are you doing here!" Chyna answered the door with an arm across his breasts.

Swagga pushed his way inside. Chyna slammed the door, and then ran around Swagga to block him from going any further.

"You fuck 'im yet?"

Chyna glanced back toward the bedroom. "Yes, I fucked him and I was about to do it again until you showed up." Chyna held up a condom.

"He still fucked up off that shit you put in his drink?"

"Yes. But it's about to wear off. You should leave."

Swagga could not pull his eyes away from the set of perfect titties. "How did you fuck 'im?"

Chyna sat down on the sofa. "I rode his dick. You happy now?"

"And it's all on film?"

"Yes. But you won't get it till I get all of my money."

Swagga walked up on Chyna. "Show me how you sucked his dick. You did suck it, right?"

"Swagga, you are really wasting my—" Chyna paused as the words Swagga had just said clicked in his mind. Chyna looked up at Swagga and saw how his eyes were roaming from nipple to nipple. "What do you mean '*show you how I sucked it*'?"

Swagga reached down and squeezed Chyna's breast.

Chyna did what any *real* woman would do, moan.

Cindy eased out of the bathroom and into the bedroom. She looked at Trevon asleep on the bed with a hard dick. She slowly crept over to the bedroom door. The voices she heard were quiet now. Slipping out into the hall, she eased toward the living room barefoot. Reaching the corner of the peach painted wall, she took a peek into the living room. Her mouth fell open. Swagga had his back toward her standing in front of Chyna. Chyna was seated on the sofa with Swagga's dick sliding in and out of his mouth. Cindy wanted to throw up. Pushing the anger down, she slowly made her way back to the bedroom.

Swagga knew Chyna was a he, but he could not deny how sexy Chyna looked. He closed his eyes as Chyna made his neck roll. Swagga started to get mad at Chyna for turning him out on this gay shit. *I should punish his ass like*

a bitch! Swagga shoved Chyna off his dick, then reached down for the condom.

Cindy stood out of sight with the tiny palm-sized digital recorder camera pointed at Swagga and Chyna. There were no words to place on her lips as she watched Swagga bend Chyna over the back of the sofa. Without blinking, she watched him shove Chyna's tiny skirt up. She recorded every second of Swagga fucking Chyna roughly up the ass.

Trevon woke up slowly. Being that he had a vague memory of where he was, he sat up quickly. The sudden move sent his head spinning. He wanted to lie back down. He held his throbbing head in his hands, placing his feet on the floor.

"Finally up, huh?" Chyna asked as he entered the bedroom.

Trevon remembered now. He rubbed his face then rose to his feet.

"If I knew you couldn't handle that drink, I would have given you something lighter."

"What happened?" Trevon's voice was deep and groggy.

"What happened? You passed out on me and fell asleep."

"Bullshit! What time is it?

"Honey, it's five minutes past nine."

Trevon looked at his watch. *What the fuck? I've been out for . . . almost four damn hours.* "Ummm . . . did we ummm—do anything?"

Chyna stood in the bathroom putting on a pair of earrings. "Um . . . no."

"Damn, I can't believe this!" Trevon sat back down. *I guess I was just dreaming and shit. My head is killing me.*

"Don't be so down on yourself." Chyna walked back into the bedroom. "I'll give you another chance, but not today."

Trevon stood back up. *This is embarrassing!* "I guess I'll get up with you later."

Chyna walked Trevon to the front door.

Trevon took a moment to gather himself behind the wheel of his XJL. Closing his eyes, he turned the engine on then turned the drive selector knob to R. He was not drunk, just tired. Backing out of the driveway, he turned the system on, filling the ride with "Say Something" by Drake. Once he was on the road, he slid the sunroof open.

He stopped at Burger King to get something on his stomach. Pulling from the drive-thru, his cell phone started to ring. Seeing that it was Kendra calling, he answered.

"Hello?"

"Hey you!" Kendra gushed. "You—sound tired. Did I wake you up?"

"Nah. But I just got out the bed though."

"Oh. Well, I finally got some free time, so I thought I'd give you a call. You doing okay?"

"I'm good. Just hating I have to stay at this motel tonight," he said, switching lanes.

"Glad you mentioned that. Good news! You can move into the apartment on Tuesday of next week."

"Good. I guess I need to look at some furniture and stuff."

"Let me help you," she offered. "I'm free all day tomorrow."

Trevon was open to spending more time with Kendra. They agreed to call each other tomorrow. Trevon made it to

the motel and ate his food on the firm bed while watching
TV. He still would not break down to call LaToria. Her last
parting words were still a resonance in his mind. *All of it
was a gotdamn mistake! I don't love you! I don't give a
fuck about you, Trevon! I hate you!* Picking up his cell
phone, he deleted LaToria's picture.

Bayview Condo, Fisher Island

Swagga had taken a long hot shower after his time
with Chyna. It was now 10 p.m. and he was back visiting
Cindy. He knew she was upset from the issue at the beach,
so he figured he would drop in to see her. Yaffa was with
him, visibly upset that Swagga had wandered off earlier
without letting him know.

Swagga told himself that his involvement with Chyna
was a one-time affair. Reaching the thirtieth floor, he
pulled out his secure key card for Cindy's room.

Yaffa stood behind him with his eyes scanning the
hallways as Swagga slid the card through the scanner.

"Why this shit ain't open?" Swagga tried the card
twice more then tested the polished chrome door latch.
Locked. "I know this is the right card!" Swagga tried the
card once more then banged on the door. Placing his ear
against the door, he heard the faint sounds of music.

"Call 'er," Yaffa suggested.

Swagga snatched his mobile phone out of his fitted
jeans and called Cindy.

"What!" she answered on the first ring.

Swagga took the phone from his ear to look at it.
What! Dis bitch must got me mixed up wit' somebody else.
"Bitch! Open the fuckin' door. That's what!" Swagga
ended the call and then waited for the door to open.

217

Swagga stomped his way inside the moment Cindy opened the door. He became vexed when he saw a white dude kicked back on the sofa with a bottle of Heineken between his long legs.

"What the fuck wrong with that card reader?" Swagga shouted.

Cindy folded her arms with her eyes beamed on Swagga. "Ain't shit wrong with it. Your card has been cut off."

Swagga balled up his fist. "Bitch! You trippin'! I paid for this roof over your head! And who the fuck is he!" Swagga pointed toward Cindy's guest.

"None of your business!" she spat.

Swagga walked up in her face. "Ain't in the mood fo' no games, bitch! You fuckin' that clown? Huh?"

Cindy glowered back at him. "The games haven't even started yet!"

Swagga grabbed her by the upper arm and shoved her toward the bedroom. Cindy's guest started to protest, but remained silent when Yaffa brandished his .45.

"You don't own me!" Cindy shouted as Swagga shoved her on the bed.

"I own this condo! That Range you drive. Bitch, I even bought the clothes and shoes you wear!" Swagga slammed the door shut. He rushed up on her with his fist clenched. "What the fuck you tryin' to play me for!"

"You played yourself!" she shouted.

"What are you mad about? Some dumb shit I bet!"

"Fuck you!"

Swagga kicked the lamp over. "You know what! I'll just replace your dumb ass. How about that? You and your Justin Timberlake looking ass cracker can get the fuck out! And toss me the keys to the truck."

"Ain't going no fuckin' where, nigga!"

Swagga backhanded Cindy across the face. "Bitch!" he said, wrapping his hand in her dreads. He yanked her up, causing her to cry out in pain. "I don't care how much of my *black* dick you suck, fuck or take up your funky ass. Don't ever feel you have the green light to call me a nigga!"

Cindy felt her dreads being pulled from her scalp. She pleaded with him to let go of her dreads.

"Now get the fuck out!" He pushed her to the floor.

Cindy got up slowly. Her eyes went to the pillow on the bed. *I swear I want to put a hot one in his ass!* She could do just that with the .380. She thought of the plan that she and Chyna had in the making. Swagga's unannounced visit to see Chyna had been perfect.

Cindy was going to blackmail Swagga to keep his affair with Chyna from going public. She could stand to lose the condo and the Range Rover.

When I'm done juicing this nigga, I'ma be in a mansion and pushing a Bentley!

"Fuck you! You can have all your shit!" Cindy screamed at him.

LaToria was content to be back in Miami. Needing to clear her mind, she had not driven straight home from the Miami International Airport. Cruising down the street with "Right Thru Me" by Nicki Minaj, had her thoughts on Trevon. The trip to New York with Jurnee had done little to fade Trevon from her mind. If anything, she grew fonder of him. She was missing Trevon, but her solid stubbornness prevented her from calling him. She knew she was in the wrong.

I just don't know how to deal with how I feel.

She was sitting at a red light on Biscayne Boulevard when she spotted Swagga's midnight blue Bentley GT. She flicked her hi-beams on and off to get his attention.

Yaffa noticed the lights on the shiny black Escalade. "Yo, ain't that Kandi's truck?"

Swagga's mood flipped instantly. He sat up. "Yeah! Turn around, yo!"

LaToria saw the brake lights light up on the GT in her side mirror. When the light turned green, she pulled off then slowed to turn into a parking lot. A few minutes later, she saw the Bentley pulling up behind her. She got out.

"Hey, Yaffa," she said as he walked up to Swagga.

Yaffa made sure no funny shit was popping off, then walked back to sit on the hood of the GT.

Swagga found himself stuck on words in front of LaToria. She was looking fly in jeans and a black tank top.

"You playing hard to get, huh?" she said.

Swagga looked confused. "Am I missing something? Last time I saw you—"

"I was just tripping, okay? Let it be in the past."

"Oh, so you gonna give me another chance?"

She smiled. "Only when you can focus on me and only me."

Swagga looked at the traffic on Biscayne, then down at LaToria's sexy feet. Here was his chance to correct the wrong he had done breaking her heart. He cleared his throat. "Yo, I was really feeling you. When I asked you to marry me, I was for real. I just let these niggas clown me and I made the wrong choice by fuckin' with that bitch Déjà Pink."

"And what other reasons?"

"I can't front. It's a hard dime to swallow about the fact you do porn. It's hard for me to think what we have is real if you fuckin' other niggas."

"Swagga, why didn't you voice this to me? You kept your feelings inside and straight up made a fool of me by fucking with Déjà Pink."

"Yeah, I know I was in the wrong. But for all it's worth, I'm sorry."

"I don't believe you." She smiled.

Swagga took the chance by stepping closer. He eased his hands on her hips. "It's true. I'm really sorry."

LaToria allowed his hands to slip down to her ass.

"You know I miss you," he said, pouring it on. He wanted her badly. "I'll ex all these other hoes out and put my all in your hands. Word up. I wanna make it like it was and even more, baby."

"How will I know you're serious?"

Swagga pulled her closer. "Stop doing porn and marry me."

LaToria had to be honest with herself. *Do I really feel like this? I'm bugging. I really miss Trevon.* "Let's not rush things, okay?"

"I can deal with that. But listen—" He squeezed her ass. "Can I come see you tonight?"

"Swagga, it's too soon to be—"

"Chill, baby. I just wanna dip my tongue in that sweet thang between your legs."

She laughed. "Whatever! I know that tired game. You'll break me off, get me all worked up then next you'll be fucking me."

"Nah. Word up. I just wanna eat it. Shit, tie me up and sit on my face."

"Hmmmm. I like that idea."

"So what's up?"

"I'm for real, Swagga. You ain't getting none and don't even ask me to suck your dick."

Swagga couldn't care less. His infatuation for her was that strong. LaToria caved in and told him he could come to her crib.

"I'ma ride wit' you. I'll tell Yaffa to come pick me up in the morning."

Yaffa knew Swagga would be okay at LaToria's crib. He tried to caution Swagga about dealing with LaToria, but his words went unheeded.

Swagga showed his yearning for LaToria the moment they stepped inside her crib. He removed all of her clothes while they stood in the living room. Sitting her on the sofa, he told her to slide to the edge and open her legs. LaToria felt a small touch of guilt as Swagga circled his tongue around her nipples. *Why am I doing this? I should be giving myself to Trevon.* She gripped the edge of the sofa as Swagga slid two fingers in and out of her pussy. He stroked her slowly while licking all over her big titties.

"Eat it," she moaned. "Suck on my pussy lips."

Swagga licked his way down her body. "Pussy wet as hell!" he said, pulling his fingers out of her. He got down on the floor then turned her over on her knees. Pulling her cheeks open, he slid his tongue slowly over her asshole. He waited until she begged him to stop until he licked his way to her pussy.

Swagga broke his personal record for oral sex. For thirty straight minutes, he licked and sucked on her pussy and ass. After three orgasms, she was deeply in the mood. She was sucking her own nipple as Swagga took his clothes off. Her pussy was dripping wet. He stood above her stroking his big dick. He rubbed it over her nipples.

"Help me out, baby," he moaned. "Please, I wanna be inside you."

LaToria wrapped her hand around his dick. With her free hand, she reached inside her purse for a rubber.

Swagga rocked in and out of LaToria doggy style while smacking her bouncing ass. Sweat coated her body. He took his time fucking her, leaving not an inch of her soft body untouched.

"Dis my pussy!" he moaned as he cupped her swinging breasts.

LaToria felt regret with each stroke. She knew she had pushed Trevon away. Even with Swagga fucking her on the floor, she still had Trevon in her heart and on her mind.

CHAPTER
TWENTY-EIGHT
October 1, 2011
Saturday, 2:30 p.m. - Miami, Florida

Kendra had the urge to fuck Trevon today, but she was afraid to act on that urge. She sat silent in the passenger seat of his XJL on the trip back from Hollywood, Florida. The two had spent most of the day looking at furniture. "Why are you so quiet?" he asked.

She turned in the seat. "Just thinking about you."

"Good or bad?"

"Hmmmm, I'll say good." She smiled at him.

"Thanks for helping me pick out this furniture today."

"You're more than welcome, Trevon."

He glanced at her then back to the road. She was dressed in a pair of peach leather stilettos, white Capri jeans and a peach strappy blouse that outlined her breasts.

"So, what's up for tonight?" he asked, switching lanes.

"I don't know. I was hoping you could tell me. You're the one with all the free time."

Here it comes. Now she's about to ask if I have a job. "Umm, maybe we could go out to eat?"

"I'm on a diet."

"Okay. How about a movie?"

"Nothing good is showing."

"Let's do the dog track."

"I don't gamble."

"The zoo?"

"Don't feel like walking."

"The beach?"

"Too hot."

Trevon laughed. "I give up. How about you make a suggestion."

Kendra rubbed her hands together. "Let's go to a play?"

"Too boring," he said, balling up his face.

"Miniature golf?"

"I hate golf."

"Bowling."

"Nah."

Kendra crossed her arms. "You're just saying no to all of my ideas because I said no to yours."

"That would be—childish," he said, grinning.

Kendra took a deep breath. *Okay, here I go.* "I have one more idea," she said, taking off her glasses.

"What is it?"

Kendra turned to face him, then slid the glasses back on. "Turn off at the next exit and let's get a nice room and just . . . do what comes naturally."

Kendra made her intentions known for getting the room by her actions. It started with her pushing him up against the door when they entered the suite. She kissed him hard, pulling his shirt up out of his slacks. Trevon returned her actions by squeezing and groping her soft ass. She felt raunchy as she shoved a hand down into his slacks. He moaned when her hand wrapped around his dick. This was the part he enjoyed the most. The beginning.

"Do to me," she said and gasped against his lips, "what you do for a living."

"Repeat what you just said again?" Trevon asked, wondering if she knew about his occupation.

Kendra squeezed his large dick and then released her grip. She took a step back and removed her clothes. "I know what you do for a living, Trevon."

"How? But—"

"I've seen the film, okay? We can talk about it later. But right now . . . I want some dick. No, I want *all* of it!" she said, taking her lace trimmed bra off.

Trevon took his shirt off, never removing his eyes away from Kendra. She only broke the stare to look down at his dick when he stepped out of his boxers.

Oh. My gawd! He's HUGE! Kendra walked up on Trevon. Her free breasts swayed. She kept her thong and stilettos on. Trevon lowered his eyes and saw a wet spot in front of her thong. She squatted in front of him, taking his long dick into her hands. Gently, she began to stroke it.

"Kendra," he moaned, lying his hands on her soft shoulders.

"So big," she purred with both hands working along the length of his manhood.

Closing her eyes, she parted her soft lips, easing them over the swollen tip of his hot, juicy dick. She felt propelled to taste him right away.

"Please," he murmured. "Don't tease me, baby."

Kendra eased more of him into her mouth. She took half of it in and slowly slid it back out. When the tip touched her lips, she eased it back in.

Trevon lifted one foot up on the bed then slightly pumped into her mouth. Kendra took him deeper. Her pace was slow. In and out.

"Yesss . . . suck it good. Swallow my dick all the way down. Ahhhh . . . now lick it for me," he gasped as she swallowed his flesh.

Kendra was shocked at how easily she obeyed Trevon. She licked all over his dick, mainly on the tip to taste his precum. It was delicious.

Trevon closed his eyes as Kendra took him back inside her mouth. She sucked him for a few more minutes then stood up. Trevon took control by telling her to lie down on the bed. Her large dark nipples stood at attention.

"Slide your ass off the edge a bit. Yeah, like that." Trevon grabbed her ankles and held them up in the air. "Slide your thong to the side."

"Forgetting something?" she said. "Look in my purse."

Trevon looked at his bare dick. "Damn, my bad."

Kendra slid her thong off as Trevon pulled a box of condoms out of her purse.

When he returned, she played with his dick to get him back up. She slid back off the bed as his hands held her legs up high. Trevon gently pushed her legs back to see how flexible she was.

"Put it in!" she gasped when her knees touched her shoulders. Her wet pussy was fully exposed. Her outer lips were slightly swollen.

Trevon told her to guide him in. She grabbed his dick, slipping it up and down her wet opening.

"Mmmmm," she moaned. "This feels so good!"

"Damn . . . pussy tight!" Trevon felt the tightness giving away as he pushed himself inside her.

"Oh, shit! Oh shit! Oh shit!" She pulled at the sheets as his dick parted her walls.

Kendra was afraid to look down to see how much he had left to put in. He was already touching spots that no man had ever touched.

"GOD!" she groaned, tracing her lips with her tongue.

Trevon looked down when his stomach touched the back of her legs.

He was deep and solid inside her. "You want this dick?"

"Yes!"

"Fast or slow?"

"Slow! Please, start slow." She looked up into his face as he slowly pulled out.

Trevon long dicked her. He felt so right being inside her tight pussy. He started out slow. In and out, he slid his dick into his parole officer.

"Uh! Uh! Yessss . . . give it to me, Trevon!" she moaned. "Mmmmmm . . . dick so good!"

She felt her juices flowing between her ass cheeks. Trevon was working it.

He fucked her at a faster pace, loving how her ass bounced. Kendra took the dick with pain and pleasure. In and out he ran dick up in her with her juicy ass hanging off the bed. Kendra's pussy snapped and popped around his dick. Slowing down, he slid her up on the bed, then pushed back inside her. Her eyes rolled easily as he started pounding at her body. She felt his balls slapping her ass. Her ankles were up by his ears. Looking into his face, she moaned endlessly as he fucked her. Her nails dug into his shoulders. Beneath him, she tightened her pussy around his sweet pumping dick. Trevon was lost in the sensation of fucking Kendra. He paid no mind to her nails raking his back apart. Reaching back, he squeezed her ass, still pumping and switching up his strokes and tempo. Not wanting to cum too soon, he slowed to a stop and turned her over.

She held her breath as he slid his hard meat deep inside her. Face down, ass up, he fucked her thoroughly. Gripping the pillow, she put a dip in her back. Trevon gripped, rubbed and smacked her stretched-marked jiggling ass. She felt herself reaching that much needed climax as he long stroked her from behind. Her move to fuck Trevon was turning out to be a wise move. She was out only to cater to her needs. No emotions were being dealt with.

"Yessss! Give me all that dick!" she blurted with his dick still running up in her.

Chills danced up and down her arms as she enjoyed the sensation of her pussy being stretched. "Pussy good, ain't it?" she said, breathing hard.Trevon had a firm grip on her waist, fucking her as if his freedom was on the line.

"Let"—Kendra gasped, pulling at the sheets—"me ride you!"

Trevon forced himself to slow down and stop. Pulling out, he looked down at her juicy pussy, then lowered his mouth to taste her.

"Oooohhhh baby! Lick it! Mmmmm suck it . . . gawd yes!" Kendra cried as he sucked on her pussy. "Nigga, don't stop!"

Trevon wormed his tongue deep into her runny pussy, slurping and sucking. She wiggled her butt against his face, pulling at the pillowcase. "Oooohhhhh. I'm fintah cum! Cum all . . . in your mouth!" She pushed her pussy hard against his flicking tongue. Her eyes were shut tight, toes stiff in her stilettos. A long moan ran past her lips as she reached her climax. Trevon freaked her by letting her juices fall into his mouth. Catching her breath, she turned over to her back and pulled him on top of her. She licked all around his lips and chin, tasting and smelling herself. Pulling his condom off, she motioned him to push his dick between her breasts. Licking her lips, she pushed her titties together. Trevon braced himself on the wall. His knees were under her armpits and his dick between her breasts. She teased him by flicking her tongue over his tip when it neared her lips. He found a slow pace and fucked her breasts. She begged him to cum as his dick kept bumping into her chin. It did not take long for him to get his rocks off. Kendra released her titties, then grabbed his dick to shove it down her throat. Palming his ass, she swallowed his dick until he came in her mouth. She held no regrets.

Kendra kept it all the way one hundred with him when they later took a shower together. Trevon was surprised to hear her say that all she wanted was the dick. It was nothing personal nor emotional.

"I can't believe I just had sex with a real porn star!" Kendra said, drying off in the bathroom.

"I'm not a star," Trevon said, reaching for a towel.

"You will be with that monster you have between your legs."

"Maybe we could make our own movie one day. Oh, nevermind. I can't do any videos outside of my contract with Amatory."

"Wouldn't matter. That's one thing I will never do." Kendra could not pull her eyes off his swinging dick. The dick was seriously good to her, but not good enough to cause her to deal with emotions. Truth be told, she would be willing to fuck him again, but she wanted to be sure he understood the foundation of their secret sexual relationship. Kendra would not let her lust come before her job. The risk she was taking now was bad enough as it was.

Leaving the room, he took her back to her SUV parked a block away from his motel. She waved goodbye and told him she would be in touch.

Back in the motel room, he sat alone on the bed watching TV. He felt no connection for Kendra. This made him realize that sex with emotions was a powerful element. The latter is how he felt toward LaToria. In the nicest of terms, Kendra expressed that she was not dealing with any emotions toward Trevon. *I need more out of life.* He turned the TV off. *There's gotta be more to life.*

Swagga was making it a new game to sneak out of his mansion without Yaffa at his side. He made it back home around nine in the morning after Yaffa picked him up from Kandi's crib. He told Yaffa all the vivid details of how he fucked Kandi and she was back on his dick. It was ten minutes past 10 p.m. when Swagga heard the shower running in Yaffa's bedroom. That was Swagga's cue to get missing. Laughing, he sped off in his Bentley GT knowing Yaffa would bitch and moan when he returned. Pushing the Bentley through the streets, he wondered how Yaffa would react about the truth behind Chyna. Deep in his own scheming plots, Swagga had no idea about Chyna hooking up with Yaffa on the down low.

Unknown to Swagga, Yaffa had caught on to how he was sneaking out. His actions made Yaffa suspicious. *What is this fool doing that he doesn't want me to know about? I'm willing to die for this nigga and he out keeping secrets!*

Yaffa kept a good distance from Swagga's GT as he followed him to an upscale neighborhood in Coral Gables. BMWs, Audis and Benzs were parked in the driveways of the expensive looking homes. Turning his headlights out, he pulled to the curb when he saw Swagga coming to a stop up ahead. Swagga slowed down then turned into a driveway. Yaffa waited a few seconds then pulled away from the curb. Driving at a creeping speed, he spotted Swagga standing under a light at the front door.

"Now ain't this some shit," Yaffa said, noticing Chyna's BMW in the driveway.

Yaffa knew what was up. "Nigga creepin'." Yaffa drove off. He was not feeling how Chyna had lied to him. He had asked to see her, but she fronted like she was not feeling well. Yaffa hated being lied to.

I got a trick for that ho next time she calls me.

"Where the tape at?" Swagga asked Chyna. The two were at the kitchen table.

"It's in a safe place," Chyna replied.

Swagga leaned back in the chair crossing his arms. "When can I see it?"

"Where is my money?"

"Ho, I wanna see if you fucked that nigga or not!"

"I told you I did it. You saw him on my bed before you left."

Swagga wanted the film now. "Look, I'll have your money tomorrow, okay?"

"All of it?"

"Fifty stacks."

"Yes, fifty thousand." Chyna looked at Swagga for a moment. "Why are you so—out to clown Trevon? What did he do to you?"

"Nigga just in the way."

"How?"

Swagga looked around the kitchen. "He's fucking my ex."

"Your ex?"

"Yeah, he was fucking Kandi. The porn star."

"I heard about you two dating and then you got caught cheating."

"Yeah, but I'ma get her back."

"What about Cindy?"

"Fuck that ho! She ain't shit."

Chyna stood up and went to the sink. "So, all this is over you wanting to get back up with Kandi?"

"You can say that," he said, looking at Chyna's tight pert ass.

Chyna turned the water on to rinse out a glass. "Why did you fuck me, Swagga?"

"Yo! I came here to see the tape, not talk about no bullshit."

Chyna turned the water off. "How is it bullshit? I done sucked your dick twice and let you fuck me up the ass! Now I wanna know what's up between us?"

"Ain't shit up, ho!" He jumped to his feet. "Got me mixed up, ho!"

"You can kill that fake ass gangsta shit!"

"Look, just have that tape ready for me tomorrow!"

Chyna pushed from the sink and walked up to Swagga. "Fuck me before you leave. Please," Chyna pleaded, grabbing Swagga's shirt.

Swagga tried to push Chyna's hands away.

"Just one more time, Swagga," Chyna pleaded. "Can't nobody fuck me like you can."

"Bitch, you buggin'."

"Am I?" Chyna reached down and grabbed his dick. "Why is it hard? You been looking at my ass? I know you want to fuck me again. This time you won't have to rush. Come on, baby. Fuck me tonight." Chyna leaned in and slowly licked Swagga on his chin.

Cindy had to give Chyna an A plus in the game of seduction. She was hiding in the dark living room filming Swagga and Chyna. When she saw Chyna stroking Swagga's dick, she knew Chyna would break him down. *Look at this dumb ass nigga! LaToria sure as hell ain't gonna want his gay ass back once she see's this. Yeah, suck that dick, Chyna. Make his bitch ass moan like the bitch he is!* She zoomed in on Chyna with the tiny palm-sized Hi-Def camcorder. The focus was on the maleness dangling between Chyna's legs.

CHAPTER
TWENTY-NINE
October 6, 2011
Thursday 4:30 p.m. - Miami, Florida

Five days later, life for Trevon was on a positive level. Yesterday, he was given the keys to his own two-bedroom apartment. It had a small fenced in yard, front and back, with all of the windows and doors barred. He would have to get used to the bars, but he knew it was needed in the neighborhood. Kendra had assisted him with getting the utilities turned on. She also sat with him and showed him how to pay the bills. Janelle had dropped by yesterday to check on him. She gave him a housewarming gift in the form of a $1,000 gift card from Target. She said she was happy for him and encouraged him to stay positive.

Last night he had fallen asleep at peace under a roof and in a bed he could call his own. The black and green fabric furniture was brand new along with the 52-inch plasma TV. He was not living the baller status, but he was far from being homeless. He was in the living room talking to his sister, Angie when there was a knock at his front door.

"Hey, sis, let me call you back, okay. Love you." Trevon got up from the recliner and went to the door. Peeking through the blinds, he saw Kendra's state owned Ford Taurus. He unlocked the door.

"Hey handsome," she said. Smiling, she entered the air-conditioned apartment. She was dressed for work. On her cargo belt, she carried her weapon, cuffs, mace and two pairs of rubber gloves.

"You ain't bring me nothing to eat?" he kidded with her.

Kendra laughed. "You better learn how to cook and stop hitting those fast food joints." She nodded at the KFC box on the kitchen table.

"I'll learn. So what's up?" He sat back down on the recliner.

"Just dropped by to see how you're doing. I have another guy on my case load that stays in this area. I'll write this up as an official surprise visit, so no one else will try to give you a hard time."

"Thanks."

"I see you moved the furniture around again." She stood in front of the TV looking around.

"It's more roomy this way."

She nodded. "Let me see your bedroom." She smiled. "Gotta check for drugs and guns."

"Yeah, right." He grinned, getting back to his feet.

"You burning incense? Smells good in here." She sniffed at the sweet scent while walking down the hallway behind him.

"Nah. Just rubbed some Muslim Oil on the air conditioner vents. A habit from prison."

"I might have to try that."

Trevon entered his bedroom coming to a stop at the foot of the bed.

"Nice," Kendra said. "The color set we picked out looks good in—"

Her words were broken when a small black blur scampered out of the bathroom and under the bed. Kendra took a step back with a scared look on her face. *A rat!*

"Trevon, I think you have a rodent issue!"

Trevon shook his head. He squatted. "Rex. C'mere, boy!"

Kendra jumped when Trevon's puppy darted out from under the bed.

"This is Rex." Trevon stood up with the squirming puppy licking his chin.

"Awwww, he's adorable. What kind of dog is it?" She reached over to rub the puppy on its shiny black coat.

"A bull mastiff. I just got him today at the mall." Trevon placed Rex back on the floor. The puppy scampered off into the hallway.

"I'm really happy for you." She sat on his bed. "I don't want to see you back in prison."

"That makes two of us." He held up two fingers, sitting down beside her.

She smiled. "Have you broken this bed in yet?" She bounced up and down.

"I just moved in yesterday."

"So." She laughed. "Who's your next door neighbor?"

Trevon shrugged. "Haven't met them yet?"

"Just be careful, okay? I know you're going to do you, but don't get caught up with the wrong crowd. Doing porn—stick with it is all I can tell you." She stood and looked at her watch, knowing she could not stay too long.

"I want to go see my sister up in North Carolina."

Kendra stood up. "Let me think about it, okay?"

Trevon slid his hands down her waist.

"I can violate your parole for touching me like this, Mr. Harrison." She grinned.

"Yeah, and if you do, who's gonna tap this pussy like me?"

Kendra pushed his hands away, laughing. "Let me get out of here before I start tripping."

Trevon stood up and grabbed ahold of her ass.

"I need a favor," she said, rubbing his chest. "My baby's father bought a new bed for my daughter and I want you to help me put it together."

"When?"

"Ummm, come by around nine o'clock. Can you make it?"

"Yeah."

"And bring some swimming trunks. We can get in the pool when we're done. If you want to."

"Will I see you in a thong bikini?" He palmed her ass hard.

Kendra giggled. "If you'll behave, I might swim naked." She slid a hand down to grab his dick. "I want a whole lot more of what you got between your legs."

At the same time, LaToria and Jurnee were having a quiet meal at Scarpetta on Miami Beach.

"I made a mistake," LaToria said, picking at her food with a worried look on her face.

"How?"

"By getting back involved with Swagga. He's been up under me ever since we got back from our trip."

"Are you two fucking?"

LaToria lowered her eyes to the table. "Yes. But I haven't done it with him in two days. He's been calling me all day, but I won't answer his calls."

Jurnee took off her shades. "Why did you give him another chance?"

"I don't know. But I sure as hell regret it."

"Been thinking about Trevon?" Jurnee asked. "And don't lie."

"Day and night. I want him back."

"Back? I thought you two were never together."

237

"You know what I mean. I just—he got me so open, Jurnee. I've never felt like this toward no man. I—even told him about my past and stuff."

"Everything?" Jurnee asked.

"I didn't hold nothing back. I just felt so comfortable with him. And it ain't just the dick."

Jurnee held up her hand, grinning. "I didn't say a word."

LaToria dropped her spoon on the plate. "I miss him, too," she pouted.

"Call him."

"No."

"See, you're acting stupid again. You say you want to be with him, but you won't even call him! Seriously, how do you feel about him?"

"He's special. What I feel—like I said before—I've never felt this way toward any nigga! I think about him in my dreams! I—"

"You're in love, LaToria. Just come out and face it, okay?"

LaToria had no idea how to deal with matters of the heart. "What do I do?"

Jurnee looked across the table at her lover. She truly wanted to see LaToria happy. "Here's what you're *going* to do. Go and see him at his place. Talk to him and let him know you're sorry for kicking him out. Then speak from your heart, girl. Just tell him the truth."

Up in Fort Lauderdale, Swagga was getting pissed by not being able to reach Kandi. Sitting in the recording booth, his mobile phone rang. Thinking and hoping it was Kandi, he answered before the first ring ended.

"Yeah?"

"Hello, may I speak to Swagga?" The male's voice was Caucasian with a country twang. He took the phone from his ear to look at the caller ID screen. The number was blocked.

"Dis Swagga! Who is this?" he said, trying to recognize the male voice.

"I can be a friend or I can make your life a living hell."

"Fuck you! Suck my dick!" Swagga ended the call. He took off his platinum bracelet, then turned the bass up on the soundboard. Behind him, his phone rang again. This time it showed an incoming media message. There was a text message that read: *Don't do that again!*

We know your secret. Want to keep it that way? View this clip and we'll talk.

10/6/11 THUR 8:51 p.m.

Swagga quickly pulled up the video clip. His anger turned to shame when he saw himself fucking Chyna in the ass. The mobile phone rang in his hands. The number was blocked. He sat down on the bed. Taking a deep breath, he answered the call.

"How much you want?"

"Now, we're talking?"

"Just tell me what you want and I'll get it."

"Here's the deal. If you try to play me, I'll crush you. Your secret will be on all of the websites from YOUTUBE to FACEBOOK. All of them!"

"Yo, I'm not gonna play you. Just tell me what you want, okay?"

"I want two million. That's not too much for you to handle, now is it?"

"No, just talk to me. I'll pay you the money."

"You have twenty-four hours. Starting now. I want the money in this form. I want one million in hundreds. Half a million in fifties and the last half a million in twenties. Do I need to repeat it?"

"Nah, I got it. A mill in hundred, half in fifties and another half in twenties."

"Correct."

"Yo, how will I know you won't leak that film after I pay you?"

"That would be foolish. This two million is just the start. I'll call you soon."

Swagga lowered his head. *How could this have happened? I got to pay this motherfucker!* Swagga replayed the clip. By the unsteady frame, he knew someone had hid and filmed him with Chyna.

Bitch set me up!

Coral Gables, Florida

Stan, the concierge from Cindy's condo ended the call with Swagga.

"See! I knew this would work!" Cindy stood behind Stan rubbing her hands up and down his bare chest. Stan no longer had to fantasize about fucking Cindy. He was given that pleasure only hours before Swagga showed up and kicked Cindy out.

"What about Trevon?" Chyna asked, sitting at the table with a plate of chicken and rice.

"He doesn't have any money. He's a nobody. But he sure as hell got some good dick!"

"I bet it was. Too bad I didn't get my chance," Chyna playfully pouted.

Cindy had come up with the plan to blackmail Swagga. She knew he would do *anything* to keep his new homosexual tendencies from the public. *Serves his black ass right for kicking me to the curb!*

"Think he'll give us the money?" Chyna asked as Cindy sat down at the table.

"Positive!" Cindy replied. "His ass would've paid more, but this is just for starters."

Chyna hoped Cindy knew what she was doing. *All I want is my money to get this operation done. I'm not too in favor of all this blackmailing mess.*

Back at Swagga's mansion, Yaffa was finding it a challenge not to confront Swagga about Chyna. Until he had the true facts, he was ignoring all of Chyna's phone calls. Swagga was down in the studio with his producer. Yaffa sat alone in the kitchen cleaning one of his handguns. His mind was working on why Swagga was being so secretive with dealing with Chyna. He was dropping oil into the barrel when Swagga came running down the hall and out of sight. Another set of feet followed him.

"Yo!" Yaffa jumped to his feet.

D-Hot slid to a halt, bending down with his hands on his knees.

"What the fuck is goin' on?"

"Don't know!" D-Hot panted hard out of breath. "He was in the booth. Got—got a phone call. Then he—he just snapped. Ran out of the studio. Something ain't right."

"Shit!" Yaffa patted his pockets for his keys. "Damn!" He snatched his .380 off the table. His keys to his SUV were in his bedroom. Yaffa was rushing past D-Hot when he motioned him to stop.

"What?"

"Swagga. He had a gun in his hand."

"Muthafuck!" Yaffa moved as fast as he could toward the garage. He was slowed down by having to punch in the security code to enter the garage. Once inside, he headed straight for Swagga's candy orange Audi R8 GT. Bringing the 560 horses to life with a twist of the key made a racy rumble. As the garage door slowly slid up, Yaffa pulled out his cell phone. Working quickly, he pulled up the GPS tracking app to find out where Swagga's Bentley GT was heading. Once it showed up on the screen, he tossed the phone aside then put the Audi in gear. Smoke billowed from the rear tires, but Yaffa locked the brakes when he pulled up beside his Lexus. Jumping out, he ran around his SUV and yanked the door open. He hit a hidden switch under the dash and a concealed floor panel flipped over in the back of the Lexus. Slamming the door, he rushed to the rear door and reached inside the stash spot, pulling out a deadly looking weapon with considerable length and power.

Back inside the Audi, he looked at his phone and saw the icon for Swagga's Bentley heading south on I-95. Revving the RPMs he smoked the rear tires with hopes that he could catch up with Swagga.

Swagga manhandled the Bentley GT, weaving past cars at triple digit speeds. Anger was pushing him to react. He could not let his secret get out about Chyna. Glancing down at the indigo blue speedometer, he saw the needle sitting on 150 mph. Racing toward Coral Gables, he was tempted to push the ride up to its top speed of 200 mph.

All this bullshit over that sucka ass nigga Trevon! With no set plan, he slowed to 88 mph. He knew he would get arrested if he was caught speeding and carrying a gun. He picked up the Glock 19, thinking deeply if he would have the heart to use it.

CHAPTER
THIRTY

Kendra rushed to the front door when she saw the car lights in the driveway. She was alone in her four-bedroom home in southwest Miami. Trevon was five minutes late, but Kendra would not stress. She met him at the front door and greeted him with a hug.

"Glad you could make it!" She held his hand and led him into her house. "Ready to do some hard labor?"

"Putting a bed together shouldn't be too hard."

"I hope it isn't. I want it up tonight so I can surprise my baby with it."

"Where is she now?"

"With my niece." She stopped at her daughter's bedroom. Trevon looked inside and saw the materials for the bed.

"It's one of those fairytale canopy beds."

Trevon took off his lightweight jacket then looked at the time. 9:08 p.m.

"Let's knock it out," Kendra said and dove into the task.

She surprised Trevon with her knowledge of tools. Whatever tool he requested, she handed him the correct one. Kendra was dressed for the job. Boots, sweatpants and a solid colored T-shirt. Trevon's gear was a mix of boots, jeans and a white wife beater. The two made the job fun. With that being true, they finished the job within forty minutes.

"Beautiful!" Kendra stood at the foot of the canopy bed. "My baby is going to love it! Now I won't have to force her to go to bed." She turned to face Trevon. "Thank you for your help."

"It's nothing," he said, being modest.

She reached for his hand. "Come." Kendra led Trevon back into the hallway. . Reaching a closed door, she stopped and turned to face him.

"Trevon," she said, squeezing his hand. "It's been a long time since I had a man in *my* bed." She looked off for a moment then looked at his face. "It's nothing based on emotions, but at the same time, I don't just let any man in my bed. I—when I saw that film of you, I just had this strong urge to be with you."

"Do you regret what we did at the room?"

"No."

Trevon took a step closer. "Close your eyes."

She did so without thought. *Damn, he got me so gone! But I like it.*

"Take all of your clothes off. Strip. Everything. And keep your eyes closed."

Kendra started with her boots. *Mmmm, this some ol' new shit!*

Trevon watched as she teasingly slid the sweatpants off. His dick grew at the sight of her pink panties. Next, she pulled the T-shirt off to reveal the matching pink bra. Kendra reached behind her back to unhook her bra. She took it off slowly. Her nipples were stiff.

"Keep going," he ordered.

Kendra was breathing hard as her body began to tingle. *I can play my games, too!* She kept her eyes closed. Turning her back to his voice, she bent slightly at the waist and slid her panties off. To her satisfaction, she heard him groan.

"Keep 'em closed." He eased up behind her and squeezed her breasts. He kissed her on her shoulder.

Kendra licked her lips, pressing her ass back against him.

"I love your big titties!" he groaned into her ear. "Can I fuck 'em tonight?"

"Yes!" She nodded.

"You have a nice ass, too!" He moved one hand from her breast to her bare ass. "It's so soft—and smooth and round."

Kendra gasped as Trevon's finger slid down her soft belly. She knew she was going to fuck him again when his fingers pushed through her thick, bushy pussy hairs. She parted her legs so he could touch her.

"You got some good pussy," he whispered against her ear. With one hand rubbing her titty, he used the other to dip two fingers inside her.

"Mmmmm, Trevon!" She squirmed. "Gimme that dick! Omigoodness. I'm so hot right now."

"You wanna ride this dick tonight?"

"Yesss!"

"Wanna do it doggy style, too?"

"Mmm hmmm."

"Damn. Feel how hard my dick is!"

Kendra reached down and behind her. "I want it!"

Trevon spun her around, scanning her juicy frame up and down. She was all woman. Kendra pushed her bedroom door open and pulled Trevon inside. At the foot of her large bed she helped him undress. Her bedroom was set in a relaxing mood with tan and white sheets and covers on the bed. Trevon caught sight of himself in the mirror atop of the glossy brown dresser with chrome handles. He saw

Kendra twirling her tongue in his navel while undoing his belt.

"Yessss!" she exclaimed, freeing his dick from his prison of clothes. Trevon closed his eyes, rolling his neck as Kendra licked pre-cum off his tip.

"Come get it, big boy." She stood up and slid on the bed.

Trevon kicked out of his jeans and boxers then removed his socks. The sight of him caused Kendra to bite her bottom lip. If she was ever forced to identify him in a police lineup, she would insist to identify him by his dick. She could not remove her eyes nor hands from it. Once he was on the bed, she pulled him on top of her. Her tongue darted over his lips as he spread her legs apart. She was jacking his dick in a rush. Whining and squirming beneath him. The lights were left on. Digging her nails into his strong back, she looked down at his dick still in her grip. Her lust was building as he hooked her legs over his swollen biceps.

Condom! she shouted in her mind. A box sat on the dresser, but she was too deep in the moment to pause. *Shit! I know he's clean. Hell, my tubes are tied so I might as well get it raw. Mmm . . . I can't wait to feel him blowing his top off all up my candy box! Hell, why not?* Kendra squeezed his dick and moaned out his name while guiding his dick up and down her wet pussy lips.

"Kendra!" he moaned above her. He could feel his dick inching inside her softness. He pushed deeper, wanting to see how far she would go.

"Oooohhh babeeeee!" Kendra released her grip on his dick. His meat slid inch by inch inside her. She tossed her head side to side. Trevon's first stroke had her begging him to go hard.

"Fuck me right now! Uhhh . . . all so big inside my pussy!"

Nude Awakening

Trevon pounded into her. Illicit words flowed past their lips as they worked as one to reach that top. Kendra was reduced to soft whimpers as his balls smacked the back of her ass. He purposefully long stroked her with all nine-inches; her ankles were now up near his ears. They went at it hard. She slapped the bed, shouting and taking the dick. His piston-like thrusts had their flesh contacting in loud repeated slaps.

"Ooohhh! Oooohhh! Trevon! Trevon! Take it—take it babeeee!"

Above her, Trevon continued to drive his organ in and out of her wet hole in a blur.

"Mmmm! Shit! Dis pussy . . . fire!" Trevon sped up.

"Oooo, you big dick muthafucka! Gawd. Make me cum, Trevon! Yesss! Fuck me harder!"

Their combined weight and strenuous movements caused the solid bed frame to develop a squeak. He was still pounding her in the same pleasing position when her cell phone rang six minutes later. It was ignored by both. Sweat began to glisten on his skin. He kept pumping in and out of her. The bed continued to squeak. Kendra's back suddenly arched up off the bed. His dick felt so good driving in and out of her. The cell phone kept ringing. Trevon lowered his lips to one of her bouncing breasts. She ran her nails up and down his back. As soon as the cell phone stopped ringing, not a second later her home phone rang. She kept her attention on Trevon and the eye-rolling dick he was beating her with. Her focus changed when she heard her niece's voice on the answering machine.

"Aunt Kendra! Aunt Kendra, pick up ! Momma had to take Carmelita to the hospital because she—"

Using strength that shocked and surprised Trevon, she pushed him up and out of her in one shove. Her motherly intuition kicked in. Rolling over and panting out of breath she fumbled with the cordless phone before bringing it up

247

to her ear. Her night with Trevon came to a sudden halt. In under seven minutes, she was dressed and rushing Trevon out in front of her. Trevon hoped her daughter would be okay. Tonight he learned a valuable lesson. Nothing was more important than family. Not even good sex.

CHAPTER
THIRTY-ONE

Trevon drove straight home, pulling up in the driveway at twenty minutes past 10 p.m. He went inside heading straight for the shower. He stepped out twenty minutes later feeling refreshed. With a towel wrapped around his waist, he stood at the sink brushing his teeth. His puppy ran into the bathroom, grabbed a pair of socks, then ran off. Trevon spat out the toothpaste, then yelled after Rex.

"I'ma put your ass back outside!" He ran into the living room. "Rex!"

He looked around the living room. Just as he started to look under the sofa, the doorbell rang. Trevon went to the window. *Must be Kendra,* he thought, lifting up a blind. *LaToria!* Trevon quickly opened the door after seeing her black Escalade in his driveway.

"Hey, Trevon," She waved when the door opened. She could not restrain her smile nor her eyes from looking over his naked torso and towel clad frame. *I'm not here for sex. I'm here to get shit straight. But mmmm . . . I can see a dick print. I hope he ain't go no bitch up in here.*

Trevon had to take a moment to find his words. "LaToria.Ummm . . . come in."

LaToria walked inside his cozy apartment. "Ooooo, how cute! A puppy!" She squatted to rub Rex.

"Grab his ass and get my sock," Trevon said as he locked the door. He looked at her holding Rex and talking to him like a baby.

"You like dogs?" he asked, pulling the sock from Rex. "Let it go!"

"I love dogs." She placed Rex back on the floor. "He's sooo cute!" she said as Rex sat down in front of the TV.

"Trevon." Her voice trembled.

"Hold that thought." He held up a hand. "Let me put some clothes on. If you want something to drink—"

"I know." She smiled. "Make myself at home."

LaToria sat down on the sofa. *Okay. Just be honest. Tell him I'm sorry and tell him how I feel. Which is? Damn, if I say I love him, he might laugh my phat ass right out the door.*

"Jurnee gave me your address," she said minutes later when he walked into the living room. "She got it from Janelle."

"I see you didn't have any trouble finding me." He sat down in the recliner.

"Ummm, Trevon, I want to apologize for all those harsh words I said to you. Also, I'm sorry for kicking you out on the streets."

"Apology accepted," he said. "I want to apologize, too."

"For what?"

"For calling you out your name. That ho comment."

"Oh, I forgot about that. But apology accepted." She bashfully averted her eyes.

Trevon had a hard time keeping his eyes off her as well. *She don't even realize how beautiful she is.* "So what's been up with ya?"

LaToria crossed her legs. "Just taking things day by day."

"I heard you went on a trip to New York with Jurnee. Did you get your groove back?"

"No." *Okay, here's my chance to get what's on my mind off my mind.* "I really didn't do much because I spent most of the time thinking about you."

Trevon pretended he had some lint on his jeans. When he looked up, he found her eyes on him. "I won't make a fool of myself by assuming what those thoughts were. I know you apologized, but we had some serious things we needed to talk about and you—"

"That's why I'm here now. I mean, I want to talk about what happened between us, okay? I'm young, Trevon. I don't have much background in this—dealing with emotional."

"It's not mess."

"You know what I mean."

Trevon rubbed his face, releasing a deep sigh. "LaToria, I left the streets when I was eighteen years old. I'm thirty-three now. In that time in prison and before, I've never been in love or in a true relationship. Just because I've never *been* in love doesn't mean I don't want it."

"What is *it?*" She gestured with her hand. "What is love, Trevon?"

"Love. Love is thinking about a person when you're with or without them. I know there is more to define it."

"I miss you," she said sincerely. "I really miss you. I've done some dumb things since you left. I . . . got back involved with Swagga."

Trevon sat back in the recliner. *I can't trip. Hell, I can still feel Kendra's pussy around my dick. At least she is being honest. And it must not be so tight since she's over here.* "So y'all back together?"

"Hell to the no! It was just a fling and a mistake."

"A mistake, huh? That's what you said we were."

LaToria uncrossed her legs. "I didn't mean it, Trevon."

"That's the point. I don't know what you *mean*," he said calmly. "Look, I know we don't have a past and we really don't *know* of each other, but I can't sit here and say I don't feel something toward you. Don't sit there and think it's based on sex, because it isn't. And for all it's worth, I miss you too."

"Really?" She tried holding back her tears.

"Yes. And I know you ain't about to cry."

She shrugged, wiping her eyes. "I'm just happy. Happy to see you."

"So, are you gonna talk about this?"

"Yes. And this time I won't run away."

"That's good to hear. Look, why did you flip out when I asked if you were on birth control ?"

"Wasn't that something you should've asked *before* you came inside me?"

"Actually, it was something *we* should've spoken on *before* it happened."

"You always know the right things to say."

"Too bad I don't always know the right thing to do."

LaToria wiped her eyes again. "You—*we* did the right thing."

"And what was that?"

"Dealing with our emotions."

"That's all I got, LaToria." Trevon touched his chest. "All I got to go on is my emotions. I can't cut things off and just call it business like you and Jurnee be doing."

"It ain't easy for me, Trevon. God knows I've made a bunch of stupid mistakes in my life. But Smooch, I'm tired."

"Tired of what?"

"Running. I'm tired of running from things I don't understand. I didn't really know or understand how my foster parents were using me, so I ran. Had I stood up to them I might not still be running like I am today."

Trevon made his way over to sit next to her. "Dry your eyes." He tenderly lifted her chin. When she looked into his eyes he slid his hand over hers.

"Talk to me, LaToria. It's important that I know if you're on birth control or not."

LaToria muttered a few words then jumped up to excuse herself to the bathroom.

CHAPTER
THIRTY-TWO

Yaffa had managed to persuade Swagga over the cell phone to pull over. The two met up at a closed grocery store parking lot on 62nd Street. Yaffa was tired of the bullshit and how Swagga was keeping him in the blind.

"What the fuck is up wit' you?" Yaffa slammed the door on the Audi.

Swagga waited in front of his Bentley in the middle of the parking lot with the parking lights on. Behind them, even at 11:10 p.m. there was a constant flow of traffic heading up and down 62nd Street.

"Tell me what the fuck is up?" Yaffa demanded, standing in Swagga's face. "You 'pose to trust me wit' your life, but lately you been on some real live bullshit!"

"I can handle my own!"

"Handle what, huh! You 'bout to go body somebody? You hard now?"

"Ain't got time fo' dis shit!"

"Make time, nigga! Now tell me what got you runnin' out da crib wit' some fucking heat?"

Swagga balled up his fist and pressed his palms against his forehead. "Some bullshit!"

"Run it to me!"

Swagga dropped his arms to his sides then took a deep breath. He had to trust Yaffa. *I'll just tell him the truth. But not all of it. Shit, Yaffa is my nigga. He'll feel how I was fooled. Hell, he still think Chyna a bitch anyway.* "I'm . . . being . . . Chyna and somebody else is blackmailing me."

"Chyna! Blackmailing you for what? If that bitch on some rape shit you can relax 'cause I got a clip of her breakin' you off in your bed."

Swagga hid his anger. "Thanks, but that ain't the case."

"Well, what the fuck is it?"

Swagga sighed, rubbing his face. "Dawg, Chyna—is a dude."

"What the fuck you just say?" Yaffa grabbed Swagga's arm. "We ain't talkin' 'bout the Asian bitch, Chyna, are we?"

"Yeah man!" Swagga yanked his arm free. "The muthafucka is a transsexual or a transvestite or whatever! All I know for sure is that the faggot got a dick 'tween his legs!"

"What! Nigga, you fo' real!" Yaffa's temper shot upward. His mind went back to the night in the park with Chyna.

"The muthafucka is a he-she, she-he—I don't fuckin' know!"

"Did you know this fuckin' shit before you had that muthafucka up in your bed?"

"Fuck no! Nigga, I ain't gay! Hell, you thought it was a bitch, too!"

Yaffa swallowed his secret about Chyna. He just hoped that Chyna had not told ANYONE about that night in the park. "What the fuck are you being blackmailed for?"

Swagga sat down on the hood of the Bentley. His shoulders were slumped. "Umm, they got a film of me with Chyna."

"A film? A film doin' what? Suckin' your dick?"

Swagga had to tell the truth. "That, and me doing something else to Chyna."

"Nigga, you got to tell me 'cause I ain't about to try to picture you—"

"I fucked Chyna in the ass, okay! There, I said it! Now the bitch said I better give up two mil' or the film hits the social networks and that shit!"

Yaffa took a step backward, rubbing his face. "Tell me you bullshittin', my nigga!"

"Shit is real."

"Fuck!" Yaffa swung at the air. "You got the money?"

"Hell no! I was on my way to Chyna's crib to beat that ho ass!"

"We can't let that film leak."

"No need to tell me that."

"Look, as for why you went and fucked the muthafucka. That's on you, dawg. But if you wanna end dis shit tonight you gotta be down to go hard!"

"I'm down for whateva, yo!"

Chyna was in her den watching TV on the sofa. Cindy and Stan were in the kitchen talking. Chyna was daydreaming about the operation and how life would be to be *fully* a woman. *I'm going to be a ho for a while and then settle down with one man. If I can find a balling ass nigga with a big dick, I'll be in LOVE! Shit, I know I'm wifey material. Hell, I got Swagga open and I still got a dick. I know how to put it down! I know I have to look Trevon up. I wanted that dick bad, like Michael Jackson!* Chyna looked down at his tiny feet. *I need to get my toes done tomorrow.*

Chyna was about to lie out on the sofa when the doorbell rang.

"I got it!" Chyna got up and went to the door.

Yaffa stood on the other side of the door with a black ski mask over his face. Swagga stood behind him gripping a Glock 19 at his side.

Yaffa took a deep breath and shouldered a custom made 12-gauge pump fitted with a silencer. He had it pointed at the doorknob. He waited. Tense.

"Who—"

Yaffa heard Chyna's voice through the door. Clenching his jaw, he pulled the trigger. The sharp clap did not match the destruction the slug did to the door. Yaffa kicked the door in and found Chyna on the floor screaming. A jagged piece of framework from the door was stuck in his thigh. He stepped over Chyna.

"Drag that faggot in the den!" Yaffa told Swagga as he rushed inside.

Yaffa ran inside like a SWAT Team Officer with the intimidating silenced shotgun hiked up in his meaty shoulder. Rounding the corner into the kitchen, he caught Cindy. She backed up against the stove with fear painted over her face. She screamed as Yaffa ran up on her with the shotgun.

"Shut up, bitch!" he shouted, pressing the warm tip of the silencer against her forehead.

"Please!" She cowered with her hands trembling over her face.

Yaffa grabbed a handful of her dreads. Cindy screamed and kicked as Yaffa drug her into the den.

"Please!" she screamed, kicking wildly.

Yaffa released his grip of her hair, then punched her solidly in the face. She moaned, curling up on her side.

"Where the film at!" Yaffa stood over Cindy with the shotgun pointed at her head. "We ain't fo' no bullshit!" He pulled the mask up knowing it was pointless.

Cindy was too shocked to speak. She had not factored in Yaffa, and what he would do to keep Swagga's actions a secret.

Yaffa reared back, kicking Cindy in her stomach. The forceful kick even made Swagga take a step back. He looked down at Chyna moaning at his feet.

"You blackmailed the wrong niggas, you dumb bitch!" Yaffa looked around the living room. "Where the fuckin' film at?"

Cindy was having trouble breathing. She looked up at Yaffa and saw no compassion in his face. A glimmer of hope sparked when she realized that Stan was missing. He had been quicker with his escape to the back of the house. Cindy would try to delay Yaffa. She moaned, curling back up in a ball.

"Please, Yaffa!" Cindy pleaded. "This isn't what you think."

"Oh yeah!" Yaffa raised the silencer tipped shotgun up to her head. "I think you betta tell me where dat film at 'fore I bust your fuckin' head open! Now talk!"

Swagga nervously stood over Chyna with his Glock 19. Yaffa's actions were a surprise to him. Swagga's intentions were just to scare Cindy and Chyna, not kill them.

"Swagga, please don't."

"Shut up, bitch!" Swagga roared at Chyna. "Don't say shit else to me!"

Yaffa turned with hate in his eyes. Chyna was on the floor grimacing from the bleeding leg wound. Yaffa wanted to see the truth for himself.

"Cover dis bitch ova here!" Yaffa said to Swagga. The two switched places.

"Swagga, I'm sorry, baby!" Cindy sobbed, pulling at Swagga's pants.

"Get the fuck off me, bitch!" he spat, kicking her hands away.

Yaffa towered over Chyna with the shotgun. "Who got tha film?"

Chyna started to cry. This was too much for him to take.

"Who got that film, ho?" Yaffa's voice filled the room.

"I don't know!" Chyna screamed. "This—it was all Cindy's idea! I swear to you. Please! Please don't hurt me!"

Yaffa jacked a slug into the chamber. Chyna winced. "Lift your skirt up!"

"Yaffa, no." Chyna looked up. "Don't make me do—"

"Lift the gotdamn skirt up!"

Chyna tried to crawl away, leaving a trail of blood on the rug. Yaffa moved slowly along, gripping the shotgun.

"FIVE!" Yaffa started his countdown.

"Swagga, stop him!" Cindy screamed. "Please! DO SOMETHING!"

"Fo'!"

"Please, Yaffa! I'm sorry." Chyna sobbed..

"THREE!"

"Yo, Yaffa!" Swagga felt that things were going too far. "Chill bruh!"

"TWO!"

Swagga was about to grab Yaffa, but stopped when Chyna rolled over.

"Lift it up!" Yaffa ordered.

Chyna reached down and grabbed the hem of the silver and black miniskirt. Yaffa's rage was jacked up when he saw the shape of Chyna's cuffed male organ. His stomach turned. A quick flashback of Chyna giving him the sweetest head kicked into his mind. It was a game of deception that he was willing to kill for. Yaffa harbored no homosexual tendencies and was one to stand behind being homophobic.

Chyna played his manhood, and for it, Yaffa had to bring some closure.

Behind them, Swagga saw the change in Yaffa's posture. Yaffa shouldered the shotgun, taking a few steps back from Chyna.

"Yaffa wait! Don't—"

Swagga's plea fell on deaf ears as Yaffa pulled the trigger. The slug punched Chyna in the stomach, gruesomely shoveling out bloody entrails and guts. Cindy began to scream hysterically crawling backward until she bumped into the sofa.

Swagga lowered his gun. Chyna lay twisted on the floor with blood pooling out like an overflowing toilet.

"Shut that bitch up!" Yaffa shook Swagga by his shoulder then shoved him toward Cindy.

Swagga was numb. Shaking his head slowly, he backed up to the wall. His eyes were focused on Chyna's lifeless body. The first he had ever seen.

"Bitch ass nigga!" Yaffa muttered in disgust at Swagga. Stepping over the pooling blood, he yanked Cindy up by her dreads. "Wanna be next, ho! Where the fuck that film at?"

Cindy was paralyzed with fear. She knew she was going to die tonight. Tears skated down her face as Yaffa kicked her in the ribs. She howled, weeping loudly.

"Please don't kill me!"

"Where is the film? I won't ask you again!" Yaffa pressed the warm tip of the silencer against her forehead.

"In—"

"Talk bitch!" He jacked the black plastic pump, staring over the barrel.

"In the bedroom. The video camera."

"Which room?"

"One on the left." She pointed.

Yaffa glared at Swagga. "Go get it!"

Swagga was frozen.

"Go get the gotdamn film, nigga!"

Swagga snapped out of his daze, breathing heavily. His steps were unsteady as he slid sideways against the wall. Reaching the hallway, he stumbled over his own feet falling to the floor. The Glock slid from his hand coming to a rest against a door.

Inside the dark hallway closet, Stan jumped in fear. He felt helpless. Terrified. He had heard the countdown and Chyna's pleas. He heard the soft clap from the silencer, and then the screaming from Cindy. Tears filled his eyes. Stan was not built for this.

Swagga regained his footing. Picking up the Glock he paused. He had heard something move behind the door.

"Hurry the fuck up! Get the gotdamn film!" Yaffa shouted from the living room. Swagga assumed his mind was tripping. He moved off, gripping the Glock at his side.

Yaffa was still towering over Cindy when Swagga ran back in with the small palm-size camera.

"Is it up there?"

"Yeah!" Swagga replied, looking at the footage of him and Chyna.

"Please don't kill me." Cindy weeped. "*Please . . .*"

"Bitch, it's ova for you!" Yaffa stated.

"We got the film, Yaffa!" Swagga stepped in front of Yaffa.

"So what! You think I'ma leave dis bitch alive to take the stand on me!"

Swagga squeezed the Glock. "We—shit is over!"

"Nigga!" Yaffa raised the black silencer up to Swagga's face. "We ain't doin' a gotdamn thang! I'm the one that bodied Chyna. Now you either wit' me or I'ma lay your bitch ass down, too!"

Swagga twitched when the barrel touched his chin. He was not going to challenge Yaffa. "Okay, chill. Let's just get the fuck outta here."

"Toss your gun ova on the sofa!"

"What?"

"Nigga, come up off it! You heard me!"

Swagga tossed the Glock on the sofa. "Happy now!"

Yaffa shoved Swagga aside. He would deal with him later. "Who else got a copy of that film?" Yaffa shouted at Cindy.

Swagga waited for her to answer. He had not thought of Cindy giving out a copy.

Cindy closed her eyes. There would be no help for her. All of her troubles were based on her fear of losing Swagga to Kandi. She had overheard Swagga telling Chyna that he in fact was setting up Trevon just to get back with Kandi. Kandi . . . Cindy hated her. Hated her enough to plant another seed of deception.

"Kandi," Cindy replied. "She has a copy."

Swagga felt blood rushing to his head.

"See!" Yaffa sneered at him. "I told you the bitch wasn't shit!"

"How the fuck she got a copy?" Swagga's voice squeaked.

"We sent it to her cell phone," Cindy lied. "She was getting a cut of the money, too."

"Fuck!" Swagga flopped down on the loveseat then averted his eyes from the body on the floor. Something was not adding up, but Swagga could not place what it was. He just could not believe Kandi was down with this shit.

"I won't go to the police," Cindy cried. "Just get Kandi's cell phone. There are no more."

"Your case is ova, bitch!" Yaffa raised the shotgun.

"Yaffa, don't kill—" Cindy's words were suddenly ended.

SPLAT!

Cindy's head exploded into a mush of blood and brain matter. Swagga threw up on Chyna's ankle and stumbled toward the kitchen holding his stomach.

Yaffa lowered the shotgun as blood pumped spasmodically from the headless body leaning up against the wall. Stepping over Chyna's body, he picked up the Glock then joined Swagga in the kitchen. He was bent over the sink dry heaving. Yaffa slammed the Glock on the counter.

"Kandi gotta get it too! Ain't no need to spare that ho! Or do you want your secret to get out?" Yaffa waited for Swagga to respond.

"Fuck—fuck that bitch!" Swagga turned the water on to rinse his foul mouth out.

"What's done is done. Let's drop in on the ho and handle this tonight!"

Swagga picked the Glock up. "I wanna go see my seed first."

"Nigga, we gotta—"

"I'm going to go see Carmelita!"

Yaffa nodded. "Okay. We go see her. Then we go see Kandi. She gotta get it!"

Stan remained hidden in the hallway closet. The silence was pushing him toward the verge of hysteria. He wanted to move, but his limbs were deadened. He waited. Silence. Six long fear-laced minutes slid by until he had the balls to open the door. His weak mind and stomach were not hardened for the sight that awaited him.

CHAPTER
THIRTY-THREE

LaToria had returned from the bathroom with a clear sign of heavy crying. She sat down beside Trevon without looking at him.

"No," she said barely above a whisper. "I'm not on birth control, Trevon. And before you even ask. I never had unprotected sex with Swagga or anyone else. That's the one thing my foster parents preached to me over and over. Safe sex."

"Okay, so can I ask why me?"

"Isn't it obvious, Trevon?"

Their eyes met for a short moment until she looked to the floor.

"Please don't force me to assume anything about you or your actions, LaToria. Tell me. Talk to me."

"I care about you, Trevon. Since the very first day I saw you in Janelle's office I had a thang for you. I just have a hard time expressing myself. I felt the only way you would see me was through sex."

"You know I don't see you like that, LaToria."

"I know, Smooch."

Trevon smiled. The pet name was going to stick. "How do you feel about me?"

"I—" She rubbed her eyes. "I want to be with you. I want . . . to fall in love with you every day for the rest of my life."

Trevon stroked his chin, looking off toward the kitchen. "What-What about the fact that we both do porn?" He looked toward her, watching her shift on the sofa. "How can we—if it comes to it. But how can we say we *really* love each other, but have sex with others?"

She bit her upper lip, pulling her words together. "I told you before that catching emotions in this line of work don't mix. I'll just have to make a big choice. You or porn."

He crossed his arms. "You would give up porn to be with me?"

"No," she said quickly. "I would give up porn to be in love with you, Trevon."

Trevon slowly got up to his feet. "What do you love about me?" He held his arms out and up at his sides. "What's so damn special about ex-con, Trevon Harrison, huh?"

"Don't make this hard on me." She was close to crying.

Trevon suddenly slapped his hands together. LaToria winced.

"Loving me won't be easy, LaToria! I got so many issues. I still have nightmares about going back to prison. I still wear fuckin' shower shoes in my own damn shower! Some days I wake up at five in the morning without the aid of a clock. Some days I go hungry because I forgot to feed myself. I got issues, okay! Issues, I doubt I can even fucking deal with! Shit is so fast to me! Cars parking by their damnself! People don't even fuckin' talk face to face no more! I'm gettin' lost out here more and more each day. And, damnit . . . I'm scared." He lowered his voice as LaToria sat on the sofa crying softly into her hands.

Trevon took a step toward her and stopped. "LaToria," he called softly. "Look at me. Please."

She gazed up, letting her flow of tears remain on her face.

"Can you take me as I am? I'm fucked up, baby. I gotta get adjusted to this new life. This freedom. If I keep fronting like I got this shit under control, I'ma crash."

"Let me help you." Her voice quivered. She stood up and walked toward him. They hugged each other tight.

"Please let me help you, Trevon." She nodded into his chest. "I want to make things work. Please."

Trevon rested his chin on top of her head. *What if she is real? Am I real about this? Real about her? Fuck what the sideline will say. I know I care a lot about this girl. She feels so right to be in my arms.*

"I miss you, Trevon." She sobbed, locking her arms around his waist.

Trevon closed his eyes. "I miss you, too."

They stood there in silence. The running air conditioner unit and their steady breathing were the only sounds heard. LaToria kept her eyes open, clutching Trevon in her embrace. This was the man she wanted to be with. She felt it now. Now she understood what Jurnee was trying to tell her. Love. You'll just *know* when you have it.

LaToria stepped out of his embrace, wiping her watery eyes.

"What time do you have? I left my watch in the bedroom." Trevon asked, hoping she would not leave.

LaToria turned her wrist up. "It's um . . .eleven thirty-three."

Trevon sat down on the sofa and lowered his face in his hands.

"You okay?" she whispered, rubbing his shoulder.

He nodded yes. "So what's really up with you and Swagga?" he asked when she sat down next to him.

"Nothing. But honestly, I'll have to get rid of him again." She reached inside her purse and pulled out her cell phone. "I haven't been taking his calls." LaToria viewed the screen to check for any missed calls since she had turned her phone off. Swagga had called her two times in the last five minutes. Plus he had sent three text messages. She deleted them all without reading them.

"Avoiding him will only make it worse," he said as she laid her phone on the arm of the sofa.

"I know," she replied. "I just don't look forward to doing it."

"What will you tell him?"

She furrowed her forehead. "I don't have to explain nothing to him!"

She understood his position. Swagga was her drama. Drama she would need to put an end to. "I'll talk to him tomorrow." She waited a moment. Then she laid her hand on his knee. "Can I spend the night with you?"

Trevon glanced at her hand, then his eyes skated up to her breasts straining against the thin material of her dress. "I got some house rules," he said in a low bedroom voice.

LaToria caressed his thigh, inching her hand up to his crotch. "And what are your rules?" She smiled, inching closer to him.

"I might have to think on it," he replied as Rex trotted off toward the kitchen.

They both smiled. She looked directly into his eyes. He laid a hand on her inner thigh the moment their lips met. She fell back into the arm of the sofa as his tongue swirled inside her mouth. Getting comfortable under his frame, her cell phone was knocked to the floor. Their kiss was building. Both were moaning. Trevon eased his hand up her warm thighs. She opened them. He felt the heat coming from her pussy before his fingertips bumped against her fishnet thong. She arched her back as his fingers slid her thong aside. She was already wet.

"Smooch!" she moaned as he lowered his lips to her neck. She loved how she felt so small under his wide body. Closing her eyes, she tugged at his shirt. "Yessss! Play in it, Smooch." She bit her bottom lip as he pushed two fingers into her wet hole. Soft seductive moans rolled off her quivering lips. His steady rhythm had her rolling and bucking back against his fingers. A sudden charge shot through her. He now had his thumb up against her clit. Riding the constant waves of pleasure pulsing from his touch, she blindly pulled his shirt off. His fingers began to plunge rapidly in and out of her soaked pussy.

Tossing his shirt to the floor, she latched her lips on his chest nipple. He moaned out her name and pulled his fingers from between her legs. Sliding off the sofa, he reached up under her skirt to slide the thong off. Her eyes were half-closed as he pushed the dressup and over her juicy bare ass. LaToria wanted him to be in control. She said not one word as he put her knees on the floor. She parted them as he stood up. He kicked his shoes off, then shoved his boxers and jeans off in one rushed movement. She could feel the cool air blowing against her exposed pussy. With her elbows on the sofa cushion, she waited for her man to enter her. She slid forward a bit as he got up behind her. His erection bumped against her luscious red ass.

Trevon looked down at her special offering. He bunched the dress higher up over her ass until it circled her waist. He inhaled deeply, taking the sweet musky aroma of her pussy into his lungs. She looked back at him with his dick resting on her ass. She knew he was special to her.

"Make love to me, Smooch. Please. I need to have you up in me."

Trevon grabbed his shaft then slipped it inside her. He rubbed her ass, pushing in slowly.

"Uhhhhhh!" she moaned, squeezing the sofa cushion. "Put all of it in . . . Yessss!"

He began with a smooth steady thrusting that sent her ass clapping. Her jiggling ass mesmerized him. Her pussy noisily filled the room as his big dick pushed out air from her tight pussy. In and out, he dicked her down, making her squeal with each forward thrust. Breathing hard and heavy, he tossed himself into her body with nothing between them. Her moans and cries made him feel whole. Gripping her waist, he murmured her name.

LaToria felt his dick reaching up into her stomach; she cried for him to cum. Smacking her ass, he started to speed up. She enjoyed it. Baring his teeth, he leaned over her back. She turned her face toward his, still screaming and moaning. Her pussy had a personality of its own as it gripped and clung to his thrusting penis. A sense of relief filled her when he began to jerk and twitch. She could feel him shooting off his cum inside her walls. Before he pulled out, she squeezed his dick with her pussy.

"Ooooohhhhh, keep doin' that!" he said, rubbing all over her ass. "That feels so good, baby!"

They both knew the chances they were taking of having raw sex. Trevon's concern was based on her getting pregnant, not the chance of catching an STD. He slid out of her, feeling weak.

"Baby," she said, tugging her dress back down. "I'm going to wash up right quick and run home to get my overnight stuff. I want to wake up in your arms in the morning."

CHAPTER
THIRTY-FOUR

"What are you doing here, Marcus!" Kendra greeted Swagga at her front door. Before he could reply, she took notice of his eyes darting from left to right. Swagga looked— scared. *I know this fool ain't at my crib high! He has to be. Didn't even correct me for calling him Marcus.*

"I just want to see my daughter right quick. I um . . . got your text about her having a high fever."

Kendra had no love for Marcus, but she did owe him a few things. Those few things were all connected to their child. She knew he had the right to know their daughter was sick. She would have never guessed he would show up. Looking past his shoulder, she saw Yaffa leaning against the Bentley GT, smoking a cigarette.

"Tell Yaffa to put that cigarette out before he comes in."

Minutes later, she stood at her daughter's bedroom door. They had left Yaffa in the kitchen. Kendra wrinkled her nose. "You been smoking weed, Marcus? I smell it all on your clothes!"

Swagga began to fidget, looking off in the distance.

Kendra grabbed his wrist. "Are you listening to me?" she snapped. "What is wrong with you?"

He shook his head. "I just need to see my baby. Please."

Kendra released him, looking at him as if he were a stranger. *Please! Oh, he gots to be on some type of drug. I've never heard him say please for nothing or to no one since I've known his ass! Please?* "Try not to wake her. She needs her rest, okay?"

Swagga nodded then followed Kendra inside. She stood against the dresser and watched him kneel by the bed. A few minutes later, he leaned over to kiss Carmelita on her forehead, and then he stood up.

"Marcus," she said as he walked toward her. "What is wrong with you?"

Swagga reached down and grabbed her hand before she could jerk it away. "I need to talk to you. Please."

Kendra now sensed that something was wrong. "You better not be playing no games with me." She pulled her hand free, looked at her sleeping daughter, and took him to her bedroom to talk.

"What's going on with you?" She stood at the corner of her bed with her arms folded.

Swagga took it upon himself and sat down on Kendra's bed. His troubles were becoming too heavy to bear. "Just listen to me, okay?" he said in a low voice. "I'm going to give you the access number and info to my three bank accounts—"

"I know damn well you ain't up in here trying to get some pus—"

"Kendra!" He stood up, placing his hands on her shoulders. "I'm not here trying to get no pussy."

"Oh."

"Just listen to me, damn." He waited until she nodded. "I'ma give you my bank info, okay? If you don't hear from me by this time tomorrow, it's all yours. I trust you'll look out for my other two kids. You're the only person I trust."

"Marcus, what is going—"

"I can't tell you. I—just got caught up in some bullshit."

"Sit down and talk to me." She grabbed his hand. "You don't have to leave."

Swagga smiled at the mother of his firstborn. "I can't. I have to—finish something."

"Fuck whatever that *something* is! You have a daughter to raise." She squeezed his hand. "I know we ain't on the best of terms, but I do care about you, Marcus. You're the father of my first and only baby."

Swagga pulled his hand free. "Kendra, I never meant to hurt you, okay?" He walked to the dresser and picked up an ink pen. "I need something to write on."

Kendra ignored him with tears welling up in her eyes. *What if he's for real? I don't want my baby to grow up without a father.*

Swagga searched on the dresser until he found something to write on.

"I'ma write a note to my attorney also."

"Stop talking like that, Marcus. You're scaring me, okay." Tears fell from her eyes. She stood frozen as Swagga wrote down his banking info and a letter to his attorney. When he was done, he laid it on the dresser after she refused to touch it.

"I need to use the bathroom right quick." He left her sitting on the bed crying. In the bathroom, he turned the water on after closing the door. He pulled out his mobile phone and called Kandi. If she did not pick up, he would leave another voice message. She did not answer.

"Kandi. Look, I know about that scheme you got going with Chyna and Cindy. Listen to me, please. Cindy and Chyna . . . Yaffa killed them and we're coming to see you. I know you have that footage of me and Chyna on your cell phone. Cindy gave you up. Just leave your phone in the mailbox. Let's get this shit over with, okay? I can't control

Yaffa no more. Please, let's end this shit. I'll still give you some money. I gotta go. Bye." Swagga flushed the toilet. Then he slid his phone back into his pocket.

Turning the water off, he stepped back into Kendra's bedroom. She had not moved. Seeing her tears made him realize his foolishness. *Why do I dog out every female that really cares about me?*

"I gotta go, Kendra."

She turned her head away, sobbing hard into her hands. Swagga stood there for a moment and quietly left the bedroom. It was now 11:53 p.m.

Coconut Grove, Florida

Swagga felt helpless as Yaffa worked the security guard at the front gate. They had pulled up to LaToria's gated home two minutes ago.

"C'mon, man!" Yaffa said, leaning out the window. "LaToria took my man here off the visitors list because he forgot her birthday."

"I can't let you guys in," the guard stated. "I have a family to feed. I can get in trouble and lose my job."

Yaffa knew he had an opening to work with now. "Look, I'm a bodyguard, and you're a security guard, so when it comes down to it we're one in the same."

The guard rolled his eyes.

"How much did you make last year?"

"Ain't important."

Yaffa kept his cool. "Thirty thousand?"

"I wish!" The guard laughed.

"Shit, I might be your genie tonight."

"How? You got thirty thousand cash up in there?" the guard kidded by shining his flashlight inside the silent running Bentley GT.

Yaffa leaned over to whisper to Swagga. The guard was fed up with the games. Suddenly, his eyes widened when Yaffa held out a handful of jewelry.

"You let us in. You can have this. This chain is worth two hundred thousand and the bracelet is worth nineteen thousand."

The guard did the math in his head. Even if he sold the jewelry for *half* its value, he would still pocket $109,500.

"He'll remember our names and faces," Swagga warned as Yaffa drove past the gate.

"He'll be stinkin' when the sun comes up." Yaffa drove down the quiet street heading for Kandi's house.

Swagga was hoping like hell that Kandi had paid heed to his voice mail. His stomach tightened when Yaffa rounded the curb. Kandi's diamond black Escalade was parked in the driveway. Yaffa drove by slowly.

"Look, yo!" He pointed at the living room window. "That bitch home. I just saw her silhouette walk by!"

"How you know it's her?" Swagga looked, but it was too late.

"Because of that big ol' ass she got."

Swagga tried to think of something as Yaffa came to a stop.

"Lemme get the shotgun out the trunk." Yaffa turned the car off and looked at Swagga. "Don't freeze up on me! The ho trying to take you down, so keep that in your mind.

We gonna run up on her hard. No games. All that talkin' shit is fo' the movies! You ready?"

Swagga pulled out the Glock 19 and chambered a round.

"Dawg, if that footage of you fucking Chyna hit the Internet, it's over for you!"

"Fuck it, let's get it!" Yaffa got out first. He was ready to kill again.

After tonight, I'll be my own man. No more running behind this gay ass, down low nigga! I need all the clips of him fucking Chyna in the ass! Once I get it I'ma show muthafuckas how to blackmail a nigga.

CHAPTER
THIRTY-FIVE

LaToria stood under the shower thinking about Trevon. She could not wait to get back to him. A smile was on her face as she turned around to let the pelting spray rinse the suds off her back. She would give anything to have Trevon standing behind her.

Swagga stood behind Yaffa at the back door. It took Yaffa almost two minutes to pick the lock. He carried the silenced shotgun.

"A'ight, here we go," Yaffa whispered over his shoulder when the knob turned in his hand.

Swagga laid a hand on Yaffa's shoulder. "Let me do this. I'll get the phone from her."

Yaffa stood up from his crouch. "We ain't got all night."

"I know that." Swagga eased past Yaffa, slipping into the living room.

Swagga motioned Yaffa to wait in the hallway as he stood at Kandi's bedroom door.

He heard the shower running. *Why is this bitch still here? Maybe she didn't get my message?* Stepping into the bedroom, he looked down at the gun in his hand.

This ain't me. He thumbed the safety on just as the shower was turned off.

The sudden silence caught Swagga off guard. He looked toward the bathroom when he bumped into the nightstand by the bed. The lamp flipped off and hit the floor before Swagga could catch it.

"Trevon?" LaToria called from the bathroom. "Is that you, Smooch?"

Swagga's face balled up slowly. *Trevon! Smooch! Dis bitch not only trying to fuckin' blackmail me! She stillfuckin' with that nigga!* He felt he was being played all the way around. He thumbed the safety off then stormed into the bathroom. LaToria was wrapping a towel around her wet body when Swagga shoved his way inside. She screamed, backing up toward the toilet.

"Boy!" she shouted as her nerves settled. "What in the hell are you doing? Better yet, how did you get in here?"

Swagga stood by the sink breathing hard with his dreads over his face.

"I'm calling the police!" she said, taking one step forward. She froze and took a step back seeing the gun Swagga held down by his side.

"All this shit is a game to you, huh?" He took a step closer to her. "You still fucking Trevon behind my back. Playing me like I'm some sucka ass nigga!"

"Swagga, you need to calm down, okay?"

"Fuck you!" He raised the gun up to her forehead. "Don't be scared now. That bullshit plot you tried to run wit' Cindy and Chyna ain't gonna work, ho!"

"Swagga, I don't—"

"Shut up, bitch!" He pushed the gun into her forehead causing the back of her head to thump against the wall. "Where your cell phone at?"

"My-my purse. On the bed," she answered.

Swagga grabbed the back of her arm and yanked her out of the bathroom. She tried to plead with him and explain.

"Gimme the phone!" He shoved the gun back in her face. "Don't make me ask you again. I swear to God I'll bust your head wide the fuck open!"

LaToria was shoved backward on the bed. She began to weep softly as she looked inside her purse.

"Hurry up!" he shouted.

LaToria dumped her purse upside down. *Oh God, it's not in my purse. All he wants is my phone and I don't have it.* She checked thoroughly by spreading the contents from her purse over the bed.

Swagga roughly shoved her aside and looked on the bed. "Where is it!"

She shrugged with tears in her eyes. "I . . . I thought it was in—"

Swagga felt she was not taking him serious. Gripping the gun, he suddenly swiped it toward her forehead. The polymer-frame struck her forehead making a sickening sound. LaToria fell back on the bed with her hands covering the bleeding gash at her hairline. Swagga jumped on the bed and yanked her head up by grabbing her hair.

"Bitch!" He dug the gun into her temple. "Where the phone at!"

"Please!" she cried, trembling. "It's not in my p-p-purse."

"I can see that!"

LaToria whined. *Please, God! Help me please! I don't—wait! Trevon! I must've left my phone at his place.* "Trevon!" she gasped. "I left it at his place."

Swagga sneered. "Oh, your ho ass been fuckin' him, huh?" He reached down and shoved the towel up. He slapped her ass as hard as he could. "You like that?" Again he smacked her ass. "I'ma treat you like the ho that you are! Then we gonna call yo' nigga and get that phone." He smacked her ass twice more.

"Swagga, please! I—"

"SHUT UP!" he shouted. "I tried to give you a way out! I guess you was too busy suckin' Trevon's dick to answer my call!"

LaToria felt the gash throbbing and leaking blood. She was on her stomach with Swagga on her back. She began to sob harder when he started caressing her ass.

"Yo, Yaffa!" he shouted with the gun pointed at the back of her head.

Yaffa ran into the bedroom and came to a halt. His eyes were like a magnet to LaToria's exposed ass.

"Want a shot of this?" Swagga palmed her ass.

Yaffa walked up to the bed. "Business first."

Swagga got up off the bed. "Don't move!"

"You got the phone?" Yaffa was still looking at LaToria's ass.

"It ain't here. That nigga Trevon has it."

"You sure?"

"Yeah. I figure we can have some fun with this ho, then handle business later."

Yaffa stroked his beard as his dick got hard. *Look at all that ass! Shit, I might as well fuck the ho*! Yaffa looked at Swagga. "Let's tie her ass up, so she won't try no bullshit."

LaToria felt her world spinning as Swagga laughed at the idea of raping her. She felt helpless. Swagga ran out of the bedroom. Any ideas of pleading with Yaffa were a proven waste of time.

"Yaffa. Ple—"

"Ho, save that shit fo' God."

Twenty minutes earlier, Trevon lay on his bed in the dark. Music was playing, deepening his thoughts about LaToria. He looked forward to sharing *his* bed with her. He felt she was the woman for him. *This is what I want. I won't call it love, 'cause it's too soon. We'll just have to—*

His thoughts were broken by a soft scraping sound coming from the hallway. He sat up. "What the" Looking toward the hallway, he saw Rex moving backward dragging a glowing square shaped device in his mouth. Trevon jumped out of the bed to catch the puppy before it ran off. "Gimme that!" Trevon scooped Rex up and pulled LaToria's cell phone from his mouth. Trevon took Rex back into the kitchen and placed him behind the small gate. Walking back to his bedroom, he looked at the phone and saw the icon for a voicemail. The ID next to the number said 'Swagga'. Trevon sat at the foot of his bed. *This nigga still calling her. Okay, she said she ain't been fuckin' with him the last few days. If I listen to the message then . . . Fuck. I'ma see what this nigga talking about.*

Trevon pulled up the voice message mailbox then played the message. His mind started to run as Swagga's voice filled his ears. *She got a scheme going . . . Chyna? It can't be the same Chyna I know. Dead!* Trevon replayed the call again. Was Swagga running game just to get LaToria's attention? He thought about the risk. He thought about going back to prison.

Swagga hurried back into the bedroom with strips of torn drapes from one of the windows.

"Tie her hands," Yaffa took a step back with the shotgun aimed at LaToria. "Tie that shit tight, too 'cause I'ma fuck the dog shit out of dat ass!"

Swagga turned to LaToria, slapping her twice across the face. "Take the towel off!"

"Damn!" Yaffa lowered his weapon at the sight of LaToria's nude frame. Her titties jiggled erotically as Swagga yanked her arms above her head.

"You want 'er on her face or back?"

"Um . . . back." Yaffa said and looked at her pussy. "Gotdamn! She gotta mitten 'tween them legs!"

Swagga showed no sympathy to LaToria. Doing this would hurt her emotionally. He tied her wrist together above her head. He then tied a second knot to the headboard and slid the gun over her quivering lips.

"I guess I can finally fuck you raw." He stood up then looked at Yaffa. "Yo, Snoop said it best. 'Ain't no fun if the homie can't have none.' I'ma let you dig this ho out first." Swagga trailed the gun down her chin, between her breasts, and then pressed it hard into her belly. "You gonna die regretting trying to fuckin' play me."

LaToria closed her eyes, forcing a new line of tears to roll out of the corner of her eyes. She opened them when Yaffa yanked her chin toward him.

"You'll enjoy this," he said, squeezing her face. "At one point, you'll love this dick busting that pussy open." He released her then started removing his clothes.

LaToria began to choke up on her tears. She felt she could go to another place by keeping her eyes closed. Reality rushed back in when she felt Yaffa's immense weight on the bed. She felt his knees easing her thighs open. She tried to keep them closed.

"Don't do that again. If you do, I'ma choke your ass out and still fuck ya!"

LaToria popped her blurry eyes open. She relaxed her legs.

Yaffa tossed her ankles up on his shoulders then leaned forward, bending LaToria like a contortionist. Changing his mind, he threw her legs aside, and moved his bulk up on the bed. "Suck it, ho! Swallow this snake before I put it in ya!"

LaToria knew she had no choice. She parted her lips as he forced himself into her mouth.

Swagga was in the kitchen looking for a drink when his mobile phone rang. His attention was drawn since it was a number he had never seen before.

"Yeah! Who dis?" Swagga answered, feeling tough.

"What's up, playa?"

"Who dis?"

"Funny how you don't know my fuckin' voice. You all on my dick doing a bunch of bitch shit over some pussy. Yeah, I'm fucking LaToria. And to make it a small world, guess who else I'm fucking, Marcus Brooks?"

"Nigga! How you know my na—"

"Your baby momma told me, nigga! Yeah, Kendra."

"WHO THA FUCK IS THIS!'

"Trevon."

Swagga gripped his mobile phone. "I'm tryin' to see your bitch ass!"

"Fuck you! I'm seeing you now." Trevon laughed. "Yo, make sure you turn that light off when you leave the kitchen."

Swagga spun around and looked at the darkened window behind him. *Oh shit! That nigga outside!* Swagga ducked down and ran back to the bedroom.

Yaffa was rubbing his dick across LaToria's lips when Swagga came stumbling into the bedroom.

"Trevon here!"

Yaffa rolled his heavy bulk off LaToria. "Here where?" Yaffa asked, dressing quickly and snatching up his silenced shotgun.

"Some fuckin' where out back!"

"You see the nigga?"

"No!"

"Well, how the fuck you know he here then?"

Swagga told him about the phone call.

"What we gonna do?" Swagga panicked.

"Call his ass back!" Yaffa shouted.

Swagga made the call.

"Tell 'im we'll kill the ho if he don't give us her phone!" Yaffa looked down at LaToria. "Shit ain't ova, bitch! I'ma still get some of that pussy. You can count on it!"

Swagga held up his hand when Trevon answered.

"We want that phone, nigga!" Swagga demanded.

"Then I guess we have to make a trade then. But now that I think on it, I shoulda dropped your bitch ass when I had you in the scope."

Swagga glanced toward the window and then edged closer to the wall. "Fuck you! Play games if you want to and we'll murder this ho!"

"Do that and you won't get the phone. We both lose. So what?"

Swagga balled up his fist. *This nigga in on the shit, too! If I kill Kandi, he'll still be able to blackmail me. Hell, he might want the ho exed out any damn way!*

"What's up, nigga? Don't bitch up on me now. You want the footage of you and Chyna, and I want LaToria."

Swagga rubbed his face. "Yo, we'll make the swap in a public place."

"Where and when?"

Swagga glanced at Yaffa. Yaffa closed his eyes, thought for a moment, then shrugged.

"Yo ..." Swagga was forced to run the show. "We 'bout to walk out of here with this bitch. We see or hear anything, you can watch the ho on film 'cause that's the only place you'll see her."

"Like I said—" Trevon's voice was calm. "We make a trade. Just tell me where and when."

Swagga motioned Yaffa to untie LaToria. "Just fall back and wait. And if we see any headlights when we leave—the bitch is dead!"

"This goes down tonight."

"Yeah nigga! Expect my call. That's after me and my nigga get our rocks off up in this ho!" Swagga ended the call then rushed to the side of the bed to help Yaffa untie LaToria.

"Gag her mouth!" Yaffa suggested. "I'on wanna see dem lips movin' unless they're on my dick!"

Trevon was facing his fears all over again. Hidden in the bushes, he saw Yaffa stepping out the front door. Seconds later, LaToria appeared with Swagga close by her side. Trevon clenched his empty hands into a fist. Swagga's last words fueled Trevon. He would not turn his back on LaToria. He had no idea what was going on. All Trevon cared about was getting LaToria back. No matter the reason for her troubles, Trevon was committed. Without LaToria in his life, there was no peace. That same rage he felt toward his sister's rapist filled him once again.

Swagga shoved LaToria into the front passenger seat of the Bentley GT. Then he pushed his frame into the backseat. Yaffa got behind the wheel.

"You see 'im anywhere?" Swagga's head turned left to right and behind him.

"Chill nigga! If you just calm the fuck down!" Yaffa looked around the quiet neighborhood and saw nothing out of order. Pulling from the curb, he glanced at LaToria. Her body was so fucking amazing! The tight tank top with no bra and the tiny boy shorts were pouring nothing but lust into his mind. No matter what, he was determined to fuck her tonight.

"Yo, umm . . . drive 'round the block right quick." Swagga sat up between the seats.

"What the fuck fo'!"

"Find Trevon's car! It's a white Jag. Let's slow this nigga down."

"Good idea. Now keep your gun on that ho so she won't try no dumb shit up in here."

It took them one trip around the block to find Trevon's white XJL. Yaffa rolled up slow on some *Boyz N the Hood* type drive-by shit. Steering with his knee, he eased the silenced pump shotgun through the window. He jacked off two quick shots. The first blew the front left tire out and marred the smooth polished rim. The second slug punched a volleyball-sized hole in the driver's side door.

"Go! Go! Go! Go!" Swagga shouted as Yaffa pulled the pump back in. The Bentley GT sped off leaving the XJL useless.

Trevon was filled with frustration when he ran up on his Jaguar. Picking his speed back up, he ran toward the front security gate. *What am I doing? These niggas are for real!* Trevon cut through someone's front yard when he heard a sharp clap like he had before. He kept running. *I need help! I can't be on this ego street shit. LaToria's life is at stake.* Rounding a corner, he saw the security booth two blocks away. He kept running.

Out of breath, he reached the booth and slowed down when he saw the guard laid out on the ground. "Oh shit!" Trevon walked up on the body. The guard's upper chest was gone.

Trevon looked away. *This is too much!* He took a step back and reached for his cell phone. It rang. He answered it quickly when he saw it was Swagga.

"Yeah!"

"Finish changing that tire yet?" Swagga laughed. "We had to slow you down a bit. We'll be in touch though. I think my nigga wants some pussy, so we'll have some fun before we call you back."

"Don't—" Trevon looked up to the starless sky as the line went dead in his ear. He was driven now. Pushed to the edge. Walking back up on the body, he made a quick search. Two items drew his full attention. The first was the guard's fifteen-round clip Glock 9mm still in the holster. The second was a set of keys clipped to the guard's belt. Transportation. Trevon took both.

Trevon sped off on the yellow and black Yamaha R1. His high rate of speed gobbled up the pavement, making the yellow lines blur into one single unbroken strip. The responsive bike obeyed his slight adjustments. He would not let LaToria down. Not today, not tomorrow.

CHAPTER
THIRTY-SIX
October 7, 2011
Friday, 1:48 a.m. - Coral Gables, Florida

Stan sat in the back of an ambulance staring down at his feet. He could still smell the blood and picture the horrid sights of Cindy and Chyna. The house was now a double murder crime scene. Since Stan had made the initial call to 9-1-1, he was questioned first by two homicide detetectives. He had nothing to hide. He told the detectives who the two bodies were and how they had been killed. Stan also gave them the most important information. The shooter.

"He killed them both," Stan said in a flat tone. "Swagga's bodyguard shot Chyna first. Then he—killed Cindy."

"Swagga? The big time rapper?" the youngest of the two detectives asked.

Stan nodded yes.

Ten minutes later, a warrant was issued for Swagga and Yaffa's arrest. Stan felt the lower pocket of his jacket. He still had Cindy's cell phone. On it was the footage of Chyna in bed giving Swagga oral sex and the two clips of them having anal sex. Cindy had not given up her cell phone and Stan would not let her death go in vain.

Yaffa and Swagga were tipped off about the warrant by D-Hot. The Broward County police along with the Dade County police were waiting at Swagga's mansion in Fort Lauderdale. The news had Yaffa and Swagga shook.

Yaffa had driven back to the grocery store parking lot at 62nd Street.

"How the fuck!" Swagga shouted.

"D-Hot said something about there being an eyewitness." Yaffa lowered his forehead on the steering wheel. "We should have searched the crib."

"Man, fuck!" Swagga punched the roof. "Ain't going down for this!"

Yaffa jerked up and turned in the seat. "What! You gonna turn State against me, nigga? You snitchin'?"

Swagga flexed his grip on the Glock. *Think I won't! I ain't kill no damn body!* Swagga turned his head, punching the roof again. "How the fuck we gonna get outta this? All I wanted to do was set Trevon up with Chyna. Now I might be facing a double murder!"

Yaffa turned forward. "What we gonna do with this ho?"

LaToria sat in the front seat filled with fear.

Swagga closed his eyes wishing all this bullshit was a dream. *All this bullshit over a dick sucking porn slut!* He opened his eyes, mentally drilling the headrest where LaToria sat. He raised the Glock, lightly pressing it into the headrest.

"We need to split up and soon." Yaffa glanced at Swagga. "Ain't no need to body the bitch now. We might need her."

"How?" Swagga lowered the gun. "Fuck her! I sure as hell ain't 'bout to carry her with me. I'm going on the run."

Yaffa looked at his watch. It was ten minutes past two in the morning. He had not planned for this outcome. He had to think his way out of his predicament. He was mad at himself for being greedy. He had jumped head first at the chance to blackmail Swagga on the low once he knew what was going on. *I should just body both of them right now! Swagga ain't worth shit to me no more. I wonder if his dumb ass realizes that?*

"How much dough you got on you?" Yaffa asked.

Swagga patted his empty pockets. "Not a damn penny!"

Yaffa ran a palm down his face. "This some real live bullshit!"

"You should've thought of that before you went on your killin' spree!"

"Nigga, fuck you! Keep up that slick ass talk and I'll add your bitch—"

"Bitch, what?" Swagga jabbed his gun under Yaffa's chin. "All this bullshit got out of order because of your trigger happy ass! We—you ain't have to kill no damn body! Now look at us." Swagga waited for Yaffa to say something. "Shit don't supposed to be like this!" He slowly pulled the gun from Yaffa's neck.

"We got to split up, yo," Yaffa said, remaining calm and keeping his hands on the steering wheel.

"Not until we get that fucking phone!" Swagga reminded him.

"A'ight. How you wanna do this? We ain't got all night. The police is at yo' crib and you know damn well they got an APB out on this car."

Swagga looked around the parking lot. His Audi R8 GT surprisingly had not been stolen nor jacked for its forged triple chrome Asanti rims. A homeless woman trudged by sluggishly pushing a rusted shopping cart with her belongings.

"Let's do this shit and I'm getting the fuck outta this country," Swagga stated.

"Okay. I'ma drive the other car. We can put the ho in the trunk."

LaToria mumbled behind the gag, shaking her head.

"Where we going?" Swagga asked.

"Remember that vacant warehouse where we shot your last video?"

"The one at the harbor downtown?"

"Yeah. Let's go there. Call Trevon and make the swap."

"And then what?"

"We kill 'em if we can. If not, your yacht still down there, right?"

"Yeah."

Yaffa looked up at the rearview mirror. Catching Swagga's eyes he smiled. "I hope those boatin' lessons of yours can get us to Cuba."

Swagga returned the smile. "Damn right I can! Yo, I fogot I even had a fucking yacht. Yeah, let's get this bullshit over with."

Yaffa followed closely behind in the Audi R8 GT as Swagga drove toward the warehouse. If Yaffa could set it up right, he could finish off Swagga and Trevon and maybe later have his fun with Kandi. Yaffa had no intentions of letting Swagga live. In no way could he trust a man that slid his dick up another man's ass. *Fuckin' faggot ass nigga!* Yaffa kept his eyes scanning the rearview mirror for any signs of the police. Picking up his cell phone he called Swagga.

"Yeah!" Swagga answered, driving at the posted speed.

"I got a plan."

"I'm listening."

"A'ight. When we get to the warehouse we'll also swing by the boat harbor to get your yacht ready."

"What about the ho in my trunk?"

"We gotta use her to bait Trevon out. I'ma be in the cut. Once I see his face and I know the phone is wit 'im, I'ma take his ass out."

"Then we bounce to the boat?"

"Yeah. Shit, we can be in the Bahamas in three hours or less."

"Three! Try an hour and about thirty minutes! My boat can top out at forty-five knots. But yo, I thought we were going to Cuba."

"Man, fuck Cuba! Once I hit dem islands, I'ma get missin' like a Muslim at a pig pickin', straight up!"

"Whateva. Let's just finish this shit up and then we can talk about where we going and shit."

"Yeah. Yo, Trevon ain't call you back yet?"

"Nah."

"Odd, but fuck it. Maybe he busy puttin' that spare tire on."

They both laughed even in the center of their building troubles.

Yaffa slid back behind an empty wood crate near the back of the huge warehouse. Looking toward the entrance he saw Swagga sitting in the Bentley GT with Kandi. Going down to one knee he laid his shotgun on the ground then pulled out his cell phone to call Swagga.

"Where the fuck you at?" Swagga answered.

Yaffa could see Swagga searching for him. "Close by. Yo, you get the yacht ready?"

"Yeah."

"Okay, call the nigga. Call 'im three-way."

"Hold on."

"A'ight." Yaffa waited while watching Swagga making the call. A few seconds later, the line clicked back over with the line ringing.

"You ready to do business or keep playing games?" Trevon got right to the point.

"Nigga, I'm the one with the bigger chips in this game, so I think you need to play your position!" Swagga spat. "But yo, let's get this done and over with. You got the video and I got your bitch. Now, you come here without the phone or come here with the police. The ho is good as dead and I put my word on it! Ain't got shit to lose, so offing this ho ain't gonna stress me."

"Fuck the police! You doing a lot of talking, but you ain't saying shit I wanna hear."

"And what the fuck do you wanna hear, tough guy?"

"Tell me where you're at so we can make the swap. It might take me some time to get to wherever you are, but I'll come. Kinda slowed me down by using my ride for target practice."

Swagga smiled. "Yeah, that was my idea. You dealing with a nigga that likes to think on his toes."

"Yeah, and one that likes to put his dick in another man's ass."

"FUCK YOU NIGGA!"

"Nah homie, I don't get down like that."

Swagga punched the dashboard causing LaToria to flinch. "Bring your bitch-ass to the boat harbor on Miami Beach! Come to warehouse seven-two-ten. You got thirty minutes to get here, nigga!" Swagga killed the line ending Trevon's connection.

"Nigga sound too calm," Yaffa spoke. "Too fuckin' calm."

"Fuck him! I'ma kill his ho ass when I see 'im!"

"Yo, drive about halfway inside this warehouse and turn around. We'll be able to see 'im when he come through the gate. We'll let him see Kandi. Once he's in the open, I'ma take his ass down."

"Good. But make sure I get the phone from him."

"A'ight. I'll holla. My battery only got two bars left."

Yaffa sat down on the floor in the pitch-black warehouse. Swagga was parked about fifty yards away with the engine still running. Trevon's calm demeanor nagged at him. Something was not right. Standing up, he searched for any headlights outside of the warehouse. Though the trap was set for Trevon, Yaffa was beginning to feel like he was the one in a trap. Ten minutes had gone by. Yaffa's third eye was telling him that something was not in order. Wanting to remain hidden, he pulled out his cell phone and called Swagga.

"What?" Swagga answered in an agitated tone.

"Call Trevon."

"What for? Ain't been but ten fuckin' minutes!"

"Call, man. Fuck!"

"Shit, hold on, yo!"

Swagga took the mobile phone from his ear and dialed Trevon's number. Seeing the call going through, he clicked over to put Yaffa on three-way.

"It's ringing now, so—"

"What the fuck! Gotdamn, dis nigga—"

"Yaffa! Hello? Yaffa, what's up, yo?" Swagga took the phone from his ear to see if he had lost the signal. To his shock, both calls had dropped. He snatched up the Glock 19 and dialed Yaffa's number. The line started to ring. No answer. "What the fuck?" Swagga hit redial. No answer. Dropping the phone in his lap, he scanned the pitch-black warehouse. Nothing. *What did Yaffa mean by 'dis nigga?' He probably just bullshitting to fuck with my head. Well, this shit ain't funny worth a fuck!* Swagga lowered the tinted window.

"Yaffa! Answer your damn phone and quit the games, nigga!"

LaToria still had her mouth gagged and now her hands were tied in front of her. If only Swagga would let her speak, she could tell him that she had no idea what was going on. She feared for her life. The added pain of maybe losing Trevon was too much to take. Tears flowed down her cheeks. Life was not fair.

Inwardly, Yaffa scolded himself for slipping. When Swagga called Trevon he heard ringing in his ear and behind him. Trevon had been watching them. Yaffa was up against the crate with a gun up under his chin.

"Breathe too hard and I'ma put one through you," Trevon promised. "Now slowly drop your piece then stay still. Now do it."

"A'ight I'ma—"

"Nigga, you don't need to talk, so shut the fuck up."

Yaffa lowered the shotgun. *Shit! Dis nigga got the upper. Not all the way he don't. We both can't hardly see shit. Okay, I gotta be smooth. Put the shotgun down and slip my .380 in my palm and then it's fair game.* Yaffa heard Swagga yelling out his name. He laid the shotgun down and carefully reached under his left pant leg. He did it smoothly without pausing.

Swagga drummed the steering wheel. Unable to control himself, he lowered the window once more.

"Yo Yaffa! Answer your phone! Shit ain't fuckin' funny no more!" His voice echoed off the rafters above. He waited. "Yaffa! A'ight now. Fuck around and leave your ass in this muthafucka!" Swagga had the window halfway up when a gun went off.

"Oh shit!" He ducked, dropping the gun. "Man, fuck this!" Swagga put the Bentley GT in gear and floored the gas pedal. The rear tires responded instantaneously. Smoke billowed, clouding the rear quarters as the Bentley sped off at a fishtail cant.

Trevon was fighting for his life having knocked the .380 out of Yaffa's hand. The chrome .380 glinted from the moonlight, drawing Trevon's attention. When the .380 fired, Yaffa took the opening to elbow Trevon in the chest. Trevon's weapon was knocked from his grip as Yaffa slammed him against the crate. Yaffa outweighed Trevon by 65 pounds. The two traded blows that would have sent the average man to the hospital with internal bleeding. Trevon kept Yaffa close, hitting him hard with quick solid jabs on his face. Trevon's natural power slowly began to wear down Yaffa's bulk. Yaffa grunted, ducked, then fired a blind uppercut in the dark. It grazed Trevon's chin slightly dazing him. Yaffa grabbed Trevon by his waist, and then used all his mass to shove Trevon off balance. They began to tussle. Two bulls.

Hearing the car peeling off galvanized Trevon. It was simple. Lose the fight—he would lose LaToria. Trevon grabbed Yaffa's head in a headlock and used Yaffa's momentum to fall backward. Yaffa realized his mistake a second too late. Trevon squeezed Yaffa's neck as they fell backward. The top of Yaffa's head met the hard concrete with a sickening thud. Trevon quickly untangled himself from Yaffa, frantically searching for the Glock on his hands and knees. Yaffa moaned. Slowly, he rolled over with blood leaking from the gash on his forehead.

"Fight ain't over, nigga!" Yaffa struggled to his feet but fell to one knee. Pushing the throbbing ache in his head aside, he rose to his feet. "Come on!" He swung at the air and nearly spun off his feet. "Where your bitch ass—"

CLICK CLACK!

Yaffa turned to the sound of a slug being jacked into his shotgun. Ten-feet away he saw Trevon standing under the dim cast from the moon.

"You ain't tryin' to go back to prison for that bitch!" Yaffa shouted. "They'll give you life dis time, boy!" Yaffa staggered forward. "You ain't built like me! Look at 'cha! Shakin' like a lil ol' bitch!"

"I might be." Trevon raised the shotgun. "But this time, I'ma keep my eyes open."

Yaffa spat and then rushed Trevon like a bull.

CHAPTER
THIRTY-SEVEN
Friday, 2:37 a.m.
Fort Lauderdale, Florida

By official documentation, the Miami U.S. Marshals Fugitive Task Force was posted in Swagga's mansion. Lieutenant Colonel Frank Robinson walked into the kitchen with a cup of coffee. He wore a dark brown suit and tie with the unmistakable five point U.S. Marshals badge on the left side of his blazer. Robinson's slightly receding hairline matched the tired look on his face. In his late 50s, he was nearing the end of his career and refused to go out with a tarnished record of not catching whoever he was sent after. The crime scene at Chyna's house was gory. Hearing that one of the suspects was the famous rapper, Swagga, had him driven. Robinson, being white loathed when the crime involved black on white. He nodded at his fellow Marshals, and then placed his cup of coffee on the table where Yaffa's broken down .45 still sat.

"Gentlemen and ladies." He kindly acknowledged the three female Marshals's standing to his right. "All of you have been briefed. All of you have seen the crime scene. The local authorities have requested our immediate assistance and that's what we're here to do." He loosened his tie.

"We're all set to make the call, Mr. Robinson." Everyone turned their attention to a young Asian U.S.

Marshal sitting at the table with a dull black briefcase-size GPS tracking system.

Robinson headed over to the GPS tracking system and took the cell phone that was wired to it. He dialed Yaffa's cell number.

"No signal, sir. It's turned off," the Asian tech stated.

Robinson pulled out a sheet of paper. On it was Swagga's cell number. He dialed the number.

"We got a signal, sir! Try to keep him on —"

"Shhh. I know," Robinson assured the Marshal.

"Yeah," Swagga answered.

"Hello. May I speak to Mr. Marcus Brooks?"

"Dis the fuckin' police?"

"I'm Lieutenant Colonel Frank Robinson of the U.S. Marshals Fugitive Task Force. I um . . . got wind that your bodyguard kinda got out of hand. You two had some issues down in Coral Gables and I—"

"Yo! Ain't fuckin' kill no damn body!"

"That's what I've heard thus far," Robinson lied. Stan had not seen who had actually shot Cindy and Chyna. "We all need to sit down and discuss what has happened so we can clear this up. Is your bodyguard with you?"

"No, and you can forget about me turning myself in!"

"That's not a wise move, Mr. Brooks. At this very moment I'm giving you a chance to call your attorney and come in on your own. I'm willing to respect your status as a rapper. But mark my word, you don't want me to hunt you down. Now, how do we move about this situation, Mr. Brooks?"

"Man, fuck you! If I see the police I'ma kill this bitch, Kandi!" The connection ended.

"Did we get a trace?" Robinson asked, lowering the cell phone.

"Yes! We need thirty seconds and you got us fifty-one. He's at the Marina on Miami Beach."

"Let's move, people!" Robinson shouted. "Tamika, find out who Kandi is. If he has kidnapped someone, I want to know!"

"I'm on it, sir."

In the hall, D-Hot raised his hand to get Robinson's attention. He had taken a big risk to call Yaffa to warn them, but he now saw his mistakes. Swagga and Yaffa were in too deep. D-Hot willingly aided the Marshals by telling them about Kandi.

Swagga jogged quickly with the Glock 19 shoved under LaToria's rib. They headed down the brightly lit floating dock walkway under the starless Miami night. Coming up on boat slip number eighteen, he yanked her to a stop. Swagga's glossy black and silver-hulled 108-foot Sunseeker Predator floated with its prow pointed toward the Atlantic Ocean. The powerful triple 2400 hp engine was idled back, but still emitting a deep throaty rumble. Swagga shoved LaToria across the stable gangway onto the sleek sports yacht. By gunpoint, he forced her into the lavish salon appointed with glossy black mahoghany walls and white plush carpet.

"Hurry up! You know where my room is at!" He pushed her violently past the custom-built travertine marble top bar, toward a set of steps. Reaching the door to his master stateroom, she paused.

"Go in, bitch!"

"Please untie my hands," LaToria pleaded.

"Fuck no! You better be glad I took the gag out. Now get in there!"

"Swagga, please! I don't know what is going on—"

"Go!" he said firmly with the barrel of the Glock between her eyes. LaToria fumbled with the polished brass knob until it opened. She was roughly forced into the stateroom. Swagga stood in the doorway scanning the room for items that she could use to aid her escape.

"Try something stupid! I promise I'll dump your ass overboard with your hands and feet tied." Glaring at her, he eased out with the gun aimed at her. The door slammed shut and was locked.

LaToria wiped her watery eyes. The stateroom was spacious. On the bulkhead wall was a 60-inch flat screen TV. The room smelled of fresh leather and wood, but the setting did nothing to relax LaToria. She began to pace in front of the bed covered with black, white and blue satin and cloth sheets. She heard Swagga moving about above her. LaToria's fear ran wild. Hearing Yaffa and Swagga speaking on Cindy's death had her on edge. She began to sob when she felt the big yacht moving from its slip. At that point, she made up her mind to fight. Crying was not going to help. Wiping her eyes once more, she moved around the room in search of anything she could use to catch Swagga off guard. Desperation replaced her fear as the 108 Predator accelerated to its cruising speed of 35 knots.

Swagga sat at the bridge controls with his eyes moving from the glowing monitors. He steered the 108 Predator on a course to freedom, Cuba. Looking at the radar, he saw his line of travel was free of any other vessels for forty miles out. Glancing back over his shoulder, he had a hurting feeling at leaving so much behind.

"Fuck it." He turned back around. Adjusting his course toward Cuba, he gripped the African mahoghany throttle, pushing it all the way forward. The sexy 108 Predator responded quickly for its massive length. When it reached its top speed of 45 knots, Swagga reached above his head to turn on a small TV monitor. The screen flashed on with a glowing icon that required a thumb print signature. Swagga carefully placed his thumb on the blue square. It took two seconds for the security system to activate. The screen changed to a list of every room on the yacht. Swagga touched the title 'Master Stateroom.' A second later, a hidden camera showed LaToria searching inside his walk-in closet. With the yacht cruising on its own, Swagga amused himself by watching LaToria with the Glock on the control panel.

The U.S. Marshals were converging with force toward the signal from Swagga's mobile phone. Robinson now had the rundown on Kandi aka LaToria Nicole Frost. Four Marshals had driven to her home in Coconut Grove and instantly drew their weapons when they found the slain security guard at the gate. Proof of LaToria's kidnapping was discovered when her back door showed signs of a forced entry. The stakes were high. Robinson sat in the co-pilot seat of a U.S. Marshals helicopter listening to guard units make their way closer to the signal that pinpointed Swagga's phone. The helicopter was a mile away flying in a waiting position.

"Do we have a visual of the suspect?" Robinson spoke into the hands free headset mic that bumped annoyingly against his lips.

"Team Crow to home," came a quick reply.

"This is home," Robinson replied as the helicopter banked over downtown Miami.

"We have a blue Bentley GT parked at the Marina. No suspect in sight. Repeat, no suspect in sight."

"Are we positive the GPS is still tracking?"

"Yes sir. No doubt about it."

"Okay, send four men to the car. If the phone is there…"

"We'll find him."

"Search those warehouses, too."

At the same time, Trevon was running down the floating dock walkway. Yaffa had died at Trevon's feet from a single shot to his chest. Leaving Yaffa behind, he had run out of the warehouse and spotted the Bentley's taillights heading toward the Marina. In the heat of the moment, the motorcycle was forgotten. He took off running behind the Bentley.

Running down the dock, he yelled out LaToria's name and began to panic. An older white couple stood on the raised covered flybridge of a 60-foot Hatteras motor yacht.

"Excuse me!" Trevon pleaded. "Have you seen a guy with dreads walking with a light-skinned female?"

The man quickly shook his head side to side and then ushered his wife below the deck.

"Shit!" Trevon spun around. No one was walking along the walkway. "LaToria," he moaned, moving further down the boat slips. He assumed this was the right dock since Swagga's Bentley was parked in the parking lot. He was afraid to yell for help. Yaffa's .380 in his waistband was his main deterring factor. Reaching the last of the boat slips, he looked out toward the ocean. He then looked at the countless yachts moored in their slips. "Swagga!" he shouted, not giving a fuck who he woke up. Suddenly, he remembered his cell phone. He hit redial. Pacing, he waited as the line rang. No answer. "Fuck!"

"Yo playa!"

Trevon spun around to the voice, reaching back for his gun.

"Whoa, yo!" the black man said.

Trevon froze. Behind him standing in the cockpit of a sleek speedboat was a black man with a wild afro. Like

Trevon, he too was armed. Trevon slowly eased his hands into the man's view.

"I need help." Trevon watched the man ponder his words with doubt.

"Help? You just woke me up yelling for Swagga and now you want help?"

"You know him? Did you see him? He, he had a girl with him and —"

"Bruh, Swagga bounced outta here 'bout fifteen minutes ago. His slip is right behind ya."

Trevon glanced at the empty boat slip. "Please man! I need your help."

"You wanna use my phone. Nah, I see you got one. But you might wanna —"

"Swagga kidnapped my girl, yo!"

"Really? We talkin' 'bout a multi-millionaire platinum sellin' rapper takin' your girl. Who is she? Ciara?"

"I'm serious, yo! He and his bodyguard. I think they killed two people tonight. I know they killed a security guard 'cause I seen the body, okay?" Trevon looked back out to the ocean. "I need to go after him."

"Dawg, if what you said is true, you might need to call the police."

"I can't."

"Why not?"

"I killed his bodyguard, Yaffa. Please help me, man."

"Listen, lemme make one phone call and I'll put it on the speaker so you can hear I'm not callin' the po-po. If what you said is true, I'll help you."

"Please!"

"Hold on."

Trevon stepped closer to the fast-looking speedboat as a helicopter flew overhead.

"Yo. Lemme holla at Felix right quick."

Trevon waited impatiently with his attention on the one-sided conversation.

"Felix, what's up old man? Yeah, it's me. I need some info. Yeah. . . . Look can you call our people down at Metro Dade and see if there is an ongoing investigation with a double murder in um . . ."

"Coral Gables." Trevon assumed the killings had occurred at Chyna's crib.

"Coral Gables. No. I don't have anything to do with it. Okay, I'll hold. Oh, and check on a security guard being found at . . ."

"He worked the front gate at Quovadis Estates in Coconut Grove. And the girl that's been kidnapped is LaToria Nicole Frost." Trevon's patience began to wear thin as the man relayed his words over the phone. *Who is this nigga? Acting like he Scarface and shit and who in the fuck is he talking to? Shit! I can't believe I just told a total stranger that I killed a man. Fuckin' stupid!*

"Are you serious? The U.S. Marshals! Okay. Man, he could be anywhere by now. I can't stand by and do nothin' . . . Yeah, I'll be careful . . . Okay. Look, you can have someone call them so they'll know who we are. Yeah, I'm gonna help. Shit, you know how I do."

Trevon got anxious when the man laid his gun down. "Will you help me?"

"Yeah. Untie that line by your foot and get in."

Trevon moved quickly. "My name is Trevon."

"I know. Trevon Harrison. The po-po found your Jag shot up and you're wanted for questioning. Take my advice. Turn your cell phone off."

Trevon jumped down into the 46-foot skater speedboat. "Man, who are you?"

"Menage Unique Legend. And yes, it's my real name. Now buckle up."

CHAPTER
THIRTY-EIGHT

"Swagga's yacht is a hundred and eight foot Predator. Ahhh . . . top speed at I think . . . 45 knots!" Menage informed Trevon as they cruised out into the deep water. The speedboat was cruising at 20 knots.

"Will we be able to catch up?"

"You don't know about boats, do ya?"

"Never been on one."

"I figured that. Well, once I get out of this no-wake zone, I'll show you better than I can tell you. But first, we gotta find out where Swagga is goin'."

"How will we do that?"

"Common sense. Head south." Menage nodded. "Plus I can use this," he said, tapping a small radar screen. "If I was Swagga, I'd be haulin' ass at top speed and bein' so late, there ain't many boats out. Matter of fact, look at the screen."

Trevon leaned over and saw a green dot heading south with a bunch of numbers around it.

"I bet that's our boy."

"What's all the numbers for?"

"It's their position, speed, course and all that other shit."

"How far ahead are they?"

"Umm . . . 'bout seventeen miles."

Trevon looked ahead at the inky black ocean. To his right the skyline of downtown Miami did nothing to ease his mind.

"Hold on, bruh. We outta the no-wake zone." Menage gently eased the gold plated throttle forward. The prow of the speedboat leapt up in the air as the speed increased. The two 1300 hp engines roared to life kicking up a ten-foot high rooster tail of water, traveling at 40 knots, then 50, 60, 65, 70, 75, 85. Catching a wave sent the speedboat airborne for three seconds. The rough landing jarred Trevon in the high-backed seat. He assumed the speedboat could take the pounding since Menage sat next to him smiling, showing off his platinum teeth.

Back at the Marina, Robinson stood beside Swagga's car as the Miami police roped the area off. The ground unit with the aid of a K-9 had discovered Yaffa's body in the warehouse. Robinson held Swagga's mobile phone in his gloved hand. He was not happy. His mood stood a chance of changing as two Marshals ran in his direction.

"He's gone, sir. Slip eighteen is empty."

Robinson smiled. "I want the type of vessel he owns! I want to know the color, its speed, everything. Dave, get the Coast Guard on the line. We'll need their help. Secure the scene at the warehouse and let's MOVE, people. This man is on his boat with a hostage and I doubt he's on a pleasure cruise. He must—he must be stopped before he reaches Cuban waters!" Robinson turned his attention back to Swagga's mobile phone. He looked at the last missed call. Someone had called Swagga only minutes before the Marshals had surrounded the car. A cool breeze off the water blew against Robinson's face. Looking out toward the ocean, a sour feeling began to boil in his stomach.

Ignoring it, he jogged back over to the helicopter as the ocean breeze rustled the dry palm tree blades.

Swagga gripped his hard dick with his focus on the security monitor. LaToria's ass cheeks were spilling out of the tiny pink boyshorts. She was now in the bathroom rambling under the sink. He could have his fun with her, then dump her ass overboard. Swagga had no more compassion for her. Picking up the Glock, he slid the slider back to make sure a round was in the chamber.

The yacht moved stable through the five-foot swells on its plotted course to Cuba. Swagga stood up. It was pointless to look ahead out of the window. The visibility was pure ink black. Swagga instead looked down at the widescreen thermal night vision screen. His path was still clear. Leaving the controls, he moved down to the main deck. He could hear the waves crashing against the hull and the smooth hum of the engine. Each second was pushing him closer to freedom. Stopping at the wet bar, he sat down and started to think. *Okay. Once I get to Cuba, then what? I know one thing, I gotta get my money. I hope Kendra will do what I told her to do.* "Fuck this shit!" Swagga stood back up. The trip to Cuba would not take much longer. "Might as well fuck this bitch one mo' time."

D-Hot sped down I-95 South in a green Porsche 911 GT3. He drove with one hand while frantically searching through his cell phone for a number. D-Hot blew past the exit for Homestead doing 98 miles per hour.

"Got it!" he shouted when he found the number. He pushed dial and prayed for the call to go through. Suddenly, the radar detector began to buzz. D-Hot eased back off the gas, slowing the Porsche. "Pick up, fool!"

"What!"

"Swagga! Yo, dis D-Hot!"

"Yo."

"Bruh listen! The U.S. Marshals are on your ass! They even got the gotdamn Coast Guard tryin' to stop you!"

"How the fuck they—"

"Look, you ain't gonna make it to Cuba."

"That bitch ass nigga, Yaffa! He talking to the police?"

D-Hot shook his head. "Yaffa is dead," he said morosely. "He was found inside a warehouse near the Marina. They think you might've did it because they found your tire marks in the warehouse. Dawg, what in the fuck is going on? And why did you kidnap Kandi?"

"Man, ain't got time to explain all that shit!"

"Okay listen. I wanna help you, but you gotta promise not to harm Kandi."

"If you want me to turn myself in, you can kill that bullshit! I'ma take my chances reaching Cuba."

"Nah. Listen, we gotta trick 'em, okay? You gotta do this shit right 'cause . . . just trust me, Swagga!"

"Okay, I'ma listen to you, but—"

"Swagga! Trust me, and I'll have you out of the country by this time tomorrow. Now listen. You know my mansion down in the Keys?"

"Yeah."

"Okay, here's the plan . . ."

"Yo, why are we slowing down?" Trevon shouted over the speedboat's engine and loud wind.

Menage pointed to the headset on Trevon's left. Trevon slid it on and repeated his question.

"Coast Guard just called me on the transponder."

"And?"

Menage pointed to the left. Trevon faintly saw a fast moving blinking blue light. "Coast Guard. They told me to stay out of the way. They're goin' to stop Swagga before he can reach Cuba. They also have a helicopter on the way."

Trevon balled his hands into a fist as Menage slowed the speedboat to 30 knots.

"Let 'em do their job, yo. They know your girl is being held hostage. Real talk, we'd be in the way."

Trevon studied the small radar screen. Swagga's yacht was still heading toward Cuba at 45 knots. The symbol for the Coast Guard's vessel told Trevon its speed was 40 knots. Its angle of approach would cross paths with Swagga's yacht about twenty miles from Cuba. It was pure tension building as Trevon watched the two symbols getting closer.

"How far is that Coast Guard boat from reaching or catching Swagga?"

Menage glanced at the radar screen. "Um 'bout seven or eight miles. Look! There's another Coast Guard ship comin' in up from the Southwest. Ain't no way Swagga will reach Cuba."

Trevon was still worried about LaToria. What would Swagga do once he saw that he could not reach Cuba? Trevon feared the worse.

CHAPTER
THIRTY-NINE

Swagga began to panic when the U.S. Coast Guard ordered him to bring his vessel to a halt. He grabbed the throttle and made a hard emergency stop. The sudden action threw him forward as the big yacht slowed its speed. The digital speedometer glowed brightly on the console, 45 knots, 40 . . . 35 . . . 30 . . . 25 . . . 20 . . . 15 . . . 10 . . . 5 . . . 2 . . . 1 . . . 0.

Rushing out of the bridge, he paid no mind to the radio. The Coast Guard was giving him orders to comply with them fully. Someone was also asking about LaToria. Swagga knew what had to be done.

LaToria had managed to free her hands with the aid of a straight razor. Her emotions were high when the yacht began to suddenly slow. She moved to the window. Nothing but pitch black darkness greeted her. *Why did this fool stop?* She frowned when an odd humming noise filled her ears. The yacht was still slowing down. The humming grew louder.

Robinson nodded at the pilot when he heard the Coast Guard had gotten Swagga to stop.

"Closer, sir?" the pilot asked Robinson.

"No. I don't want to spook him. Keep us out of visual range. The Coast Guard has it under control."

The pilot kept a loose racetrack oval pattern orbit at 1,000 feet above the Atlantic waters.

"Think he'll give up, sir?"

Robinson sighed. "I sure as hell hope so."

"We can't get any closer." Menage turned his speedboats engine to a low idle.

"How far away are we?" Trevon asked.

"'Bout four miles. Here." Menage reached down by his feet and unlocked an odd-looking pair of binoculars. "Use these. You should be able to see a bit of what's goin' on."

Trevon took the thermal vision binoculars.

"Can you see his yacht?"

"Not yet," Trevon replied, slowly scanning left to right.

"Look toward your right. He should—"

"Okay, okay, I see it! Damn, where the fuck is the Coast Guard?"

"Still movin' in, dawg. Just watch. Trust me, I know how you feel."

Trevon unfastened the harness belt then stood up. "Why did he stop?"

"He gave up. I'm sure he has a radar picture of the Coast Guard runnin' him down. Plus, I bet they're talkin' to 'im right now."

"Too easy," Trevon murmured. "Something ain't right."

Aboard the U.S. Coast Guard vessel approaching from the Southwest stood Lieutenant Janayia A. Martin. She was one of the few African American women that held command of a Coast Guard vessel.

"What are our range and bearing on the stopped vessel?" she asked the navigation Petty Officer First Class. She rechecked what she heard with the radar overlay and the plotter. A large 20-inch screen displayed a thermal image of the sleek yacht floating dead in the waters five miles away. Stepping behind the coxswain, she nodded at the farthest symbol toward the north.

"Make sure that vessel stays out of this area until this issue is over." The communications officer seated next to the coxswain acknowledged the order and made the second warning to Menage's speedboat. Lieutenant Martin looked back at the thermal image of the yacht. She wanted everything done by the book.

"How far is the yacht from Cuban waters?" She already knew, but she felt it was a must to keep her crew on their toes.

"Uh, approximately ten and a half miles, ma'am," the navigation officer replied.

"What's our ETA?" Lieutenant Martin turned toward the coxswain.

Before the coxswain could reply, the Chief Petty Officer jumped out of his seat. "Bastard's on the move again!"

"Ma'am, vessel is increasing speed quickly," the coxswain stated.

"Course?" Lieutenant Martin calmly asked while making a mental note to speak to the CPO about his unprofessional outburst.

"Cuba ma'am."

"Can we catch up before the vessel reaches Cuban waters?"

"Yes ma'am. But—"

"I know, Petty Officer First Class Neal. Catching him is one thing. But making him stop is another."

"Lieutenant Martin. We got another big problem." The CPO stood over the thermal monitor shaking his head. "Look."

Lieutenant Martin gasped. Even though the image was a dull grayish picture, she knew it was the worse case to see red and yellow. The yacht sped toward Cuba with a bright glowing fire licking from its bridge.

"Get us there now!" Lieutenant Colonel Robinson ordered the pilot. Robinson felt his stomach shift when the ex-military pilot banked the helicopter in a hard turn. It was now a race. Robinson did not need the aid of binoculars to spot the burning yacht down on the ocean.

Back aboard the U.S. Guard vessel, Lieutenant Martin ordered to coxswain to steer as close to the burning yacht as possible. "Look for anyone on board. The suspect is a black male and we also have a hostage!" She ran to the port side window as a black and gray U.S Marshals helicopter buzzed overhead. "Where is the Coast Guard? Hello?" she shouted.

"Delayed, ma'am. The fuel lines have some sort of problem. Second helo's ETA is twenty minutes."

"Damn it! This will be over in five!"

"Second Coast Guard vessel is now on station."

Lieutenant Martin looked out and saw the second U.S.C.G. vessel on the starboard side of the speeding yacht. The three vessels continued a course toward Cuba.

313

"Jesus!" Robinson muttered helplessly at the sight below the helicopter. The Coast Guard could do no more than escort the burning yacht. The helicopter's powerful searchlight along with the two from the Coast Guard vessels played over Swagga's yacht. All eyes were looking for any signs of life.

"Get us closer!" Robinson jabbed down toward the yacht. "And keep the light on the damn boat!"

Four miles to Cuban waters, ma'am."

"I know!" Lieutenant Martin shouted back at one of her crew. She gripped the rail fitted along the port bulkhead as the vessel bounced in the burning yacht's wake.

"Coxswain! Get us ahead of the yacht on its port side," she ordered, turning to the CPO. "Put the searchlight on the bridge and turn on the loudspeaker!"

The coxswain glanced nervously at the speeding yacht with fire spreading quickly along it's forecastle. Like everyone aboard, he knew their actions were useless. In truth, there was nothing else the two Coast Guard vessels could do. Their only plan of action was to hope someone aboard the yacht was alive. If so, they would be encouraged to jump. The loudspeaker boomed over the roar of the three boats and the helicopter.

"IS ANYONE ON BOARD?"

"Three miles to Cuban waters, ma'am!

Robinson slammed his fist in his palm when the Coast Guard vessels began to decrease their speeds. They were now a half a mile from Cuban waters.

"Sir," the pilot spoke. "We're too close to Cuban airspace. I don't think there is anyone alive down there."

314

Robinson could not peel his eyes from the yacht. "Shit!"

Seconds later the pilot began to slow, bringing the helicopter into a hover.

"Sorry sir." The pilot nursed the controls. "I can't go any further."

Lieutenant Martin felt defeated as the burning yacht sped off into the night.

"It's in Cuban waters, ma'am."

She could not respond. Sighing, she turned to her CPO. "We'll sit here until—"

"Ma'am!" The navigation officer looked up from the radar. "You might want to look at this!"

"What is it?"

"That speedboat we were tracking. It's on the move again. And I mean moving!"

"Where is it heading?"

"Cuba, ma'am. Um, this can't be right. Jesus!"

"Jesus what?"

"Ma'am, I'm reading the speed at 94 knots . . . 98 . . . .Uh . . . 100 ma'am! 110 . . . 115 . . . 1—16 . . . . One hundred sixteen knots and holding. Damn, he's moving!"

"Whoa!" Robinson shouted at the sight of the speedboat ripping between the two Coast Guard vessels. All that was left behind was the wake.

CHAPTER
FORTY

LaToria banged on the door, coughing and gagging from the smoke seeping around the door. "Somebody help me!" She kicked and pounded the warm door with her fist. She had screamed her voice out when the Coast Guard was around. *They had to have seen me!* Backing away from the door, she rubbed her burning eyes. "Please . . ." She sobbed. "Please! Somebody help me!"

Menage's speedboat easily caught up with the yacht now engulfed in flames.

"You sure you wanna do this!" Menage shouted with the speedboat bouncing in the yacht's wake. Smoke burned his eyes.

"I gotta get up there!" Trevon was free of the harness on the seat.

"Look, I'ma get as close as I can. You'll have to jump on the swim platform!"

"What's that?"

"That wooden flat piece on the back! Yo bruh, if you slip off . . ."

"I know, we only get one chance!"

"Ready?"

"Yeah."

Menage eased the speedboat closer then slid alongside the port stern of the yacht. The ride was bumpy due to the water crashing against the speedboat. Menage misjudged his speed and caused the boats to touch.

"Shit!" Menage yanked the wheel to the left decreasing speed.

"C'mon, man!"

Menage gripped the throttle and turned back toward the yacht, matching its speed. "Okay, when I get close, you gotta jump quickly. I won't be able to hold dis bitch steady this close to the yacht."

"Okay, okay let's go!" Trevon stood up in the cockpit. The heat from the fire warmed his skin twenty feet away. He placed one foot up on the edge of the speedboat.

"Wait!" Menage shouted. "Put on a lifevest!"

"Fuck it!" Trevon was focused on the jump. "Closer!"

Menage eased up closer. "Fuck!" Menage felt the wheel jerk in his hand . He could not hold the speedboat steady. Trevon fell back over the seat, knocking the .380 out of his waistband.

"A'ight yo!" Menage vented. "On three! One . . ."

Trevon stood back up. "Damn! The gun! Fuck." He moved back to the edge.

"Two!"

The yacht continued to burn.

"Three!" Menage jerked to the right, purposefully crashing into the port stern of the yacht. "Jump! Jump!"

Trevon launched himself off the speedboat, landing hard on the wooden swim platform. He fastened a life holding grip on the rail lining the stern, then pulled himself up. Flames greeted him.

"LATORIA!" he shouted. Looking behind him, he saw the speedboat veering sharply away with a gaping hole from the crash with the yacht. Trevon was on his own. Taking a deep breath, he ran into the smoke.

LaToria could feel the heat building. Burning to death made her shiver. Smoke was now billowing around the door. Closing her eyes, she sat on the bed. Sobbing, she placed the straight razor on her wrist. A large wave caused the yacht to land hard in the water. She flinched, nicking her wrist with the razor. It drew blood.

Gripping the ivory handle, she allowed her tears to fall. The end. The razor hovered inches over her wrist. She bit down on her bottom lip. Mentally, she started to count.

Five, four, three, two . . .

"LaToria!

Her head snapped up. Slowly, she stood looking toward the door.

"LaToria! You in there!" The handle jiggled.

"Trevon!" She dropped the razor and ran to the door. "Trevon! Please get me out of here!" She pounded the door.

". . . back!"

"Baby please!" She heard him shouting something behind the door. "I can't hear you!"

"Step back! . . . kick it in!"

LaToria tried to piece his words together when a loud crack sounded. She jumped back as Trevon kicked the door in. Words could not match her relief when he stumbled into the stateroom.

"Come on! We gotta get off this boat now!"

Trevon grabbed her by the hand, yanking her off her feet. He did his best to shield her from the flames. They moved toward the stern and out in the open air. Behind them a small explosion rocked the yacht down below the deck. He gripped LaToria's hand, edging down to the swim platform.

"We gotta jump!" he shouted.

LaToria cried. "I can't swim!"

Trevon could not spoil her hopes by telling her the same. He could not swim. Squeezing her hand, he looked into her eyes.

"Do not! No matter what. Do not let go of my hand. I love you."

Her scream rang in his ears as they jumped off the burning yacht and into the deep Atlantic.

CHAPTER
FORTY-ONE
Friday 3:53 a.m.
Sugarloaf Key, Florida

Swagga rode the Jet Ski out of the surf without slowing. When it grounded on the sandy bottom, he was thrown off tumbling onto the dark private beach.

"Ahhh fuck!" He rolled over, holding his sore left wrist. Stumbling out of the water, he ran up to the back of D-Hot's oceanfront estate. Swagga's teeth chattered from the cold water that soaked his clothes. He kept running up the beach until he neared the back gate of D-Hot's home. Before his hands could touch the gate, three vicious pit bulls charged the gate on the opposite side barking loudly. Swagga stopped, breathing hard.

"D-Hot!" he shouted, pulling out the Glock. "Better come get these gotdamn mutts before I—"

A sharp whistle issued by D-Hot calmed the dogs as D-Hot came running past the resort-sized glass tile pool.

"Hurry up, yo!" Swagga stared back out at the Atlantic briefly, assuming he would see the police or something. All he saw was the white caps of the surf easing back and forth on the sandy beach. D-Hot ushered him through the gate and inside his elegant 11,000 square foot home.

"I need some clothes, yo!"

"Bruh, I got all that shit ready! You gotta hurry and change. I got you a plane ticket leaving outta MIA on a private jet."

"Where am I going?"

"Rabat," D-Hot said, rushing Swagga into a bedroom.

"Rabat? Where the fuck is that?"

"Morocco."

"Morocco?"

"Damn bruh! Did you even go to school? Rabat is the capital of Morocco. It's a kingdom in Northwest Africa."

"All you had to say was Africa."

"Look. I got some good people over there that will look out for you. I'ma get your lawyer on this shit and wait"—D-Hot grabbed Swagga's wrist—"Did you let that girl go?"

"Yeah fool!" Swagga said, yanking his wrist free. Swagga would not tell him about setting his yacht on fire after he lowered his Jet Ski in the water.

"Okay, change your clothes and let's get out of here. The jet is fueled and ready."

Swagga hurried with removing the wet clothes. D-Hot advised him to switch all of his assets to his account before the government placed a freeze on it. Swagga trusted D-Hot and sat down at his computer to do so. D-Hot stood over Swagga's shoulder as he made the transaction.

"What's that for?" D-Hot saw Swagga send $4.5 million to Kendra.

"Gotta look out for my seed, nigga, that's what!"

"Oh. Shit, I was gonna see to that."

"Yeah well, I wanna be sure that my firstborn is straight."

D-Hot hid his resentment. He wanted all of Swagga's money. D-Hot watched the screen closely as Swagga wired the high-end eight-figure amount to a new account. D-Hot's account.

"Thanks yo!" Swagga later gave D-Hot a thug hug then ran out to the garage.

Swagga slid behind the wheel of a silver metallic Aston Martin Virage then sped off toward Miami. D-Hot stood on second wing grand view deck, watching the taillights of his Aston Martin fade into the night. D-Hot smiled, but then started laughing. Turning around, he pulled out his Vertu Ascent smartphone along with the calling card Lieutenant Colonel Frank Robinson had given him earlier.

CHAPTER
FORTY-TWO

Out on the Atlantic, Lieutenant Martin stood observing the U.S. Marshals' helicopter landing perfectly on the stern of her vessel. She instructed the CPO to escort the visitor to her office.

Seven minutes later, there was a knock on her steel door.

"It's open."

Her CPO, Richard Wensell escorted Robinson inside and made the introductions. When Wensell started to leave he was told to stay.

"Yes ma'am," Wensell said and sat down in a chair beside Robinson.

Silence. The three exchanged eye contact without words.

"Um, how soon will we reach port?" Robinson asked Lieutenant Martin.

"Eight or ten minutes," she replied.

Robinson looked at the pictures and awards that belonged to Lieutenant Martin. He was surprised the ship was being run by a Black female. He loosened his tie.

"Excuse my manners, Mr. Robinson," Martin said. "But would you like a cup of coffee?"

"No ma'am. Thanks all the same."

She nodded.

"So, some night, huh?" Robinson began. "How are those two you pulled out of the water?"

"They're fine. Just a little shocked. The ocean was cold and neither of them could swim. My two rescue swimmers jumped off this vessel as soon as those two jumped off the yacht."

"I saw that," Robinson said. "Pretty amazing, those two swimmers."

"Thank you for keeping that spotlight on them until we were able to turn around," Lieutenant Martin added.

Robinson shrugged. "I couldn't sit back and do nothing."

"Well, this will be the high of my career as well as the end." Martin's tone was sullen.

"End?" Robinson said. "What you did . . . running with your light off. If you hadn't followed that yacht those two would have drowned. Even if they could swim, it was what? Twenty-five miles from the Cuban shore."

"I violated another country's water, Mr. Robinson," she reminded him.

"Tough shit! I violated their airspace and I don't regret it. You—you did your job like you were trained to do. To save lives. The rules can come second."

"That may be true, Mr. Robinson, but I have to face reality. There will be an outcry from Cuba as we know it. And the game will go like this: I will take the scapegoat title and just do what I can to spare my crew. I'll take what's coming to me."

Robinson looked at Wensell.

"Uh, excuse me, Lieutenant." Wensell cleared his throat.

"What is it, Chief Petty Officer?"

"That sheet on your desk. That's not a standard resignation form, is it?"

Lieutenant Martin frowned, easing a folder over the form. "That is personal, Chief Petty Officer!"

Wensell blew off her rebuke. "Ma'am, that would seem odd being that our vessel um . . . had some electrical problems."

"What electrical problems?" She frowned. "I heard of no such thing."

"The kind that caused our navigaton and GPS system to malfunction. This is why we entered Cuban waters by mistake because we were unaware of the vessel's true position."

Martin crossed her arms. "Need I remind you that another Coast Guard vessel was out on this operation, Mr. Wensell? One that I'm sure had a working GPS unit. Now tell me how I can explain why I didn't heed to the call from the—"

Robinson cleared his voice. "If I may?"

"No, Mr. Robinson." Martin stood. "I'm going to ask you to step out of my office for a moment because—"

"Lieutenant! Please!" Wensell stood and placed his hands on Martin's desk. "Just listen to us, okay! If you don't like it, hell I'll turn in my resignation papers, too." Martin remained on her feet.

"You may speak, Mr. Robinson," she said, glaring at Wensell.

"Ma'am, the other ship couldn't call you because while . . . um . . . my pilot—he flew too low on a turn and clipped the um . . ." Robinson glanced at Wensell for help.

"Their landing skids clipped the main communications antenna on Captain Alterman's vessel," Wensell explained. "It was really dark and . . ."

"Shit happens." Robinson shrugged.

Wensell slid the folder off the resignation form and looked up into Martin's eyes. "We look out for our own, Lieutenant. What you did tonight took a helluva lot of balls and I'm proud to serve under you, ma'am." Wensell snapped a quick salute while balling up the resignation form in his left hand.

Trevon sat next to LaToria with his arm around her waist. She was still shivering. "You wanna lay down?" he asked.

She quickly shook her head no, pressing her body closer to his as they sat on the small bunk. Both had been seen and treated in the sick bay and given a U.S.C.G. jumpsuit to wear.

"Why didn't you tell me your ass couldn't swim?" she said into his chest.

Trevon shrugged. "I thought I could learn. We sure as hell couldn't stay on that damn boat."

LaToria sat up. "You came for me."

"Damn right I did!" He tilted the brim of the Coast Guard cap up so he could see her eyes. "Think I wasn't?"

"You said something to me before we jumped."

"What? Don't let my hand go? Something you did before we even hit the damn water. And when I did reach you I was kicked in the face." Trevon was glad to be able to smile at what happened.

"Smooch, I was so scared! When that Coast Guard dude grabbed me from behind—"

"Your crazy ass started yelling about a damn shark. I'm sitting there drowning and like . . . sharks ain't orange. Yo, it was—"

"You said you loved me, Trevon." LaToria looked into his eyes.

"Yeah, I did, huh?"

"So you wanna—"

They both looked toward the door when a knock sounded.

"Come in." Trevon stood.

Lieutenant Martin stepped inside followed by Lieutenant Colonel Robinson. Martin informed LaToria and Trevon who Robinson was, then asked if they were open to talking with him.

"Yeah, we'll talk." Trevon sat down as Lieutenant Martin sat down on another bunk beside Robinson.

"Are you two okay?" Robinson began. He wanted to come off as a friend and not an asshole. Trevon stated that they were fine, just tired.

"Ms. . . . LaToria Frost?" Robinson nodded.

"Yes."

"Ma'am, was Swagga alive when—"

"I was locked in that room, okay? I don't know—"

"Tell me what happened when he stopped the boat."

"I heard a funny humming noise. He was moving around a lot, but he never came down to the room."

"A humming? Was it another boat?"

"No."

"How long did the sound last?"

"It . . . Shit! I know what it was! It was that crane thing!"

"A davit," Martin explained. "It's a small hydraulic winch used to lift small tenders or personal water crafts onto the yacht or down to the water."

"So if it was used that means Swagga got off," Robinson guessed.

"And setting his yacht on fire was the perfect diversion." Martin stood up. "I doubt he's still out there, but I need to start a search for him."

Silence loomed for a few seconds when Lieutenant Martin left the small room. Robinson leaned back rubbing his neck. "I'm trying to piece this all together. I'll start with the two bodies in Coral Gables. Do either of you two know about that?"

Trevon knew to keep his mouth closed. LaToria followed Trevon's actions.

"Okay." Robinson nodded. "I do know that your car was shot up, Mr. Harrison. And I assume you took that dead security guard's gun and motorcycle. We found it near the warehouse. It's being checked for your fingerprints. We also found the guard's gun, and that too is being fingerprinted. And this brings me to the body. Shotgun wound to the chest. Odd that we also found a casing from a .380, but where is it?" Robinson clasped his hands together resting his elbows on his knees. "What you did tonight, Mr. Harrison, I'm still replaying it all in my mind. Through a pair of binoculars I watched you jump off a speedboat onto the back of a burning yacht in Cuban waters I might add."

"We were in Cuba?" LaToria asked in disbelief.

"We all were." Robinson sat back up. "Like I was saying, Mr. Harrison, your actions were commendable. Had you been some part of the military, you would have been given a medal. Tell me. You jumped on the yacht without knowing if Ms. Frost was alive or not? And I'm sure you realized that the only way off was to jump. And son, you can't even swim." Robinson held his hand out. "I'd like to shake your hand, Mr. Harrison."

The two men shook hands.

"Reality, which sucks at times," Robinson said, shrugging. "You have a record, Mr. Harrison, and I know about what sent you to prison. Again, you took the law into your own hands and that brings me back to the body at the warehouse. Now, would you like to tell me what happened? Yaffa looked pretty roughed up, and I see you have a bit of swelling around your left eye. Wanna talk about it? And yes, we got the shotgun. I forgot to mention . . . and it too is being fingerprinted."

Tevon felt trapped. He remained silent.

Robinson smiled. "I was hoping for that reaction, Mr. Harrison. Now, let me tell you why. See, in my report, due to the close proximity of the blast, my report is that Yaffa suffered his um—last moments on earth from a self-inflicted wound."

"What about Swagga?" LaToria asked.

Robinson pulled out his cell phone. "As soon as I get a signal, I'll continue to hunt him down."

CHAPTER
FORTY-THREE
Friday 4:20 a.m. - Miami, Florida

Trevon and LaToria were moved directly from the Coast Guard vessel and driven to the U.S. Marshals office. The trip was made in the back of a black tinted supercharged 2011 Dodge Durango. Escorting the Durango were two similar painted Ford Taurus sedans. The three vehicles sped through the lit streets of Miami. Trevon suddenly sat up from the second row seat he shared with LaToria.

"Hey! What happened to the guy with the speedboat? I forgot his name!"

Robinson shook his head. "The Coast Guard said they received a distress signal from him. Said his boat was taking on water. The other Coast Guard ship took a risk and headed to his last location. They found him on a life raft. He's okay."

"Yes!" Trevon sat back, sliding a hand down his face.

Reaching the U.S Marshals building, Trevon was surprised to see a familiar sports utility vehicle in the underground parking lot. The instant they exited the Durango, Janelle appeared near the elevator.

The two women hugged each other once they were inside the building. Trevon joined them as Janelle began asking them what was going on.Trevon saw Robinson standing off in the corner with his back toward him talking on his cell phone. He headed over. He wanted to make sure the Coast Guard had done everything possible to find the guy with the speedboat. As he neared Robinson, he slowed to a stop due to parts of the conversation he was hearing.

"Okay, you know where I can find Swagga? And I assume you'll want some amount of a reward. Yes, I do understand and I'm pleased that you called. . . . Yes, Ms. Frost is alive and well. . . . I'm sorry, but I can't give out that information. . . . Yes, I'll see that it's done. . . . Okay. Now, the whereabouts of Swagga. Sir, we will try to apprehend him alive, but since he's armed I can't promise you anything. . . . I do understand. . . . Yes. Yes. Okay. You said it's a silver Aston Martin Virage. And he's at the Miami International Airport. . . . Say it again. . . . Okay, you said it's a private section near the west end of the runway? Yes. Sir, if he's there we'll find him. . . . Yes, I heard you. His jet will pull off in twenty minutes. Thank you, sir. Goodbye."

Robinson ended the call then turned around. Walking toward LaToria and Janelle, he motioned his tactical officer to follow him. "We just got a tip," Robinson whispered to the tactical officer. "Get the team ready to move in ten minutes or less."

The tactical officer nodded, then ran off to get the Fugitive Task Force Unit suited back up.

"Ladies," Robinson said, standing in front of LaToria and Janelle. "We just received an anonymous tip on Swagga's whereabouts."

"Where is he?" LaToria jumped up. "I wanna be there when y'all arrest his dumb ass!"

Janelle touched LaToria's arm. "Calm down."

"He's trying to catch a private jet at the airport. He won't make it," Robinson assured them. "As for you being there." He shook his head. "Not gonna happen. I need you and Mr.—" Robinson looked around the small room. "Where is Mr. Harrison?"

"He was standing over there behind you," LaToria said and looked at Janelle.

Janelle shrugged. "I guess he went to use the bathroom or something. I'm sure this building has cameras."

Robinson again scanned the room. It was hard to overlook Janelle's stunning beauty. Robinson had checked her out. Amazed how she was so flawlessly dressed at four in the morning. He had noticed everything. Taking a step closer, he looked down at the seats.

"What's wrong?" LaToria asked.

"Ms. Babin, can you tell me why your purse is on the floor?"

Janelle gasped. "I had it sitting right next to me while I was talking to Kandi."

Robinson squatted and picked up the purse. "Ma'am. Please see if anything is missing."

"Why would anything be—"

"Please, Ms. Babin." Robinson handed Janelle the purse. "It would greatly satisfy me if you would check to see it anything is missing."

"Fine!" Janelle searched inside the purse. *This man is tripping! Why would Trevon want to take something out of my purse? This is so stupid. Ain't nothing in here but my phone and credit cards and it's all here. Oh and my—wait! Where are my . . .* Janelle looked up with a lost look on her face.

"My—my car keys are missing."

Robinson cursed, and then ran down the hall yelling at another Marshal to initiate a Code Red lock down on the building. No one was allowed to enter nor exit the building until the Code was clear.

"Ohhh Trevon." LaToria sat down and buried her face into her hands. She hoped he was not missing to repeat what had cost him fifteen years in prison.

EPILOGUE
December 25, 2011
Sunday 8:35 a.m. - Selma, North Carolina

Three-inches of snow covered the grounds outside and it still fell lightly as LaToria stood looking out the window. A cap of snow sat on the hood and roof of her Escalade. She felt alone without Trevon.

Behind her sat Trevon's family at the kitchen table along with Jurnee, Janelle and her newly wed husband, Victor. Angie was telling stories about Trevon's childhood days. Laughter flowed endlessly from the kitchen, but LaToria had other things on her mind. Life was on her mind. The journey with Trevon had changed her inside. After reaching an agreement with Janelle, LaToria would film her last three porn films next year and call it quits.

Her relationship with Jurnee was still strong, but now it was based solely on friendship and not sex. Keeping her life private, LaToria was one of the few that knew of Jurnee's new boyfriend, Michael. Like Victor, he too was an author. Reaching up to rub the tears from her wet eyes she thought of Swagga.

Swagga had gotten his money back from D-Hot. The two were the farthest from being friends. D-Hot returned the money willingly, so as to keep his snitching ways from being uncovered. Swagga and his high-powered legal team were able to brush aside the attempted murder charge. Cuba would not release the burnt wreckage of the yacht. No one could prove how the yacht was set on fire, thus clearing

Swagga from facing a trial in court. The case was still pending and was set to be thrown out at the next hearing in a few weeks. Swagga was surprisingly keeping a low profile spending time with Kendra and his firstborn.

"LaToria," Angie called from the table. "It's time to eat, girl. Your seat is ready."

LaToria wiped her eyes again. "I'm coming."

Rex barked and trotted up to the door. When LaToria did not open it, he moved around her and placed his paws up on the window sill. He barked again.

The roads were too slick to drive, so Trevon had to walk to the store. He was okay with it because he was free! Trevon had wised up. He never left the underground parking lot, and instead pushed his anger aside and thought about what he stood to lose. LaToria, Angie, and his mom. Swagga was not worth the effort. Two Marshals had found him leaning against Janelle's Aventador with his head toward the ground. Robinson had kept his word and kept Trevon free of any criminal charges.

Kendra had spoken to Trevon in private and told him it was best to end their affair. Trevon agreed fully. He was still on parole and just hoped that no bullshit would stir up from Kendra's renewed bond with Swagga. A smile spread on his face when he saw Rex loping toward him in the snow. LaToria stood in the doorway waiting for him.

"You still crying from them onions, baby?" Trevon asked when he stepped inside.

"Yeah, and I hope you got my crunchy peanut butter." LaToria took the plastic bag from him, anxious to feed her odd craving.

"How you feel?" he asked, taking his coat off.

"Pregnant."

"Mm hmm." Trevon squeezed her ass. "And it's getting bigger."

"Stop, Smooch!" She giggled. "Your mom is in the kitchen."

Trevon smiled as he sat down at the table with his loved ones and friends. He was thankful for so much when his mom began to pray. He even had a best man lined up for his wedding to LaToria next July, Menage Unique Legend. Yeah, life was all good for Trevon even through all the drama he had to endure to reach it. No Justice. Nah, he had peace. Peace of mind and a grasp on that element titled love.

At the same time across the country in Auburn, Washington was Stan. He had moved back home, leaving the hurt and loss of Cindy behind. In his hand, he watched the clip of Swagga having sex with Chyna. This was the one key item he had not told the police. With his mind made up, he typed a quick text message.

Trevon,
Merry X-mas. I hope all is well.
FYI, Chyna did not xxx U. It was Cindy.
Here is the root of your troubles with Swagga. I'm moving on. Here are two video clips that people have died for. Maybe U will know what to do with them.
A friend of Cindy R.I.P.

Stan dialed in Trevon's cell number then pressed the SEND button.

WAHIDA CLARK
PRESENTS
BEST SELLING TITLES

Trust No Man

Trust No Man II

Thirsty

Cheetah

Karma With A Vengeance

The Ultimate Sacrifice

The Game of Deception

Karma 2: For The Love of Money

Thirsty *2*

Lickin' License

Feenin'

Bonded by Blood

Uncle Yah Yah: 21st Century Man of Wisdom

The Ultimate Sacrifice II

Under Pressure (YA)

The Boy Is Mines! (YA)

A Life For A Life

The Pussy Trap

99 Problems (YA)

Country Boys

WAHIDA CLARK PRESENTS
COMING SOON!
LICKIN' LICENSE II
A NOVEL BY
INTELLIGENT ALLAH

WAHIDA CLARK PRESENTS
COMING SOON!
STILL FEENIN
A NOVEL BY
SERENITI HALL

UNCLE YAH YAH

21ST. Century Man of Wisdom

VOL 2

COMING SOON!

AL DICKENS

WAHIDA CLARK PRESENTS

TRUST NO MAN

A NOVEL

CA$H

HOW TO

R U I N

A BUSINESS

WITHOUT

REALLY

TRYING...

"What every aspiring entrepreneur should not do when starting a business"

CASH MONEY CONTENT
PRESENTS

Justify
my
THUG

New York Times Bestselling Author of *Payback With Ya Life*
WAHIDA CLARK

WWW.WCLARKPUBLISHING.COM